Winging It

Lucky in Love Book 2

Jen Desmarais

Renaissance

Diverse Canadian Voices

PressesRenaissancePress.ca

First edition 2025

Cover art by pinkpiggy93.
Cover design and Interior design by Éric Desmarais.
Edited by Max Emberley, Cassandra Pegg, Wayam Essa
and Anne Coderre.

Legal deposit, Library and Archives Canada, June 2025.

Paperback ISBN: 978-1-990086-86-1
Ebook ISBN: 978-1-990086-89-2

Renaissance Press - pressesrenaissancepress.ca

Renaissance acknowledges that it is hosted on the traditional, unceded land of the Anishinabek, the Kanien'kehá:ka, and the Omàmìwininìwag. We acknowledge the privileges and comforts that colonialism has granted us and vow to use this privilege to disrupt colonialism by lifting up the voices of marginalized humans who continue to suffer the effects of ongoing colonialism.

Find our cover artist :
Instagram: http://www.instagram.com/pinkpiggy93
Tumblr: https://pinkpiggy93.tumblr.com
Patreon: http://www.Patreon.com/pinkpiggy93

Printed in Gatineau at
Imprimerie Gauvin - Depuis 1892
gauvin.ca

Renaissance gratefully acknowledges the support of the Canada Council for the Arts

Conseil des Arts
du Canada

Canada Council
for the Arts

For Éric,
whose encouragement and enthusiasm pushed
me to write. Thank you for letting me play in your
world of Everdome.

Note To Reader

I would like to note that although this is a low-stakes romance, there are still some heavy themes, such as injuries, ethical dilemmas over killing a literal monster, and bullying. There are also sexual situations between consenting and enthusiastic minors (both 15 year olds).

Please note that there is no homophobia in this book. This was not the reality in 2003 (or today), but that is not my story to tell. My story is about two boys who are falling in love with each other.

Chapter 1

**FRIDAY THE 6TH OF JUNE, 2003 -
WESTMEATH, ONTARIO**

Tommy's heart pounded faster in excitement, and he couldn't help but bounce a little in the backseat of his mother's car; the shining steel and glass towers of Westmeath were visible in the distance. Despite his two black eyes and sore ribs, he couldn't stop himself from wiggling. The seatbelt prevented him from moving more than that. In any case, too much motion made his bruised ribs hurt.

His mother, Lilah, turned around in the passenger seat and smiled gently at him. He noticed that her blonde hair, so much like his own, was starting to turn white.

"We've still got at least half an hour until we're there. You're going to wear yourself out before we even reach city limits," she said with a chuckle.

Tommy tried to focus on the back of his father's greying head instead of the view out the front window. It worked for maybe ten seconds before his gaze was drawn again to the horizon. A grin burst across his face, and he winced at the tug on his freshly healed split lip. "I can't help it! I get to see Carter, Kennedy, Jason, Elyse, and everybody!"

It felt weird that after three months of hiding his relationship status from his parents, he could be open about it now. He'd told them yesterday afternoon at the hospital.

He and Carter had met over March Break, when Tommy had been visiting Westmeath to attend an exclusive science camp run by Door Technology. Carter was one of his sister's best friends, was Tommy's age, and had also been attending the camp.

Halfway through camp, Tommy had realized his feelings for the other boy were more than platonic, and they'd been dating ever since.

Long distance relationships suck, Tommy thought, picturing Carter's face as he had seen it two nights ago during their video call.

The laptop had been custom-made by Veronica, the best friend of his soon-to-be brother-in-law and Tommy's sponsor for the March Break camp. It had allowed him to keep in touch with not only his sister, but his boyfriend, who had been gifted one as well.

Even then, seeing his face isn't the same as being physically in the same room as him. Tommy bit his lip anxiously, avoiding the cut. Although the boys had reunited for an eventful STEM competition less than a month ago in early May, he looked forward to hugging his boyfriend again.

He'd been planning on telling his parents he was seeing Carter when they arrived today, but life had other plans. At least the talk had gone well, albeit awkwardly.

Before camp, his relationship with his mother had been tense, to put it mildly. When she had picked him up after camp, he wasn't ready to be completely open with her.

He winced and touched his temple; a dull ache was developing behind his left eye. *Guess I was right to not bring up Carter at school*, he thought bitterly. His STEM team had found out they were dating by accident while in Toronto, but *they* had kept his secret after returning home.

No, his team hadn't been the problem. Tommy scowled out the side window at the outskirts of Westmeath. His ex-friends, the ones he'd been hanging out with before the camp, had snooped around his room and found the love letter Carter had sent him.

He had been involuntarily partnered with Cindy Lou, the leader of his old group of friends, on a science project. Tommy had thought Cindy Lou was over the rift between them. They'd been working on the project in Tommy's room earlier that week, and when Tommy had left to go to the bathroom, she had found the letter, taken pictures of it, and returned it, all without Tommy noticing.

They had presented their project in class Thursday morning. That afternoon, while Tommy had been waiting for Faith at the bus stop, the gang of his ex-friends had jumped him.

The highway widened to six lanes while he tried to get his panic under control. Just thinking about the fight made his heart race, and breathing too hard made his ribs hurt. *It wasn't so much a fight as a beating,* he thought bitterly.

Apparently, Cindy Lou had been under the impression that they had been dating and had had a minor fight. Tommy shook his head. *How could we be dating? She didn't ask me out!* It hadn't mattered to them. He'd been labelled a cheater and was beaten for it.

A large transport with the logo of Door Tech, the company who had run the camp, drove past them in the fast lane on the left, making Tommy smile. They were almost there!

"I hope I pass the qualifying test this week for the Door Tech summer camp," Tommy said anxiously.

He kept his eyes on the transport, the lone difference in the multitude of cars ahead of them. The transport moved quickly into their lane several cars ahead of them and then into the right lane.

"I'm sure you'll be fine," Lilah said calmly. "You've been studying with Carter, Elyse, and Faith for the past two weeks."

"And I'll be able to go if I get in?"

"Dear, the March Break camp was so good for you. You came home with a determination and focus that was lovely to see. We aren't concerned about letting you come to Westmeath for the summer camp if Kennedy and Jason are alright with it," Lilah said. "And you'll be closer to Carter."

"What the—?" Tommy's dad, Gerard, jerked the steering wheel to the right, sliding into the space next to them and braking hard.

He stared out his window as a large hand, resembling that of a gorilla, landed where their car had been a second before, followed by a foot. Tommy leaned closer to the window to look up at the rest of the body, which was that of a bear. His eyes widened. "Is that real?" he gasped.

The monster didn't stay beside them for long, charging forward on all fours and knocking cars aside.

Gerard slowed even further, making room for the other cars. Two figures on a motorcycle sped past on the shoulder.

Tommy wrinkled his nose and scoffed. "What's their hurry?"

Lilah turned to see what he was looking at and drew in a sharp breath. "Of course," she murmured.

A yellow Hummer had cut in front of the motorcycle, trying to avoid the traffic.

It looked like the motorcycle was going to run right into the back of the car when a dark grey ramp appeared. It was just wide enough for the bike, which rose quickly with it.

Tommy's jaw dropped as the ramp kept going, growing pillars and struts over and around the gridlocked traffic and vanishing behind them. The motorcycle didn't slow down at all and was soon out of sight, chasing after the monster. "Were they *superheroes*?" he asked, shocked. "Superheroes are real, and in Westmeath?"

"Sure looks like it," Gerard said distractedly. The traffic around them had started moving again, slowly.

"I think they're funnelling people off the highway," Lilah said, peering ahead. "We'll have to navigate the back roads to get to Oldtown."

"The map's in the glove compartment," Gerard said, shoulder-checking before he changed lanes.

"*Holy shit!*" Tommy exclaimed, pointing out the front window, where a massive bullet was heading directly for them.

"Language," Lilah said calmly.

Tommy glanced at her hand, which had gripped her husband's arm so tightly that her knuckles were white. Looking forward again, he saw a person in black appear on top of the bullet, and then the whole thing disappeared. He rubbed his eyes and then gasped in pain.

He'd forgotten about his injuries.

A few heartbeats later, there was a muffled *thump*, and the highway shook slightly.

"What—?" Tommy muttered. "That was weird, right?"

"Depends on your definition," Lilah said lightly.

"By anyone's definition!" Tommy exploded.

"We're in an enclosed space. Please lower your voice, dear."

Tommy started laughing. "Ouch," he gasped, clutching his ribs. "Don't make me laugh!"

Lilah frowned. "Are you okay?"

"Yeah, I'm fine. The hospital wouldn't have discharged me this morning if I wasn't."

"Are you sure? I wish I could've seen the X-ray too," Lilah said, obviously concerned. "What if your ribs are broken and they missed it?"

Tommy shrugged. "They did a lot of tests throughout the night. They said I was fine."

"But—"

"Mom, if it gets worse, I'll go to the hospital here, okay?"

"Promise?"

"I promise." Tommy sighed inwardly.

"Are you sure that you should be having Carter over for a sleepover tonight? What if he bumps into you in the night and makes it worse?" Lilah worried at her bottom lip. "I'm still not one hundred percent comfortable with this sleepover in the first place."

"I'll make him come with me to the hospital for the long wait if it gets worse. Really, Mom. I'll be fine." He ignored the second half of her comment.

They left the highway. Lilah pulled out the map and directed Gerard while Tommy sat quietly in the back, trying not to distract them. The shops on the street started to look familiar, and then his dad turned left onto a street lined with bungalows.

"Do you think they're home from work?" Tommy asked excitedly. "It's almost dinner. They should be home by now, right?"

"They might have had to pick up people from the airport," Lilah said as they turned into a driveway. "I think Kennedy mentioned something about Michelle and Evanna arriving today."

"But their car's here?"

"They probably borrowed Zoe's because of the car seat," Lilah replied after a moment's hesitation.

"Should we go to Zoe and Gabrielle's if they're not home?" Tommy asked. Zoe was Jason's sister and lived next door with her wife and their almost two-year-old daughter, Brooke.

"Kennedy said that your fingerprint would still work and to let ourselves in," Lilah said. "We can unpack and start dinner."

Lilah knocked on the front door while Tommy and his father got their bags; one large suitcase for his parents and his medium-sized one, plus his backpack and guitar case.

When he got to the door, Lilah took his suitcase so he could use his thumbprint to unlock the door and disable the alarm.

The house was silent when they entered. Tommy felt like he was intruding. "You're sure Kennedy said we should let ourselves in?" he asked, peeking down the hall to the bedrooms.

"Quite sure." Lilah turned to her husband. "Jason said we would be most comfortable in the guest room in the basement. There's a queen-sized bed down there instead of the double up here. I'd like to unpack before they get home."

"Yes, dear," Gerard said, lifting the suitcase and following her to the basement stairs in the kitchen.

"Do you need any help lifting that down the stairs?" Tommy asked.

Gerard paused and looked back at his son. "Even though I retired this year, I don't have one foot in the grave *yet*," he said wryly. "And you're in no shape to help lift anything."

"Right." Tommy had forgotten about his injuries again. "I'll just... go. To my room." He turned down the hall and entered the first room on the left, the one he had stayed in when he'd visited in March.

He unpacked quickly, filling drawers and closet with clothing, and putting his schoolwork on the desk. After tucking his suitcase into the closet and leaning his guitar against the bookcase, he sat at the desk and opened his laptop, connecting easily to Jason's Wi-Fi; the password had been scrawled on a piece of paper left on the table.

It was a relief not to have to listen to the dying screech-whirr of a robot. His parents had to connect to the internet via their phone line. MSN opened easily and Tommy changed his username from MyNameIsNotTommy to TommyIsInWestmeath.

He didn't have to wait long. Carter's icon flashed first, followed quickly by the group chat that the two competitive STEM teams had made once they returned from Toronto. Oldtown High and Parry Sound High teams had hung out together all weekend, and they hadn't wanted to lose the friendships they'd made.

Tommy grinned then winced; the tug on the split in his lip was more pronounced this time. He double-clicked on Carter's name, opening the chat window.

CarterIsARockStar had typed, "You're here TODAY? Can I come over?"

TommyIsInWestmeath replied, "Yes, bring your pyjamas. We get two nights together before school!"

He opened the group chat while he waited for Carter to respond and scanned the messages quickly to see what he'd missed.

It started with Chris, one of the seniors at his school, telling the Oldtown group about Tommy's fight the afternoon before, followed by concerned questions from both sides.

Tommy groaned, exasperated, and typed, "Hospital discharged me this morning. I'm fine, just look a bit like a panda." He put an emoticon of a panda bear.

CarterIsARockStar had replied in the private chat, "You sure your parents will be alright with me sleeping over once you tell them I'm your boyfriend?"

TommyIsInWestmeath replied, "Actually, I told them last night. They didn't understand why I was attacked. If anything, they got even more angry at them after I explained *why*. Mom's still hesitant but hasn't said no outright yet. J and K will back us up."

"OMG are you ok? I know you wanted to wait until I was with you to tell them."

Tommy could picture Carter's furrowed brow. They'd walked through several scenarios of telling his parents they were together. He replied, "I'm ok. Not how I wanted it to happen, but they were more concerned about the gang thinking I was dating Cindy Lou. Tbh, I think they suspected. It's not like I was subtle, talking about you every chance I got, just to have the shape of your name on my lips."

CarterIsARockStar put three laughing emoticons and then typed, "Packing and omw."

Tommy sighed happily. He'd get to hug his boyfriend soon. He returned his attention to the group chat and typed, "I'll ttyl. C's on his way."

The group chat exploded with hearts and kissy faces, making Tommy laugh and then groan from pain. "Jeepers, that's annoying," he gasped.

He heard his name being called by Jason and joined the others in the living room.

Kennedy let out a cry, flying across the living room to greet him. "What happened?" Her hands fluttered around Tommy's face without touching him.

"My ex-friends happened," Tommy mumbled. "Sorry."

"Sorry? What are you sorry about? Tommy!" Kennedy grabbed his hand and laced their fingers. The tiny amount of touch from his sister made him feel better.

"Sorry for looking like this for your wedding," Tommy said sheepishly. He ran his free hand through his hair, brushing the bangs off his forehead just for them to flop back down. "I didn't mean to."

"Did you start the fight?"

"No. I didn't even end it. Chris and Bryan pulled them off me." Tommy looked at the floor, not wanting to meet her eyes, identical to his own. He'd been mistaken for Kennedy's twin often enough, even though she was eight years older, and he was always flattered by the comparison. "Cindy Lou is pissed at me for being happy away from her. Something about her thinking that we were dating?" he scoffed. *As if!* "Which is ridiculous. She instigated."

"Can I hug you?" Kennedy asked quietly.

"Gently," Tommy cautioned.

He got a careful hug that he could barely feel and a kiss on his forehead.

The doorbell rang and Tommy pulled back, feeling giddy. "Carter's here!" he said, a grin spreading across his face, the cut on his lip hurting at the stretch yet again.

He felt stiff as he walked to the door and opened it to see the gorgeous face of his boyfriend. His heart thumped harder in his chest, and he resisted the urge to throw himself into Carter's arms.

It would have hurt.

Instead, he raked his eyes over every inch of Carter's face, from the short, curly brown hair with shaved sides to his grey eyes, his thin nose, and down over his soft-looking lips. "You're a sight for sore eyes," Tommy murmured.

Carter huffed a surprised laugh. "Too soon," he said with a grin.

Holding out his hand, Tommy drew Carter into the house.

"Carter, why don't you put your bag in Tommy's room?" Jason suggested. "We're about to have a talk in the kitchen."

"Hang on," Tommy said, noting Carter's tense posture. He held Carter's bronze hand tightly. His mother had come to the kitchen doorway, and his father stood up from the couch. "Mom, Dad, this is my boyfriend, Carter."

"Nice to see you again," Lilah greeted him with a smile.

Gerard pasted a stern expression on his face that made Tommy roll his eyes. "What made you decide to date our son?"

Carter cleared his throat. "Well, sir, he asked me."

Tommy chuckled softly.

"Not what I meant." Gerard waved a hand. "What are his qualities that drew you to him?"

"Oh, that's easy." Carter smiled at Tommy. "He's brilliant. And he's beautiful. Caught my eye the moment I saw him. We have fun together. He wrote a song for me." Carter brushed his thumb over Tommy's knuckles softly. "I've lost track of time talking to him more than once over the laptops."

"Stop teasing the poor kid, Dad," Kennedy said when Carter paused for breath.

"Oh no!" Lilah exclaimed, drawing everyone's attention. "I just remembered! Faith is supposed to be your date for the wedding! What are you going to do?"

Kennedy laughed, Tommy joining in despite the ache.

"Don't worry, Mom. She knows. Elyse is Carter's date for the wedding, and this way the four of us can hang out," Tommy said. The four fifteen-year-olds had grown close over the spring, studying together virtually for the STEM competition.

Tommy followed his father, who squeezed his hand warmly as he passed, toward the kitchen, and was stopped by Kennedy when Carter disappeared down the hall to put his bag in Tommy's room.

"You okay?" Kennedy whispered to him.

"I'm glad I told Mom and Dad that I had a boyfriend at the hospital, even though I had planned on telling them here. It was stressful enough just introducing them to Carter properly. But really, nothing could have been as bad as yesterday afternoon," Tommy said seriously. He resisted a shudder. "Dee," he said, using his childhood nickname for her, "I'm worried about what might happen when I go back. The STEM club can't be my body-guards all the time."

"We'll cross that bridge when we get to it," Kennedy said.

Tommy wanted to take comfort from her words, but he couldn't see how everything would be alright. It's not like he could stop being happy. He sat beside her, and when Carter returned and sat beside him, he took his hand.

Carter squeezed Tommy's hand gently and smiled at him.

"Tomorrow is the Community Ball," Jason said. He took a deep breath and looked at Tommy. "I'm not human."

Tommy chuckled. *That was oddly abrupt. What's he playing at?* he thought and looked over at Kennedy to share in the joke.

Kennedy smiled, but nodded, and Tommy's chuckles died away. He furrowed his brow in confusion. *Wait, what?* None of the people around the table were the kind to pull a prank like this. He trusted them, and, therefore, what Jason said must be the truth. He returned his attention to his almost brother-in-law.

"My ancestors were created from the Aether, which you could call the stuff of magic and chaos. There's a barrier between our universe and the Aether, but sometimes it leaks through, and when that happens, it creates a living being. If there's a human around, that person's will shapes what is born. If the being is non-sapient, we call it an Aether-creature, and if it is, that's when you get my people, Aetherborn. I wanted to tell you before the ball, because not all of us look human."

Tommy nodded slowly, thinking about the stories Grandma told him about magical people when he was younger. *Maybe they were Aetherborn!* His schoolmates told stories about aliens in the woods. *Maybe those were misunderstood Aetherborn?* The mon-ster they saw when they arrived in Westmeath popped into his head. *Should I say monster?* "That thing we saw on the highway when we arrived, the gorilla-bear, was that...?"

Jason winced. "It disappeared once it was killed. That's not something that an Aether-creature does." Jason cleared his throat. "My point is, you're going to see a lot of different Aetherborn tomorrow night, a lot of whom are especially important to both us and the Community. We wanted to prepare you in advance so that you can get all your questions out of the way and won't be startled."

"I'm sorry, I'm still not quite over the fact that magic exists." Tommy stared into space for a minute, his thoughts racing. He had a lot of questions for Grandma regarding her stories. Then he thought about what he had seen on the highway. It was hard to believe, but the superheroes cinched it for him. *Cool!* "I mean, we *did* see a motorcycle ride a vanishing ramp into the air this evening. And there was that gorilla-bear-not-Aether-creature. Okay... Magic exists. And you're not human. Is there anything else I should know?"

"Some Aetherborn have special powers, for the lack of a better word. Most of us are stronger than an average human. Some live much longer. Some have names for their kind, others don't." Jason shrugged. "My family falls into the latter category, with no specific name. We also have a human lifespan, but I am most definitely stronger." He grinned.

"How many Aetherborn are there?"

"In the world?" Jason asked with a chuckle. "I have no idea. There are Communities in pretty much every major city. None are as large as the Community here in Westmeath, though. There are twenty-thousand Aetherborn, give or take, who live in Oldtown."

"Twenty-*thousand*?" Tommy gasped. "Have I met any? Other than you, of course. And I guess your sister?" he questioned.

"Me," said Carter quietly, drawing his attention.

Tommy gaped at his boyfriend, thinking about the time they'd spent together and wondering if he'd ever shown any powers. *Maybe he doesn't have powers?* But then he remembered that when Carter had butted heads with the bully, Greg, during Door Tech's camp, he had challenged him to... "Arm wrestling!" Tommy said with a smile.

Carter chuckled, his body losing its tension. "Yeah."

"I have so many questions," Tommy started, mind whirling.

"Any for me?" Jason asked.

Tommy shook his head. "I can't think of any right now. Was there anything else you wanted to talk about?" he asked impatiently. He wanted to drag Carter to his bedroom, *now*!

Kennedy chuckled. "Go on. I'll knock when dinner's ready."

"Be careful," Lilah said, getting up to check the oven. "Don't hurt yourself worse."

"Mom..." Tommy frowned, defensive.

"You don't have to worry about me hurting him—" Carter started to say.

"No, dear, I know you wouldn't hurt him," Lilah reassured Carter. "I'm just being a little overprotective." She waved them out of the kitchen.

Chapter 2

FRIDAY THE 6TH OF JUNE, 2003 -
WESTMEATH, ONTARIO

With his heart in his throat, Carter trailed after his boyfriend into his bedroom. *Tommy seems alright with the idea of me not being human, but is he really?* He sat on the bed, his heart sinking into his belly when Tommy chose the desk chair instead of sitting beside him.

The room hadn't changed since Carter had first seen it: bare walls, a double bed with a desk next to it, a three-shelf bookcase next to that, and a dresser near the foot of the bed. Tommy's guitar was tucked beside the bookcase, and his schoolbooks were on the desk, but beyond that, the room didn't look lived in.

Carter shifted uncomfortably, his eyes tracing the bruises and cuts that covered Tommy's face. "How did they find out?" he whispered.

Tommy's brow furrowed in confusion, his head tipping to the side like a puppy, so Carter gestured at his face.

"Oh, that." Tommy grumbled under his breath for a second before replying, "Cindy Lou found your letter to me, or so she said while kicking me when I was on the ground. She was under the impression that she and I were dating or something."

Carter ached to hold him. He clenched his fists in the comforter on the bed, physically keeping himself back. "It was my fault? I'm so sorry."

Tommy shook his head. "I *love* your letter. Don't you dare be sorry. I can't believe she thought I was dating her even though I didn't talk to her for three months."

"That's ridiculous," Carter said with a laugh. Then he sighed. "I feel so helpless. Are you going to be okay?"

"I'm in Westmeath now. I've got you and the STEM team at school, and my family here. I'm safe here."

"Implying that you're not safe there," Carter pointed out.

Tommy shuddered. "I don't want to think about home right now. Or this week. Or at all, really."

"What can I do?"

"Don't treat me like I'm about to faint, be gentle when you touch me, and answer all my questions about Aetherborn," Tommy replied, a twinkle in his eye.

Carter chuckled. "I'll do my best. If there's anything I can't answer, we'll ask Jason later. Shoot."

"Do you have powers? You're obviously stronger than you look." Tommy leaned forward, resting his elbows on the arms of the chair.

"I'm about equivalent to Jason's strength, even though I don't look like I should be," Carter said hesitantly. "I can beat him in an arm wrestle occasionally. I don't exactly have powers. Most Aetherborn don't, and if they do, they don't talk about it except to their close friends. Zoe is an exception. She can manipulate water, and everyone knows about that."

"Jason's sister Zoe?" Tommy asked, eyes wide. Then he started laughing. "Ow. Let me guess, Brooke inherited her power?"

"She's the youngest Aetherborn I've ever heard of to develop powers," Carter said seriously. "She's doing a fantastic job controlling them. She can create water," he started chuckling, "and *become* water."

"What?"

"Yeah, gave Kennedy and Jason quite a shock when they were babysitting. I haven't seen it personally, but I heard that when she's angry, she loses control and just...melts."

"No way!" Tommy thought for a second. "Does that mean Jason has powers? He didn't say anything about them in the kitchen."

Carter smirked. "Now *that* is the question, isn't it? I have a theory."

"A theory?" Tommy asked.

"I think Jason is the Phantom," Carter whispered.

"I'm sorry, who?"

"I keep forgetting you don't live here," Carter said, shaking his head. "The Phantom is one of Westmeath's superheroes. He has shadow powers."

"Wait, wait, I think I saw him this evening!" Tommy said. "I saw two people riding a motorcycle, and then it sort of, I don't know, rose above the cars on a vanishing ramp? They were chasing after a monster."

"Yeah, that sounds about right." Carter smirked. "You know who I think the other person with him was?"

"No..." Tommy trailed off. "Kennedy?"

"The Wraith didn't show up until after they began dating," Carter whispered, eyes flicking to the door. "And Kennedy started taking private lessons with Judy right after the assassination attempts. It all fits."

"But you don't have proof," Tommy finished.

"Not yet, but with you living here for a week and knowing about Aetherborn, maybe you can find some."

"I'm not going to go poking around," Tommy said, frowning.

Carter pulled back, shocked. "I wouldn't ask you to! No, I just meant regular day-to-day conversations. They're bound to let something slip."

"Oh. That's alright then." Tommy smiled. "To get back on track, you said you don't *exactly* have powers. What does that mean?"

"I don't have powers that I can turn on and off." Carter took a deep breath and stared at his hands. "My skin is rock."

Tommy was silent for a second. Then he scoffed, "No, it isn't."

Carter's mouth twisted up in a smirk. "I assure you, it is."

"Rocks are all dusty and bitter. I've licked, kissed, and bit your entire torso. You taste amazing," Tommy said firmly.

Carter remembered the day he was referring to, in their hotel room in Toronto after he had found out his older roommates had alcohol and had changed rooms. Carter shifted a little on the bed, his body reacting both to Tommy's words and the memory. "You have," he confirmed, his voice hoarse. "But you couldn't get any hickies to stay, remember? My skin is rock because I'm a rock giant."

"But you're not *that* tall," Tommy said, confused. "And your dads are short! Are they rock giants, too?"

"They are." Carter debated with himself for a moment before continuing, "Rock giants don't have children the same way that humans and other Aetherborn do. When we have children, they are always rock giants because of how they're conceived."

"When you say, 'the same way,' do you mean...?" Tommy blushed and his eyes dropped to Carter's lap. "But I've felt...?"

Carter flushed. "We still *look* human. I'd just be shooting blanks. Rock giants conceive by the melding of sloughed-off skin cells. It's how my dads are both my biological fathers. The baby rock giant is a creation of love and is granted life after bonding with their parents through skin-to-skin contact for a length of time. It varies from couple to couple, or so I'm told. Never more than a year."

Tommy's jaw dropped. "That is so cool! Do you have pictures of yourself as a baby?"

"Of course I do!" Carter said. "My dads were so excited to have me. I think they have a full photo album from before I began breathing, which took five months."

"Wow. That is so different from my baby-making knowledge."

"Too different?" Carter asked softly, his belly in a tight knot. *Will this drive us apart?*

"Definitely not." Tommy traced a design on the back of his laptop, not looking at the boy on the bed.

"Then why are you sitting all the way over there?" Carter whispered.

Tommy let out what Carter could only describe as a whimper, and then he was in Carter's lap. "I'm worried I won't be able to control myself and hurt myself worse," he breathed, inches away from Carter's lips.

"I won't let you hurt yourself," Carter murmured, and tipped his chin up to press their lips together gently.

Tommy walked his knees higher up on the bed.

Carter got the hint and hauled Tommy toward him. The added weight on his lap sent delicious tingles throughout his body.

Tommy groaned and slipped his tongue into Carter's welcoming mouth.

Feeling slightly dizzy from lack of oxygen, Carter pulled back from the kiss, trailing his lips along Tommy's jaw.

"Oh my *God*, I've missed this!" Tommy moaned, threading his hands through Carter's curls, and tugging him closer.

With his scalp tingling in the best possible way and needing to touch more skin, Carter ghosted his hands up under Tommy's shirt. He pulled back from sucking on a sensitive spot just for the second it took to pull the t-shirt over Tommy's head and throw it on the floor.

And then Carter looked down.

"What the ever-loving bloody *fuck* did those bastards *do* to you!" Carter shouted, taking in the black-and-blue-and-red mottled torso on top of him. "Is that a shoe print?"

Tommy scrambled off him, grabbing his shirt and trying to find the opening. "Sorry, I—"

"*You* have nothing to be sorry for." Carter was so angry that he had never felt less aroused in his life. "Do they know?" he asked, gesturing at the door, meaning Tommy's family. He leaped to his feet. "I bet they don't." In two quick strides, he was ripping open the door, blood pounding in his ears and practically seeing red. He rounded the corner to the kitchen, where the four adults were still sitting and talking.

"Have you *seen* his body?" he demanded, gesturing wildly. "His chest is practically one big bruise! Someone *stepped* on him!" He stopped his tirade when he saw that Jason and Lilah were smirking, Gerard was chuckling, and Kennedy was covering a smile with her hand. "What's so funny?"

"How do *you* know what his chest looks like?" Jason asked, eyes twinkling.

"When I—" Carter cut himself off, realizing what he was about to say to Tommy's *parents*, and the other three joined Gerard in laughter. "Oh, shut up. Like you're any better."

SATURDAY THE 7TH OF JUNE, 2003 - WESTMEATH, ONTARIO

Carter returned to consciousness slowly, his ears ringing and the phantom bruises on his ribs fading so quickly that he wasn't sure they had even been there. It took a little longer for his brain to catch up, his mind gliding over the events of the day like skates on ice.

He'd woken up in Tommy's bed that morning, only their fingertips touching. Carter hadn't slept very well; he'd been so afraid of hurting Tommy worse.

Martial arts was first thing in the morning. He and Tommy had planned to sit in on Jason and Kennedy's private lesson, but Judy suggested Carter join in. She said that it was good for them to incorporate other people into their training.

Maybe they'll make me a superhero too, when I'm older! Carter had thought excitedly. *If I'm right about my theory,* he amended.

They went to lunch with Kennedy's family at Mortimer's. The diner was owned by the wizard, Jesse. Most Aetherborn were slightly afraid of the older man, but Carter enjoyed his sarcastic humour.

A flash of green shimmered across his memory next; Kennedy trying on her wedding dress at the tailor, Seams Likeable.

The white lace over the green shifted slightly, as if in shadow one second and not the next. *Another clue,* he thought. *Why else would she go all the way to Baker, Ontario to get lace made with a shadow illusion?*

His brain slid from that thought to the community centre, where the Investiture Ball was being held.

Jason preferred to call it the Community Ball. It was a formal event that inducted Kennedy into the Community before her marriage to Jason, who was one of the Arikis, or leaders.

Carter had stuck close to Tommy and his parents, introducing them to the people who wanted to meet the family of the bride-to-be. He'd been surprised at just how many people he knew in the Community.

The speeches hadn't taken long, and Gerard had left to get some punch. That was when the chaos started.

Flashy stun grenades knocked out a dozen people by the food tables, including Gerard, and Blue Blood gang members—one of a few in Westmeath—swarmed into the ballroom like a S.W.A.T. team. Judy had taken charge, telling people where to go, and Carter had helped to get people out. Lilah held onto his arm for a long moment. "Protect my Gerard," she'd whispered at last, giving Carter a hair elastic from her purse. "For Kennedy."

Carter had been a part of the extraction team that got the unconscious people out, and then three more grenades had landed at Jason's feet. Two were kicked back out, but there was no time for the third.

Making the split-second decision, Carter threw himself on top of it and knew no more.

Until now.

His eyelids felt heavy. The flashback through his day had taken only a few seconds. His brain was conscious before his body could make sense of the signals it was sending.

Eventually, his eyes cooperated and opened. He was lying on

his back on the floor in one of the safe rooms. Tommy was sitting beside him, holding his hand. Evanna was chattering away at Tommy about the different people she had met so far at the party, and Brooke was curled up on his lap.

"Hey," Carter rasped, his throat feeling like a desert. "Is there water?"

"I'll be right back," Tommy said and squeezed his hand before getting to his feet. "Stay with Carter, girls."

The girls scooted closer to him as he sat up, one on each side. "Do you want to cuddle?" Carter asked them. "I can put my arm over your shoulders."

Brooke nodded silently and half-climbed into his lap. "Water?" she asked him, her head cocked to one side.

"No!" Carter said quickly. He didn't want to have the equivalent of a bucket of water dumped on him. "A cup of water."

"Okay," Brooke replied in a little voice and curled into his chest.

"Yes, cuddles, please. Mama is protecting the room. I'm not really scared," Evanna confided with wide eyes. "I know that Kennedy will find me, but I don't want to get taken away again."

Carter digested that information slowly, his brain feeling sluggish. Tommy had returned with a little paper cup of water by the time he'd figured out what to say. "Nobody's going to take you away," he murmured to the small blonde girl pressed against his side. "And you've got more than Kennedy who'll go looking for you."

"I don't need more than Kennedy. She found me last time, when I was on the moon," Evanna said solemnly.

Carter mouthed, "The moon?" at Tommy, who shrugged.

"You were on the moon?" Tommy asked the little girl, sitting on her other side. She promptly climbed into his lap and rested her head on his chest.

"Well, not *on* the moon. I could see it through the window. It was *huge*."

"Oh," Carter said, suddenly remembering. "You're talking

about when you were kidnapped in September. Were you out in the country for the moon to look so big?"

Evanna frowned, obviously confused. "I don't know where I was. There were lots of windows and a ramp, and we walked through a glowing door, and then we were in a cave. I fell asleep, and then I was at Jason's."

Tommy shrugged. "Sounds kinda like a warehouse, maybe? Were there lots of crates?"

"Yes. They were filled with all sorts of things." Evanna reached out to touch Carter's chest, closed her eyes for a moment, and smiled. "You're all better now."

Carter stared at her. "Did you *heal* me?" he whispered.

"Your bone hurt here," she said, patting his chest. "And your head had a booboo. I helped them feel better."

"Thanks." To toss healing around like that... Carter remembered watching the bruises fade unexpectedly from Tommy's face that afternoon in Seams Likeable under Evanna's gentle touch and the anxiousness he had felt. Healers were often exploited. The idea of someone taking this little girl and forcing her to heal made him feel sick. "You should ask your mama before you heal someone," he whispered. "You have a very special gift."

Evanna beamed at him and cuddled into Tommy.

"Don't you four look cozy," Gabrielle said, coming up to them. She held out her hand to Brooke. "We can go back into the ballroom now. All the bad people have gone away, and Jason has an announcement to make before the dancing."

They joined the hundreds of other Aetherborn filing back down the hallway to the large ballroom. Jason and Kennedy, neither looking hurt, were standing on the dais with the reassembled microphone.

Once everyone had entered, Jason started speaking. "We want to thank everyone for being so calm. There was no loss of life and only minor injuries, all of which were treated by Reverend Mitchel and Doctor Sallah." He paused to let the cheering die down.

Carter frowned, puzzled. *Why did the Blue Bloods attack us? It makes no sense. I'll talk to Jason about it tomorrow.*

"Now comes the bad news," Jason continued. "There are too many gang members for us to deal with in the usual way."

Carter smirked. The "usual way" was to strip them to their underwear and deliver them to a public park near a police station.

"Which means that we have called the police. We understand if anyone wishes to return home. We will assist you, of course. Please raise your hand and move to the interior doors."

Carter looked around the ballroom. Nobody raised their hands, and nobody moved.

Kennedy clasped her hands together and brought them to her lips, visibly overcome with emotion.

"Here is the official story we will be telling the police," Jason said with a grin, "Reverend Mitchel, Brent, and I stepped outside for a breath of fresh air. We saw the Phantom and the Wraith fighting the Blue Bloods and called the police."

There was scattered laughter amidst the applause.

"There should be no reason for the police to enter the building, but we will station guards at the doors to stall them if they try. The three of us will be giving our statements outside. The rest of you, enjoy the dance!"

The band started playing "Boom Boom Boom Boom" by VengaBoys.

Kennedy clapped her hands together excitedly. "Conga line!" she called. "Carter, you're the lead!"

Carter jumped in surprise.

"What asking?" Brooke said, pulling on his hand and blinking up at him with big hazel eyes.

Carter laughed. "She's asking me to lead the dance. Do you want to help me?"

"Yes!" Brooke lifted her arms, and Carter picked her up, putting her on his shoulders. He tucked the frills of her skirt behind his head and glanced at Zoe, who smiled and nodded at him.

"We're going to lead the others around the room!" he shouted up at Brooke. She giggled and kicked her legs, grabbing onto his ears to stabilize herself.

He felt hands grab his waist, and he started dancing across the room, leading a long, snaking line of people.

What a way to get the party started!

Chapter 3

SATURDAY THE 7TH OF JUNE, 2003 -
WESTMEATH, ONTARIO

Tommy spun Evanna around in a circle to the beat of "Slide" by The Goo Goo Dolls, holding her tightly with one arm under her bum.

"Dip me!" she shrieked, and he obliged, dropping her down until her blonde hair almost touched the ground.

"Spin!" she demanded, and he turned in a circle.

He caught a glimpse of Carter, dancing with his own taskmistress Brooke. She was content to sway in a slow circle, cuddled up against his chest.

Tommy took a closer look on the next dip and grinned. The little girl was asleep in Carter's arms, despite the loud music.

When the song ended, Gabrielle and Michelle came and took both girls. Brooke didn't wake during the transfer, but Evanna pouted.

"Mama, I'm dancing with Tommy!" she exclaimed.

"It's hours past your bedtime, dearheart," Michelle replied patiently.

"I'm not tired!" Evanna protested, a huge yawn escaping her.

"That's not the point," Michelle said. "You want to be able to play with Brooke tomorrow, don't you?"

"And Tommy?" Evanna turned her big blue eyes on him pleadingly.

"I'm sure I'll see you tomorrow, too," Tommy reassured her. "I don't know what the wedding plans are, but it's Sunday. I think the Johnsons usually have Sunday dinner together."

"And we can play?"

"And we can play."

Evanna clapped her hands and went calmly with her mother, who mouthed, "Thank you," as she left.

"Finally, I get to dance with you," Carter said, snaking his arms around Tommy's waist from behind. He felt lips against the back of his neck and shivered despite the warmth from the crowded ballroom.

The song was a slow one, Shania Twain's "You're Still The One." Tommy put his hand over Carter's and spun him gently under his arm until they were face to face. "Something I've been looking forward to all evening," Tommy murmured, draping his arms over Carter's shoulders. They pressed their foreheads together, and it felt like they were dancing in their own little bubble, sharing space and air.

When the song ended, the band started playing the heavy beat of "Survivor" by Destiny's Child. Carter took Tommy's hand. "I've got an idea," he said, leaning in and speaking near Tommy's ear. "Want to see the teen room?"

"Yes!" Tommy replied, nodding for good measure.

"Great!" Carter pulled him through the masses of writhing dancers until they reached one of the interior doors. All sound vanished the instant they stepped through.

"Whoa!" Tommy shook his head to clear the ringing, the result of leaving a loud space suddenly. "Is that magic?"

Carter looked thoughtful. "I bet it is. I hadn't really thought about it before." He pulled out his cell phone.

"What are you doing?" Tommy asked, curious.

"Sending a text to Kennedy so she knows where we are," Carter said absentmindedly. "I don't want them to panic trying to find us, especially after that attack earlier." He hit send and took Tommy's hand again. "Come on, this way!"

Tommy was led past an elevator to a set of stairs. "It's only one floor up. I don't like the elevator because you don't get to see the view."

"The view?"

Carter stopped on the second set of stairs and opened the window. Once it was wide enough, he hoisted himself up and walked through onto the roof. "Come on."

"Is this the way to the teen room?" Tommy asked, climbing through the window.

"No. Don't worry, I told Kennedy I was taking you here first. Close your eyes."

Tommy smiled and shook his head as he obeyed. "You're not going to lead me off the edge of the roof, are you?"

"Have a little faith."

"Faith isn't here."

"Smart-ass." Carter took both his hands this time, leading him slowly over the roof. "There's a bit of a ramp here, feel for it with your toes... There you go." They walked a bit further.

"I had no idea the roof was this big," Tommy remarked.

"It's because we're walking so slowly. Don't worry. Okay, wait here. Don't open your eyes yet!"

Tommy heard a thump and some rustling of the gravel of the roof, but other than that, everything was silent. He couldn't even hear the traffic on the streets around them.

"I'm coming back to you now," Carter said softly so as not to startle him. "Come here, okay, back up slowly... Sit down."

"On the ground?"

"I put out a blanket. Sit, please."

"Okay." Tommy could feel Carter's strength as he guided him to sit. Then Carter moved around and sat on the other side.

"Twist a quarter turn to the left and lie back," Carter said.

"Okay." Tommy did as he was asked and felt a pillow under his head. He relaxed.

"Open your eyes."

Carter's voice was right next to him, but Tommy barely noticed because all he could see were stars. The vastness of space never failed to make him feel breathless. He was an insignificant speck on one planet of billions in the universe. The Milky Way slashed across the view, and he wished he could paint so he could remember this feeling forever. "I didn't think you could see the stars this clearly in the city!" he gasped. "It's almost like being home!"

"It's one of my favourite places in the summer," Carter said. "I don't think the mosquitoes have figured out that this place exists, so they never bother people up here. Sometimes someone with a telescope shows up if there's something cool to see, and they usually let us look too. I've seen craters on the moon, Jupiter's storm, and Saturn's rings! But when there isn't a special event, it's nice to just come up here and feel tiny, like a speck in the universe."

Tommy turned his gaze away from the stars to look at his boyfriend, his face upturned and lit by starlight. "Beautiful," he whispered.

"It is," Carter agreed.

"I meant you."

Carter turned to face him, their noses inches apart. "How are you?"

"Fine?" His voice cracked and soared on the tail end of the question.

"I mean, you just got introduced to a heck of a lot of people, some obviously not human. Then the ball got attacked, your dad got knocked out, and your boyfriend had a concussion and broken ribs. I'm just saying..." Carter trailed off meaningfully.

"Okay, yeah, I see your point." Tommy thought about the evening. "If I'd met some of those people before being told about Aetherborn, I probably would've been terrified. I mean, Sanaa looks like a demon!"

"She's a cambion," Carter supplied helpfully.

"Right. She's kinda scary, but she's so good with the little kids. Everyone tonight has been awesome. That's not bothering me at all." Tommy paused. "The attack was a lot. Seeing you laid out on the floor like that... You were so pale." He closed his eyes, holding back tears. "I was worried for you."

"Thank goodness Evanna was in our safe room," Carter said lightly. He sighed. "You must have felt the way I did when I saw your bruises yesterday. I'm sorry you worried. I probably shouldn't have jumped on that grenade. I just figured I'd be better off taking the hit than if it knocked out half the defending force, including Jason and Kennedy."

"I *do* appreciate that." Tommy leaned in and brushed their lips together. The plushness of Carter's lips sent his head spinning pleasantly. "I'm doing okay now."

"Good," Carter breathed, pulling their bodies closer together. "Sometimes I come up here, and someone else has already claimed this spot," he confided quietly.

"Yeah?" Tommy swallowed nervously. "What were they doing?"

"They weren't looking at the stars."

"Show me."

Carter drew in a deep breath. "Tell me to stop."

"Not sure I'll need to," Tommy murmured.

"But you will?" Carter looked deep into his eyes. "Promise you will if it gets to be too much?"

"I promise," Tommy replied, his voice hoarse.

Carter brought their lips together softly. The kiss quickly heated up, their tongues meeting and dancing together.

A surge of movement, and Carter was kneeling over Tommy, hands in his hair, tilting his head gently to the side to deepen the kiss.

"I've missed you so much," Carter gasped, his fingers sliding from Tommy's hair down to his chest. "Want to touch you."

"Yes, please!" His fingers fumbled with his shirt buttons, and Carter took over, methodically working his way down Tommy's body. "You too?" Tommy asked, and when Carter finished one shirt, he started on the other.

Halfway down, he got impatient and yanked it over his head, sitting up and placing his weight directly over Tommy's hips.

Tommy's hands flew to Carter's thighs and gripped him firmly. "I like that."

"Me too." Carter ran his hands down Tommy's chest, arrowing to his pants. "Can I?"

Tommy's eyes snapped open, meeting Carter's. Though he was backlit by stars, somehow Tommy could see every micro-expression on his boyfriend's face: excitement mixed with nervous energy, hope, and trust... Carter didn't move a muscle as he waited patiently for Tommy's answer. "Yes," Tommy whispered, his pulse thundering loud in his ears.

Carter rewarded him with a brilliant smile, the white of his teeth shining in the light of the quarter-moon low on the horizon. Button and zip were released slowly with shaking hands, Carter checking in after each inch. A surge of motion and then he was over Tommy again, kissing him deeply and making his head spin.

The softness of Carter's curls against Tommy's hands kept him grounded as Carter left his mouth, licking and kissing along his jaw, down his neck, over his ribs, down his belly...

"Alright?" Carter rasped, looking up at him.

Tommy fought to calm his breathing. "A little nervous, but yes."

"You have nothing to be nervous about," Carter said with a chuckle. "I get it though. I'm nervous too. Still okay?"

"Can I keep my hands in your hair?" Tommy asked.

"Definitely." Carter sobered. "I'm serious. Tell me to stop."

"I promise," Tommy repeated, and Carter began kissing down his chest again. His heartbeat picked up once more.

"You're gorgeous," Carter murmured into soft skin, and then let his actions speak for him.

"Holy shit," Tommy gasped when Carter moved back up his body again, taking his time now to kiss every spot where there had been a bruise. "That was... God, Carter!" His brain couldn't function more than that, so he shakily pulled Carter the rest of the way up and enthusiastically joined their mouths again, shivering with delight. "I definitely saw stars, by the way," he said.

"Yeah?" Carter looked very pleased with himself.

"You said that the people you saw up here weren't looking at the stars. Well, I saw stars."

Carter rested his chin on his hand. "You're adorable," he said, grinning.

"Now it's your turn," Tommy said, giving Carter's shoulders a little push.

"You don't have to," Carter replied weakly.

"I really want to," Tommy replied. "The only way you'll stop me is if you tell me no."

"I won't." Carter rolled onto his back, Tommy following him over. "Trust me."

Later, after they had folded up the blanket and put both it and the pillows into the rainproof container, they walked back to the window. Carter pointed out a door as they passed and said, "That's the accessible roof entrance. Normal people don't use the window."

"We're anything but normal," Tommy agreed immediately. His cheeks were starting to hurt from the goofy grin on his face. A glance at Carter showed that he wasn't alone in the giddy feeling.

They stepped back through the window and continued up the stairs, stumbling a little because of how close they were walking to each other.

"There's the elevator again," Carter pointed out. "The bathrooms, the roof door, storage on the right, and teen room on the left."

There was music, chatter, and laughter coming from the room. Carter's eyes sparkled. "Let's see who's here today!" he said, pulling Tommy into the room.

The room was shaped like a large box. There were three large, squashy couches on the long wall with two others opposite them, and a round table with many chairs around it at the far end. Next to the table, there were two couches facing a TV. Directly across from the door, along the wall, were several old arcade games, including *Dance Dance Revolution*.

At first, Tommy was a little overwhelmed by the sheer number of teenagers in the space after being outside alone for so long. He started to recognize some of the faces; Elyse and Adrien he had expected to see, but then he spotted George leaning over the back of one of the far couches, and Lauryn was sitting with Alicia at the table playing a card game.

Tommy turned to Carter, eyes wide and his smile wider. "The entire Oldtown STEM team is Aetherborn?" he asked incredulously.

"Of course they are!" Carter chuckled. "Most of my school is. There are a few humans, maybe fifty or so, but chances were good that the whole team would be Aetherborn."

"Do the humans know that you're not, umm... like them?" Tommy asked hesitantly.

"Some of them, but not all." Carter tugged on Tommy's hand. "Don't tell me you're shy all of a sudden?"

"Nah, just a little surprised."

They walked further into the room, and Elyse looked up from her conversation with another girl that Tommy didn't know. "There you two are!" she exclaimed. "Are you having fun?"

"My niece really loves you, Carter," Adrien said. He was cuddled up on a couch with a beautiful girl. "You're good with kids."

"She's a sweetie," Carter replied. "Easy to love." He sat on the couch next to Adrien, not letting go of Tommy's hand.

"It hasn't quite sunk in that you're related to Brooke," Tommy said to Adrien, sitting as close to Carter as possible.

"I'm her favourite uncle," Adrien said with a grin. "And only because Carter isn't related. Yet." He winked.

The others from the STEM team left what they were doing and gathered around them, dragging chairs or sitting on the floor.

"This is my girlfriend, Arielle," Adrien said, introducing the girl sitting beside him with a gentle squeeze.

"I've heard so much about you that it feels like I already know you," she said, reaching out one elegant hand for Tommy to take.

Her grip was firm, surprising him. Then he remembered

that Jason had said that most Aetherborn tended to be slightly stronger than humans. "Nice to meet you. How did your baseball tournament go?"

Arielle's eyebrows rose. "It went well, thank you. We came second."

"Nice." Looking around at the shocked faces, Tommy said anxiously, "Was I not supposed to ask about that?"

George chuckled. "I'm just surprised you remembered."

"Adrien was checking his phone for updates all weekend in Toronto." Tommy was confused. "Of course I'd remember."

"You're a sweetheart," Arielle said, smiling at him.

"I have a question," Tommy said, attempting to change the subject. "Back in March, Jason told me he was in charge of the Oldtown Council. And then the Council was introduced today..." Tommy faltered.

"What's your question?" Alicia asked.

"The Council feels like kind of a big deal?" Tommy finished quietly.

The teenagers chuckled.

"Oh, you're serious?" Alicia said apologetically. "Sorry."

"Jason's kinda like the king of the Aetherborn Community," Carter said with a smirk. "Zoe recently joined him as co-Ariki of the Council, but she does the financial stuff. Jason's the one that people go to."

"So, Kennedy's marrying royalty?" Tommy asked, jaw agape.

"Pretty much," Carter replied.

"Hang on, back up," George said, holding his hands out. "Tommy knows now? We can talk about it?"

"Jason told me about Aetherborn last night," Tommy said, smiling.

Everyone relaxed, an invisible tension that had been running through the room dissipating at his words.

Steve, one of Carter's oldest friends, burst through the door two seconds later, flopping onto the floor next to them. "This is nice."

He tapped his fist against George's and leaned against Elyse's chair. "What are we talking about?"

"I was just about to tell Tommy that I would never take him for *granite*," Carter said with a straight face.

Everyone laughed.

Alicia leaned in. "Just think about it for a while, really *muse* it over."

"This is really *dragon* on," George said with a smirk as Tommy's jaw dropped again.

"You must have been hanging onto that one for a while. The *elf* control!" Adrien said, reaching out and slapping George's knee affectionately.

"You're just *wind*-ing us up," Lauryn said quietly.

"It'll all *blow* over in a few days," Arielle said.

Tommy looked at her closer and saw the resemblance between her and Lauryn in the shape of their eyes. "Are you two..." He trailed off to let the girls fill in.

"Wind spirits," Arielle said, nodding.

"I was going to say sisters?" Tommy asked weakly. *Wind spirits?*

"We're cousins." Lauryn smiled at Arielle. "Close enough to be sisters, though."

"Aww," Arielle cooed, a hand to her heart.

"I hate this game. It's *soul-draining*," Elyse said, bringing the conversation back to the kinds of Aetherborn.

Tommy frowned and cocked his head, unsure what she meant.

"Succubus," whispered Carter in his ear.

"Is that why guys keep hitting on you?" Tommy asked her. "Chris and Bryan couldn't stop talking about you for a week after we returned home. Bryan's girlfriend was super jealous."

"No, that's just because she's beautiful," Alicia said with a toss of her long black hair. She smiled at the younger girl, who blushed when everyone else nodded in agreement.

"Bah, I don't see *eye to eye* with you," Steve said, his eye gleaming impishly.

It took Tommy a moment to realize what he meant, and then

he couldn't believe he hadn't noticed the single eye over Steve's nose. It was oddly natural and bizarre at the same time. *My brain must be combining my memories with reality,* he reasoned, but it still made him uncomfortable that he had missed something so obvious. What else had he been missing?

"And you play sports?" Tommy asked, curious. "Is your depth perception affected at all?"

Steve shrugged. "I'm used to it, and my team figures out work-arounds. Mistakes happen."

George chuckled. "Like the time you tried to tackle that dude in rugby last week and fell flat on your face because they were further away than you thought."

Steve flipped him off, and everyone laughed.

"Is it hard to play physical sports against teams from human schools?" Tommy asked. "You'd have to restrain your strength constantly."

The entire group shrugged as one.

"Most of us are just a little above average strength. Even Carter can't pick up a car and throw it at someone," George teased.

"It's something we've been doing our entire lives," Adrien added.

"You didn't notice when you were here in March," Elyse said, rolling her eyes. "And Carter wasn't exactly subtle, showing off when he arm wrestled Greg."

"You didn't notice in Toronto either, although I think you were a tad distracted," George said mischievously.

"It's amazing what humans don't notice when we're not looking," Tommy said easily, making the others laugh.

"You're alright, kiddo," Adrien said, ruffling his hair. "And you're right. In Oldtown especially, there are runes in the buildings to help prevent humans from noticing Aetherborn traits. It took you a bit to see Steve properly, eh?"

"Yeah, it did."

"It's hard to see past the glamour at first."

"That's really cool." Tommy relaxed in Carter's embrace, letting the conversation flow over him as the rest of the group started talking about people he didn't know. Tommy was again struck by the enormity of things he had missed. He'd shared a hotel room with a dragon, elf, and rock giant and never suspected a thing. It didn't bother him that they were different, only that he hadn't known. He understood that Jason hadn't known him back in March, and had insisted on keeping the Community a secret, but it still hurt a little.

He wondered what the humans living in Oldtown would feel when, or if, they found out about the hidden magical world right under their noses.

"Where's Leo?" Tommy asked Carter, looking around once the others had drifted away.

"He's one of the humans in Oldtown," Carter said. "He knows about Aetherborn, but Steve and I didn't tell him until a few years ago."

"So, he comes to the dances at The Hawaiian, but he's not included in Community events," Tommy guessed.

"Exactly." Carter leaned back, spreading his arms wide over the back of the couch. "When we tell someone who we are, it means we trust them completely." He paused and then added quickly, "You were a different case. I had to wait until Jason was ready to tell you. Otherwise, I would have told you the day you asked me to be your boyfriend."

Tommy smiled, draping his legs over Carter's, snuggling up to him. Carter wrapped one arm around Tommy's shoulders and put the other on his knees. "That means a lot to me. Thank you."

A loud cheer erupted from the people watching the TV. Tommy couldn't quite see what was on the screen.

"What are they doing?" Tommy asked.

"Someone must be playing a video game. There are some old systems like Atari and Nintendo that were donated. There's a VCR too. There are old VHS tapes on the wall behind us, for if we ever want to have a movie night," Carter said.

"Nice. And this place is open until...?"

"Three. It keeps the same hours as The Hawaiian." Carter nuzzled into Tommy's neck. "Want to go dance some more? Get some food?"

"Yeah, sounds great."

"We're heading back to the party," Carter said, raising his voice to reach every corner of the room. "Who thinks they can beat me in a dance-off?"

"Not me, but I'll enjoy watching you win," Tommy said, kissing Carter on the jaw.

Carter beamed at him. "I'll teach you how to dance," he offered.

"You already have," Tommy murmured, thinking about their time together under the stars.

"Come on, kids, you can't throw down a challenge like that and then not follow through," George said, slapping Carter's leg as he walked by. "Up you get!"

"Yeah, yeah, we're coming," Tommy said, getting up.

"Excellent." Adrien scooped Tommy up and tossed him over his shoulder. "We're family now, you and me. Us Johnson in-laws need to stick together."

"Unhand the human!" Tommy gasped from his upside-down position.

"Once we get to the ballroom," Adrien said cheerfully.

"Yeah, this way we know you'll actually get there!" Alicia added with a chuckle.

Tommy didn't say anything to that but met his boyfriend's sheepish expression with a matching one of his own. *They know us well,* he thought.

Adrien returned Tommy to his feet just outside the ballroom, the magical doors keeping the thumping beat of the music from permeating the hallway.

"Let's dance!" Tommy said, grabbing Carter's hand and pulling him back into the ballroom, the rest of the teens whooping behind them.

Chapter 4

MONDAY THE 9TH OF JUNE, 2003 -
WESTMEATH, ONTARIO

Carter shivered and shifted across the bed, trying to find Tommy's warmth.

Instead, he fell off the edge of the twin bed.

His eyes flew open, and he rolled, grasping at his sheets to slow his momentum. Even so, he landed on his back with a loud *thump* that was audible throughout the apartment.

Carter? Are you alright? Both his dad and father mindspoke to him at the same time.

Carter groaned from his position on the area rug beside his bed. *I'm fine. Just fell out of bed,* he projected back to them. He squinted up at the digital alarm clock on his bedside table and groaned again. *Only five?* He considered climbing back into bed, but it didn't have Tommy in it to cuddle. Getting up for the day, he pulled out his clothes, taking Zhanna's advice.

Zhanna was one of the two ladies who ran the tailor shop Seams Likeable, and on Saturday, she had given him a package and told him to wear a pair on Monday. When he'd opened the package to find seven pairs of short boxer briefs in the jewel tones he liked, he'd been confused. When Tommy had told him they were the same, other than the colour, as the ones his mother had been convinced to buy for him, he'd been even more confused.

But the ladies were rumoured to be able to see the future, so when he got dressed, he chose the burgundy pair and slipped them on before pulling on his cargo shorts.

Okay, these are seriously comfortable, Carter thought, impressed. He got his school things together in his backpack and pulled out his knife throwing kit. *I've got some time, might as well get some practising in.*

"You're up early," his dad said from the kitchen. "You want breakfast?"

"I'll have some after I throw knives. My stomach is still too sleepy to eat," Carter replied.

"Have fun."

"Of course." If his dad was up, his father was already in the bakery's kitchen, getting started on the fresh breads for the day. Carter smelled them as he entered the stairwell, and it reminded him that he owed Kennedy some cream puffs.

They'd made a bet about who would shower faster after martial arts on Saturday, and he'd lost. She'd bought him a new dark orange shirt anyway, but he had promised her cream puffs. "I'll do that after school today," he muttered to himself.

Carter turned left at the bottom of the stairs, leading him outside to where he had set up his target. If he turned right, he'd enter the bakery right behind the cash. He put his knife kit down and took a couple of breaths to prepare himself. The knife kit was custom-made for him; the five throwing knives each fit perfectly in his hand. Sometimes, when he threw them, he felt like pieces of his soul were soaring through the air with them, longing to take flight.

There were no clouds, as far as he could see. It was so clear that the blue of the sky looked fake.

He chose his first knife and set his stance for the new throw that he'd started working on recently. After he threw all five, he let his mind wander back to when Tommy had first seen him throw knives over March Break. Carter grinned. That afternoon had turned out quite well.

Carter stood alone in his backyard, heart pounding, the sun

shining off the snow around him. He stared down at his phone, still showing the completed transfer of the video Tommy had taken of him throwing his knives into the target. He tapped it, hiding the notification, and slid it into his pocket.

He blew out a long breath. "Holy shit," he murmured to himself, running both hands through his curls, and lacing his fingers behind his head, tilting his face up to the cloudy sky.

"What now?" Carter whispered to himself.

"That was super hot," Tommy had said. Carter couldn't believe his ears at first. And then Tommy had panicked at being overheard and had run away.

Carter bit his lip. "Will he ignore what just happened?" He hoped not. "I hope I read him right and that he *is* into me."

The sky offered no answers.

Sighing, Carter headed for the target and removed the knives. He was proud of himself for not letting his nerves get the better of him; all five knives had hit the centre of the target despite his distraction. Tommy had smelled so good when they'd checked the angle of the camera that his knees had almost buckled. The hint of his shampoo or deodorant was intoxicating, and Carter had to resist the urge to bury his nose in Tommy's neck to inhale deeply.

Carter closed his eyes, almost swamped by desire just thinking about it. He gave himself a shake. "Slow down. He's your friend. Don't rush things just because you have a crush. You don't know what's going on in his head." He walked over to his throwing position and squared his shoulders, balancing his first knife carefully in his hand.

Taking several deep breaths, Carter cleared his mind until Tommy's face was no longer foremost in his thoughts. "Hard to do, like telling someone not to think of a pink elephant," he muttered to himself. He threw his first knife; it landed too low. His second was too high.

Distracted? his father's voice rumbled in his head.

Carter sighed. *You could say that, but it would be an*

understatement, he mindspoke back, turning to face his father at the back door of the bakery.

William Batudev leaned against the frame of the red brick building, his arms crossed over his chest. *You were broadcasting.* His breath made a cloud of steam in front of his face that dissipated quickly.

Oops, Carter thought to himself. "Was I? Sorry. Any advice?"

"Not in so many words. A general feeling of being upset was coming through." His father furrowed his brow. "Did you and Tommy have a fight?"

"Far from it." Carter sighed. "I think he likes me, but he doesn't want to admit it to himself."

Eyebrows rising, his father said, "Of course he likes you. You're friends, aren't you?"

Carter chuckled. "Are you doing that on purpose? *Likes* me, likes me."

His father grinned, white teeth flashing in deep olive skin. "I knew what you meant. What are you going to do about it?"

"Wait, I guess. Even if I'm right about him liking me, I'm not going to force him to say it. That's not fair to him." Carter sighed. "Father, I *really* like him."

A low rumble like an earthquake left his father. "I know. I remember how giddy you were on Saturday after you met him," he teased.

Carter flushed and smiled. "The crush I had because he's pretty has turned into a full-blown attraction because he's amazing," he admitted.

"Oh yeah?"

"Yeah. He's so brilliant; he's always the first one done in every lesson, and then he offers his help to anyone struggling. He's got a great sense of humour, and we spend a lot of time laughing together. Brooke adores him." Carter found himself staring off into space.

"And he's cute," his father added, a smirk playing at the corner of his lips.

"Oh my God, *so* cute!" Carter groaned dramatically. "And he smells so good? I want to breathe him in all the time. The self-control, father. You have no idea."

The rumbling chuckle echoed through the backyard again. "Have you told him any of this?"

"Noooo. Not in so many words. But I did let him know I was interested before he took off today. Hopefully, that will encourage him to say something."

His father regarded him thoughtfully. "And what happens when he goes back home?"

"Gah!" Carter exclaimed, flailing his arms. "I don't know, okay? I just know I like him, and I'll take whatever he's willing to give me, whether it's friendship or more. I'm going to miss him when he goes home no matter what."

"Any kind of long-distance relationship is hard, even friendship," his father said solemnly. "It's a tough position to be in."

Carter's shoulders sagged. "Yeah, it is."

"I'll leave you to it. Switch to practising your Katas instead?" his father suggested before disappearing back inside. *Or take a cold shower?*

Carter blushed. *Father!* He stared at the knives and wrinkled his nose. "He's right though. I'm distracted, and I could do my Katas in my sleep." He packed up his knives and took them upstairs to his room before stripping out of his clothes and putting on sweatpants.

He pushed his desk chair in and made sure he had enough space before settling into the first stance.

Half an hour later, his phone let out a muffled *ding* inside the pocket of his crumpled-up jeans. Carter dug his phone out and read Tommy's message: "I didn't mean to say it out loud but I'm glad I did. Can you come over and stay for dinner? I would like to say some more things out loud, intentionally this time."

Carter's heart leaped with excitement. *Dad! Father! Can I go to Tommy's for dinner?* He mindspoke to get a faster response.

Of course, his dad replied instantly.

"Omw," Carter texted back and dashed out of his room. In the hall, he realized he was only half dressed and hurried back in, yanking on his clothes from the day and putting on his outdoor gear at the front door.

Does he mean what I think he means? Carter thought to himself as he half-jogged the short distance to the little bungalow where Tommy was staying. His heart was thumping so loudly that everything else sounded muffled.

He rang the doorbell and didn't have to wait long before Tommy opened the door. "Hi!" Carter said in greeting, beaming.

"Let's go to my room," Tommy said.

Carter studied the other boy out of the corner of his eye as he unlaced his boots. Tommy looked nervous but determined.

As soon as his boots were off, Carter found himself being pulled by the hand down the short hallway to what must be Tommy's bedroom. It was small, the dominant feature being the double bed, and had no decor on the walls. *Right, only temporary,* Carter thought to himself sadly.

Tommy pulled out the desk chair for him and then rambled on about Carter having been patient with him. Carter was about to open his mouth to say something, he wasn't sure what, when Tommy raised a hand.

"Let me..." Tommy said, pulling out his guitar and grabbing a piece of paper off the desk that Carter hadn't noticed. It was dark with scribbles around some words. Tommy settled himself on the bed with the guitar and tuned it quickly.

Carter forced his heart to calm down. He didn't want to miss a single note.

"I wrote this when I got home..." Tommy said, and Carter blinked in surprise. *He couldn't have been home for more than an hour, and he wrote an entire song?* "I didn't get a chance to write music, so I'm going to make it up on the spot..." Tommy continued apologetically. Carter leaned forward, intent on the boy on the bed.

And then the music started.

Tommy's voice was low, but not so quiet as to be drowned out by the guitar. He played simple chords, letting the sound die away before strumming again. A bright red crept over his cheeks as he sang the chorus, about wanting to kiss him, and Carter felt his heart soar.

Tommy must have felt more confident after that because he added a rhythm to his strumming, one that made Carter want to dance. But he stayed in his chair, focused on every word. The chorus sounded even better the second time with the added rhythm. Tommy met his gaze as he moved through the bridge, singing about Carter's intelligence.

Carter squirmed with delight as he listened to the last chorus, feeling overwhelmed by how much he liked this boy in front of him. This boy, who stammered through an apology about lying about liking guys. Who asked him to be his boyfriend.

What else could he say but yes? They'd work through the challenging stuff together.

Carter shook himself out of the memory and checked his watch. It was nearing six-thirty, so he gathered his knives together, checking each one for nicks before storing them in their case.

His dad had toasted a slice of yesterday's bread for him, and Carter slathered it with peanut butter, folding it in half to eat as he walked over to the Johnson house to collect Tommy.

The principal of Oldtown High, Ms. Chang, had agreed to let Tommy sit in on classes during the week. Tommy's parents had told him during Sunday dinner, and both boys had been too excited about that to pay much attention to the unexpected arrival of a new houseguest, Kathryn Johnson, Jason's grandmother.

After the rain from the day before, everything felt shimmery and new. Carter skipped up the steps at the front of the house, Kennedy holding the door open for him as she left for work. She gave him a quick hug as they passed each other.

Carter joined the adults sitting at the table in the kitchen, happily accepting a fresh muffin that Kathryn had made that morning.

"Has anyone told you what your ring means, Sir?" Kathryn asked him during a lull in the conversation.

"It means I'm a Knight of Gaulan, according to a dinner-theatre show in Toronto," Carter said, taking a big bite of the muffin. "Wow, this is really good," he mumbled, mouth full.

"Nothing else was said when you received it?" she asked, amused.

"Just something about Everdome claiming what's hers." He and Tommy had spent more than one night over video chat trying to make sense of that.

She sighed and rolled her eyes before saying, "Sounds vague and ominous, but probably all you need to know, Sir Knight." She bit into a muffin and walked off, her words leaving him feeling a little nervous.

Tommy stumbled into the room, still half asleep, but smiled brightly when he saw Carter. "I missed snuggling with you last night," he whispered in Carter's ear, giving him a hug. "Let's go."

"Breakfast, dear," Lilah said, and Tommy grabbed a muffin, lifting it in acknowledgment.

She rolled her eyes but nodded as they left, shouldering their backpacks after putting on their shoes at the door.

"Did you find out anything more about Kathryn after I left last night?" Carter asked the minute the door closed behind them.

"Apparently Jason found letters written by her to Hammond, his father, this spring. Kennedy wants Mom to read them for some reason," Tommy said, shrugging. He hooked his thumbs under his backpack straps and Carter copied him. "I still have no idea how Kathryn looks thirty."

"Oh, they said something about that when I was waiting for you. She learned a spell to keep her young." Carter wondered how he'd feel about staying the same age while everyone around him grew old and died. There were some Aetherborn that were like that, like Judy, his martial arts instructor. "I'm glad I've got a human lifespan."

"I'm glad you do too," Tommy said and then blushed. "I mean… If we… Never mind, forget I said anything."

Carter grinned and bit back his words. He wanted to say, "Are you thinking about forever already? We're on the same page," but he didn't want to make Tommy any more uncomfortable than he already seemed to be. Instead, he said, "What do you think of Kathryn?"

"She's interesting, in an odd way. Like calling you 'Sir' every time she talks to you," Tommy said.

"I like that," Carter said thoughtfully. "Makes me feel mature."

"Should I call you Sir?" Tommy asked, his voice dropping to a whisper.

Carter shivered. "*That* has an entirely different feel to it."

Tommy smirked. "I'll keep it in mind."

They turned a corner, and the school came into view: a huge, grey stone building that took up an entire block.

"Whoa!" Tommy said, jaw dropping.

"It's one of the original schools in the city, although it was renovated at some point in the late seventies," Carter said. "They got rid of the asbestos, added the north wing and the second floor, and made the whole thing more accessible."

"Isn't that around the time that the tech companies really started in Westmeath?" Tommy asked.

"Yup. Hammond was in charge then. When more humans started moving to Westmeath, the tech campuses bought up the land. He started investing heavily in the real estate of Oldtown to keep it from being bought out too. The Council owns nearly all the land in Oldtown now. Then he invested in the schools, renovating the ones that already existed, and building new schools so that Aetherborn would always have a safe place to learn." Carter stopped talking. "Sorry, you don't want a history lesson. I've been hanging around Jason too much lately."

"No, I do!" Tommy reassured him. "How are the Aetherborn

safe at school if there are humans as well? The thing Adrien mentioned on Saturday at the ball?"

"It's the same spell that'll be used during the wedding; it's a glamour ward that's built into the architecture. If you don't know about Aetherborn, you can't see the ones that don't pass."

"They're invisible?" Tommy asked and tripped over a crack in the sidewalk.

Carter caught him. "Not invisible. They're just not noticed. Same goes if you know about Aetherborn and don't have good intentions."

"So back in March, I never noticed that Steve is a cyclops because I didn't know about Aetherborn?" Tommy asked.

"Exactly. If you'd met him on the street in broad daylight, you might've noticed something was up, but the community centre, schools, churches, mosques, and temples, even Judy's and the other stores in the area all have it built into their architecture."

They had reached the block the school was on. Carter could see the distinctive purple leather jacket belonging to a member of the Blue Blood gang at the other end and frowned. "Why are *they* hanging around our school?" he growled. He couldn't quite make out the girl or boy that the gang member was talking to.

As if they'd heard him, the gang member started walking away.

"I don't like this," Carter said, frowning. He pulled out his phone and texted Judy about what he'd seen before turning it off. "All set. Are you ready?"

"Excited and nervous," Tommy replied.

"Exactly how I felt on my first day. You know what your sister said to me?"

"'You're amazing! Just be yourself, and everyone will love you.'" Tommy mimicked Kennedy's hair flip at the end, and Carter chuckled.

"Yeah. How'd you know?"

"I know her pretty well."

"Your imitation was spot on." Carter reached out to Tommy. "Is this okay?"

Tommy took his hand eagerly. "More than."

Carter beamed. "This confidence?" He gestured at Tommy. "I love it."

"It feels good too."

Holding hands, they walked into the school.

Inside, there were people everywhere. Carter pulled Tommy to one side and shouldered his way through the throng. When they reached a set of glass double doors, the school's duckling mascot engraved across them, Carter pushed one open. It swung closed behind them, and the noise level dropped dramatically.

One of the secretaries, an older woman with her grey hair pulled back in a bun, held up a finger to them, indicating that they needed to wait. They sat on the chairs opposite the main desk, and Tommy looked around the office.

"What are you thinking?" Carter asked, playing with Tommy's fingers.

"I'm thinking about how that one hallway had enough people to fill my entire school, and that you could fit three offices in here, and I'm suddenly feeling very small-town," Tommy said anxiously.

Carter chuckled. "It's just a little different. You'll get used to it quickly."

The door to one of the enclosed rooms opened, and two girls walked out, followed by a petite woman. Both girls had tears trickling down their cheeks.

Chapter 5

MONDAY THE 9TH OF JUNE, 2003 -
WESTMEATH, ONTARIO

"You can come back once you've changed," the woman said to the teary-eyed girls in a nasally monotone. "Run along now."

Tommy was on his feet the instant the door closed behind the woman. "Lauryn! What's wrong?" She was on the STEM team, but he didn't know Lauryn's friend. He couldn't imagine that either girl was the type to get in trouble.

Lauryn tried to compose herself, with mixed results.

"Do you need a hug?" Carter asked the girls, standing beside Tommy.

The girl Tommy didn't know nodded, and Carter held his arms open for her to bury herself in his chest. He made shushing noises as he rocked her. "What happened, Emily?"

A scowl appeared on Lauryn's face, and Tommy could feel a light breeze brushing through his hair. "Ms. VanCamp thinks our skirts are too short."

A snort escaped Tommy before he could stop it. "I'm sorry, what?"

Lauryn put her arms straight down, the very tips of her fingers reaching past the bottom of her skirt. "'Skirts must be below your fingertips,'" she mimicked in a nasally monotone. "'Return to school once you are dressed appropriately for learning, girls!'"

Carter snickered. "Great impersonation."

Tommy chewed at his lower lip as he thought. "What is the dress code for boys?" he said at last.

Emily wiped her tears with the palm of her hand. "You're fine, don't worry about it. Ms. VanCamp has it out for the girls at this school."

"That's not what I meant." Tommy locked eyes with Carter, willing him to understand. "Is there anything in the dress code that says that boys can't wear skirts?"

Carter beamed at him. "No, there isn't."

"I don't follow," Emily said, confused.

Lauryn's jaw dropped. "You're kidding. You'd switch with us?"

"Of course I would." Tommy frowned. "It's a ridiculous rule. Girls wearing short skirts don't distract from learning."

"Of course you think that. You're gay," Carter said, chuckling when Tommy stuck his tongue out in response. "But you're right. When I'm in a classroom, I'm not paying attention to what people are wearing."

"I have to get my schedule, and then we'll switch, alright?" Tommy said to the girls.

The secretary beckoned him forward, handing him a map of the school and a printout of his class schedule.

Carter peeked over Tommy's shoulder at the list of classes. "Oh hey, you're following me around."

"I was hoping I could join a music class," Tommy said softly to him.

"We'll go see the music teachers at lunch," Carter promised. "I'm sure one of them will be happy to have you, and you can replace your drama or computer class."

"Awesome." Tommy brightened.

"Let's go, girls," Carter said. He took Tommy's hand firmly in his and gestured for the girls to lead the way.

"How are we going to do this?" Emily asked, a light blush on her cheeks.

"The accessible bathroom should be large enough for all four of us," Lauryn suggested.

"I promise to be a gentleman," Carter said with a wink, making the other three laugh.

The bathroom was large enough, and they exchanged their lower clothing without any trouble.

"I'm so glad I took Zhanna's advice and wore the new underwear," Tommy said, giving his hips a little wiggle. Lauryn's purple-and-green patterned skirt swished around his hips, not revealing the emerald green boxer briefs underneath. "Everything feels contained."

Carter chuckled. "I know what you mean." He struck a pose, Emily's dark burgundy skirt complimenting his grey Rush t-shirt nicely. "How do I look?"

"Handsome as always," Tommy said with a smile.

"You guys are the best," Lauryn said, giving them each a hug.

"Oh, my phone!" Carter said suddenly.

Emily started putting her hands in her pockets, trying to find his phone for him. "How many pockets do you need?" she asked.

"Two, one for my wallet, one for my phone." He took both when she pulled them out. "Where do you keep your things? There aren't any pockets in these!"

"My backpack." Emily shrugged. "Or I carry a purse."

"Backpack it is, then," Tommy said, tucking his wallet in the front pockct.

"We'll meet outside this bathroom at the end of school to change back," Lauryn said. "Thanks again."

"Not a problem," Tommy said, grinning. "If I'm going to attend a different school for a week, I might as well make a statement. First impressions are everything, right?"

Emily smiled back at him. "They are. This was really great of you. Are you sure you're gay?"

"Very," Tommy said gravely.

Carter laughed. "Thankfully." He squeezed Tommy's hand, pulling him in for a light kiss.

"You two are so cute together," Lauryn said with a smile.

They left the bathroom to go to their classes. The halls buzzed with whispers as the boys passed, hands clasped, heading for Carter's locker before their first class.

"I think I'm going to get lost if I ever have to navigate by myself," Tommy said, trying to figure out where they were on the map without getting bumped by anyone.

"We're right..." Carter glanced at the map for two seconds and pointed at a spot in the wing, "...here. Don't worry, you'll get used to it before the week is up. Here's my locker."

They stowed their backpacks and took out their science books, agendas, and pencil cases. The whispers around them were getting louder, allowing Tommy to hear snippets of them.

"Who's that with Carter?"

"Why are they wearing skirts?"

"Is there some kind of drama event happening today?"

"I didn't know Carter was seeing anyone."

"You already know Ms. Rubens, of course," Carter said as they continued along the hallway. "I think we're starting the space unit today."

"Oh, awesome! We started that last week," Tommy said, bumping his hip into Carter's. It was easy to ignore the whispers around them when all he wanted to do was focus on his boyfriend.

The crowded hallway thinned out as people went into their classrooms.

"You won't be bored, will you?" Carter asked.

"I doubt it!" Tommy said with a chuckle. "Even if it's the exact same material, Ms. Rubens will teach it differently than Mr. Travese."

"True." Carter stopped outside an open door. "Are you ready for your first class at Oldtown High?"

"I'm ready for anything," Tommy said with a smile.

After Carter's computer class, which both boys found ridiculously easy, was lunch. Carter had Tommy navigate them to the cafeteria using his map.

The school was straightforward; it was two floors in the shape of an L. The office was in the corner on the main floor. The cafeteria was at the far end of the original building and pulled double duty as the auditorium. It had a permanent stage at one end, with a drum kit and an upright piano. There were still a few set pieces up from the play the week before.

"You don't have to worry about vandalism?" Tommy asked Carter quietly as they joined the line of people waiting for their food.

"No. Is that a thing at your school?"

Tommy shrugged. "It must have been at one point. Nothing is ever left out for students to access."

"Hmm. Well, here, people can go up and have a jam session if they want or just try out the instruments. The higher-level students help the newbies. Everyone's super encouraging." The line moved quickly, and Carter chose a pre-wrapped egg salad sandwich.

"I don't think I could ever do that!" Tommy said, adding a shudder for good measure. He picked up a tuna sandwich.

Carter took the sandwich away from Tommy and put it back with a wrinkle of his nose. "Don't. They're terrible." When Tommy had selected another sandwich, he added, "Aren't you performing at the wedding on Saturday? How are you going to deal with it then?"

"I have no idea." They reached the cash, and Tommy said to the man behind the till, "Put his on my bill, please," indicating Carter's sandwich.

"Aww, thanks, babe," Carter said, kissing Tommy's cheek.

They re-entered the main room of the cafeteria, and Tommy looked around at the sea of faces. "Where do you want to sit?" he asked.

"Mondays are my best friend days," Carter said. "Leo, Steve, Elyse, and her best friend Karine. They should be over here to the left... Sweet, they saved us seats."

They sat at the table, and Tommy nodded at the others. He recognized Karine from the Community Ball on Saturday but hadn't caught her name then.

"Why are you wearing skirts?" Leo asked, a puzzled frown on his face. "Is this a wedding thing?"

"You didn't hear?" Karine asked, turning to him. "Two grade ten girls were going to be sent home because their skirts were too short. These two switched with them." She sighed dramatically. "So romantic!"

Leo chewed on a fry thoughtfully. "It's romantic for a boy to offer to wear a skirt for a day?"

"If it keeps a girl out of trouble," Karine retorted.

Carter nudged Tommy and gestured at the aisle with his head. Adrien was heading for them, and he was wearing a skirt, too.

"Did Arielle get sent home?" Carter asked.

"No, but we heard about what you started and wanted to join." Adrien sat beside Tommy and draped his arm around his shoulders. "Thanks for sticking up for Lauryn."

"Of course," Tommy said.

Adrien grinned. "There's a petition going around the caf to get that rule removed from the dress code. Until it's removed, all boys who sign it will wear a skirt in solidarity."

"That's genius," Carter said excitedly. "Heck yeah, I'll sign it!"

"Can I, even though I'm not a student here?" Tommy asked.

"I don't see why not. You're here for a week." Adrien squeezed Tommy's shoulders and got up. "I knew I could count on you two. See you at lunch tomorrow."

"What did you two start?" Steve asked, mouth agape.

"Look around!" Tommy exclaimed, finally noticing how many guys were wearing skirts, and how many girls were wearing baggy shorts. "This is amazing."

"We should probably make sure that some of the teachers know what's going on," Elyse said.

"Mr. Coolidge seemed pretty great when I met him in Toronto. We can tell him," Tommy said. "And I wanted to go talk to the music teachers at lunch today."

"Alicia's got music last period," Elyse said. "I don't know when the grade nine classes are though. Karine?"

"I've got music first thing in the morning," Karine said brightly. "I play the flute. What's your instrument?"

"Guitar. First thing is science, though. I don't want to miss that. I'll ask about the grade eleven class. That's during drama, right?" Tommy asked Carter.

"Yeah, but I think you'd get a lot out of drama. Why not ask for the grade twelve class before lunch? George is in that one." Carter balled up his plastic wrap from his sandwich, stood up, and threw it at the garbage can at the end of the aisle. It sailed in perfectly.

"Is there nothing you're not great at?" Tommy asked admiringly.

"No," the table chorused.

Carter chuckled. "Thanks for that. Yes, I'm not great at math."

"'Not great,' he says." Steve rolled his eye. "Just because you have trouble with tests doesn't mean you suck."

"You might struggle with it, but that doesn't mean you're bad at math," Elyse added.

"I think the general consensus is that you're good at math, too," Tommy teased. "You really *are* perfect."

Carter reacted with an exaggerated horrified expression. "Bite your tongue. I can't be perfect. Nobody is."

"You're perfect for me," Tommy said, squeezing his hand under the table.

"Gag," said Steve with a smirk. "If you're going to act all lovey-dovey, don't hang around with us."

"Fine," Carter said, his nose in the air. "We'll hang with the STEM crowd tomorrow."

"You *always* have STEM club on Tuesdays," Leo pointed out.

"Yeah, and?" Carter replied, sticking his tongue out across the table.

Tommy chuckled, enjoying the general atmosphere of the school, the low hum of conversation in the caf interrupted by shouts of laughter, and the teasing between the friends. It was obvious that they were close.

A new girl suddenly appeared at the end of their table. "Hello,

Carter." She pushed a perfect golden-brown curl behind her shoulder.

"Hi Patricia," Carter said, his tone emotionless. "How can I help you?"

"Always so polite!" Patricia giggled. She sat on the bench where Adrien had been and scooted close to Tommy. "Are you going to introduce me to your new friend?"

"Patricia, this is Tommy."

"Pleased to meet you," Patricia said, holding out her hand to Tommy. He shook it awkwardly. "You must be Kennedy's younger brother. I can see the resemblance."

"Yes, I am."

"How wonderful that you're here for the whole week before the wedding! What do you think of our little school?" She batted her eyelashes at him.

He wondered if she had something in her eye. "This school is amazing! I feel so welcomed by everyone."

"I bet you are!" Patricia said, giggling again and putting her hand on his arm. "You're such a nice guy, to help out a girl you don't even know!"

"I already knew Lauryn," Tommy said, eating the last bite of his sandwich. He handed Carter his plastic wrap. "Do you want to throw this one, too?"

Carter grinned at him. "Of course. Practise makes perfect."

"I thought you said you didn't want to be perfect?" Tommy teased.

"I was wondering..." Patricia tried to insert herself into the conversation.

Tommy held up a finger and watched Carter execute another perfect toss into the garbage. "Nice! Sorry, what was that?"

"I was *wondering*," Patricia said again, a hint of impatience in her tone, "if you had a date for the wedding."

"Oh, yeah, my best friend Faith is driving up from home with her brother." Tommy smiled across the table at Elyse. "We're going to have so much fun! She's coming up on Thursday evening and should be here in time for the party."

"That's awesome!" Elyse replied.

"There's a party on Thursday night?" Patricia asked, leaning eagerly into Tommy's space.

"Oh, sorry, it's just for the wedding party and family and a few other guests," Tommy said apologetically.

Patricia huffed and got to her feet, crossing her arms. "You—!" She stomped her foot and pivoted, walking away from them.

"Should I not have brought up the party?" Tommy asked Carter, who was silently shaking with laughter beside him.

"You know she was flirting with you, right?" Elyse asked, amused.

"No!" Tommy looked helplessly at Carter. "Sorry?"

"You have nothing to be sorry for. I've never seen anyone flirt with a brick wall before. You completely blocked all her attempts!" Carter started laughing again.

"I didn't know I was," Tommy said, eyes wide, which made Carter laugh harder.

"Not to burst your bubble, but you know why Patricia came by, right?" Elyse asked.

Carter wiped tears from his eyes and got himself under control. "No, why?"

"Granted, this is only a rumour, but Patricia's sister was being groomed by Claude to be Jason's wife." Elyse dropped her voice to a whisper. "Heather was supposed to meet Jason at The Hawaiian the night that Jason brought Kennedy there for their first date."

"No kidding!" Carter said, visibly taken aback.

"What does that have to do with today?" Tommy asked, confused. "Who's Claude?"

Karine smirked. "I guess Patricia figured that if she can't be the sister-in-law to the Ariki, she could get with the brother-in-law to the Ariki. Claude was a member of the Council."

Leo groaned. "Your Aetherborn politics are too complicated for me."

The petition arrived at their table, and they all signed it before passing it on.

"I guess Patricia wasn't at the ball on Saturday?" Tommy asked.

"I didn't see her there," Elyse said thoughtfully. "The family is probably a little miffed that Claude's promises didn't amount to anything."

"Claude had no right to promise anything of the sort." Carter frowned. "He must have thought he could control Jason better through a pliable wife."

"He must have *hated* Kennedy," Tommy said with a chuckle.

The rest of the table fell silent.

"What?"

"He tried to have her killed," Carter said quietly.

Tommy remembered Jason mentioning that there had been assassination attempts when they had first met. "Yeah, my statement stands." He shook his head. "That guy sounds like a real piece of work. I assume he's in jail?"

"Ah, no. He died." Carter made a face. "Don't mention him to Jason, if you can help it. He feels responsible."

Tommy's jaw dropped. "Was he?"

"It's complicated, and I don't think I ever heard the full story, but Claude was a shapeshifter, and he had an accident while he was in giant form. When he shrank..." Carter made a disgusting squishing noise and drew his finger across his neck.

Tommy hadn't realized how dangerous Westmeath could be. A brief worry crossed his mind, but his sister's confidence that he would do well here eased it. *I can ask her for the full story after the wedding,* he thought.

"And on that pleasant note, we should get going if you want to talk to the music teachers." Carter got to his feet and offered his hand to Tommy.

"Can I try to navigate?" Tommy asked eagerly, unfolding his map.

"Of course."

Tommy's parents were in the living room when he arrived at the house after school, reading something in a binder.

Lilah wiped her eyes surreptitiously and smiled at him. "How was your day, dear?"

"It was fantastic!" Tommy beamed. "Today, I joined Carter in all his classes, but tomorrow I'll be able to join the grade twelve music class before lunch, so I'll bring my guitar. The school is *huge*! I had no idea what to expect! Oh, and Carter and I sort of started a revolution." His cheeks flushed a little. *Would they approve?* He told them about the petition and the skirts.

"I'm very proud of you," Lilah said with a smile. "I have some skirts you can wear."

"Uh, thank you, but I'm going to ask Kennedy," Tommy said. "I want to at least be fashionable."

Gerard chuckled at Lilah's shocked expression.

"Just for that dig, young man, you're going to sit down, and we're going to talk about safe sex," Lilah said with a smirk. She picked up two pamphlets from the end table and handed them to him.

"Oh, come on, we had that talk last year!" Tommy said with a sigh, taking the folded papers and glancing between them. There was one on STI transmission and one on gay sex.

"Yes, but that was when I thought I had to prepare you for pregnancy prevention, not anal sex."

Tommy felt his face flush. "Um. Right." He was determined not to give her the satisfaction of knowing just how much those words flustered him. "Where did you get these?"

"There was a Planned Parenthood close to where we parked this morning. I popped in and asked for some resources for you," Lilah said.

"Thanks, Mom." Tommy forced a smile. "I appreciate you thinking of it."

"Oh!" Lilah put a hand to her heart. "You're welcome, dear. Why don't you read those, and if you have any questions, you can come to me."

"Thanks, I will." Tommy got to his feet and picked up his backpack. "I'm going to work on some homework first. Love you."

Lilah looked like she was going to cry again. "Love you too, dear."

Tommy escaped to his room, tossed the pamphlets on his bed for later, and pulled out his books from the day.

He had split up his assignments from home while he'd been in the hospital so that he wouldn't feel too overwhelmed by the end of the week.

He'd finished that day's assignments and was reading the pamphlets on his bed when he heard someone come home from work. He paid them no mind, figuring that if they wanted to talk to him, they'd come see him. He furrowed his brow, reading the bit about STI transmission through saliva again.

Shit, he thought, trying not to panic. *I wouldn't be surprised if Hunter or one of them had something, considering what they get up to at those parties. They all spat in my face last week, and I had open wounds...* He read a little further, but his eyes kept skipping back up to the paragraph about testing times. *I was tested for everything under the sun at the hospital, but I won't hear back for two weeks!* He flipped the other pamphlet open, his heart sinking with each word. *If I do test positive, I've exposed Carter! I didn't know we had to use condoms for oral. Even kissing him might have exposed him to something if I had an STI in my mouth.*

A knock sounded on the door, making him jump. It was Kennedy, he saw with relief. "Dee, you're home!" Tommy shot to his feet and drew her into his room, closing the door behind her.

"Sounds serious. What's the favour?" Kennedy said, amused.

Tommy chuckled, feeling his tension melt away. "You know me well. Can I borrow skirts to wear to school for the rest of the week?"

Kennedy blinked in surprise. "Not that well, apparently. Sure you can, but *why*?"

"We're protesting!" Tommy exclaimed, bouncing a little on the bed. He told her about the injustice of the girls being sent home and the petition to change it.

"Sounds like you had a busy day," Kennedy said with a smile. "Do you want short or long skirts?"

Tommy grinned. "As short as you've got."

"I got ya covered." Kennedy sat quietly for a moment, as if waiting for him to keep talking. "If that's everything..."

"Ummm, no, there's something else." He blushed and felt the anxiety come back. "Mom got me some pamphlets." He reached for his reading material on the bed.

Kennedy frowned. "Did you want me to talk to her...?"

"No, no, this is just like the talk she gave me last year, except now that I have a boyfriend, she thought it might be good to have more specific information." He showed her the pamphlets. "There's lots of really important information in here, stuff I'd never even considered. Dee..." he trailed off uncomfortably. "In the fight, I was spit on. If one of the gang members had something, I might've gotten it. It takes two weeks to get results, and even though the hospital did a full blood test..." He raised his eyes to hers miserably. "What if I gave it to Carter?"

"Hang on, I'm fighting the urge to drive back to Parry Sound and beat those kids into a pulp." Kennedy drew a deep breath. "Alright. Let's see what the symptoms are." She flipped through the pamphlet on STIs and checked in Tommy's mouth. "I don't see any sores or lesions, but if you want to be sure, we can go see Doctor Sallah tomorrow morning before school."

"Yeah, that would give me peace of mind," Tommy said. "I don't want to stop kissing him when I only have a week here. I can hold off on—" He blushed again as he cut himself off, but he desperately needed to know how worried he needed to be. "Did you know you're supposed to use a condom when doing oral?"

"No, I didn't." Kennedy was silent for a minute and then

shrugged. "Jason and I are monogamous. Doesn't really matter." Her eyes widened as she figured out what he was saying. "Oh! And you're worried because of the spitting! Oh, Tommy." Her eyes filled with tears. "Please don't let these worries colour your first experience. It's supposed to be happy!"

Tommy gave her a lopsided grin. "I like how there's absolutely no judgement from you."

"Why would there be?" Kennedy winked. "At least you're *dating* Carter. *My* first was just a summer fling. And I didn't know to use barriers." Her eyes widened dramatically. "Jeepers, I was lucky," she said thoughtfully. "You should tell Carter what's going on. I'm sure he'll understand. And if it turns out that you do have something, treatment should be quick for both of you."

"Thanks. I will. What was it you wanted?"

"Help me open presents! Please?"

Chapter 6

**TUESDAY THE 10TH OF JUNE, 2003 -
WESTMEATH, ONTARIO**

Carter paced in front of the main doors of the school, waiting impatiently for Tommy to arrive. He checked his phone again, but there were no further messages from Kennedy past the, "On our way!" she'd sent five minutes before.

Jason's little car pulled to a stop in front of the door, and Tommy hopped out. He opened the back door and pulled out his guitar and backpack before poking his head back in. "Thank you so much, Dee!"

Carter faintly heard her reply, "What are big sisters for? Love you."

"Love you too," Tommy replied and closed the door. He sauntered up to Carter with a small smile. "Doc gave me the all-clear for kissing," he said quietly once he got close enough that no passing students would overhear. "He couldn't tell me more, just that we should put a hold on anything else until I get the results back next week. He did say he would call the hospital in Parry Sound and see if he can get the results earlier."

"If you do have something from those good-for-nothings, wouldn't I already have gotten it from you?" Carter asked, pressing their foreheads together.

Tommy shrugged a little. "There's no guarantee. I'm sorry."

"You're so Canadian. There's nothing to be sorry about." Carter pressed a light kiss to the corner of Tommy's lips, aching for more, but class was about to start. "Come on, we'll drop our things in my locker before science."

Holding hands, the boys hurried down the almost empty hallway.

"You're not afraid to kiss me, are you?" Tommy asked quietly when they were almost at the classroom door.

Carter preferred actions over words. He backed Tommy into the wall beside the door, their books falling to the floor as he thoroughly kissed him. He pulled back, both breathing heavily. "I will *never* be afraid of you," he promised fiercely.

"Okay," Tommy gasped, a tiny smirk curling his lips. "Is that how I get bone-melting kisses?"

"You could just ask," Carter replied with a chuckle.

The warning bell rang, and they scrambled to pick up their things.

The morning passed quickly. Carter waited at his locker for Tommy to get out of his music class. The STEM club and any-one hoping to attend Door Tech's Ontario-wide summer camp were being treated to lunch at The Hawaiian before being picked up and brought to the Door Tech test. The students would be allowed to leave their things in one of the conference rooms.

"I'm here! Sorry, class ran a little later than the bell because we were having such an interesting discussion about the difference between Renaissance and Baroque compositions," Tommy said excitedly.

"Oh, I know this one!" Carter paused dramatically, trying to keep a straight face. "If it's not Baroque, don't fix it!"

Tommy collapsed in laughter against the locker. "That's exactly what I was thinking during the entire conversation!" he gasped, taking deep breaths. "I was too shy to say it though."

"George would've appreciated it," Carter said, handing Tommy his backpack and shouldering his own.

"True," Tommy agreed easily. "But there were a lot of other people in the class, and I felt very young and out of my depth."

"I understand." Carter took Tommy's free hand. "Want me to carry your guitar?"

"I've got it. The Hawaiian's only a block away, isn't it?"

"A block and a half. Ish." Carter's belly flipped as he thought about what was coming after lunch. "Are you ready?"

Tommy gave him a sympathetic smile. "You're going to do great. You kicked ass on the STEM competition test this spring, you attended the March Break camp and won the grand prize, *and* we've been studying. You've got this. Would I lie to you?"

Carter blew out a long breath. "My brain accepts that. Not sure my stomach does though."

"I'm not sure I speak stomach. Growl burble rumble, grumble growl roar," Tommy said, grinning. "Translated, that means, 'Stop stressing, you're amazing.'"

Carter laughed. "*Je t'aime*," he said happily, squeezing Tommy's hand. Saying the phrase they had come up with in Toronto at the STEM competition reminded him that his offhand comment had won their team a special award for speed in the final event. His confidence grew a tiny bit. "You're amazing, too."

The Hawaiian had set up two of the conference rooms for all the students, opening the walls in between them.

"Is there another Aetherborn high school?" Tommy asked, looking around the large room filled with people.

"There's a French public school in Oldtown," Carter said, nodding. "That's why the buses are picking us up here instead of at the school."

Tommy frowned. "What about the Aetherborn kids who don't pass?"

"What about them?" Carter asked.

"The special wards in the architecture here can't be moved with them, so they'd never be able to attend camps like Door Tech's, right? That kinda sucks for them," Tommy finished sadly.

"Yeah, it does. Maybe we should mention that to Jason when we get home." Carter looked down at himself and chuckled. "And we should probably get changed."

"What, you don't think I look pretty?" Tommy asked, popping his heel up.

Carter admired the short blue and black ruffled skirt his boyfriend was wearing. "You look great in that, and you know it, but I'm not sure the Door Tech experts will appreciate it as much as I do."

Tommy chuckled. "Yeah, alright."

They found a spot to put Tommy's guitar and their bags and dug out their pants, bringing them to the bathroom to change with all the other boys.

"Nice skirt, Tommy," Adrien said.

"It's Kennedy's."

"Of course it is!" Adrien laughed. "I can't imagine your mom wearing that."

Tommy made a face that made the rest of the boys laugh.

"Where'd you get yours, Carter?" another boy asked.

"You're assuming I didn't own this already," Carter replied with a straight face.

"Oh. Sorry." The boy looked ashamed.

Tommy nudged Carter in the ribs. "Didn't you get that one from Elyse?"

"Yeah," Carter said with a chuckle. "But I don't like assumptions. I've enjoyed wearing skirts so far this week. I might consider buying one or two of my own for the future. If they have pockets."

"I miss pockets," Tommy said mournfully, making the others laugh again.

"I never realized how much I relied on pockets until this week," George said. He tossed his skirt to Adrien, who caught it with a grin. "I like not dealing with zippers when I need to pee, though."

"Very easy access," Adrien said with a nod and a wink. "You might be onto something, Carter."

"That's all well and good," said one of the other boys, "but how do you keep everything from, you know, just hanging out?"

"Have you been to Seams Likeable?" Carter asked. "I highly recommend their boxer briefs. They're super comfortable."

"I only wear boxers," replied the boy, wrinkling his nose.

George, Adrien, and Tommy all shook their heads at him.

Carter chuckled. "So did I. These are life-changing."

"Really?" The others in the bathroom all looked thoughtful. "I'll have to look into that."

"Me too," chorused several others.

"Check them out!" George exclaimed, pulling his pants down to his thighs and turning to the side. "Perfectly contained, and the material is soft, feel it!"

Carter exchanged amused glances with Tommy as several guys felt up George's thigh.

"Pizza's ready!" someone shouted through the door, and Carter quickly did up his pants and took his skirt off the counter.

"Ready to go?" he asked Tommy.

"Yeah." Tommy looked around for his skirt, and Carter pointed at the floor under the counter. "Oops." He checked it for any wetness or dirt. "Good thing these floors are clean."

"I wouldn't want to eat off of them, but I think they're cleaner than my room," Carter said as they headed back to the conference room.

Tommy chuckled. "Mine too, back home. I think the only reason my room here isn't a mess is because I've only been here a few days." He folded his skirt and put it in his backpack, Carter copying him.

"I can't imagine Lilah allowing you to let your room get messy," Carter said. "She seems really strict."

"She is and she isn't." Tommy followed Carter to a seat with the rest of the Oldtown STEM club students. "Mom doesn't allow food in bedrooms, so there's no mould growing on leftover plates or anything, but she doesn't force me to vacuum or dust, so there are more than a few dust bunnies under my bed."

Alicia laughed. "Who doesn't have dust bunnies under their bed?"

"Who has time to vacuum?" Elyse said in agreement.

They settled into a comfortable banter, and before they knew it, Adrien, George, and the other seniors split off onto a separate bus.

"Does Door Tech not offer the summer camp for the graduating students? Where are they going?" Tommy asked as they boarded their own bus.

"There's a separate camp for them, so their test is somewhere else," Alicia said. "It includes a college credit. I can't wait to take it next year!"

Once the bus was full, a cheerful woman climbed aboard. "Welcome, camp hopefuls, my name is Maria! This year, the Westmeath test and meet and greet will take place on a boat cruise on the Ottawa River. We'll be boarding at the northern docks and heading west to Hen Island before we return along the same route. The test will take place once everyone has boarded and will take forty-five minutes. After that, we have six experts who will give brief talks of five minutes each, and then you will have the chance to talk to them while you mingle." She smiled at them. "Are there any questions?"

When no hands were raised, Maria sat in the front seat behind the driver. Carter realized that the bus had started moving while she'd been talking and tried not to panic. "Only forty-five minutes?" he hissed at Tommy. "That's not much time!"

"Just do as much as you can," Tommy whispered. "I have faith in you."

"That almost makes me feel worse," Carter admitted. "What if I fail?"

Tommy squeezed his hand. "That's a possibility for me, too. Or my parents could decide to not let me come. All we can do is our best, and hopefully, everything will turn out the way we want."

"I guess so," Carter said. "Distract me?"

"In public?" Tommy replied innocently. "Didn't know you were into that." He grinned evilly, and Carter stuck his tongue out.

"How are you feeling about meeting the wedding band and practising with them tomorrow after school?" Carter asked.

Tommy shuddered. "Nervous. Do you know how hard it is to play guitar when your hands are shaking?"

"No." Carter chuckled. "I can see how that would make things difficult though. Let me try to think of a solution."

"I don't really need a solution," Tommy replied. "I just need to get out of my head."

"Yeah... You're right." Carter smiled, a plan beginning to formulate. "You're bringing your guitar to school every day this week, right?"

"Yeah. Why?"

"Just thinking out loud."

Perfect! And we're eating lunch with the drama club tomorrow! They'll be totally on board with putting on a lunchtime performance in the caf! Carter resisted the urge to bounce in his seat. *I'll get Alicia in on it just in case he needs a little boost.* Alicia's power as a muse meant that if she knew all the parts of a song, she could broadcast them to her fellow performers. It came in handy during impromptu jam sessions, but only if the performers weren't beginners. Carter was confident in Tommy's skill; he'd be able to play any song Alicia chose, and hopefully that would help him get over his anxiety.

While Carter was planning, the bus wound its way through the city to the northern docks, where the tourist boats berthed.

Maria stood up when they stopped moving and smiled brightly at them. "Stay close to me until we get on the boat. We don't want to leave anyone behind!"

A few people laughed, and they filed out onto the busy docks.

"This way!" Maria called out, and they followed her like a flock of adopted ducklings.

Well, more than half of us are *Ducklings,* Carter thought, amused, thinking of their school mascot. *I guess it's a suitable metaphor.*

There was a short ramp onto a large boat, which was already

packed with students from other schools in the city and from across the river in Demers, Quebec.

Carter's throat tightened in panic at the vast quantity of candidates vying for positions in the exclusive summer camp. And this was just the Westmeath group!

"Please take a test, Scantron, and a pencil set," said a voice, and Carter glanced up to meet the smiling face of Quinn. They had been the tutor assigned to his group over March Break. Their hair, which had been electric blue then, was an equally eye-catching shade of purple now. "Hello Carter, Tommy, Elyse. Good to see you three," Quinn said.

"You remember me?" Carter said, surprised.

Quinn's smile widened. "You were all rather memorable. In a good way," they added quickly.

"Thanks," Tommy replied. "It's good to see you again, too, Quinn." He made sure Carter collected the proper equipment and led him to the table. "You going to be okay?" he asked as they sat down. "You're moving a little robotically."

Carter gave himself a shake. "I'm not used to being memorable."

Tommy chuckled. "You'd better get used to it. You're remarkable."

"You have to say that. You're my boyfriend," Carter said, picking at the plastic pencil set containing two pencils, an eraser, and a basic calculator.

"That has nothing to do with it," Tommy argued. "I bet everyone at the Everdome dinner theatre remembers you. And the judges at the STEM competition certainly remember you. The teachers from March Break probably do, too."

"I'm used to flying under the radar," Carter said, lowering his voice. "Most of us try to avoid the spotlight."

"Memorable is a good look on you," Tommy said, preparing his workspace. "Better get ready," he advised.

Carter quickly organized his things and started filling in the bubbles of his name. The repetitive darkening of the circles helped calm his mind to a quiet hum of nerves. He noticed that his test was marked D. Tommy had C. "The questions must be in different orders to prevent cheating," he murmured.

Tommy nodded and was about to reply when a man tapped the microphone at the front of the boat.

"Good afternoon. Please complete the tests to the best of your abilities. Wrong answers and no answers will both give you a zero score; you won't be docked extra points on those questions. You have forty-five minutes, and your time starts... now!"

Carter's stomach lurched at the same time as the boat engines turned over. He opened the test booklet and read the first question. *Okay, I know this one. I got this.*

The time passed quickly. Before he knew it, the man was calling a five-minute warning. Carter flipped through the test. *There are still ten questions left to answer!* he thought frantically. He decided to read them each quickly and make educated guesses for the answers, but he could feel his heart sinking even as he filled in the little bubbles. *Best case scenario, I'll only get thirty out of forty.*

They called the end to the test, and Carter put his pencil down along with everyone else. He'd managed to finish filling the last bubble just in time. Once his papers were taken, Carter put his head down on the table.

"You okay?" Tommy whispered, putting his hand on Carter's knee.

"Could be better, could be worse," Carter groaned, not lifting his head from the worn plastic table.

Tommy squeezed his knee. "I'm sure it wasn't as bad as you think."

"How many questions did you finish? Properly finish, doing the calculations and everything?" Carter asked.

"I didn't get to the last question."

Carter sighed. "I had *ten* unfinished," he said gloomily.

"I'm sure there are plenty of others here who had even more than that," Tommy said, rubbing Carter's thigh. "The experts are about to start their talks. You'll like this."

"I'm not sure I can concentrate on them," Carter said mournfully.

"Stop feeling sorry for yourself and look up," hissed Elyse on his other side.

Carter raised his head slowly and then sat up straight when he saw who was standing at the microphone, smirking at him. It was Veronica Giles. His jaw dropped. "You know, I sometimes forget that she's brilliant," he murmured to Tommy.

Tommy chuckled quietly.

They listened avidly as Veronica talked about advances in robotics. She was followed by a man named Dominic Peters, who lectured about nanotechnology. After that, Dr. Amita Dubois discussed agricultural sciences, winking at them as she stepped away from the mic. Carter knew her as Kennedy's boss at the Westmeath ARC. Another man, Julian Trevino, followed her, lecturing about geology. An archaeologist named Carol Jenkins followed him, talking about her most recent dig. Last was a wildlife biologist named Wayne Edgerton.

"They really got a wide variety of experts, didn't they?" Elyse whispered.

Carter and Tommy nodded silently.

The man in charge stepped back up to the microphone after Wayne finished. "Thank you to our amazing experts!" he said enthusiastically, leading the students in applause. "You now have the opportunity to talk to them for the rest of the cruise. You have two hours. Enjoy yourselves!"

Most of the students immediately got to their feet, eager to be the first ones to get one-on-one time with an expert.

The Oldtown group exchanged wide-eyed glances, and while they stood up from the uncomfortable chairs so the crew could put the tables away, none of them made a move toward the front of the boat and the rest of the crowd.

"I hope they had a chance to spread out a little bit before they were mobbed," Tommy said to Carter.

"No kidding," Carter said. "Hey, I'm going to go find the

restroom. It looks like we've got some time before things calm down a bit."

"Do you want me to come with you?" Tommy asked quietly. "You're still looking a little pale."

"No, I'm good. I'll find you when I'm done." Carter asked a crew member and was directed to the lower level. He used the facilities, washing his hands when he was done. Rather than join the others upstairs, he moved to the railing and looked out at the slowly moving shore. He took several deep breaths of the fresh, river-scented air as he felt his roiling emotions calm.

"Mister Batudev," a pleasant voice greeted him. "What are you doing down here when the party is upstairs?"

"I could ask you the same question, Ms. Door," Carter replied, turning to face Margery Door, the owner, founder, and retired CEO of Door Technology. Her daughter, Ellen, oversaw West-meath's facilities, but it was Margery who had built the empire from scratch in the late seventies. "Is everything alright?"

"You're sweet to ask." Margery smiled. "While I'm a big fan of parties, when there are a lot of people all trying to get your attention at once, it can be a little overwhelming."

Carter narrowed his eyes. "You weren't introduced. Everyone's trying to talk to the experts."

Margery laughed. "You're sharp, aren't you? Ellen was impressed by you during her camp, and Captain Herrington wrote a glowing review of your efforts during the last challenge of the competition."

"You remember that?" Carter asked.

"I make a point of remembering important information," Margery said. She joined him at the railing, resting her elbows on the high bar. "I was concerned about you, if I'm being honest. I was watching the test from the pilot cabin. You seemed... Despondent."

Carter chuckled bitterly. "That's a good word for it."

"Why?"

"I didn't finish." Carter shrugged a shoulder up. "I really wanted to go to the camp this summer."

"Because of Mister Fairfield?"

Carter paused to think about that. "I was excited about the March Break camp before I knew Tommy was attending. I think he pushes me to work harder to try to keep up with him. Not on purpose, of course. I guess part of my excitement for this summer camp is because of him. But there's so much *more* than that! I learned so much in March. It was such an incredible experience, and I... I just wanted to be immersed in that environment again. It's why I joined our STEM club after the camp."

Margery smiled. "It's nice to share interests with someone you care about. I'll let you in on a little secret." She lowered her voice even though there was no one else around. "The test was only a small part of the entrance exam. Each expert will make their recommendations after the meet and greet. We'll also be taking your past achievements into account."

"That's encouraging," Carter said with relief. "I don't really do well on tests."

Margery leaned in. "Neither do I!" she said and winked at him. She leaned back again. "I find testing to be a quick way to gauge how much information is crammed into your brains, but intelligence can be measured in many ways. You can't judge a fish by how well it climbs a tree or a bird by how well it swims."

"Am I a fish or a bird?" Carter asked with a chuckle.

"Whichever you want. You have no limits. How's the revolution going, by the way?"

Carter gaped at her. "You know about that?"

"I think it's admirable that you're fighting for women's rights to wear what they want."

"It was Tommy's idea," Carter said quickly. "Not the revolution, I think that was Adrien's, but he suggested that we switch with the girls that were going to be sent home."

Margery chuckled. "And you went along with it."

"Of course! It's a ridiculous rule," Carter said indignantly.

"I like your attitude. Both of you," Margery said thoughtfully. "Keep it up, and you both will be involved with Door Tech for a long time."

"I... Wow." Carter's brain scrambled to keep up. "Thank you."

"Don't let it go to your head now," Margery said with a smirk.

Carter stared at her for a moment. "Either you knew it wouldn't, or you're testing me."

"Why can't it be both?" She shrugged. "Shall we return to the party?"

Carter offered her his arm, and she accepted it with a curtsy.

Chapter 7

TUESDAY THE 10TH OF JUNE, 2003 -
WESTMEATH, ONTARIO

Tommy kept an eye on the stairs down to the lower level while he chatted, first with the other Oldtown kids, and then with Carol Jenkins, the archaeology expert. Carter had been downstairs for over half an hour, and Tommy was starting to worry.

He felt relieved when Carter finally reappeared, arm linked with Margery Door, and Tommy understood why there had been a delay in his return.

Since he was at the back of the group around Ms. Jenkins, he was able to leave without being noticed and joined Carter and Margery. "I'm pleasantly surprised to see you here today, Ms. Door," Tommy said with a smile. "Thank you for rescuing Carter from the depths."

Margery laughed softly. "He is excellent company."

"I agree." Tommy beamed at her.

"It's nice to see you both. Go and enjoy your conversations with the experts. I chose them because of their high-quality work and because they are excellent conversationalists." Margery winked at them. "It's a good quality to have."

"I'll keep that in mind," Tommy replied, bowing slightly.

"Aren't you two chummy with the retired CEO," Veronica murmured to them when they reached her. There was a brief lull when the group of students she was talking to headed to another expert. "That Toronto competition gave you some excellent contacts. Are you going to try for it again next year?"

Tommy and Carter both nodded vigorously.

"Mr. Travese said that we'd start preparing for it in September next year, so I think we'll do even better than we did this year!" Tommy said enthusiastically.

"You know he probably didn't think the school stood a chance until you joined the club, right?" Carter said, smirking.

Tommy was taken aback. "But it was a team effort! Everyone pulled their own weight, even the subs when Chris and Naomi got sick."

"Do you think they'll still try out even if you're in Westmeath next year?" Veronica asked.

"I hope so. I think Faith has a really good chance to make it on the team, and Naomi and Sabrina will be seniors next year. Naomi will be an excellent leader." Tommy tried not to get too excited over the idea of living in Westmeath. He still couldn't believe his parents were considering it. He knew this week was a bit of a trial run, to see how well he integrated with the school, and he felt like it was going well, but...

"If you're here next year, it'll be you, me, and Elyse competing for the junior positions," Carter said. "I'll never make it on the team against you two!"

"Simply being a replacement for four years will look amazing on post-secondary applications," Veronica pointed out.

"But I want to actually compete," Carter said wistfully.

"Should I tell my parents that I don't want to come—"

"Don't you *dare*!" Carter cut Tommy off with a glare.

Sudden screams broke through the murmur of voices. Everyone ran to look out the left side of the boat.

"Where are we?" Tommy asked.

"Right around the western docks," Veronica said grimly. She pulled out her cell phone and an earpiece, dialling quickly. "Jay, situation. Western docks, on the water. I can't see from where I am, the Door Tech hopefuls are in my way."

"I know where you can get a better view," Carter said quietly. When Veronica nodded, he led them down to the lower levels.

The bathrooms were closed off near the back of the ship, but Tommy barely spared them a glance. There was a ship off the left side that had large shapes hovering around it. He squinted, trying to make out what they were.

"Okay, I'm in a better position." Veronica said as soon as she reached the railing. "Just two. Naturally. Okay, I'm seeing a cargo ship on the river being attacked by what looks like flying moose. I'd say about a dozen of them. There's something wrong with their noses..."

Tommy watched Veronica flip her cell phone sideways and extend it until the screen grew three sizes.

"Hacking the ship's security. Oh, ew." She made a face. "They've got a mosquito's stinger, which should *not* be allowed at that size." There was a pause. "Yeah, thanks for that. You know what I mean when I say stinger, so I'll keep using it."

"It's a proboscis, not a stinger," Tommy whispered to Carter, who nodded in agreement. The flying moose were terrifying, and he hoped they stayed far away from their ship. On the other hand, he was fascinated by the physics behind them; wings that frail should not have been able to support a moose's weight.

Veronica glanced up from her phone screen at the boys. "How close are you? No, we're safe. The monsters are targeting the cargo ship, not the tourist boat. Yes, I'll let you know if anything changes."

Veronica was silent for a minute, watching her phone, and then she focussed on the boys. "I can't answer any of your questions, so don't ask. If you want to help, keep an eye on those monsters and tell me if any of them leave the ship to go somewhere else. I'm trusting you, not because I want to, but because I must. Keep your mouths shut about anything you might overhear."

Tommy gulped and nodded along with Carter. "Is this like the gorilla-bear monster on Friday?" Tommy asked nervously. "The one on the freeway?"

Veronica glared at him. "Is that a question?"

Tommy winced. "Sorry." He turned to the railing, focussing on the cargo ship and the moose flying around it. "Moosequitoes," he muttered to Carter, who nodded again.

"Are you thinking what I'm thinking?" Carter asked in a whisper, his breath tickling Tommy's ear.

"You think she called the Phantom," Tommy replied, equally quietly.

"She called him Jay," Carter whispered back. "It fits. Plus, she's Jason's best friend."

Tommy nodded.

"Great, you've named the monsters and half nicknamed the villain. How are we going to stop these things?" Veronica said suddenly into her headset. She was silent for a moment, and although Tommy strained to listen to the other side of the conversation, he couldn't hear anything over the engines. "You could jump and slash over and over again," she suggested.

Silence again, and then she said, "Let me check." She clicked away on her phone. "No harpoons. But there is a cannon on the next dock..."

Tommy's eyes widened. *What would happen if the cannon missed? Could it hit us?*

Veronica whistled suddenly. "You'd have to have memorized not only the specs, but the science behind it. Why go through that kind of effort?" A pause. "How about you let me make you a proper gun?" She asked with a smirk.

"She's obviously very familiar with the person," Carter whispered.

"Whoa!" Tommy exclaimed suddenly. "Did you see that?" He squinted, trying to get a better look at the other ship. He thought he'd seen a flash of darkness. "There it is agai—What!?" The monster he was looking at vanished into thin air.

Veronica made a gagging noise and said, "Less flirting, more shooting."

Tommy and Carter exchanged amused glances and kept themselves busy by counting down the number of monsters left as they disappeared one by one. Tommy tried to see what was happening to them, but the bulk of the other ship was in the way.

There were only three monsters left when they stopped attacking the ship.

"They're heading for the dock!" Tommy told Veronica, who nodded in acknowledgment.

Despite how much they tried, they couldn't see what was happening beyond the ship.

"Are they gone? Oh wait, that's a question." Tommy bit his lip and lowered his voice so that only Carter could hear him. "How do we ask if everything's okay if we can't ask any questions?"

"I've hacked the dock's security. If she shows up, I'll have a picture and ID in twenty minutes. Go ravage a fry truck," Veronica said. She closed her phone and took the earpiece from her ear. She smiled at the boys, who stared at her eagerly. "The monsters are gone." She led the way to the stairs and turned to face them at the bottom. "Not a single word about any of this, you understand?"

"I promise," Tommy said immediately.

Carter nodded. "My lips are sealed."

"Good." Veronica climbed the stairs quickly, leaving the boys at the bottom.

"*What* just happened?" Carter hissed. He ran a hand through his curls, messing them up more than the wind already had.

"I know!" Tommy grinned. "That was so cool!"

"I never even suspected that Veronica was in on it!" Carter whispered. "I can't believe we were here for that!"

"We should head upstairs now," Tommy said. "I haven't talked to Doctor Dubois or any of the others yet."

"Yeah, we definitely need to do that." Carter quickly filled Tommy in on Ms. Door's conversation with him.

"Jeepers!" Tommy grinned. "Well, you've got this in the bag, then. You can charm anyone!"

WEDNESDAY THE 11TH OF JUNE, 2003 - WESTMEATH, ONTARIO

"Hungry?" Tommy asked as Carter met him outside the music room door, their homemade lunches in his hands.

"You have no idea." Carter said with a grin. "Come on, it's drama club day."

"Okay," Tommy said. He lifted his guitar. "What should I do with this?"

"Bring it along. They might ask you to play something." Carter offered his arm to Tommy, who took it.

"Not sure how I feel about that," Tommy said, his stomach flip-flopping uncomfortably. He was suddenly not hungry.

"You've got to get used to playing in front of people someday. Why not today? Remember what I said about everyone being super supportive?" Carter led them into the cafeteria and to a back corner near the stage, waving at multiple people along the way.

"Yeah, I remember," Tommy said, swallowing hard. "You really think I can do it?"

"I know you can." Carter pulled Tommy down at a table. "Hey all! This is Tommy."

A chorus of hellos echoed around the table as Carter introduced each person. Tommy recognized a few of the faces from the previous day, including Alicia.

"Are you in everything?" Tommy asked her. "Drama, STEM, music…"

Alicia laughed. "I'm not in any sports. No time. I play too many instruments."

"What do you play?" Tommy asked.

"Guitar, bass, piano, drums, vocals. I'm a one-girl band!" she added with a chuckle. She leaned in closer. "It means I can 'inspire' my bandmates if they forget a chord or something." She winked.

Tommy took a bite of his sandwich. "Really? How does that work?"

"It's kinda like telepathy, but with music. The person has to know *how* to play the chord, but I can tell them *which* chords to play. Do you want to try it out?" Alicia grinned at him.

"Oh, I don't know..." Tommy hesitated.

"Think it over while you finish eating," Alicia suggested.

"Not sure I'll want to eat before performing in front of all these people," Tommy said with a wince. His stomach had started flipping again.

"Suit yourself. You can eat after." Alicia raised her voice to the rest of the table. "Hey all, Tommy's going to play us some songs! What should he play?"

Tommy's protests were drowned out by song suggestions from the group. Alicia nodded, writing some of them down. After a moment, she turned back to Tommy. "Okay, we have our set list. You ready?"

"Just like that?" Tommy squeaked.

"Just like that." Alicia smiled.

"Can I start with a song I know?" he asked tentatively. "I had to memorize a French poem last semester, and I chose a song by Garou instead and learned how to play it. His voice suits my range."

"That's perfect!" Alicia crossed something out and scribbled in the name. "Which song?"

"'*Je n'attendais que vous*,'" Tommy said.

Alicia finished writing it. "Excellent, I know that one. You'll get a chance to see how I can help you out with a song you know before we move on to the new ones."

"Can I see?" Tommy asked, reaching for the paper.

"Nope!" Alicia stood and climbed the stairs onto the stage. "Come on."

Tommy looked pleadingly at Carter, who grinned encouragingly at him and gestured to the guitar case at Tommy's feet. "Okay," Tommy said, trying to pump himself up. Alicia sat behind the drum kit and picked up the drumsticks, giving them a twirl and pounding out a rhythm across the kit. "Jeepers, she's good," he said, awe-struck. "I've never played with accompaniment like this before." He started panicking.

"Alicia is probably the best person to play with," Carter said encouragingly. "You've got this." He took Tommy's face in his hands, bringing their foreheads together. "Look at me. I'm right here. Sing to me. Can you do that?"

Tommy gulped and nodded tentatively. "I'll try."

"Nobody's going to laugh or boo you. Just have fun up there, okay?" Carter smiled.

"I'll try," Tommy repeated robotically. He picked up his guitar case and stood up, walking to the edge of the stage, and placing it on the corner. He opened the zipper with shaking fingers and took out the guitar strap, placing it around his neck and then hooking it onto the guitar. He listened to each string to check the tuning and then climbed up onto the stage with Alicia.

The drama table erupted into cheers, re-drawing the attention of the nearby tables, who had turned back to their lunches when Alicia had continued playing drums, off in her own little world.

Tommy wiped his sweaty hands on his short red-and-black checked skirt and thanked his past self for choosing to wear a black dress shirt; the sweat would be less likely to show through.

Alicia dropped her rhythm to a slow beat and spoke into the nearby microphone. "Let's give Tommy a warm Duckling welcome for his first time on our stage!"

There was a round of applause, and more faces turned to look at them.

Oh my God, Tommy thought frantically. *I don't think I can do this!* He saw George walking quickly down the aisle toward the stage and wondered what he was going to do.

"Our first song is '*Je n'attendais que vous*' by Garou," Alicia continued. "Oh, thank you George."

George brought a microphone stand from backstage and set it up in front of Tommy. It had one mic pointing toward his guitar and one at his face.

"Tommy, take it away!"

Heart pounding in his throat—or was it his stomach? —Tommy let his gaze fall to the upturned face of his boyfriend and took a deep breath. *Pretend you're in your bedroom, singing just to Carter. You can do this.*

The first chord popped into his mind, along with the lyrics, and he opened his mouth and started to sing. Alicia sent him the correct chords at exactly the right time, and Tommy felt himself relaxing into the beauty of the song. The soft sounds of a piano joined, and Tommy glanced to his left to see George behind the upright. He smiled, grateful for the support of his friends, and kept playing, his anxiety fading into the background as he finished the song.

The applause as the last chord faded startled him. He raised his eyes from Carter's rapt expression to see that everyone in the cafeteria was facing toward him; some had even risen from their seats and moved closer.

Tommy took a deep breath and turned to Alicia, who was smirking at him with mischief in her eyes. *Uh oh,* he thought.

"Our next song will really get you moving!" Alicia said excitedly. "You've all heard it on MuchDance 2001, you've danced to it at school dances, you've heard it on the radio because, hey, Canadian band, am I right? Put your hands together for 'Get Down' by B4-4!"

Oh sweet, I love this song! Tommy thought. He nodded to Alicia and turned to face the audience again. George led them in, and Tommy cupped the microphone in both hands, singing the opening verse directly to Carter, who grinned at him.

The chorus meant that Tommy needed to play as well as sing, and even though he didn't know the chords, they popped into his head, sending the correct signals to his fingers so that he could play properly. He grinned, thrilling at the energy coming from performing for a crowd of happy, dancing teenagers. The next verse came up, and Tommy knew that the bridge after it didn't involve guitar either, so he swung his guitar in a smooth move onto his back and took the microphone out of the stand, walking closer to the edge of the stage to sing directly to the upturned faces. When he got to Carter's, Tommy put his hand out and gave a little tug, letting Carter know he should join him on stage.

Jeepers, this song is sexual, Tommy thought as he sang the bridge, George jumping in on back-up vocals. Carter started dancing beside Tommy the second he got up on stage. Tommy tossed out the last line with a straight face, making the crowd laugh, and swung the guitar around to his front again, instantly starting the chorus.

In the next verse, Alicia gave Carter some of the lyrics to sing together with Tommy, and they played it up to the crowd, making them whoop at the suggestive lyrics.

Carter did some pop and locking moves, Tommy backing up to give him space as he sang the chorus again. *He's so good at that!* Tommy thought, trying to keep his thoughts on his performance and not his boyfriend's.

They finished the song with a flourish that had the audience cheering.

Tommy exchanged grins with Carter and his bandmates, excited to see what was next.

"I'm glad everyone enjoyed that! And thank you, Carter, for your incredible dancing!" Alicia shouted over the applause. "We have one last song for you today. It's slower, but it's by the king of rock and roll, Elvis himself! Put your hands together for 'Can't Help Falling in Love!'"

Tommy's cheeks flushed as he looked at Carter, who had returned to his seat, his friends in the drama club clapping him on the shoulders. *I've already fallen for him,* he thought, his heart aching with joy. He sang the song from his soul, barely noticing his fingers following Alicia's instructions, eyes locked on Carter's. He hoped Carter understood that he meant every word.

When he was done, he bowed to thunderous applause and gestured at Alicia and George, who joined him for another bow at the front of the stage.

"Encore!" said someone, and it was picked up by others, but Tommy shook his head.

"Sorry, I need to eat, now that I don't feel like I'm going to vomit from nerves," he said into the microphone, making people laugh. "Thank you for being a fantastic first audience!" Tommy walked down the stairs and put his guitar away in its case before rejoining Carter at the table.

"That was amazing," Carter leaned in to murmur in Tommy's ear, making the hair on the back of his neck stand up. "I loved being up there with you."

"You made an already great experience even better," Tommy replied. "I really do need to eat though. I'm suddenly ravenous."

Carter laughed. "Fill your belly, and then we'll go find a corner and make out a bit. I have some excess energy that I need to get rid of."

"So do I, but I'm not sure a corner will be enough," Tommy said huskily.

"Oh," Carter said softly, his pupils visibly dilating. "Maybe we should wait until we get to my place after band practice this afternoon."

Tommy hesitated only a moment, the lack of answers about his bloodwork filling his mind before he relaxed. This was Carter. He understood. "I'm down for that," Tommy replied, goosebumps erupting all over his body in anticipation. They hadn't had much time alone together this week, what with all the wedding activities.

"That was so amazing!" Patricia said, plopping down on the bench as close to Tommy as she could get and putting her hand on his knee. "I didn't know you could play like that!"

Tommy's back went ramrod straight, the feeling of her warm hand on his bare knee making his skin crawl. "I didn't know I could do it either. I don't think I could have done it without Alicia and George, and, of course, Carter."

"Yes, your dancing was awesome, Carter," Patricia said, leaning forward to speak to him on Tommy's other side, her hand slipping from his knee.

Tommy breathed a sigh of relief and bit into his sandwich.

"That last song was so powerful," Patricia simpered. "Were you singing that to someone special?"

Mouth full, Tommy could only nod.

"Oh!" Patricia smiled happily and put her hand to her heart. "That's so wonderful!" She kissed Tommy's cheek and got to her feet. "I knew you could feel the connection between us!" She bounced off, Tommy still chewing vigorously on his mouthful of sandwich and giving Carter a desperate look.

"Uh oh, should I be worried about you getting a girlfriend?" Carter teased.

Tommy glared at him and rolled his eyes, swallowing his food. "I'm not going to dignify that with an answer."

Chapter 8

**WEDNESDAY THE 11TH OF JUNE, 2003 -
WESTMEATH, ONTARIO**

They left the wedding band's studio close to dinnertime. Carter glanced sideways at Tommy's ecstatic expression and felt his heart dance.

The band had listened to the song Tommy had written only once, talked amongst themselves for a few minutes, and come back with a bass line, rhythm for the drums, and backup guitar and vocals. They'd practised it all together twice and then recorded it for Tommy to be able to give it to Jason and Kennedy as a wedding present.

Tommy looked like he was on cloud nine and had been ever since the band had responded so enthusiastically to the song.

"I'm really proud of you," Carter said, squeezing Tommy's hand.

"Thanks." Tommy beamed at him. "And thanks for the encouragement at lunch, too. That was such a rush!"

"It was fun to be on stage with you," Carter said, doing a smooth dance step on the sidewalk before bumping his hip into Tommy's. His stomach did a little flip as he said, "You said that the Elvis song was being sung to someone special...?"

Tommy's brow furrowed. "You, of course."

"Right." Carter blushed. "I meant... Oh, never mind. It's just a song, and you didn't even pick it."

They walked in silence until the Johnson house came into view.

"I meant every word," Tommy said quietly, his cheeks pink. "Although I'm not sure I'm ready to say it outside of songs yet."

Carter's heart leaped, and a grin burst across his face without his permission. "Me too."

They smiled at each other until Tommy looked away. "I don't really have workout clothes."

"That's okay. You can borrow something from me," Carter offered.

"In that case, I won't bother changing, and I'll just drop off my things," Tommy said.

There was a quick round of hugs at the house, and then they were back on the sidewalk, Lilah's admonition to return immediately following the nine o'clock drop-in class ringing in their ears.

It didn't take long to walk to Carter's, and they trotted up the stairs to the apartment above the bakery, following the spicy scent of tomato sauce into the kitchen, where they washed their hands.

"Sweet, homemade spaghetti!" Carter exclaimed, dipping a finger into the sauce on the stove before his father batted him away. He grinned and licked his fingernail, humming happily at the flavours of tomato and basil as they crossed his tongue. He offered the pad of his finger to Tommy, who sucked it into his mouth, eyes widening.

"Wow, that's really yummy," Tommy said. "Can I help set the table?"

"Carter can show you where the glasses are," William said. "Dinner should be ready in two minutes. I was just keeping it warm for you and Sam."

Sam's heavy tread sounded outside the door.

"Perfect timing," Tommy said cheerfully, putting the glasses down carefully on the heavy oak table in the dining area.

"Hi Dad," Carter said in greeting, putting forks on placemats. "Closing go alright?"

"Same as usual," Sam replied, washing his hands. "How did your meeting with the band turn out, Tommy?"

Tommy smiled happily. "*So* good!"

"I look forward to hearing the song properly on Saturday," William said, serving a plate of spaghetti. "I feel like I've been hearing it for months as you worked on it."

"You have," Tommy said with a chuckle. "I wrote it at the beginning of April when I was waiting to hear about the results of the STEM competition test."

Sam shook his head, accepting the plate his husband handed him. "I still can't believe you wrote that song in a day."

"Half an hour, actually," Carter said proudly, taking the plate from his dad and putting it on the table.

"My music teacher, Mr. Gordon, gave me notes on how to make it better. It's not like it was *complete* in half an hour!" Tommy protested. "A little less food than that for me. I'm not used to doing exercise as intense as martial arts."

"Class isn't for another three hours," William said, his ladle poised over the pot of pasta. "Are you sure?"

"Are you nervous?" Carter asked quietly, leaning close to Tommy so his dads wouldn't hear.

"A little," Tommy admitted. "Okay, a lot. My stomach is all tied up in knots because it's something new and I don't know what to expect and what if I'm *really bad* at it?" he squeaked out all in one breath.

Carter bit back a laugh. "Then you're bad at it. No big deal." Louder to include his parents, he said, "If you're hungrier closer to class time, I'll heat up a bowl for you."

William nodded, and Tommy shot Carter a grateful look.

Dinner was always loud at the Batudev house, with Sam telling them the news he'd heard from various customers and Carter telling his dads about school. Tonight, Tommy joined in, thrilling Carter with how easily he fit in and regaling them with his time in the spotlight at lunch.

After dinner, Tommy helped dry the dishes with Carter.

"Are you going to The Hawaiian before class tonight?" Sam asked as he washed the dishes.

"We hadn't really talked about what we wanted to do," Carter said, glancing at Tommy.

"Whatever you decide, leave us a note. William and I are going on a date!" Sam's eyes sparkled.

Carter grinned at his dad, content to bask in their happiness at being together. "Have fun, but not too much fun," Carter said, repeating the oft-heard refrain.

Sam rumbled a laugh, the air shaking a bit with his amusement. "Back at you, kiddo." He shook his hands over the sink and dried them on the hand towel hanging from the stove. "Maybe set an alarm so you don't miss the class?"

"Already done," Carter said easily. "I know how easy it is to get caught up talking and lose track of time."

"Talking." Sam raised an eyebrow and smirked when both boys blushed. "I trust you to be safe and consensual."

"Oh my God, Dad!" Carter muttered, his face suddenly feeling like it was on fire. "Just go."

The air shook with Sam's laughter again as he left the kitchen.

Tommy leaned in and whispered, "How do we know if we're having too much fun?"

Carter grinned. "If anything dangerous gets involved."

"Ah." Tommy stared at the overhead cupboards as he dried a plate. "I can't think of anything dangerous that I'd want to do."

"Are you dangerous?" Carter asked, a smirk on his lips. "Because I'd want to do you."

Tommy's jaw dropped. "Jeepers, what a line!" he said, a chuckle escaping him. "I guess I'm dangerous until we find out the blood test results."

Carter sobered. "That's not... I was just teasing. I'm sorry, I didn't mean to bring that up."

"No, it's okay." Tommy put the plate away gently. "It's good to keep in mind in case we get carried away. I know that I *want* to get carried away."

"Me too," Carter murmured, his heart beating faster as his mind raced with possibilities.

"Have a good night, boys," William said, popping his head into the kitchen. "We're heading out."

"Bye, Father," Carter said, automatically shielding his mind in case he accidentally projected his thoughts. "Bye, Dad."

The door closed behind them, the lock clicking into place.

"How fast can we get these dishes done?" Tommy asked.

"Let's find out." Carter was impressed that, despite their obvious mutual desire, Tommy wasn't cutting corners on their responsibilities. The dishes *could* drip-dry, but there'd be water spots on the glasses and silverware.

It only took them five more minutes before everything was put away and the towels hung to dry on the stove.

"Soooo, what do you want to do?" Tommy asked, a smirk at the corner of his mouth.

"Bedroom. Now," Carter said hoarsely. He grabbed his backpack as they passed through the front hall and tossed it onto his desk chair when they got to his room. He took his phone out of the front pocket and put it on the bedside table, double-checking that he had, in fact, set an alarm. "We've got almost two hours. You said something at school about wanting to do more than make-out?"

"Not in those words, but yes." Tommy moved into Carter's space, their breath mingling.

Carter bit back a groan. "I was intrigued by Adrien's implication yesterday that skirts were easy access."

Tommy smirked. "Oh, you caught that, too?" He gave Carter's shoulders a light push toward the bed.

Letting himself be moved, Carter sat on the edge, barely having time to move the extra material out of the way before Tommy's weight was on him. His eyes closed involuntarily as Tommy took his time kissing every thought from his brain.

"Yes," Carter murmured, Tommy's fingers dragging the hem of his shirt higher. "More," he gasped, fingers tight around the other boy's brief-clad hips. "Please," he whispered, sharing breaths spicy with tomato sauce. "Tommy," was said last, almost reverently, as he rested his cheek on a sweat-slick chest.

After changing, they finally laid down facing each other, fingers and legs intertwined. Carter's mind buzzed pleasantly, overwhelmed that he got to be with his boyfriend like this. He traced his fingers over the bare skin of Tommy's arm, enjoying watching goosebumps appear in their wake.

"I'm pretty sure I'm in love with you," Tommy said shyly, his cheekbones turning a light pink to match the flush on his chest from their exertions.

Carter's heart danced a jig. He brought Tommy's fingers to his mouth, kissing each one lightly. "I want to wake up to your face every day until we're old and grey."

"And then you won't want to look at me anymore," Tommy deadpanned.

Carter laughed. "I'm in love with you, too."

Tommy smiled bashfully, ducking his head into the pillow for a second before Carter tucked his hand against Tommy's cheek and pulled their lips together again.

The alarm interrupted them quite a bit later.

"Rude," Tommy muttered at it, making Carter laugh again.

"Come on, I promised Zoe I'd be there tonight to help out," Carter said, stretching as he sat up.

"I'm not saying we should neglect our promises," Tommy protested. "Just disappointed that the time passed so quickly."

"Agreed." Carter got out of bed and crossed to his dresser, pulling out two pairs of comfortable workout shorts and shirts, tossing one set at Tommy. "What?" he asked, seeing as Tommy hadn't moved yet.

"Just admiring the view," Tommy said cheekily.

"I'll do a reverse strip-tease for you," Carter said, slowly rocking his hips to a beat only he could hear. He almost fell over putting on his shorts, making them both chuckle.

"I always want to watch you dance," Tommy murmured, finally

getting off the bed and sauntering closer, still in just his boxer briefs.

"Get dressed or I won't be responsible for my actions," Carter said. He trailed his fingertips down Tommy's chest and then clenched his teeth, turning away to pull on his shirt. "I'm going to go write a note to my dads."

Tommy laughed. "Alright."

Carter headed into the kitchen and wrote a quick message on the whiteboard on the fridge. He was writing his name as Tommy entered and wrapped his arms around Carter's waist, dropping a light kiss on the back of his neck. "I'm glad you're as clingy as I feel after being intimate," Carter said, squeezing Tommy's hands, grabbing two apples from the basket on the counter, and passing one to Tommy.

"Who says I'm clingy?" Tommy teased, rubbing the apple on his shirt, and taking a bite. "By the way, not sure it was the best idea to give me your clothes. I'm going to be able to smell you the entire class, and it's doing funny things to me."

Carter laughed and kissed Tommy's cheek. "You could just not wear a shirt," he suggested with a smirk. "I certainly wouldn't mind." He locked the door behind them, and they headed out into the night. Judy's dojo wasn't far. They walked the familiar distance and up the three flights of stairs, tossing their apple cores in the compost bin at the top.

There were several people in the coat room and a loud buzz of voices coming from the main studio space. They took off their shoes and socks and entered the dojo. Carter's jaw dropped. The room was full of teenagers.

"Is it always like this?" Tommy murmured as heads turned in their direction.

"Oh good, you're here," Zoe said, pouncing on Carter and pulling him off to the side. Her face was calm, but there was mischief behind her eyes. "Did you happen to mention attending class tonight while at school?"

Carter wracked his brain. "I don't know. Maybe?" He watched

people crowd around his boyfriend. "I'm guessing the teen drop-in class is usually a little quieter than this?"

Zoe chuckled. "That's an understatement. I hope you're prepared for this."

"Do I have a choice?" Carter cracked his neck. "Trial by fire, it is."

"I think we'll get along just fine." Zoe said with a smile. She raised her voice as she turned to face the class. "Alright everyone, the most important thing you'll learn is to respect your teacher—that's me, Zoe—and the teacher's assistant, Carter. That means bowing before you step onto the mat and listening when we correct you. If you're here for the class, great, you can stay. If you're just here to gawk at the newbies, get out." She glared around the room. Nobody moved. Zoe smiled. "Let's start with some stretching!"

THURSDAY THE 12TH OF JUNE, 2003 - WESTMEATH, ONTARIO

Carter flipped open the folded newspaper and thrust it at Tommy the minute they were on the sidewalk in front of the Johnson house. He watched, amused, as Tommy took in the headline "Monsters Attack Niche Gala" and the full colour photo on the front page of Jason and Kennedy in their formal wear at the Royal Canadian Museum of Natural and Cultural History—or Niche's—masquerade ball the night before. They were feeding each other cupcakes, oblivious to the dinosaur perfectly framed behind them.

"Cool statue," Tommy said. "I don't get it."

"It's not a statue," Carter said with a chuckle. "Read the story."

"Not a statue?" Tommy parroted. He scanned the article. "The dinosaurs were the same sort of monster-creature as the gorilla-bear and the moosequitoes? No mention of the Phantom or Wraith."

"Nope." Carter grinned and winked conspiratorially. "But what a coincidence that the monsters were at an event where Kennedy and Jason are present, and it just so happens to be the *one* time that the superheroes *don't* show up to fight them."

"That is quite the coincidence." Tommy studied the image. "They look amazing. I'm disappointed I didn't get to see them in person last night."

"As if your mom didn't take a bunch of pictures before they left." Carter smirked. "Are you telling me you regret our time together last night?"

Tommy couldn't help his grin. "Definitely not."

"Good." Carter plucked the paper from Tommy and took his hand. "Because I'm looking forward to next time."

Tommy flushed but looked pleased. "Yeah, me too," he said, his voice cracking.

The school came into view, and Carter frowned at the guy in a purple jacket on the sidewalk. "I'd recognize that silhouette any-where. What the heck is Greg doing on this side of town? Seeing him on Tuesday on the boat cruise was bad enough."

"At least he didn't try to talk to us then," Tommy said. "Isn't that Leo with him?"

"It is," Carter said grimly. "And Patricia."

"What an odd trio." Tommy pulled on Carter's hand. "Let's go see what he's up to."

But when Greg saw them coming, he left, walking the other way. Patricia didn't see them and headed directly into the school, but Leo leaned against a tree, obviously waiting for someone. He jumped when he saw them.

"Just the guys I was looking for!" he said with a tight smile. "You need to hear this."

"Is it about that Blue Blood you looked awfully chummy with?" Carter said, trying to keep the anger out of his tone.

"Dude, chill." Leo rolled his eyes. "This is the first time I've seen the guy. He was trying to recruit Patricia and me as spies for him at school."

"What? Why would Greg want that?" Tommy asked, confused.

"You know him?" Leo asked, surprised.

"He's a Door Tech kid," Carter said absentmindedly, his mind whirling. "The Blue Bloods must be trying to infiltrate the school since they can't get into Oldtown the usual way."

"He said he only wanted information," Leo said, raising his hands.

"What kind of information?" Carter asked.

"I said 'no', and he ran away." Leo crossed his arms. "Should I have said 'yes' and reported back to you?"

"Might be a good idea," Carter said, considering it. "You could be a double agent."

"I'm not sure I'm capable of that," Leo said. "I'm a terrible liar."

"But could you do it to keep your friends safe?" Tommy asked, raising his eyebrow.

Leo drew in a sharp breath and stood up straighter. "Yeah, I can do that. Okay, next time I see him, I'll let him know I changed my mind."

Carter smiled. "You're the best. Come on, let's get to class."

The day passed quickly, despite the excitement running through his veins. Kennedy and Jason's "not-a-bach-party" party was happening that evening at FunZone, and the STEM club, plus a few extras, were all attending.

He always ate lunch outside on Thursdays, hanging out with his skateboarding friends. They had brought bagged lunches from home and sat at the top of one of the half-pipes of the skate-boarding park in the back of the school.

"You can do this, too?" Tommy asked, eyes wide.

"I'm just learning. It's fun! I board-hop for now, at least until I can ask my dads for one for Christmas." Carter brushed the crumbs from his skirt, a black pleated one with silver threads. He pulled safety gear out of his backpack and unclipped his helmet from a shoulder strap, putting it on before getting to his feet. "Hey Angie, mind if I try?"

"Sure." She hopped off and passed Carter her board.

Carter stayed away from the half-pipe and kept to the flat ground around it. As much as he wanted to show off in front of

Tommy, he didn't want to try anything new today. A broken bone would put a damper on the party. He coasted a bit, core muscles clenched to keep his balance, bent his knees, and jumped the board an inch off the ground. He raised a fist in the air at his success, grinning widely.

"Hey, good job!" Angie said, taking her board back. "You've been practising."

"No, I haven't had time." Carter unbuckled his helmet strap. "Just wanted to show off."

Angie grinned down at Tommy. "You must bring him luck."

Tommy laughed. "He doesn't need luck. He's already great at so many things."

"Your own personal cheering section," Angie teased Carter. "I need to get myself a boyfriend so I can have one of those."

Carter nodded solemnly. "I highly recommend it."

After school, they rushed home to change and then met the rest of the teenagers going to FunZone at The Hawaiian.

"What's FunZone like?" Tommy asked. Carter had his head on Tommy's lap, enjoying the fingers running through his curls.

"It's like an arcade, cinema, and roller-skating arena all smushed together," Lauryn said, bouncing a little on the couch opposite them.

"Don't forget the roller coaster and lasertag," said Steve as he passed by.

"There's go-karts and a climbing area, too," Adrien said from the table next to the couches.

"All of that in one building?" Tommy asked, jaw dropping.

"And a restaurant," Carter added. "It's epic. One of the largest Aetherborn-owned establishments outside of Oldtown. It has wards, so people like Kennedy's friend Sanaa will be able to come tonight."

"Really? That's awesome. I liked her." Tommy dug his fingers gently into Carter's scalp, making him hum with delight.

"I wish I could purr," Carter said lazily. "Feels good."

"We should probably start heading over," Adrien said, ruffling

Tommy's hair as he passed. "It's not as far as Door Tech, but still a good half-hour walk."

"Yeah, yeah," Carter said, sitting up. His head felt heavy from all the gentle caresses. He gave himself a shake. "Let's go have some fun!"

The late afternoon sunlight filtered through the real buildings, blinding them from the left every once in a while as they headed north to FunZone. The giant three-storey building became visible several blocks away, and Tommy's jaw dropped. "It looks like the blocks I used to play with as a kid!"

Carter gazed fondly at his boyfriend, enjoying the amazement playing across his face.

Jason and Kennedy greeted them at the door, handing out cards for free plays throughout the building.

"Dang, this is some party!" whistled Adrien after they had entered the building. "Gabrielle and Zoe didn't go all out like this when they got married."

"Weren't they eighteen?" Carter asked. "How would you feel about getting married next year?"

To everyone's surprise, Adrien blushed and glanced shyly at Arielle. "Ummm..."

Arielle smiled at him. "My parents don't want me to get married until I've graduated from college."

"Whoa, dude!" George teased. "Look at you, being all adult-y!"

Continuing to rib each other, they headed further into the arcade.

Chapter 9

The bright lights, loud sounds, and scope of FunZone was overwhelming. It was the size of a full city block and contained an indoor roller coaster and go-karts, a computer and console game room, a full arcade, a cinema, lasertag, a climbing gym for all ages, and a roller-skating arena. Tommy glued himself to Carter's side, taking everything in without saying much at first.

Then Carter spotted the *Dance Dance Revolution EXTREME* machine and dragged him over to it. "It has two platforms!" he said excitedly. "We can play together! And I don't know these songs by heart like the ones at The Hawaiian, so we'd be on an even playing field. Come on, please?"

"Would you be willing to play against me?"

Tommy turned to face the new speaker, Kathryn Johnson, Jason's grandmother. She smiled. "I know dances from many realms, but I've never seen them performed in a game. Will you show me?"

"Oh, Carter's amazing," Tommy said, feeling like he was gushing. "You should watch him."

"I was asking you." Kathryn put her hands on her hips. "Then I won't lose too badly."

Tommy huffed a laugh, shaking his head. "Alright, you're on."

They chose "Stomp to my Beat", and Tommy was surprised to find himself keeping up. It was a much faster version of the song than he was used to, but he liked the way the rhythm got into his head.

At the end, barely out of breath despite not missing a step, Kathryn smiled at him. "You did well. Trust your instincts and you'll be even better."

"Uh, thanks?" Tommy said. He wasn't sure how to act around Kathryn. She looked like Jason's older sister but sounded like Grandma Denise; it was confusing. It must have been even worse for Kennedy as her soon-to-be in-law. Somehow, she still seemed at ease with the woman. He'd always been envious of Kennedy's confidence with people.

Kathryn smiled and bowed as she left.

"My turn!" Carter said.

"I'll play against you," Elyse offered.

The three of them played several rounds before Carter's phone chimed with a text.

"Faith is here!" Carter said excitedly, looking up from his phone.

"Oh my gosh!" Elyse bounced in place.

"Let's go meet her at the door!" Tommy exclaimed.

The three of them sprinted through the arcade and down the stairs to the first floor.

"You made it!" Tommy exclaimed, reaching his friend first. Faith had her long dark hair pulled back in an intricate braid. "You *have* to see this place!"

Elyse threw herself into Faith's arms for a hug. "There's an air hockey table, we need to play!"

"You're on!" Faith said to Elyse, and then to Tommy, she added, "You look so much better! I'm so relieved. How has your week been?"

Carter took over, saying, "He's been impressing the teachers, throwing a concert at lunch, and starting a revolution about skirt lengths at school. Are you nervous for your Door Tech test? It's next Tuesday, right?"

"Extremely nervous. I hope I finish all my questions. I know they're going to be different from yours, but maybe you can give me hints about what they're like?"

"They're not too different from what you'd expect," Tommy said. "Read the questions carefully."

Faith nodded her understanding. "I heard that Captain Herrington will be one of the experts! I'm going to die!"

"You'll be great," Elyse reassured her.

"Ha!" Faith scoffed, and abruptly changed the subject. "I'm glad you're having a good week, Tommy."

"And my parents might be sending me to Oldtown next year!" Tommy said, leading her into the building.

"No way!" Faith exclaimed, jaw dropping. "For real?"

Tommy nodded solemnly. "I'd miss you and the others, of course, but I would feel safer here."

Faith grimaced. "Yeah, the whole school is talking about the fight. Mostly rumours, which you'd know if you'd been online!" She slapped him lightly on the upper arm.

"Sorry. It's been hectic here, what with wedding stuff and schoolwork," Tommy apologized. "I haven't even opened my laptop since Friday."

"It's a good thing some of the others have more time." Faith grinned. "George told us about your concert and Alicia about the monster attack during the Door Tech event. Adrien mentioned that the teen drop-in class you went to last night was packed." She wiggled her eyebrows. "Are you becoming popular?"

Tommy laughed. "It's only because I'm new. They'll get bored of me sooner or later. The most interesting thing about me is my boyfriend."

Carter scoffed. "Right, because the guitar playing isn't swoon-worthy, and that's not even mentioning your smarts."

Elyse rolled her eyes. "I'm going to stop the complimenting there, because it'll go on for a while," she said, interrupting Tommy's rebuttal. "Come on, I think it's almost time for dinner."

They introduced Faith to the other teens when they reached

their table, slightly separate from the adults, and she was greeted with a round of hugs.

"Thanks for keeping me up to date on things," Faith said. "It seems Tommy has forgotten how to use a computer." She scowled at him playfully.

"He forgets most things when he's around Carter," George teased.

"Hey!" Tommy protested.

"He forgot to come to The Hawaiian last night before the drop-in class," Adrien pointed out.

"He came for dinner with my dads!" Carter chimed in to defend Tommy.

"I bet your dads barely saw him," George said with a wink. "You know, with all the kissing."

"Oh my God," Tommy squeaked, covering his face with his hands. "Is *nothing* a secret in Oldtown?"

There was silence for a moment.

Carter leaned closer as the table burst into laughter. "They were teasing. You just confirmed it."

Tommy's embarrassment deepened. "Sorry," he murmured, cheeks burning.

"I don't mind. They're all friends." Carter smirked at him. "I guess you forget your filter around me, too."

"Ugh," Tommy groaned, sitting back. "More like my common sense."

Carter brought their foreheads together, one hand warm on the back of Tommy's neck. "Hey, it's okay. Yeah?"

"Yeah." Tommy stared into Carter's grey eyes, ignoring the ribbing of the others as he lost himself in flecks of green and gold. "Jeepers, you're beautiful."

"You're only just now noticing?" Carter teased, but there was a light flush on his bronze cheeks from the compliment.

"I notice every time I see you," Tommy murmured.

"That's enough lovey-dovey gazing into each other's eyes," Elyse said, poking Carter in the ribs and making him flinch.

They ordered their food just before Jason stood up to give a welcoming speech. "Welcome and thank you for coming to our party," Jason said, his voice projecting to every corner of the restaurant. "I know most couples would have Bachelor and Bachelorette parties separately, but Kennedy and I are different. We wanted to celebrate together. Besides, how would we split up to celebrate? Kennedy has woven herself into the Community so tightly that she's taken all my friends!"

Jason paused with a grin, and Tommy chuckled along with everyone else. "The fact that none of you, not even my sister, are disagreeing with that proves my point." Jason paused for more laughter.

"Kennedy's capacity to love is unparalleled, and it's one of the many reasons I knew she was the one for me." Jason's sappy smile at Kennedy was contagious. Tommy enjoyed watching them together; their love was practically tangible. "But on to what's happening tonight. After dinner, there's going to be a huge game of laser tag, and everyone's invited. There'll be some rules to make sure the littles are safe, but I hope to see each and every one of you, either on my team, or at the other end of my laser." Jason glared around the silent room.

Kennedy laughed. "Not if I see you first!"

"See, this is why your friends sided with Kennedy," Jesse joked. Tommy still couldn't quite get over the fact that his sister was close friends with a *wizard*.

"Because she can shoot a laser gun better than me?" Jason nodded solemnly. "Excellent reason."

Chuckles rippled around the room.

"After the game, everyone is free to do their own thing. Enjoy your dinner!" Jason sat down to a round of applause.

"Sweet, that game is going to be *epic*!" Adrien exclaimed.

It was.

The little kids were given a light laser wand attached to a wrist band. Everyone's jerseys were a thin cloth that had integrated nanotechnology. Veronica had worked on the prototype, and Tommy couldn't wait to pick her brain about it.

Tommy teamed up with Evanna, who was an incredibly enthusiastic shot, if not completely accurate.

She led Tommy through the maze, her tiny hand holding tightly onto his, squeezing whenever she was startled by someone appearing ahead of them. It worked decently as a warning; Tommy was able to shoot the other team more often than he thought possible. He was grateful for the healer running around; it was George on his team, and he saw him often.

Occasionally, Jason let out a feral yell, drawing everyone's attention, and Evanna shook her head and led him behind whatever ambush the other team had prepared for those who thought Jason was an easy target.

That's not to say he wasn't; Jason was easily the largest person on either team, although Sanaa was taller, and George was getting there, but he was also a terrible shot. Amita, Kennedy's boss, on the other hand, never missed. Tommy made a point of always aiming for her first whenever he came across an ambush.

The scores were close. Amita had the most hits, followed closely by Kennedy. His team won by a very slim margin, thanks to Kennedy's guidance.

After the giant game, people split off into different areas of FunZone.

Tommy, Carter, Elyse, and Faith followed the little kids and their parents into the climbing gym, slides, and ball pit area.

He was surprised by how much he had missed his nephew. He'd only been away from him for a little less than a week. *How am I going to manage the homesickness if my parents let me move to Westmeath for the school year?* His heart twisted as he watched Carter catch the little boy at the bottom of a slide and swing him up in the air. *Arthur would grow up without knowing me.* It was a high cost, but to get to stay with Carter... Tommy was willing to pay.

They spent the next hour or so chasing the kids up stairs and down slides until little Arthur collapsed into his mother's arms. Sarah smiled as she pulled him close, planting a light kiss on his tousled curls, before letting her husband take him.

Phillip swooped the little boy up onto his shoulder, where Arthur rested his head with a wide yawn. "Alright, little munchkin. I think it's time for bed. You've had a big day."

That prompted the other families to start collecting their children. Denise, Tommy's grandmother, who was supposed to be staying with her son and his family, had said that she was going to be staying with Kathryn instead; they had a lot to catch up on.

"Very full house at Jason's," Carter murmured to Tommy as they said goodbye to the families.

"I didn't know that they knew each other," Tommy replied.

Elyse shrugged. "Small world."

"Apparently."

They made their way over to the go-karts, where most of the others had congregated, and had fun driving in circles until they were dizzy. When FunZone closed at midnight, Tommy was almost delirious from exhaustion and excitement.

"You sure you're going to be alright for school in the morning?" Kennedy asked the teens in general but fixed her gaze on Tommy.

"I'll be exhausted, but I'll nap after class before the rehearsal dinner," he said. "I had so much fun!"

"Napping is an excellent plan," Carter said seriously. "Your place or mine?"

Tommy barely stopped himself from giggling uncontrollably. "Yours will be quieter."

FRIDAY THE 13TH OF JUNE, 2003 - WESTMEATH, ONTARIO

Six-thirty in the morning came all too soon. Tommy dragged himself out of bed and into the bathroom, where a not-quite-warm shower woke him the rest of the way.

Nobody else was awake when he entered the kitchen, and he grumbled good-naturedly as he toasted some bread for breakfast.

Denise joined him while he was eating. "Did you sleep well?" she asked, opening cupboards.

"Coffee is in the corner cupboard," Tommy said, pointing it out. "I slept like the dead. You? Or did you talk all night?"

"We stayed up late enough," Denise replied, blushing slightly as she followed Tommy's directions.

Tommy nodded in understanding. "Lots to catch up on."

Denise paused for only a moment before pulling out a mug. "That's right. It's been over twenty-six years since I last saw Kathryn." She set up her coffee. "How's the skirt revolution going?"

Tommy glanced down at the dark pink ruffled skirt he had paired with his black David Usher band tee. "I think it's going alright. Ms. Chang, the principal, is holding a meeting before school today. She talked to the teachers after school yesterday about it. I'm pretty sure the teachers are all for removing the length rule. I mean, Mr. Coolidge, for one, joined in and wore his wife's skirts all week."

Denise smiled. "Sounds promising."

Tommy crossed his fingers. "I hope so." He popped the last bite of peanut butter toast into his mouth.

"Would you like some coffee before you leave?" Denise asked, turning to pour hers.

"Ah, no thanks. I've got to run."

"Make sure to bring an umbrella. It's supposed to rain this afternoon," she said.

Tommy paused mid-shouldering of his backpack. "I'll grab a plastic bag for my guitar then. Thanks, Grandma." He kissed her on the cheek before grabbing a black garbage bag from under the sink. "Love you."

"Love you too, darling."

The walk to Carter's was short, but the humidity was already creeping up, and Tommy could feel sweat beading along his hairline. "Great. That's *so* attractive," he muttered to himself. He spotted Carter leaving Oven Baked by the front door and stopped to wait for him.

"You're early," Carter said in greeting, slipping his hand into Tommy's free one. "I thought I'd have to drag you out of bed and dress you myself."

Tommy grinned at him. "You'd have enjoyed that."

"I had to give myself *something* to look forward to," Carter said with a chuckle. "Otherwise, I'm not sure I could have gotten up."

"Just the thought of seeing you was enough for me," Tommy said shyly.

"Oh my *God*," Carter groaned dramatically. "That was so romantic. Hang on, let me think of something." He walked silently for a few moments, their hands swinging between them. "This week has been a dream come true, getting to see you every day. I can't wait to do it forever."

Tommy tripped over his feet, his jaw hanging open. Carter caught him by the elbow, and Tommy righted himself. "That gave me shivers," Tommy confided. "I want that, too."

When they reached the school, it was busier than usual, despite their early arrival. They put their things in Carter's locker and followed the wave of people to the cafeteria.

They found seats with the STEM club and talked boisterously until Ms. Chang's arrival. She didn't make them wait long.

Her presence at the door of the cafeteria was heralded by a silence that grew until the sound of her heels clicking on the polished floors echoed throughout the room. She walked up onto the stage and faced the crowd.

"I'm not sure I need a microphone today. You are such an avid audience!" Ms. Chang said.

Tommy smiled. The silence was a little unnerving. He hoped it didn't bother her.

"After discussing the skirt length rule with teachers, parents, the school board, and the Community elders, I have come to a decision." Ms. Chang paused, looking solemnly out over the sea of upturned faces.

Carter sucked in a deep breath and tightened his grip on Tommy's hand.

"The rule is outdated and targets girls unfairly." Ms. Chang raised a hand as a cheer went up and silence fell once more. "The Community, especially, was impressed by the efforts of the boys to prove that this rule should be abolished. Therefore, it is with immense pride in the students at this school that I announce that the skirt length rule has been removed from the dress code. Congratulations." She smiled as the students all stood as one, clapping and whooping at their success.

"This is so great!" Carter exclaimed. "I can't believe we started this!"

"I'm just glad that the girls don't have to worry about such a silly rule anymore." Tommy was astonished by how much power he felt, having evoked such a change. "Remember, Adrien and Arielle started the petition. It wouldn't have gone anywhere without that."

"We *all* did good," Adrien said, hooking his arms around their shoulders. "And that's the way to start a revolution, boys!" He grinned at them.

"We should probably get to class," Carter said. "It's at the other end of the L."

"Don't make up excuses," George said dramatically. "We all know you just want alone time."

Tommy rolled his eyes, but kept his mouth shut, worried he'd say too much again.

On the way past the office, the vice-principal called out to them. Tommy stopped, hesitant to come face-to-face with the person who had been the cause of the revolution.

"I hope you boys are proud of yourselves," Ms. VanCamp said in her nasally monotone.

"We are, actually," Carter said, crossing his arms.

Ms. VanCamp huffed. "This is ridiculous! I was protecting those girls from predators. You," she gestured at Carter, who was wearing a tight, short, red skirt that showed off his ass and legs very well, in Tommy's opinion, "don't have to worry about him," she gestured at Tommy, "assaulting you because he can see your thighs!"

Carter barked a short laugh. "Of course I don't have to worry about it. We practise consent."

Ms. VanCamp, who had opened her mouth to continue her tirade, stopped, visibly confused. "I don't understand."

"Consent is when two people communicate about what is acceptable to both of them," Tommy said helpfully. "Maybe if you're concerned about assault, you can institute a consent workshop or two."

"That's a good idea," Carter said, nodding. "I'm sure the Arikis would agree. They'd probably want to host it at the community centre."

The vice-principal fluttered her hands, flustered at the casual mention of Jason and Zoe. "Of course I know what consent is!" Her voice rose in pitch. "I don't understand what you mean by 'practising' it."

Carter smirked at her for a moment. Tommy bit his lip to stop himself from laughing as she grew increasingly flustered. Finally, he elbowed Carter in the ribs. "Be nice," he whispered.

"Tommy's my boyfriend. He isn't going to assault me because we check in with each other before trying something new," Carter said, relenting. "It has nothing to do with whether I'm wearing a skirt or not."

"Oh!" Ms. VanCamp deflated a little. "I'll take the workshop under advisement," she said quietly. "It might be good for everyone."

Carter nodded solemnly. "I look forward to it next year. If that's everything?"

"Yes, yes, get to class, boys." Ms. VanCamp disappeared behind the glass doors to the office.

"Well, that went better than I expected," Tommy said cheerfully. "Hand?"

Carter held his out, and they continued to science with hands clasped between them.

The morning passed quickly, despite Tommy's attention wandering occasionally due to lack of sleep. He met up with Carter at his locker to store his guitar, and they headed to the cafeteria to grab lunch.

Carter insisted on returning the favour of paying for his lunch, and they each grabbed egg salad sandwiches to eat with the same group from the beginning of the week: Steve, Leo, Elyse, and Karine. Tommy had just picked up the second half of his sandwich when someone slid into the space next to him, pressing up against him.

Oh no, not again, he thought to himself.

"Hello." Patricia simpered at the group. Her hand slid up his thigh from his knee, and Tommy put his own in his lap to stop her from passing his skirt. She didn't seem to mind and gripped his fingers tightly. "It's okay, Tommy dearest, we can go at your pace," she said in a fake bubbly voice.

"Patricia—" Tommy started to say, but she cut him off.

"I do hope you let that country girl know that you won't need her as your date to the wedding now that you have me," she said, batting her eyelashes at him.

"You've got the wrong idea—" Tommy said, but she cut him off again.

"I love weddings. I can't wait to meet your parents!" Patricia gushed.

"Let go of me," Tommy said clearly.

Surprisingly, she did. "I don't understand what's wrong, Tommy dearest, but—"

"That's because you haven't let me speak." Tommy glanced around the table, drawing courage from his friends. He took a deep breath. "Patricia, I never said anything about inviting you to the wedding or having feelings for you. For one thing, Faith is already here, and for another, I'm gay."

Patricia looked shocked. "But... But you said that song... That it was for someone special?"

"Yeah, my boyfriend," Tommy explained patiently.

"I haven't seen you with anyone but—" Patricia cut herself off with wide eyes and leaned forward to see past him to Carter. "*You!*"

Carter smiled. "Sorry, he's mine."

Patricia opened and closed her mouth a couple times, her face getting redder the longer she sat beside him.

"How can you not know? Are we too subtle?" Tommy asked, confused. *If I had a loonie for every time a girl thought she was dating me, I'd have two loonies. It's not a lot, but it's weird that it's happened twice.* "It's not a secret or anything."

"You'll regret this!" Patricia hissed. "Nobody makes a fool of me and gets away with it."

"Tommy didn't do anything to you," Elyse protested.

"Yeah, you kinda threw yourself at him," Steve pointed out.

Patricia snarled at him, took one last look at Tommy, and left the table.

"Jeepers, that was dramatic," Tommy said with a shiver. "Should I start wearing a rainbow flag or something?"

Carter chuckled. "Or something. I could stake my claim on you right here and now if you like."

"What would that entail?" Tommy said with a grin. "Making out with me on stage?"

"Ooh, good idea." Carter pretended to consider it for a second. "No, that's a little too extreme. Can I do something?"

"I trust you." Tommy took a bite of his sandwich, and then wished he hadn't, because Carter got to his feet and climbed onto the table.

"Hey!" Carter shouted, his voice echoing through the cafeteria. "It's come to my attention that some people weren't aware that Tommy Fairfield is my boyfriend. He's mine. Back off!" He jumped back down to the raucous cheers of the cafeteria.

"And that's *not* extreme?" Elyse said, raising one eyebrow.

Carter shrugged. "Effective, though."

Tommy chuckled after he managed to swallow his bite. "I love you," he whispered in Carter's ear.

Carter gave him a quick kiss. "Love you too."

Chapter 10

**FRIDAY THE 13TH OF JUNE, 2003 -
WESTMEATH, ONTARIO**

"We are going to get *soaked*," Carter announced, looking out the main door of Oldtown High.

"When Grandma said it was going to rain, I thought she meant regular rain, not a deluge!" Tommy said, hugging his guitar to him.

"Does Denise have weather magic?" Carter asked, eyebrows rising in surprise.

"She says it's called arthritis," Tommy said wryly, making Carter laugh. Tommy put his backpack on the ground and started digging through it, pulling out a black garbage bag. "I'm just glad I listened and brought this to protect my guitar."

"Nice." Carter nodded his approval and then squinted through the glass. "Hey, am I seeing things, or does that purple blur look like Greg?"

Tommy joined him at the door. "The shape is bulky enough to be him. Let's go see what he wants."

Greg was standing under the protection of an old maple tree. His brown hair was dark with water and plastered to his head. He looked miserable.

"Hey," Carter said as they joined him under the canopy of leaves.

Greg didn't look surprised. He stuffed his hands in his pockets and glared at them. "About time," he grunted.

"Oh, you actually *want* to speak to us today?" Tommy said. "You ran away quickly enough yesterday morning."

"I can leave again," Greg said, scowling.

Carter raised his hands pacifyingly. "What's up? Are you alright?"

Now Greg looked surprised, which Carter thought was interesting. "'M fine." Greg scuffed the toe of his sneaker into the grass at the base of the tree. "Heard a rumour. Was trying to corroborate it before I handed it off to you, but..." He shrugged. "You Oldtown kids are tighter than I thought."

"Probably has something to do with the purple duds," Carter pointed out. "You do know that over a hundred of you guys attacked a private party in Oldtown last Saturday, right?"

Greg flushed. "I wasn't part of that."

Tommy chuckled. "We know, or you'd be in jail or juvie right now."

"If—" Greg exclaimed, furrowing his brow in anger.

"My *point* is," Carter interrupted. "Nobody in Oldtown is going to talk to you because you're wearing *that*."

Greg ran a hand over the purple leather of his sleeves. "I... I don't want to be a part of this anymore. But once you're in..." He sighed and rolled his eyes. "And I'm a legacy." He coughed and turned away abruptly. "That's not why I'm here. There are rumours of an Oldtown gang forming, one that disagrees with the people running things."

"There are people that don't like what Jason and Zoe are doing?" Carter said, incredulous. "What do they want instead? They are open to suggestions."

"How should I know, I couldn't even get confirmation of the gang, let alone what they want." Greg sighed again. "I was trying to do you a favour, to repay what my father... Ah, well." He stuffed his hands in his jacket pockets, immediately taking them out again. "I'll see you this summer?" He sounded hopeful.

"Provided we all get in, yeah, we'll see you at Door Tech," Tommy said.

Greg snorted. "As if you two wouldn't." He looked sad for a second, eyes worried. "I hope you have better luck finding anything out about the gang." He walked out from the shelter of the tree, instantly getting drenched. "Glad you're still together."

"Why do you care?" Carter asked Greg's back.

He didn't turn around or answer them.

Tommy shrugged. "Maybe he's just a romantic at heart."

Carter grinned. "Seems out of character, but I've heard weirder things."

"What do you think of his story about the gang?" Tommy asked as they started walking to Carter's.

"I can't imagine anyone being upset enough with how Jason's running things to start a *gang*," Carter said with a shrug. Water dripped down the back of his neck, and he shivered.

"He certainly does a lot for the Community," Tommy agreed. "I can't think of anyone who doesn't benefit. Other cities *wish* they were run like this."

"Maybe..." Carter trailed off, gathering his thoughts as he stared at the agitated puddles they walked past. "We say that there are plenty of opportunities to speak to Jason, but maybe there are people that don't feel heard? And then there are those of us who are close to the Council members. It's easier for us to affect change because we can talk to them whenever we want."

Tommy frowned as he thought about that. "You think that people could be upset because others get special treatment? Or because they're not related to someone on the Council?" He shook his head.

"A lot of resources do go to people who don't pass, or to the people who were kidnapped last year," Carter pointed out.

"But they can walk around without fear. Those seem like pretty silly reasons to form a gang. We must be missing something."

"We should bring it up to Zoe after the wedding. Everyone's a little stressed right now," Carter said.

"Understatement." Tommy hitched his guitar up higher. "This wet plastic is *not* easy to hold onto. I'm glad it's not much further."

"At least you've got something to protect it," Carter pointed out. "Do they make waterproof guitar cases?"

Tommy shrugged. "Probably. I might ask for one for Christmas if I end up coming here, so I don't run into this problem again."

"You didn't bring your guitar to school in Parry Sound?" Carter asked.

"No, I used the school's."

Carter pushed open the door to Oven Baked, and they stepped inside with sighs of relief.

"Look what the cat dragged in," Sam greeted them with a low rumble of laughter. "You'd better go dry off before you catch a cold."

"That's not how colds work," Tommy replied flippantly and then looked panicked. "Sir," he added.

Carter laughed and tugged Tommy to the back stairs. "We'll dry off before taking a nap. Don't worry, I'll set an alarm. We won't be late for the rehearsal dinner."

"I'm not worried, you're very responsible," Sam replied, a twinkle in his eyes.

Carter groaned. "Da-*ad*! You know how that makes me feel!"

"That's why I said it." Sam chuckled. "Go on, snuggle up."

As they headed up the stairs to the apartment, Tommy blurted out, "Do you find it weird that your dads will be just downstairs?"

"Do you find it weird that we sleep at your sister's house?" Carter asked in reply. "No. I like that they're supportive of my relationship with you."

Tommy smiled at him. "I like that, too. What was all that about 'responsible,' then?"

Carter chuckled, unlocking the door. "It was his way of reminding me to be safe."

"Does he know?" Tommy asked, face neutral as he took off his shoes.

"No. That's not for me to tell. If your tests come back positive, I'll have to say something because I'll need to get tested, but until then, they don't have to know." Carter fought to get his shoes off, the water making things more difficult.

"It's not like I'm embarrassed about my status being in Quantum Cat State. You know, being simultaneously positive and negative until we get the results," Tommy said, putting his guitar and backpack against Carter's in the front hall. "Even if I test positive, I did nothing wrong."

"No, you definitely didn't." Carter struggled to get his shirt off. "You didn't do anything wrong with me either." He succeeded and balled up the wet fabric in his hands.

"Hmm?" Tommy said, eyes fixed on Carter's abdomen.

Just like that, Carter's foul mood vanished, and he chuckled. "Come on, let's get out of our wet things. We'll hang them in the bathroom and hope that the rain has stopped by the time we have to head to the community centre."

"I fully support this plan," Tommy said with a grin, peeling his shirt over his head.

Carter took his hand and led him to the bathroom where they stripped to their briefs.

"Last day of wearing a skirt. How do you feel about it?" Tommy asked, shaking out the pink ruffles before draping it over the curtain rod.

Carter's red skirt joined it. "I think I'll miss it. Might buy some for next year."

"As long as it has pockets." Tommy wrung out his shirt.

"Right." Carter laughed. "You wouldn't be embarrassed by me?"

"Why would I?" Tommy's brow furrowed as he hung the shirt up. "Because it's not 'traditional' men's clothing?"

"Yeah." Carter shrugged up one shoulder. "It's pretty different, right?"

"It *is* different, but honestly?" Tommy turned to face him, his hands running down Carter's back. "You look amazing in skirts, and if it makes you happy, then I'm all for it. But how I feel shouldn't change what you're going to wear. If I hated Rush, which I don't, but say I did… I wouldn't expect you to never wear your Rush shirts again."

"That's a good point." Carter tilted his head, grazing his lips over Tommy's once, and then going back in for a lingering kiss that made him dizzy. "We need to dry our hair."

"'Kay. Just know that I'm not exactly feeling tired right now," Tommy said, letting Carter go so he could grab a towel.

"Mmm, yes. I could feel that." Carter rubbed his hair vigorously with the towel before passing it off to Tommy. "I think I know exactly how to tire us out."

Tommy peeked out from under the towel, green eyes framed by dark brown cloth. He grinned mischievously. "Me too. Packing your sleepover bag."

"Yeah, okay, that too. I'll be coming back here to get dressed for the wedding after martial arts. Too many people needing to use the shower at your house." Carter tossed the towel at the sink and drew Tommy close again. "I was thinking something a lot more fun."

"Yeah," Tommy breathed, eyes half-closed and fixed on his mouth. "Me too. I was just—"

Carter cut him off by claiming his lips. "Less talking, more action, then more sleep."

"Okay." Tommy nodded eagerly. "Lead the way."

Carter took his hand, pressing their palms together. He could feel the calluses on the tips of Tommy's fingers from his guitar playing, and the ones on his palms from helping build his brother's house. The difference in their skin tones fascinated him, and he turned their hands, the bathroom light shimmering over them. The mood changed, softening from hot and heavy to something gentler. "I think," he said, and almost jumped at how loud his voice sounded in the quiet of the bathroom. "I think we've got a big night ahead of us, and I'm more tired than I realized."

Tommy nodded, gaze fixed on their hands, eyelids heavy. "I think you're right."

"Snuggle time," Carter said, summoning all his energy to link their fingers and pull Tommy down the hall to his bedroom. "I wanna be the big spoon this time."

"No complaints from me."

The alarm on Carter's phone woke him all too soon. He reached over Tommy's shoulder to hit snooze and pressed a kiss to his bare shoulder blade.

"Mmm?" Tommy hummed sleepily.

"Time to get up," Carter said quietly. "We have to be at the community centre to catch the shuttle to the church in…" He glanced at the time. "Twenty-nine minutes."

Tommy groaned and yawned. "Are weddings always this hectic? Go-go-go, not a moment to cuddle my boyfriend in peace?"

Carter laughed and kissed the back of Tommy's neck. "I don't know, we've managed to make some time for ourselves quite often this week." He rolled away from the warm body and twitched the curtain aside to look out the window. "It's nice and clear now. You'll be able to carry your guitar no problem."

"Great." Tommy got up and stretched, his briefs riding low on his hips and showing off the two dimples at the base of his spine. Carter eyed the waistband hungrily, biting his lip to keep from reaching out. "I'm glad Nick has agreed to store my guitar in his office, so I won't have to worry about carrying it tomorrow."

"That is convenient."

They got ready quickly and made it to The Hawaiian with time to spare, joining the others who were waiting for the shuttle. Carter glanced at the faces. "Where are Kennedy and Jason?"

"And Veronica?" Tommy added.

"Hopefully they'll meet us there," Zoe said as the shuttle drove up.

Lilah commented, "I believe Veronica was supposed to go to the church straight from work."

However, they were not at the church when they got there. After waiting for half an hour, Zoe got impatient and picked up her phone. "I'm just going to give Jason a call. If they've snuck off somewhere to have sex..." She left the threat unfinished and moved a little away from the rest as she dialled.

"Where *are* you?" Zoe's voice carried, and the rest of the conversations died down, everyone anxious to hear where the bride and groom were. She glanced back at them before turning away and lowering her voice until Carter couldn't hear her. When she returned to them, her mouth was set in a grim line. "They got held up. Jason said to run through the rehearsal without them, that he wouldn't remember anything tomorrow anyways, and then to enjoy the dinner. They'll try to make it to that."

Carter pulled Tommy a little further away from the others. "Veronica's missing too. I think they might be on a mission!" he hissed in as quiet a whisper as he could manage.

Tommy nodded slowly, his gaze on his mother. "That makes sense. Kennedy's not one to skip out on something this important unless it's something big. And Mom isn't blowing up. She probably knows. Do you think we could get her to tell us?"

"I doubt it."

They practised the ceremony quickly. There were a lot more steps than Carter realized to a wedding, and an awful lot of standing around and waiting.

Zoe and Rachel were to be the witnesses to the union, so it didn't matter too much that Veronica wasn't there, although Sylvie, Veronica's girlfriend, was there to stand in her place.

Carter found that he'd be walking with Evanna at the end of the ceremony, which made her happy. The toddlers, Brooke and Arthur, would be walking with Zoe, holding her hands.

On the way back to the restaurant, Zoe kept looking at her phone anxiously. Sylvie sat down next to her, and they put their heads together. Zoe drew back sharply, and their whispered conversation grew agitated, almost loud enough for Carter to hear over the rumble of the engine.

He felt like he was stretching his ears to their limit and caught the words "rescue" and "secret." *Hmm, the plot thickens. Who are they rescuing? And Sylvie knows?* Carter raised his eyebrows at Tommy meaningfully, who shrugged.

The rest of Tommy's family and Kathryn were waiting for them in the community centre.

"Grandma and Kathryn are holding hands!" Tommy whispered to Carter.

Carter examined the two women and how closely they were standing. "They were friends when they were younger, weren't they? Rather good friends, it seems." He winked at his boyfriend.

Tommy looked thoughtful. "That's nice. I'm glad they found each other again."

They took their seats in one of the smaller meeting rooms. Carter recognized it as being the one that had held all the gifts from the Community Ball the previous weekend. He and Tommy had helped unwrap the nearly three hundred presents. It had been overwhelming, to say the least.

"Oh, no wine for me," Carter heard Gabrielle say to the waiter. She was sitting across from Sarah, Tommy's sister-in-law, who quickly said, "No wine for me either."

The two women looked at each other and started to laugh. "You are?" they both said at the same time. "Me too!" they echoed again.

"What's going on?" Lilah asked, looking from one to the other.

Sarah smiled and put one hand on her lower belly and the other on her husband Phillip's arm. "We're going to have another baby."

"Oh!" Lilah clapped her hands and rushed to hug her daughter-in-law. "Oh, I'm so happy for you!"

Gabrielle added, "We're pregnant, too." She chuckled. "Only ten weeks, though, so we weren't expecting to tell anyone yet."

"I'm twelve weeks. We were going to say something on Sunday after the wedding," Sarah said. "We thought it would be nice to have everyone together, instead of calling the girls."

Both families were surrounded by people then, and Carter turned to Tommy, who had a furrow in his brow. "You're going to be an uncle again," he said. "Are you excited?"

"If I'm in Westmeath for school, I'll miss everything," Tommy said sadly. "This baby will barely know me."

"I'm sorry," Carter said. He took a deep breath and asked, "Does this make you want to stay in Parry Sound?"

"A bit. But not enough to ask to stay. It would be more like a silver lining if my parents don't let me come." Tommy sighed. "Maybe Zoe and Gabrielle will let me play with their baby."

"Most likely yes," Carter said with a chuckle.

"Where can they *possibly* be?" Lilah demanded loudly.

"Here, have some wine," Kathryn said, handing Lilah a glass of red. "Let's celebrate the two new lives joining us before the end of the year, as well as the union of our families."

"I'll drink to that!" Lilah said, downing half her glass. "I'm going to go white from the escapades of my youngest daughter, I swear!"

SATURDAY THE 14TH OF JUNE, 2003 - WESTMEATH, ONTARIO

They were kept busy the morning of the wedding. In between Carter's martial arts class and getting dressed, the boys helped look after Brooke and Evanna. They kept them from pulling out the French braids that the stylists had done for them or spilling their lunch on themselves. They weren't wearing their dresses yet, but nobody had time to bathe them a second time.

Somehow, they found themselves on the first shuttle to the church with Kennedy.

Carter adjusted his white tie self-consciously and wiped his hands on his matching pants. "Do I look okay?" he asked Tommy quietly.

"You fishing for a compliment?" Tommy asked with a grin. "Because you look incredibly handsome."

"Thanks." Carter fiddled with the emerald green collar of his dress shirt. "I'm not used to wearing white. Or green. I feel like I'm wearing your colour."

Tommy studied him seriously. "I think it looks amazing. Kennedy wouldn't choose a colour that doesn't work on everyone."

"Thanks," Carter said again. "You're right. Paler greens look terrible on me. You look great in that dark green, by the way."

"Nobody's going to be looking at *me*," Tommy said with a shrug. A flicker of panic crossed his expression. "At least, not until the reception," he said in a whisper.

The shuttle rolled to a stop at the church, and the reverend walked out to meet them.

"Perfect timing," the reverend said in greeting, kissing Kennedy's cheek lightly. "The make-up team arrived five minutes ago and is setting up in the bigger meeting room. You have access to the smaller rooms on either side for privacy to get changed."

"And the florists?" Lilah asked.

"They were here early this morning," Reverend Mitchel said. "Actually, Nick, I'm glad you're here. I believe you can remedy a slight problem." The two men walked into the church.

"Problem?" Lilah sounded panicked. "What's wrong?"

"Whatever it is, I'm sure Nick can take care of it," Kennedy replied. "He has an affinity with plants."

Tommy gasped excitedly. "Really?"

Kennedy laughed. "Why don't you and Carter see if you can help?"

The two boys hurried after the men, leaving the girls to walk downstairs to the meeting hall alone.

"What does 'affinity with plants' mean?" Tommy asked.

"He's a nymph," Carter explained. "He helps plants grow."

"That's so cool!" Tommy was silent, and Carter could practically see the wheels turning in his brain. "I guess the type of Aetherborn doesn't really affect their interests at all, eh? Or else he'd be a gardener or farmer or something?"

"My dads used to be geologists," Carter said with a straight face.

"Really?"

Carter burst into laughter. "No. I'm just kidding. Although Kennedy's boss is a dryad, and she works in agriculture, so I guess that's kinda related. The answer to your question is no, but sometimes."

Tommy grinned. "I guess it would be the same thing as asking me if I'm going to become a farmer just because my father is one. And Phillip did follow in his footsteps, so there you go."

"Exactly."

Dr. Sallah passed them and halted almost comically. "Tommy! So glad I bumped into you. I called in some favours and got the results back from your tests." He looked pointedly at Carter.

"I'll just..." Carter pointed after the men. "You can catch up."

"No, no, stay, please." Tommy squeezed Carter's hand hard. "I'll tell him immediately anyways. Please, go on," he said to the doctor.

"Your tests all came back negative. You don't have to worry." Dr. Sallah grinned at Tommy's whoop of happiness.

"Thank you so much!" Tommy said, shaking the doctor's hand. "You have no idea how relieved I am."

"I have some idea." Dr. Sallah winked at Carter, who grinned. "I'll see you later."

Reverend Mitchel led them to a room in the wings. "I need your utmost secrecy," he said to them, receiving nods before he opened the door. Inside were a few boxes that were filled with the stun weapons that Carter remembered seeing the Blue Bloods wielding at the Community Ball the week prior.

"Why are these here?" Carter asked, peeking into one of the boxes.

Nick scratched behind his ear. "Jason's concerned that the wedding will be attacked, right? These are just precautions." To the reverend, he added, "This is as good a place for them as any. Keep the door locked, in case any guests wander in, and give me a key. I don't get mind controlled easily."

Carter felt queasy. "Mind controlled?" He must have been distracted by Tommy during that part of the planning the night before.

"Yeah, the gang was controlled by someone off-site at the ball last weekend," Nick said.

"Keep an eye on me, then. Claude controlled me in the fall," Carter admitted. "I'm just glad he didn't ask me to do anything beyond untie Kennedy and shut up."

Tommy looked worried. "But nothing will happen, right? This is just a precaution?"

"Right." Nick clapped a hand on Tommy's shoulder. "We'll be fine."

Chapter 11

SATURDAY THE 14TH OF JUNE, 2003 -
WESTMEATH, ONTARIO

We'll be fine. Nick's words came back to Tommy as he ran into the main part of the church.

"We'll be fine," Tommy repeated mockingly, looking for Nick among the stunned and collapsed wedding guests. He finally spotted him in one of the side aisles, halfway to the front of the church.

One of the few plus sides to this situation was that Carter hadn't been affected by the mind control. He was out in the hall, keeping the little kids calm. Kennedy said she hadn't been surprised when Tommy was fine; something to do with Grandma Denise.

Tommy dug in Nick's pockets, trying to find the key to the weapons room.

They had prepared the main part of the church with stun bombs that Veronica could activate remotely in case the guests were mind controlled. That planning had paid off, and none of the guests had been harmed.

Unfortunately, Kennedy had to pull a gun out from *somewhere* and stun their dad and Rachel in the hallway. Out of the wedding party, who were out of range of the stun bombs within the main church, they were the only two who were mind controlled. Something to do with heritage or innate abilities, depending on the person. It was a very good thing that the hallway was out of the range of the mass stun, because no sooner had the mind control taken effect than soldiers with actual guns had burst into the church from another entrance.

He found the key and ran for the weapons room.

Kennedy had quickly taken charge, stunning the first wave of soldiers and urging the rest of the wedding party to move the children and unconscious people into one of the small rooms off the hallway.

Fortunately, Kathryn had not been affected by the stun bombs because she could project a shield across the hallway to protect Kennedy from the bullets shot by the soldiers.

Tommy was a little in awe of his sister and how calm she was despite the danger.

But she needed backup, which was why Tommy had been sent to grab weapons. A smaller box was beside the larger one. He made sure there were a variety of stun guns and batons and scooped it up, running back to the hallway as fast as he could.

"Thanks," Michelle said, taking a gun. Lilah did as well, and the two women flanked Kennedy, making a serious dent in the soldiers. Carter grabbed a baton and planted himself at the door. Tommy left the box outside the door in case the weapons ran out of charge and went into the room.

Evanna, Brooke, Arthur, and another little boy, one of the wedding guests, were huddled together. They were all sobbing quietly, tears trickling down their cheeks.

This won't do, Tommy thought. He sat cross-legged in front of them and said, "You are all being so very brave. Thank you for staying calm and quiet."

"I don't feel very brave," Evanna said brokenly. "I can't stop crying!"

Tommy smiled. "That's normal. This is kinda scary. Do you know why I'm not worried?"

All four children shook their heads.

"Because Kennedy's out there, and Michelle, and my mom, and Kathryn. They are the most capable women I know. They won't let anything happen to any of us. I feel so safe, don't you?"

Brooke wiped her face and nodded. "Me help?"

"Yes, you can help by doing one of the most important things, even if it seems like something small. You can sit in here with me and make sure nothing happens to Rachel and Dad." A thought came to Tommy. "Brooke, did you know that people are mostly made up of water?"

The little girl's eyes widened. "Yes."

"If any of the bad guys do make it to the doorway, you can throw them away from the door by moving their water, don't you think?"

"Yes!"

"I can't do anything," pouted Evanna. "Lilah said I wasn't to touch Gerard or Rachel."

"Well, they're not hurt," Tommy said patiently, his voice suddenly loud in the silence. The past week had been a rollercoaster of new information. Mostly, he felt excited at being let into Carter's secret world, but with that excitement came a level of danger he was still having a tough time processing.

"Leave now," Kennedy said clearly, her voice echoing in the hallway.

Tommy looked out the door to see Kennedy and Lilah calmly pointing their guns down the hall. "Where did Michelle go?" he wondered aloud.

"Mama?" gasped Evanna.

"She stepped outside to help Jason since Kennedy had everything under control here," Carter said quickly.

"Mom, Jason and I need to go," Kennedy said.

"Go where?" Lilah's eyes narrowed suspiciously.

"To stop the monster attacks."

Lilah frowned. "But the wedding? You can't just leave! And you'll mess up your hair!"

Tommy laughed. *Of course Mom would be worried about that!*

"The guests aren't going anywhere. Take care of everyone while we're gone, and we'll be back before anyone knows it. As for my hair," Kennedy shrugged, "this is so much more important."

“Actually, I can help with that.” Veronica’s voice came from further down the hall.

Tommy got up to join Carter at the doorway.

“Don’t turn around!” Lilah shrieked at Kennedy. “Jason’s there!”

“It’s a good thing I have excellent control over my reflexes,” Jason grumbled.

“How can you help with my hair?” Kennedy asked Veronica.

“I can give you your wedding presents early.”

Veronica placed a ring on Kennedy’s finger.

“Your wedding rings,” Veronica explained. “Tap it three times.”

Kennedy did as she was told and Tommy gasped as her dress disappeared, replaced by a Wraith suit, complete with a full-face mask. Glowing green lines in the shape of wards spider-webbed across the dark green material.

“Oh wow!” Kennedy, now the Wraith, exclaimed.

“I knew it!” shouted Carter. He coughed bashfully when every-one looked at him. “I knew it,” he repeated, a huge grin on his face.

Tommy bumped his hip into his boyfriend.

“Where’s the dress?” asked Lilah, her eyes wide.

“In a pocket dimension. When they tap the rings again, they’ll revert to the exact outfit they were wearing, hair untouched,” Veronica reassured Lilah.

“Does this count as seeing each other?” Jason’s voice had lowered. He was wearing a dark grey suit with matching spider-webbing and a mask.

“I hope not,” the Wraith said, putting her hands on her hips.

Lilah sighed. “No, I guess it doesn’t count.”

The Wraith whirled to face the Phantom, who was pointing at the teenagers. “We are counting on your discretion.”

Without waiting for a response, the superheroes linked hands and started running down the hall toward the stairs to the basement.

“Take care of yourselves!” Lilah called after them. Then she turned to the boys. "We need to tidy up and wake these people up. Bring them outside. They shouldn't be under the mind control effects when they wake, and they'll go away on their own."

It took Tommy and Carter the better part of an hour to clear the hallway of the stunned soldiers while Kathryn and Veronica woke up the wedding guests in the church.

"Why do you think the mind control didn't work on me this time?" Carter asked as they pulled the last guy down the hall to the exit by his ankles.

"I don't know. Maybe the control wasn't as strong as the time before?" Tommy shrugged. "Maybe your martial arts training helped to control your mind as well as your body? Or maybe alien mind control doesn't work on rock giants."

"I suppose it could be any of those."

"Jason seemed to think you wouldn't be affected when we made plans last night," Tommy said thoughtfully, dropping the legs of the guy they were dragging.

"I wonder why." Carter dusted his hands together.

"Let's go see if they're back yet," Tommy said, grabbing Carter's hand. "I wonder if we'll ever find out who sent the monsters and why."

"Maybe at brunch tomorrow," Carter said. "Or later in the week. Oh shoot, I forgot you're not here next week." He frowned.

Tommy chuckled. "I'm glad I fit in so seamlessly. You'll have to fill me in."

"Don't worry, I will. If they tell me." Carter grinned. "I can't believe I was right!"

"I'm not surprised. All your observations pointed to them. My sister's a superhero!" Tommy whispered, afraid of being overheard.

The Phantom was walking out of the little room where the kids and Lilah were playing when they reached it. He tapped his ring three times, and his white suit reappeared, the Phantom's outfit vanishing. Jason nodded at them and headed into the main part of the church.

"I am never going to get used to that," Carter whispered to Tommy.

Kennedy filled them in quickly on what they had discovered; the people behind the monster attacks were not Blue Bloods but scientists with a mind control device and a small army of soldiers.

"Wild," Carter said, shaking his head.

"I think we're going to be starting soon," Tommy said, peeking into the church. The organist had started to play.

"I'll check on the kids," Carter said, leaving Tommy with Gerard.

"You've picked a good one," Gerard confided to Tommy gruffly.

"Sorry?" Tommy asked.

"Carter." Gerard nodded at the boy, who was smiling at Kennedy. "I've enjoyed getting to know him this week. I can see that he cares about you, and that's all I want for my kids."

"You're getting sappy, Dad," Tommy teased.

"Well, my baby girl is getting married. I'm allowed to be sappy," Gerard said, clearing his throat. "And I'm not ready to lose you yet. I thought we'd get three more years of you being at home before you went away to university."

"That sounds an awful lot like you're letting me come to Westmeath in the Fall," Tommy said hesitantly.

"Your mother isn't ready to admit it yet, but she will. We want you safe." Gerard squeezed Tommy's hand. "Don't let on that I've said anything, eh? It would only upset her."

"Of course, Dad. Hi, Nick, are they ready for us?"

Nick smiled. "Yup, just waiting for my signal to start."

The others joined them soon after. Nick refreshed the bouquets and boutonnieres and returned to the church.

Moments later, the sound of a conch shell echoed through the building, and Tommy offered his arm to his mother.

"You're so grown up," she said, sniffling a little. "Let's go."

The wedding was beautiful, and it passed very quickly. Tommy met Carter's gaze when the bride and groom were saying their vows and felt like an electric bolt had speared him. *I can imagine us up there,* he thought, his heart pounding in his chest. *Is it too soon to think that? We've only known each other for three months! We're only fifteen!*

Carter smiled at him, and Tommy's knees felt like jelly. He gripped the back of the pew in front of him. *We've got time. Three whole extra years of it. And some pretty great role models.* He looked at his parents, holding hands as they stood next to him, beaming up at the altar. His gaze moved on to Gabrielle, who was across the aisle, her eyes never leaving Zoe's. She mouthed, 'I love you,' and Zoe said it back. Tommy then watched Jason and Kennedy as Reverend Mitchel pronounced them married. The expression on Jason's face as he drew Kennedy closer for their first married kiss could only be described as rapturous. Tommy looked back at Carter, almost embarrassed to witness such intimacy.

The wedding guests started laughing, and Tommy glanced around confused, only to see that Jason and Kennedy hadn't yet separated from their kiss. *I want that,* he thought. He met Carter's eyes again, grinning in amusement.

Following the ceremony, the family and wedding party were whisked away to take pictures at a fancy garden. It took a long time, and then they were back at the community centre. Faith and Elyse met them.

"Glad you two had each other," Carter said. "How did you like the wedding?"

"I want to be like Kennedy when I grow up," Faith said dreamily. "That dress? She looks like a princess."

Tommy watched his sister as she greeted the guests, her dress hugging every curve perfectly. The base colour was green, but every inch was covered in white lace. The dress was backless, which Jason obviously couldn't get enough of, as he couldn't keep his hands off her. It had tiny sleeves, a high neckline, and a train that she had tucked up after the pictures had finished. "She really does," he said, smiling. "And Jason treats her like one."

"Are you nervous about your song?" Elyse asked.

Tommy swallowed hard. "Extremely," he said. "Thanks for reminding me. I'm terrified."

He barely tasted his food and couldn't focus on the speeches. He knew he was after everyone, right before the dancing, because that was when the band would be set up, but it felt like it was taking forever, and his fingers couldn't stop shaking and—

Carter took his hands. "You're doing this for them," he said, indicating Jason and Kennedy, who were talking to Veronica. "Focus on them. Nobody else matters. Your song is beautiful. You can do this."

"Thanks."

Nick came over then. "It's time. Come with me."

Tommy retrieved his guitar and set up with the band, only half listening to their banter as they tuned their instruments. Once they were done, they took their places on the stage, Tommy front and centre. He forced himself to focus on his sister, who had been about to try to sneak out of the room with Jason before Nick called her attention to the band.

"Sorry to interrupt your getaway," Tommy said, grinning, "But I hope you don't mind a slight delay in your plans. I couldn't think of what to get you, so I wrote you a song. I hope... I hope you like it." He took a shaky breath.

Kennedy, an awed expression on her face, pulled Jason closer to the stage.

Tommy started playing then, the band backing him up. Focussing on Kennedy seemed to help ease his nerves as he sang.

Crunching through the leaves,
Your hand clasped in mine,
Lifelines interweave,
Winding like a vine.

This journey's just begun,
We're ready for some fun,
Our hearts are taking flight,
Shadows live for the light.

Run across the snow,
Leap into my arms,
You will never know,
How much my heart warms.

This journey's just begun,
Kisses, need more than one,
Our hearts are taking flight,
Shadows live for the light.

Dance amidst flowers,
Twirling in a spin,
Sunshine and showers,
Life is never dim.

This journey's just begun,
Play fights, who cares who won?
Our hearts are taking flight,
Shadows live for the light.

Lying in the sun,
Counting grains of sand,
Our life has begun,
Keep hold of my hand.

Press you up against a wall,
I come undone,
More in love with you I fall,
Hearts beat as one.

This journey's just begun,
Shine brighter than the sun,
Our hearts are taking flight,
Shadows live for the light.

Kennedy started crying halfway through; Tommy felt proud of himself. The last notes of the song died away and he swung his guitar onto his back, stepping off the stage and into Kennedy's arms.

"Oh my God, Tommy!" Kennedy sobbed. "That was so perfect!"

"Thank you so much." Jason sounded choked up. "It was beautiful. Any chance we could hear it again when we're not quite so emotional?"

Tommy chuckled. "The band helped me make you a CD. It's at home. I didn't wrap it because I thought you'd have enough of opening presents, and I didn't want it to get lost. Kennedy, that's a little too tight, oh thank you," he gasped as she hugged him.

"Jeepers, I think I need some time to compose myself," Kennedy said, pulling back and waving her hands in front of her face. "Mom? I need your handkerchief."

Tommy beamed at her. "I'm so glad you liked it."

"Liked?" Kennedy laughed through her tears. "That doesn't even *begin* to cover it."

His part in the wedding complete, Tommy felt a huge weight lift off his shoulders. He rejoined his friends, only to be swept up by Carter.

"You were amazing!" he said. "I'm so proud of you."

"Thanks. Your advice really helped." Tommy pressed their foreheads together. "Let's dance the night away!"

Interlude - Kathryn

Kathryn Johnson waved goodbye to Brooke and smiled at Gabrielle as she closed the side door quickly to keep the cool air inside the house. "I'll be back tonight to read you a bedtime story, Brooke," she called through the door, getting an excited squeal from the two-year old in response.

She crossed the double driveway to the house she was staying in, letting herself in through the side door and entering the kitchen.

"Jason thawed some ground beef for hamburgers, so I should cut some tomatoes in preparation for dinner," she said to herself, pulling out the fruit and getting a knife and a cutting board. She was still thrown by them being red instead of bright yellow like those in the realm of Everdome, where she had spent the last long stretch of time.

"Maybe make a green bean casserole to go with it." She paused, her hand on the fridge door. "No, that's not a thing here anymore. Palates have changed since the fifties." She sighed heavily. Sometimes she felt like she was back in time, living in the same house that she had come to as a young bride. She slept in the same room, but the people were vastly different.

Instead of her husband Donald, their eight-year-old son Hammond, and her father-in-law Jason, she was living with her *grandson* Jason, his new wife Kennedy, and her younger brother Tommy.

The young teenager had just arrived yesterday for the summer camp he'd be attending in August with his mother, Lilah, who was staying for the long weekend. The first day of camp was today, since Monday was a holiday, and there were games and activities all day at the Door Tech campus. About a quarter of the students at the camp were from Westmeath or Demers, but the rest were coming from across Ontario, and most of them would arrive in time for the first real day of camp on Tuesday.

Both Tommy and Kennedy reminded her of their grandmother Denise, who was Kathryn's best friend and... Kathryn blushed. *I'll see her all weekend.* Kennedy was using the gate travel system to send her to Baker for a three-day visit with Denise.

The hair on the back of her neck prickled as a bright shockwave of magic rippled toward her. "Something's happened!" she gasped, putting the knife down and gripping the edge of the counter. The shockwave passed, leaving her feeling nauseated. "Jason," she said, panicked. He'd be at the restaurant. It was early afternoon.

Leaving everything on the counter, she reached into the layer of Quintessence and stepped through. It only took her three paces to reach The Hawaiian; it wasn't far away in the physical world, and since it had been built by the same family and used by the Johnsons for so long, it also wasn't far in the Quintessence. Quintessence was a form of energy that was both adjacent and opposite of Aether; where Aether was a force of entropy, Quintessence was creation, a spiritual dimension fuelled by the souls of all living things.

She exited in Jason's office, making him jump.

"Kathryn!" he said, obviously startled. He must have seen something in her face because he added, "What's wrong?"

His phone ringing cut off any answer she might have given.

"Hang on," he said to her, picking up the phone. "The Hawaiian, Jason Johnson speaking, how can I help you?" He listened for a moment, his face turning pale. "He *what*?" Then he listened some more. "I'm coming now. I want to see everything you've got." He put the phone down and glared at Kathryn. "You knew?"

She shook her head. "*Something* happened. I have no idea what. We should get going." She paused, mid-way to opening the Quintessence field again. "Where are we going?"

"Door Tech. Tommy's disappeared. Carter, too."

Kathryn smirked. "Is that really a surprise?"

"Yes. They take this camp very seriously, for one. And when I say disappeared, I mean *poof*, gone. Elyse and one of the other boys from the camp vanished, too."

"That does make a difference. I'm coming with you." Kathryn put up a finger when Jason opened his mouth to argue. "Can you see magic? An exceptionally large disturbance just happened, and it was enough to rattle me. Someone used a lot of power, and people who do that are either careless or making a statement. You need me there." She nodded in satisfaction when Jason didn't argue further. "I'm afraid I don't know the technology district well. We should go back to the house to get your car."

Jason agreed, so she took his hand and led him through the Quintessence field back to his house.

"This is how you got into my home that first afternoon, isn't it?" he asked with a chuckle and shake of his head. He grabbed his keys and tossed her his phone. "I'm going to need you to call Kennedy, the Batudevs, and the Garridos to let them know what's going on while I drive."

Kathryn eyed the phone with distaste. "If I must," she sighed.

The drive to the campus didn't take long, and Jason was soon parking on a side street and then taking the cell phone from Kathryn.

He continued the conversation with Kennedy, "We're here now, love. Tell Lilah I *will* get to the bottom of this and get the kids back." He was silent for a moment, his long legs eating up the pavement to the main entrance of the campus. Kathryn had to half-jog to keep up with him. "Thank you for your faith in me." He chuckled. "Oh, in Kathryn? Ouch, that hurts. I love you, too."

The guards at the gate didn't want to let Kathryn in, but Jason glared at them. "I was called down here by Margery Door herself. If you want to tell her that I was delayed by you because I brought a specialist, be my guest."

Kathryn's breath caught at the name. "Sorry, did you say *Margery*?" she asked, once they were through security, a guest pass hanging around her neck. Jason was wearing his Board of Directors ID card, his face like a brewing thunderstorm as he strode to the closest, and largest, building. It couldn't be her old friend Margery, one of the other women that Robin had taken as a Fay bride along with her and Denise. What would be the odds?

"Yes. She's the one who built the entire Door Technology empire from the ground up. Dad liked her, and bought stock in her company that grew very well." Jason held the door open for her.

"Very well." Kathryn snorted. "That's an understatement. Is Door her married name?"

"I have no idea." Jason squinted at her. "Why do you ask?"

"I think—"

"*Kathryn?*" a tall redheaded woman gasped before clearing her throat. "Apologies. Now that you've arrived, please follow me to the security office. We have prepared the footage for you to view the incident."

"Oh, *Margery*," Jason murmured quietly to Kathryn.

She poked his side, causing him to wiggle out of the way. Kathryn examined the woman as they followed her to a room on the first floor. Despite the twenty-six—*almost twenty-seven,* she thought to herself—years, Margery had barely changed. Like Denise, she had matured with grace, and Kathryn couldn't help but admire her.

There was a man wearing a purple leather jacket, despite the heat of the day, with her. He greeted Jason with a nod, and while they were walking, said, "You have a child?"

"Brother-in-law," Jason said. "Your son must be Greg. Tommy's mentioned him."

The man winced. "Sorry."

Jason smirked. "Mixed reviews, I'll say that much. But he's not too bad."

Kathryn was interested to see that the man flushed darkly and avoided their eyes by ducking his head.

"Here we are," Margery said, interrupting any further conversation. She nodded to the security guard, who indicated the slightly larger screen and pressed play.

Kathryn watched closely as Tommy, Carter, their friend Elyse, and a large boy who must be Greg stood huddled around a lab bench. Elyse didn't look happy, a scowl on her face as she glared at Greg. Carter gestured wildly as his mouth moved.

"Can we hear them?" Kathryn asked, not taking her eyes from the screen.

"Sorry, no audio," the guard replied.

Jason grunted in acknowledgment.

Now Greg was talking, and then Tommy, and then the four of them were gone.

Kathryn blinked. "What was that?"

"Alien teleportation?" Greg's father asked, surprising Kathryn into looking away from the screen.

"You know about aliens?" Jason asked, eyebrows raised.

"*You* know about aliens?" he countered. They regarded each other appraisingly for a moment.

Didn't you tell me that the Blue Bloods were aware of the situation? Kathryn asked Jason in mindspeak, amused.

Yes, but only the Phantom knows the Blue Bloods know about them.

How do you keep all this straight?

I don't, at least not very well. No wonder Carter guessed.

"I would like to see the spot they were standing, please," Kathryn said to Margery. "It's possible there are some traces left behind."

"Right this way." Margery led them up to the second floor. "This is where the auditoriums and student labs are located. They were in room 208. Here it is."

Kathryn gasped and had to pause at the doorway, gripping the frame tightly as the overwhelming presence of familiar magic filled her senses.

"What's going on?" Jason whispered, giving her a hand to steady her. "What do you see?"

"I know who took them." She stared into Jason's eyes. "I can get them back, I promise. Please make my excuses to Denise for this weekend and to Brooke for tonight. This might take a while. Or not. Time is different there." Kathryn looked past him at Margery. "You might as well put 'kidnapped' on their file. They were not given a choice. We'll talk when I return."

Bring them home. I'll bring Mister Finch. You can come back here afterward to fill Margery in on the important details, Jason thought to Kathryn.

She nodded at him and opened a portal. Taking a breath, she prepared herself for travel between the realms.

Chapter 12

FRIDAY THE 1ST OF AUGUST, 2003 -
WESTMEATH, ONTARIO

There was a break in activities on the first day of the Door Technology summer camp, and Greg approached the small group of Oldtown High School kids, drawing Carter and Tommy away to tell them some new information. Elyse had followed.

"I'm still not sure that we should be trusting you with Oldtown business," Elyse grumbled, crossing her arms over her chest as she glared at Greg Finch, the some-time bully, and a Blue Blood member.

"He's the one who told us about the gang in the first place!" Carter said, gesturing wildly.

"Look, I don't care about your Oldtown politics," Greg said calmly. "I'm just telling you what I overheard."

"He has no reason to lie to us," Tommy added, standing up for Greg.

"He has no reason to tell the truth eith—" Elyse cut herself off and looked around with wide eyes. "What in the world?"

Carter felt too much heat pressing against his skin on his left. "Fire?" he asked himself, confused. His eyes widened in alarm as he turned to see the entire wall engulfed in flames. "Go! Get out!" he shouted, pushing Greg toward the door. "Find the fire alarm!"

Greg stopped short. "The door's gone," he said, confused.

"This way!" Tommy said, pulling the lower half of his shirt up over his mouth and nose. "Follow me!"

Carter was completely turned around as he followed Tommy out the door, which had the poor taste of being on the wrong side of the room. *What?*

The hallway looked different, too. It was wider and didn't have any windows. People were walking quickly toward the exit, and they joined them.

"Do you hear that?" Tommy asked suddenly.

"No," Elyse said.

"Go on. I'll catch up." He continued down the hall instead of leaving with the others.

Carter groaned. "Get outside. Stay with Greg. I'll get Tommy," he said, and hurried after him.

Tommy hadn't wandered far; he was facing a door that was closed, smoke coming from underneath it. He smiled in relief when he saw Carter. "Can you hear it now?"

Carter listened intently.

"Help!" The cry was weak and was coming from behind the door.

"The handle's hot to touch," Tommy said. "That means there's fire on the other side, doesn't it?"

Carter frowned. "It does. And if we open the door, the fire will rush out and do more than singe us." He looked around for another solution. They were at the end of the hallway, with doors on either side. He touched the one on the right and couldn't feel any heat. "Let's try this way. Maybe there's another way in."

They hurried into the room, which looked like a classroom, and spotted another door at the far end. It led to a closet, with no way out.

"The ceiling!" Tommy exclaimed, pointing up at the drop ceiling. "Maybe we can crawl over the wall that way?"

"Brilliant!" Carter exclaimed. He started shifting desks over to the wall, building a wide base to support the second level.

Tommy was staring at a piece of paper on the wall near the door. "There's nothing in between the two rooms, so we should be able to connect no problem."

"Great. Come on," Carter said, climbing onto the second desk and pushing a ceiling tile out of the way. He peeked into the space. "Ugh." He dropped down again. "I forgot that smoke rises. We can't go through the ceiling. Now what?"

"I have no idea... Wait..." Tommy looked at the floor plan again. "What's that?" He poked at a part of the wall in the closet.

"Dunno. Let's check it out." Carter ripped the paper off the wall, and they headed for the closet. "Should be right here, where this filing cabinet is. Hang on." He bent and pushed, the heavy cabinet screeching loudly across the floor and revealing a short, wooden door. "Look at this!"

"I wonder where it leads." Tommy put his hand on the wood. "Not hot." He pulled it open, and they ducked to enter a dark, low, narrow corridor full of spider webs. Their feet disturbed the thick dust on the wood floor, sending it puffing up into the air. Behind him, he could see a staircase leading down. "Maybe there's another entrance to the next room!"

They hurried down the hall, bent almost double to avoid knocking their heads on the ceiling beams.

"Here!" Tommy called back. He put his hand on the wooden door. "Warm, but not hot. Do I risk it?"

"If we want to save the person inside, we've got to." Carter swallowed hard. There was no noise from inside the room now, other than the crackle of the fire. *Smoke inhalation or given up hope?* He crossed his fingers that it was the latter.

Tommy pushed open the door, and they stood back, but no fire licked into the corridor. "Hello?" Tommy called, covering the lower half of his face with his shirt again and crawling into the room.

"Don't go too far," Carter cautioned, copying Tommy, and looking around the room.

"There!" Tommy said, pointing to the nearest corner, where a figure was huddled. "Hey, you! Can you crawl this way?"

The person unfolded themselves and started crawling toward them.

Carter breathed a sigh of relief. He kept an eye on the encroaching flames, but they were busy climbing the far wall and blackening the posters there. Then they leaped to the ceiling, quickly spreading over the tiles. "We gotta go!" Carter shouted. "Come on!"

But the person collapsed onto the ground, coughing weakly.

Definitely inhaled smoke, Carter thought as he crawled toward the person, who he could now see was a short woman. "Get on my back," he said, turning around.

She climbed on and weakly held him around his chest, resting her head on his back and coughing a little. Carter crawled back to the small door, which Tommy was holding for him.

Tommy took the woman from him, cradling her in his arms.

"Go!" Carter urged, getting to his feet in the hallway. They hurried back the way they had come.

"Back to the staircase," Tommy said. "It's our best bet."

"Agreed."

A crashing sound came from behind them, making Carter's blood freeze for a second. *That was probably the ceiling,* he thought. The stairs led them down to the corner of a kitchen.

"You know, I bet that was a cleaner's corridor," Tommy said as they hurried across the tiled floor. "I didn't know Door Tech had those."

"With the amount of dust in there, I don't think the cleaners knew about them either," Carter said, chuckling. He pushed at the door handle. The door opened a crack and then stuck on something. Carter put his shoulder against the door and pushed hard.

"Is that snow?" Tommy asked, incredulous, and Carter stared out the door at the snowy fields beyond. Some of the snowbank had fallen in through the door.

"I guess this door isn't used very often," Carter felt a little silly stating the obvious. "Surprise snowstorm in August. Maybe little Chloe lost control of her powers again."

Tommy nodded. "Wow. That's cool."

"Pass her to me. You go first, and I'll follow in your footsteps," Carter suggested, and accepted the weight of the woman, draping her over his back. She'd fainted at some point, and he hoped they could get her to an ambulance quickly enough to save her. "We'll go around the side of the building. Hopefully, that'll help orient us, because I have no idea where we are on campus right now."

"Yeah, I got turned around, too," Tommy admitted. He took a step into the snow, sinking up to his knee. "Wow, this is uncomfortable. Wish I had a shovel."

"There's a shovel near the fireplace, there," Carter said, pointing it out. "Why is there a fireplace in a Door Tech kitchen?"

"Maybe for that wood-smoke taste?" Tommy stomped his foot as he walked over to grab the shovel, returning quickly. "Let's try this again. The snow is super fluffy and fresh."

Tommy only pushed the snow to either side, so they moved quickly through the drifts, away from the building first and then circling around to the side that they agreed must be the front.

Loud voices met his ears, and Carter looked up from his feet to see people huddled together against another building, staring up at the fire and shouting at each other.

"I saw it go that way!"

"No, it went *that* way after destroying the university!"

"My friends are in there!" screamed a shrill voice that he recognized as Elyse.

"Hey, we're over here! Is there an ambulance?" Tommy called out.

Several people broke off from the group, crowding around the boys and taking the woman from Carter's arms.

"You two should get checked out by the healers as well," said an older woman. "Come with me."

"How did the fire start?" Carter asked, following behind her.

She shrugged but didn't answer.

Elyse and Greg met them at the door of the building, and the woman shooed them away. "You'll see your friends once they've been given the all-clear," she said briskly. "Get back to your dorms."

"Dorms?" Carter said in confusion. "We live in Westmeath and are staying at home during camp."

The woman put her hand on Carter's forehead, brow furrowed. "Where is Westmeath? What camp? This is Gaulan's sole university, specializing in veterinary medicine and animal husbandry. There are no camps; we're about to start mid-winter exams."

Monday the 17th of December, 1290 Post-Cataclysm - Tène, Gaulan

"I'm sorry, I don't understand you. Are you speaking French?" Tommy's voice cracked on the last word. "I thought my French was pretty... good..." He trailed off, gaze fixed out the window.

Carter joined him at the large window, jaw dropping open in shock. The white fields beyond the building were endless, but that's not what was drawing their attention. There were three large Domes floating like soap bubbles in the sky. "We're in *Everdome*?" Carter's voice came out as a squeak and was followed by a hacking cough.

The woman gave Tommy a leather bracelet and waited until he had put it on before saying, "You don't sound good, we need to get you to a healer immediately." She pulled them away from the window with strong hands.

"I can understand you now," Tommy said, and stared at his bracelet. "What is this?"

"It's been spelled to automatically translate languages," the woman replied.

"Why didn't I need one?" Carter asked, confused. "I understood you right away. Do our friends already have them?"

"Your ring of knighthood, and yes. Excuse me, I must help another patient." The woman hurried off.

The boys were seated in a room with several others. They looked around, trying to spot the woman they'd rescued, but they couldn't see her.

"I'm not even sure I'd recognize her," Carter murmured to Tommy, not wanting to disturb the other patients. "I don't think I saw her face at all."

Tommy nodded his agreement. "I don't like being separated from the others like this. We're..." He lowered his voice, "...in Everdome, which is a real place and not just a story, even though we're supposed to be at Door Tech? That makes no sense. How did we get here, and how do we get back?"

"I have zero answers." Carter squinted at the ring he was wearing. "But I think my ring is speaking to me."

"What's it saying?" Tommy whispered.

"Let me see if I can hear it." Carter put his hand up to his ear. "It is! Something about... 'Find us in the central square for further instructions.' Oh, it loops. 'Knight of Gaulan, you have been called to Tène in Gaulan to assist in the capture and destruction of the Great Beast Icaryoe, which has wreaked havoc in the capital city, where you have been summoned. We used sympathetic magic to match your departure and arrival points. Find us in the central square—' okay, I've already repeated that part." Carter slowly lowered his hand, staring at Tommy. "I'm not going to lie, I'm some combination of terrified, excited, confused, and overwhelmed."

Tommy laughed. "No kidding! Okay, we need to go talk to those people that called us here. Let's find the nurse—sorry, healer— in charge and see if we can get the all-clear to leave."

It was as good a plan as any, so they stood up, ready to go find the woman who had brought them in.

"Where do you two think you're going?" A frowning man advanced on them. "You haven't seen the healer yet."

"I'm sorry, but we need to go. My ring says so."

When the man saw his ring, he bowed deeply. "Of course, sir. You must be very busy, sir. Right this way, sir." He turned and led them quickly to a room. "I'll get the healer in here right away, sir." He backed out of the room, closing the door behind him.

"That was..." Carter floundered for the right word.

"Amazing!" Tommy grinned. "How did that Toronto show get a real ring from Everdome to give to you?"

"No, remember, it wasn't the Knights of Everdome show that gave it to me; it was the old man in wizard's robes afterwards," Carter pointed out. "And nobody else knew who he was."

Tommy gasped. "I just had a thought!" He grabbed Carter's arm. "What if that man was *Merlin*? Jesse told us that he exists, remember?"

"But *why* would he do that?" Carter said with a chuckle. "That's a little unlikely, don't you think?"

"So is Everdome being a real place instead of just a book series, and yet, here we are." Tommy gestured around them. "'Everdome claims what is hers.' I think you've just been claimed."

"Great. I'm luggage," Carter said sarcastically.

The door opened just then, and a woman in a white coat entered with a clipboard and stethoscope. "I'm sorry, sir, I have no—" She cut herself off abruptly as she looked up from the clipboard and frowned. "I was told that a Knight of Gaulan was in this room."

"He is. I mean, I am." Carter sat up straighter.

The healer looked down her nose at him. "You are a *child*. How could *you* be a knight?"

"King Demetrius was younger than I am when *he* became a knight," Carter said, raising an eyebrow. "It's not for you to decide whether I'm deserving of the honour. *Your* job is to make sure I and my consort are healthy enough to leave after saving a woman from a burning building." He held up his hand, indicating the ring. "Unless you want to tell the people who are sending me this message *why* I was delayed…?"

"You saved… Yes, sir." The healer listened to their lungs and looked into their mouths. "There are signs of smoke inhalation. You're going to cough up black gunk for a few minutes." She sprayed something down their throats that made them gag and cough violently.

"Is 'gunk' a medical term?" Tommy asked mischievously after spitting into a basin she passed him.

"If you can talk, you're not coughing hard enough," the healer replied.

"Come on, Tommy," Carter said with a weak chuckle. After a few more coughs, the healer pronounced them healthy. They left, finding Elyse and Greg in the main hall of the building.

"You won't believe where we are!" Elyse greeted them excitedly.

"Everdome!" Carter replied with a grin. "Yeah, apparently, I'm a knight here. We've got to go talk to whoever brought us here and hopefully get sent home."

"Hold up." Greg's quiet voice stopped them all in their tracks. "*How* did we get here?"

"Magic, of course." Tommy hesitated and then added, "Have you ever read *The Wonderful Wizard of Oz*? *Alice in Wonderland*? *Narnia*?" Greg nodded at each name. "In each one, the kids get to the other world by magic. How else would we be in Everdome?"

"Magic doesn't exist," Greg said shakily.

"Right." Elyse rolled her eyes. "You explain away the Domes in the sky while we go find someone who can help us get back."

"Are you going to be okay out there?" Tommy asked her, noticing that none of them were dressed for winter weather. They were all wearing shorts and t-shirts, but Elyse was shivering, even inside the warm building.

"Depends on how far it is and how quickly we get sent home," she replied.

"Let's find out." Carter turned to one of the men standing against a wall. "Excuse me, we need to get to the central square for the meeting of the Knights of Gaulan, and—"

"For Goddess's sake! Where did you four come from, the Ruby Isles? Those Sisters have no respect for the knights of the realm. Todd!" he shouted, raising his voice, and making them all jump. "Get these four some coats and pants from the portal stash... Ah yes, thank you."

Carter's stomach flipped at the mention of the Sisters. They were extremely powerful, almost god-like beings that were similar to the Fates or Norns of myth. They were said to work for the betterment of Everdome, but they were cold, disengaged, and rarely kind.

Todd handed out clothing, and they pulled them on.

"That's better. Now we can get you boots. Follow Todd," he told them, "and then come back for directions."

The storeroom that they were led to had shelves of boots for all sizes.

"Does this sort of thing happen often?" Tommy asked.

"Often enough," Todd replied with a chuckle. "Usually, it's just visitors coming through the portal from another Dome and expecting different weather, but we outfit anyone who needs it. It's not always winter here, you know. Otherwise, we'd have a lot more trouble feeding the herds!"

"Ah, yes, that makes sense," Carter said, trying on a boot. "This one's good. What do we owe you?"

"Owe?" Todd said. "Nothing at all. These are for those in need. In the future, if you are able, help another the way we have helped you." He squinted at Tommy and Carter. "Aren't you the two that rescued Hannah?"

"I didn't catch her name," Carter said. "But we did get a woman out of the building."

"Thank you. You truly are a Knight of Gaulan." Todd shook both their hands, a genuine grin on his face. He handed them bags for their shoes. "You're as prepared as we can make you. Good luck out there, sir." He bowed to Carter.

"That's going to get old real quick," Greg muttered under his breath.

Carter snorted. "You're telling me."

They headed back to the first man, who gave them a map of the city with their route drawn on it. The university was at the edge of the city, and they had to navigate to the centre.

They set out, Elyse leading them with the map, Greg following her, and Tommy and Carter holding hands behind them both. The buildings, other than the university, were all one or two storeys, built of stone and wood. They had windows and chimneys, and they seemed to be warm inside, based on the lack of condensation on the windows.

"So," Tommy said quietly. The stillness of the city was unnerving. The fire had been extinguished in the building they had arrived in; smoke escaping through the windows was the only sign that remained, and all the people had dispersed. Their footsteps squeaked a little in the snow, but beyond that, the streets and shops were quiet. "Are we going to talk about your ring and its message?"

"The ring that I was given on Earth seems to be a genuine Gaulan ring," Carter said, excitement quivering through his body. Then he remembered *why* they were there. "And I was brought here because the Great Beast Icaryoe has recombined. That's not exactly comforting."

"Which of the six Beasts is Icaryoe?" Tommy asked. "I don't remember, and I just finished that book."

"The dragon with fire wings," Carter said. He shuddered. "I'm not sure I'm ready to face off against a Great Beast. Who do you think brought us here?"

"As long as it's not the Sisters, we'll be okay, I think."

Carter's heart sank. "Didn't that guy at the university say something about the Sisters?"

"That they have no respect for the knights of the realm," Tommy replied. His expression mirrored Carter's. "Oh no."

They reached the central square, a large cobblestone town square in the centre of the city, which must have been used for events and markets. Sure enough, the three Sisters were waiting for them. There were many other men and women standing around the raised dais, all knights, Carter assumed.

"Let's get in closer. Try to talk to them before their speech," he said as they joined the other teens.

"Yeah, alright, let's walk up to the scariest beings in Everdome, tell them they made a mistake, and ask them to send us home," Tommy muttered.

"Do you have a better idea?" Elyse asked, crossing her arms.

The action made her coat puff up and cover the lower half of her face. She huffed impatiently and tugged her coat back down. "We need to get home. I don't want a mark on my record at Door Tech, do you?"

The three boys shook their heads vehemently.

"Then let's go." Elyse strode purposefully into the square.

The minute Carter stepped onto the strangely clear stonework, the three Sisters started speaking in unison.

"Too late," Carter muttered.

Chapter 13

❝Knights of Gaulan," the three Sisters said in unison. "You have been summoned due to a dire emergency. The Icaryoe has recombined. It is of utmost urgency that you defeat the Beast. We don't have to remind you what happened last time."

The Sisters stopped as one, looking around at the knights.

"What happened last time?" Greg hissed.

"Death. Destruction. Mayhem," Tommy replied flippantly, not taking his eyes from the women. "Book nine."

The Sisters were beautiful in a cold and distant way. One looked as if she had never seen the sun; she was unnaturally white and had silver-blonde hair. The second was a complete contrast; her skin was black as ebony, and she had dark red hair. The last had no hair at all and her skin gleamed like polished gold.

"Once you have burned the Beast, call to us through the rings, and we will bring the enchanted jars that will contain it. The knight who returns the Beast to us shall be rewarded handsomely. Do not fail." They turned inwards in a clear dismissal of the knights, all of whom started leaving, some grumbling under their breath.

Elyse led them up to the dais. "Excuse me," she said, trying to get the attention of the Sisters.

When nothing happened, Carter cleared his throat. "Excuse me," he said loudly.

The gold Sister slowly turned to face them. "Were our

instructions unclear?" she asked, the other two echoing her like ghosts in a creepy movie. Her brow furrowed. "Go defeat the Icaryoe!"

"Right, about that," Carter said, twisting his hands behind him in a display of nerves. "We're not from Everdome. We're from Earth. And we're kids. Our parents are going to be worried about us when we don't come home tonight. Clearly, you made a mistake when you brought us here."

The gold Sister's expression morphed into amusement. "We do not make mistakes," she said alone, and Tommy felt a shiver run down his spine; one of the Sisters speaking out of unison was extra creepy. "Show me your ring."

Carter glanced at the others and then held out his right hand.

"Emrys," the Sister spat. "That meddling fool. Your ring is genuine, and you are a Knight of Gaulan, therefore your coming here to kill the Beast is no mistake." They spoke in unison again, "If you succeed, we can return you to your realm." Then the Sisters raised their arms, clasped their hands, and vanished.

"What the *fuck*?" Greg demanded, whirling to face the others.

"My sentiments exactly," Carter said in return. He sighed. "Sorry. I had no idea this would happen, or that it would drag you into it. I shouldn't have accepted the ring from a stranger."

"Don't think like that!" Elyse said, shaking her head. "You were given a gift. I can think of no one more deserving of being a knight than you. It's just unfortunate that the rest of us got pulled into this with you."

"I'm sorry, I have to disagree," Tommy said firmly. He took Carter's hand. "There is no place I'd rather be than right here with you. If you vanished in front of me, I'd tear the realms apart to find you. This is much easier for everyone."

Carter laughed. "You would, wouldn't you? Alright, what do we know?"

"About the Icaryoe or about our unexpected travel?" Tommy asked.

"Let's focus on trying to get home. There are plenty of knights that are going after the Beast. We don't need the Sisters." Carter shivered. "I'm a little chilly. Let's go back to the university and see if we can get some answers there."

"Well, we know that Emrys gave you that ring. Emrys is another name for Merlin," Elyse said thoughtfully. "Therefore, Merlin must exist here and can get to Earth. Maybe we can find him and ask him to bring us home."

"Good. I like it. No idea how to find him, but it's optimistic," Carter said with a smile.

"The books are awfully detailed about this place, and knowing now that Everdome is real, perhaps the author has also been here. Maybe we can find S.M. Arwdur and ask them to help us get home," Tommy suggested.

"Also a good idea," Carter said. "We need to know more. I'm sure a professor, maybe of history or something, could help us. We should go to Sartorna, the Dome of knowledge, and see if they can help us."

Greg scoffed. "Okay, I'm trying to suspend my disbelief here. We've obviously been moved from Earth to Everdome without knowing how, but why couldn't it be through an alien transporter? All we have to do is find the return switch."

Elyse regarded him appraisingly. "Magic is fake, but aliens exist? Why?"

"What do you mean 'why?'" Greg snapped. "I've seen aliens. They use technology to do mind control, teleportation, and stuff. Magic?" He shrugged. "I'd have to see it to believe it."

"So, to you, the Sisters teleported just now, and they teleported us here?" Tommy asked. He nodded slowly. "I can see how that makes some sort of sense, if you discount magic."

"Do *you* have any proof of magic?" Greg asked, a sneer on his face.

Tommy opened his mouth, but then closed it without saying anything. "Nothing I can share, but trust me," he said at last. "Magic does exist."

"It's a good thought, though," Carter said.

They returned to the university building that had been turned into a makeshift hospital.

Todd greeted them. "How did it go?"

Carter wrinkled his nose. "Not great. The Sisters expect me to kill the Icaryoe. Only then will they send us home."

"Wow." Todd's jaw dropped. "Good luck with that. But you could just use the portals to go home, you know?"

"Do the portals connect with Earth?" Elyse asked, crossing her arms and raising an eyebrow.

"The Lefrane Dome has a lot of earth," Todd replied, confused. "Farming, you know."

"No, not earth, the planet Earth," Greg said, enunciating as if that would clear everything up.

"The only liveable planet here is Everdome," Todd replied, even more confused.

"Excuse me," said a woman's voice. She had grey streaks in her brown hair and lines around her eyes that showed she laughed often. She was not smiling now. "I was told I could find the knights that rescued my Hannah down here. I'd like to offer my thanks."

Todd indicated Carter and Tommy. "That's them alright."

Her eyes welled with tears. "Thank you so much! She's our only daughter." She hugged them both tightly.

"I'm not a knight," Tommy said awkwardly. "I just heard her calling for help."

"Of course we helped. Is she okay?" Carter asked.

"According to the healers, she's going to make a full recovery, thanks to you," the woman said, wiping her eyes. "I'm Aliyah. How can I even begin to repay you?"

"They're trying to get home to Earth," Todd said helpfully. "Have you heard of it?"

Aliyah's expression turned thoughtful. "It sounds familiar, like an old fairytale. Why don't you four come home with me, and we can ask my husband. He might know. Hannah's sleeping peacefully, and there isn't really room for me here to stay overnight."

"Thank you, we gladly accept your hospitality," Carter said with a slight bow.

"You won't need your coats there. Pakaha is in its spring season."

"We're going to Pakaha!" Carter squeaked. He coughed, and Tommy chuckled quietly. "Will we get to see the castle?"

"Sorry, no, the castle is nearer to the other portal. We want the city portal."

The teenagers stripped off their winter gear and thanked Todd for the loan before following Aliyah to the portal to Pakaha, which was just outside the back door of the building. There was a room just inside the door where each person had to sign in with their name, occupation, city of origin, and reason for travel.

Once they were approved for travel, they headed for the door. A guard held it open for them, and they walked out into the courtyard, which was sheltered from the wind by high walls. Even so, the four teenagers immediately started shivering in their summer wear. Tommy was thankful there weren't line-ups or delays like in train stations or airports. This was more like a run from the back door of a house to their hot tub in a bathing suit in the middle of winter.

"Hurry," Aliyah said to them, and she walked through an archway that shimmered slightly in the middle. The instant she passed through, she vanished.

"I'm not waiting around," Elyse said, and ran through.

Greg balked. "Are we sure it's safe?" he asked.

"Safer than getting frostbite," Carter said.

Tommy held out his hand. "Would this make you feel better?"

Greg knocked the hand out of his way as he walked up to the arch. He took a breath and then walked through.

"I'm glad we didn't have to force him through," Carter muttered. "I could have done it, but it wouldn't have been fun."

Tommy laughed. "Let's go. I'm losing feeling in my fingers."

Holding hands, they walked through the arch.

MONDAY THE 17TH OF DECEMBER, 1290 POST-CATACLYSM - PAKAHA CITY, PAKAHA

The air was much warmer on the other side of the archway. Tommy spotted the others nearby, talking with a guard and signing a book. There were twelve archways in a large circle, and Tommy wondered how they'd be able to tell which one led to which Dome before noticing a sigil scratched into the rock that looked like the stylized G on Carter's ring.

"I guess we have to sign out, too," Carter said. "I wonder if they have spells on the books that indicate if someone is lying or is a criminal, and they can stop them."

"Good question," Tommy replied.

After signing the book, they followed Aliyah through the city to her home.

"My husband, Pieter, is a musician," she told them as they navigated busy streets. There weren't any cars, but some sort of bicycle with a cart seemed popular. "He is one of the expert instrument makers of Everdome and works in a large shop here in Pakaha City. He has five journeymen and six apprentices who work for him," she said proudly.

"That's impressive," Elyse said politely. "Tommy plays guitar. Do you have anything like that?"

"We do. Fascinating that our instruments have the same names, even though you're not from here. Pieter is proficient in guitar, although he prefers playing the cello," Aliyah said. "I fell in love with him when he came to my village in the Wild Nations as a journeyman. He played the most beautiful love song, and my heart was his. Fortunately, he stayed in my village for quite some time, and during those months, he came to care for me as well." She smiled. "Sorry if I bored you with my sappy tale of romance."

"Not boring at all," Carter reassured her. "That was beautiful."

"Tommy won your heart with a song, too," Elyse said, nudging him with her elbow.

Aliyah smiled wider. "Falling in love over music is so romantic," she said enthusiastically. "Tommy, you should play something for us after dinner."

"Ummm, I'll try," Tommy said anxiously. "I only know a few songs by heart. I'm still a new player."

"We shall treasure them all the more because they are so close to your heart that you chose to learn them," Aliyah replied. She led them to a simple two-storey house. "We'll be a little cramped tonight. I hope you don't mind."

"We had nowhere else to go, and we are incredibly grateful that we will have full bellies and a safe place to sleep tonight," Carter said. "I'll sleep on the floor in the living room, no problem."

"We should be able to find you boys some mats for the common room, at least," Aliyah said. "And Elyse, you can have Hannah's room. Unless this young man is your intended?" She indicated Greg.

Elyse made a face. "No, we barely know each other," she replied.

"Great, so you're putting me with *them*," Greg said, rolling his eyes.

"We're going to *sleep*!" Tommy protested. "If you don't want to watch us snuggle, face away from us."

Aliyah chuckled. "You could sleep outdoors?" she teased as she opened the front door. A delicious aroma wafted out. A tall man stood at the stove, stirring something in a pot.

"That won't be necessary." Carter chuckled. "He'll be fine with us."

"That smells amazing," Tommy said, changing the subject.

"My husband, Pieter," Aliyah said, introducing them to the man in the kitchen. "I started dinner before I left. I know it's lunch for you…"

"Actually, it isn't," Elyse said, glancing at her watch. "For us, it's well past dinner."

"No wonder my stomach's growling," Carter said, rubbing his belly.

"I made *tsiroshi* with *bateen*. I hope you like it?" Aliyah asked hopefully.

"Never heard of either of those things," Greg said. "But I'm so hungry I could eat a horse."

Aliyah looked shocked. "Why would you do that?"

"It's an expression on Earth," Elyse reassured her. She glared at Greg, who shrugged.

They washed their hands in the kitchen sink and sat down at the large wooden table while Pieter served them.

Tommy dug in heartily, the aroma winning him over despite not knowing what it was that he was eating. The protein tasted like chicken and was in a spicy orange sauce that reminded him of curry. There was a blue vegetable on the side that looked like zucchini but tasted like broccoli, which was odd until he got used to it. Beside it was a yellow-white tuber with brown skin.

"Is this the *bateen*?" Tommy asked, indicating the tuber.

"No, that's a potato," Aliyah said. "Do you have those?"

"Yes, we do!" Carter said excitedly. "It's very popular in Oldtown."

Tommy took that to mean that Aetherborn ate a lot of potatoes.

"This is amazing!" Elyse gushed. "Is this traditional cuisine for Pakaha?"

"No, I learned it from my mother. She was from Lefrane." Aliyah played with the end of her utensil. "She died last year."

"I'm sorry to hear that," Tommy said.

"Her legacy lives on in your cooking," Carter added.

Aliyah smiled at them. "Thank you. It brings me joy to share one of her meals with you."

"My parents must be so worried about me," Elyse said softly. She ducked her head to hide her face. "I feel so far away, and we have no idea how to get back..." She sniffed. "I'm sorry. I don't mean to bring everyone down."

"That reminds me, Pieter, have you heard of Earth? I thought it sounded like a fairytale," Aliyah said, turning to her husband.

"I remember your grandmother telling me something about Earth. It's another realm. She said that there were rumours that your queen came from there," Pieter said thoughtfully. "She disappears every once in a while," he told the teenagers.

"Is she here now?" Carter asked eagerly. "Can we go see her?"

"As far as I know, she's in the Wild Nations, but I doubt I would have heard if she'd left," Aliyah said. "My father doesn't keep track of such things like my mother did. You can go in the morning and try to reach her. It's summer there right now, so you won't even have to change your clothes."

Tommy looked down at his t-shirt and shorts, covered with grimy smears from the fire. "Not that we even have clothes to change into, but is this really presentable for meeting a queen?" he asked, gesturing at himself and Carter, who was in the same state.

Aliyah waved a hand as if to brush his concerns aside. "Queen Es'Sem never cared about such things. However, we can help you out by cleaning your clothes and giving you something to wear tonight while they dry."

"Oh, thank you!" Elyse gushed. "I was so not prepared to travel today. If I'd known, I would have worn something more comfortable."

"I'm pretty comfortable, but the smell of smoke is really starting to get to me," Tommy said. "Sorry."

"Don't you dare be sorry!" Aliyah scolded him. "You saved our daughter! We owe you everything!"

Tommy flushed. "You don't owe us anything. You've already done so much."

"Nonsense." Aliyah stood up and started clearing the table. "Pieter, you get the boys some clothes. You can wash up and change in the room upstairs. Give us your underclothes, too. Then once you're done, I'll bring Elyse up, and she can change as well."

Carter and Tommy changed in the little bathroom, stripping out of their clothes and scrubbing their hair with soap that Pieter suggested they use. They exchanged shy, lingering glances that didn't go further than that. The clothes that Pieter gave them were a little big, but they made it work.

Aliyah took their smoky clothing and dunked them in an acrid-smelling liquid before taking everything outdoors.

"Why aren't you as worried about our parents?" Elyse asked them as they were sitting around the fireplace.

"I *am* worried," Tommy said, reaching over Carter to squeeze her knee. "But there's nothing I can do about it. And, I mean, we're in *Everdome*! Jason's going to flip when we tell him when we get back."

"If," muttered Greg. "I'm probably not even missed."

Silence fell over the little group, nobody knowing what to say to that.

Greg pushed himself up from the floor and dusted off the seat of his pants. "I can't stand the pity-silence any longer. I'm going for a walk."

"Not too far," Carter said quickly.

Greg nodded curtly and left, closing the door quietly behind him.

After a second more of silence, Tommy stood as well. "I'm going to go with him. Maybe I can help."

"Why do you care?" Elyse asked, crossing her arms. "He's been a bully to you since the day you met."

"And now he's feeling all alone in a new place." Tommy crossed to the door. "Give him a break." He met Carter's eyes, hoping he understood. Carter gave him a crooked grin and nodded. Relieved, Tommy stepped outside and closed the door behind him.

Greg hadn't wandered far at all. He was leaning against the gate in front of the house. "Heh. Thought you might follow me."

Tommy took a deep breath of the crisp spring air. Woodsmoke from chimneys wafted on the spring breeze and he shivered slightly as he joined Greg. "Really?"

"Yeah, you're too goody-goody to just leave me alone," Greg said with a sneer.

"If you're trying to get me to go away, it's not going to work," Tommy said, shaking his head. "Why do you think your family wouldn't miss you?"

"You don't pull your punches, do you?" Greg said. "What do *you* know about not getting along with your family?"

Tommy chuckled. "Quite a bit, actually. Before the March Break camp, my mom and I were constantly butting heads. She didn't approve of my friends, and I didn't appreciate her interference in my life."

"And what happened after?"

"I realized my friends were vapid social climbers with no skills other than drinking, smoking, and presumably, having sex."

Greg barked a laugh. "Yeah, that doesn't sound like you at all. Why were you hanging out with them?"

"Because they seemed cool and had parties and school was boring." Tommy shrugged. "Trust me, I regret it now. And I hate that she was right. I'm so lucky that she still agreed to let me go to Westmeath, or else I wouldn't have met Carter. Kennedy and Jason helped a lot, too."

"So, your family does care," Greg said bitterly. "You didn't get along with one person, who had your best interests at heart. Sounds like you really don't know what my life is like."

"Then tell me." Tommy said.

Greg stared silently at the house across the road for so long that Tommy thought he wasn't going to say anything. He looked up, spotting a Dome in the night sky blotting out the stars behind it. It took his breath away. Just when he was about to give up and return to the house, Greg started to speak.

"My father is a Blue Blood. I guess you probably know that already. He's not upper management, just an enforcer. A good one, too. He's the one who got me into boxing. It's been just the two of us since my mom passed when I was little." Greg fell silent again.

"Jason faced off against your dad," Tommy said finally. "Before the wedding."

Greg snorted. "Yeah. My dad was impressed. Not many people could lay him out cold."

"That's a great way of looking at the guy that put him in jail," Tommy said with a chuckle.

"Not that he stayed there long. We've got a man on the inside."

"Of course you do." Tommy rolled his eyes. "Your dad sounds cool. Why do you think he wouldn't miss you?"

"What kind of dad signs their kid up to join a gang?" Greg said bitterly. He rubbed his arms as if feeling the chill in the air or maybe wanting to touch his jacket. He'd left it inside the house.

"Maybe he had no choice," Tommy said. "Maybe he thought it was the best way to protect you. Maybe he thought he could keep a better eye on you. Did you ask him?"

"No. We haven't really talked much since he brought the jacket home for me."

"When you get home, I think you need to have a chat. And if you want out, I hope you can find a way."

"Who says I want out?" Greg said, scowling.

Tommy laughed. "Your actions. Everything about you *screams* that you want out. Those two kids that followed you around at the March Break camp... They didn't make it into the summer camp. I bet they didn't even try out. And yet here you are. Out of hundreds of high schoolers from across Ontario, *you* made it into the summer camp. You're smart. You don't seem like you want to be part of that gang. And I bet your dad doesn't want to be in it either."

Silence fell over them again.

"You really think so?" Greg asked softly. "You think I can change?"

"I know you can," Tommy said firmly.

The hint of a genuine smile played across Greg's lips. "Thanks. It's nice to be believed in."

"I'm not the first and I won't be the last." Tommy nudged Greg's arm. "Come on back inside. Pieter said I could play his guitar. You don't want to miss your chance at hearing me play, do you?"

"Are you any good?" Greg asked with a smirk.

Tommy gasped. "Was that a joke?" He grinned. "I wouldn't say that. I've only been playing for a year, and I mostly know little kid songs. But you can sing along and have fun with the rest of us."

"Alright. You've twisted my arm."

"Better than breaking your hand," Tommy teased.

"Ouch. Too soon."

Chapter 14

Carter woke to the pleasant aroma of cooking meat. He tightened his grip on his boyfriend and nuzzled into his hair. "You smell good," he murmured, eyes still closed. "Don't want to go to class this morning."

Tommy's breath fanned out over his neck as he huffed a laugh. "You don't have to."

"Right. It's summer." Something niggled at the back of his brain, but Carter ignored it, content to cuddle his boyfriend closer on the rather hard mattress. "Wait a second..." His eyes snapped open to be met with the open-concept shared area of the house they were staying in. "Oh. Right."

Memories from the night before flooded back: sitting around the fireplace while Tommy played guitar, Pieter offering Tommy the guitar as thanks for saving their daughter, Tommy refusing politely, falling asleep curled up with Tommy... Carter smiled. "I'm glad you're here with me," he whispered.

"There's nowhere I'd rather be," Tommy replied, pressing a kiss under Carter's jaw.

"Aww, aren't you two sweet," Elyse cooed from her seat at the kitchen island.

"I feel a cavity forming," Greg grumbled.

Carter reached behind him and gave the bigger boy a smack on the arm, making everyone else chuckle.

"You should get up, though," Elyse said. "We want to go to the Wild Nations today."

"Right." Tommy sat up and stretched.

Carter looked away from the dimples low on Tommy's spine revealed by the lifted shirt. *Now is not the time,* he thought.

Aliyah bustled over from the kitchen and passed the three of them their clothing. "They're a little damp, I'm afraid, but they'll dry on you."

Tommy sniffed his clean shirt. "I don't know how you managed to get the smoke out, but I'm impressed. Thank you."

"I don't mind wearing damp clothing," Carter added. "Um, these are yours." He passed Tommy his briefs and took his from Tommy's pile.

"Sorry," Aliyah apologized. "You're the same size."

"No big deal." Carter shrugged.

They took their things upstairs, Greg heading into the bathroom, and the couple taking the bedroom Elyse had slept in.

"One big positive of being here," Tommy said as he pulled on his shorts. "No matter how long or short the time, we can snuggle every night."

Carter chuckled. "Great point. But hopefully Es'Sem will be able to send us back today."

"Obviously. Hey, do you have your phone on you?" Tommy asked, flipping his shirt around in his hands.

Carter shook his head. "No, I had stored it in my locker at Door Tech. I didn't want it to get damaged during any of the activities." He did up the button on his shorts slowly, admiring the flexing muscles of his boyfriend's body as he pulled his shirt on.

"Ah, good call. You were crawling around on the floor during that one activity, weren't you?"

"It was the only way to get at the underside of the vehicle."

A knock sounded on the closed door. "I'm done in the bathroom," Greg announced.

Tommy ran his tongue over his teeth. "Kiss after brushing?"

"And emptying bladder," Carter said, tucking his shirt under his arm and heading for the door. "I feel like I'm going to explode."

They performed their ablutions quickly and spent another few minutes locked together, hands exploring each other and heads spinning pleasantly.

Carter pulled back at last, admiring the flush on Tommy's cheeks and kiss-swollen lips spread in a smile. "I love seeing you like this," he whispered, pressing a light kiss to Tommy's nose. "We should head down before we get too distracted."

"Bit late for that," Tommy murmured, his smile morphing into a smirk. "Okay. I'm gonna splash some water on my face first. No point in broadcasting it, eh?"

"Good idea." Carter mentally told his body to stand down, which wasn't easy. After taking his turn at the sink, they went downstairs for breakfast.

Aliyah had just taken a tray of muffins from the oven. "Fresh cydant muffins?" she said, indicating a cooling rack on the counter island.

"You had me at muffin," Carter said, taking one and biting into it. A cotton candy apple flavour burst across his tongue, and he hummed happily. "Wow, this is amazing!" he said after swallowing his mouthful.

"The taste is sort of familiar, don't you think?" Tommy said as he thoughtfully munched on his muffin.

"I am getting a sense of déjà vu," Carter said. He took another bite. "Don't worry, it'll come back to me, even if it takes a whole dozen."

Aliyah chuckled. "Have as many as you like."

"It doesn't taste like anything I've ever eaten," Elyse put in.

"Me neither," Greg added.

"Hmm, interesting," Carter said thoughtfully. "What have you and I eaten that Elyse and Greg haven't?"

"Cydants, apparently," Tommy teased.

Carter pushed him off his stool.

After breakfast, Aliyah led them back to the circle of portals. Tommy and Carter walked with her.

Carter kept looking from one busy area of the city to another. There were market stalls set up with fresh produce, booksellers discussing volumes with customers, and people walking arm in arm. It was so similar to the feel of Oldtown that he couldn't quite figure out why something felt off. A shadow fell across the sun, and he squinted up, only to see a smallish dome overhead. *Ah, there's the difference.*

"That is the Abrasax Dome," Aliyah said, noting the direction of his attention. "It's one of the smaller ones."

"That's *small*?" Elyse squeaked, ducking instinctively.

"Compared to the domes that grow our food, yes," Aliyah said with a chuckle.

Tommy took Carter's hand, squeezing tightly. "We'll get used to it soon." His voice cracked a little, so it sounded like a question, but nobody pointed that out.

"Have you two been together long?" Aliyah asked after a moment of silence.

"Not in person. Only two weeks," Carter replied. "But we did video calls for five months."

Aliyah frowned in confusion. "Sorry, I don't understand."

"We live in different cities," Tommy tried to explain. "Video is..." He rubbed his hand through his hair. "Wow. Umm. How about I just call it a long-distance relationship, but we were able to talk to each other every day?"

"I find it difficult to be away from Pieter for even a few days. How did you manage five months?"

Carter's shoulders heaved in a sigh. "It wasn't easy. But we didn't have a choice. We get a month together at camp. Hopefully, we won't get sick of each other."

Tommy stuck his tongue out.

Aliyah put a hand to her heart. "May the Goddess smile upon your relationship," she said. "It is obvious that you care about each other deeply."

Carter grinned at Tommy. "Yeah, I don't really know the meaning of subtle."

Tommy laughed.

"If you come back through Pakaha, please look us up." Aliyah made them promise and then helped them sign in for the correct portal. "Good luck!" she said, waving as they walked through the shimmering portal that would hopefully be their last.

TUESDAY THE 18TH OF DECEMBER, 1290 POST-CATACLYSM - SYDNEY, WILD NATIONS

The first thing Carter noticed about Wild Nations was the oppressive heat. "Aliyah said it was summer here, didn't she?" he said. He squinted through the too-bright sunshine and spotted the check-out official. "This way. I'm not sure I would've known if she hadn't said something."

Greg snorted. "Yeah, it's downright chilly here."

"Brr, where's my coat?" Tommy said with a laugh.

When they had finished signing the paperwork with the official, they started walking through the city.

"You know, for a place named Wild Nations, I kinda expected the houses to look a little more shack-like," Greg said.

"Me too," Elyse admitted. "I almost feel like we're in the Mediterranean."

"Except it's hotter, and there aren't any cars or multi-storey buildings," Tommy pointed out.

"And very few people," Carter added. "Excuse me," he said to a woman passing by. "Could you tell us where to find Queen Es'Sem, please?"

"At this time of day, she'd be up at the training yards," she said. She gave them directions and then continued on her way.

"At least we don't have to backtrack," Elyse said, fanning her face with a hand. "The sooner we get out of this heat, the better."

The houses ended abruptly, changing to a tree-lined road that offered much-welcomed shade. Beyond the trees on either side, which reminded them of olive and palm, there were plains, one with a circular track and the other with hard-packed dirt. As they got further down the road, voices could be heard from the side with the dirt, accompanied by the sound of metal hitting metal.

Approaching the top of a rise, they could see several people training in pairs. Some were working on unarmed combat, others had swords, and there were a couple of archers in the distance, shooting away from the rest.

"How do we know which one is Es'Sem?" Tommy asked anxiously.

"We walk up and ask," Carter said, squeezing his hand. There didn't seem to be anyone watching over the training, so he assumed that these people were advanced enough that they didn't need any oversight.

Only one sparring group stopped when they saw the teenagers, the woman turning to them while the man joined another pair. The woman was light skinned with pink undertones and had several scars. Her hair was light brown with sun-dyed blonde streaks, pulled back into a loose braid. She had soft smile lines around her mouth and eyes.

"Can I help you?" she asked once they were close enough to talk. She had a trace of an accent that Carter couldn't quite place.

"Hopefully," Elyse said. "We need to talk to Queen Es'Sem as soon as possible, please."

"If you're looking for training, she won't help you." She put her fists on her hips and looked each of them over. "Brawler," she nodded at Greg. "Martial arts," she said to Carter. "Dancer or gymnast," was said to Elyse. "I can't place you, though." She frowned at Tommy. "What's your background?"

"Me? I don't really do sports." When she didn't say anything, he continued, "I play guitar?"

A corner of her mouth ticked up in amusement. "You're the cheering section?"

Carter bit back a laugh. "We didn't come here for training. We're hoping she can tell us how we can get home."

The woman's eyebrows rose. "I am not surprised easily, but you've managed it."

"Australian!" Tommy blurted out. When everyone looked at him, he blushed. "Sorry. But your accent... It's Australian, isn't it?"

The woman smiled widely and nodded. "You're from Earth. Canadian, Eastern Ontario, wait... Westmeath, aren't you? How did you get to Everdome?" She started unwrapping her wrists, walking to a long, low building nearby. They followed her.

"Er, that would be my fault," Carter said sheepishly. "I was given a knight's ring by Merlin, and when the Sisters recalled all the Knights of Gaulan, the four of us got pulled through."

"Really. Show me the ring." When Carter gave it to her, she examined it carefully. "That's Everdome workmanship alright." She gave it back. "Poor kids. I'm sorry, but I can't help you get home."

The teens were silent for a moment, upset, until her words finally hit Carter. "Wait, you're the queen?" he gasped. "Should we bow or something?"

Es'Sem burst out laughing. "Don't you dare. I'm not that kind of queen."

Elyse's eyes widened. "Hang on, we were looking for you because Pieter told us there were rumours that you travelled to Earth, but your name... You're S.M. Arwdur, aren't you?"

The woman looked embarrassed, her cheeks flushing red beyond the heat of the day. "Yes, I am."

"How do you publish on Earth if you're here in Everdome?" Greg asked, narrowing his eyes suspiciously.

"I arrange for someone to bring me across the Aether. But if I stay too long, Everdome drags me back. It's not a pleasant experience. I don't recommend it." Es'Sem looked haunted. She gave herself a shake. "Sometimes Emrys brings me back to Earth, sometimes Morgana, sometimes Kathryn. I can try to reach out to one of them, but I haven't seen any of them in a while. So, I'm sorry, but I can't help you get home."

"I know who Emrys and Morgana are, but who is Kathryn?" Tommy asked. "Is she the same Kathryn from your books?"

"Did I write about her?" Es'Sem said, surprised, before shaking her head. "I suppose I must have. She's an excellent friend of mine. She brought me here in the, oh, let me see, I guess it was the seventies on Earth? The nineteen-seventies, I mean. We arrived here in Everdome before the Cataclysm."

Carter held up a hand and stopped walking. "Hang on, that's breaking my brain a little. What year is it now in Everdome? Did we go back in time, or is it after your last book?"

"Today is the eighteenth of December, twelve ninety post-Cataclysm," Es'Sem replied calmly. "We'll be celebrating our midwinter festival in about a week, which will be our twelve-ninety first year since the Cataclysm."

"But you don't look older than forty!" Greg spluttered.

"Thank you." Es'Sem grinned.

Carter exchanged amused glances with Tommy. "This Kathryn... She wouldn't be Kathryn Johnson, would she?"

Es'Sem shrugged. "I don't remember last names. They're not important. Why do you think it's her?" She opened the door of the low building, leading them into a communal area with benches, tables, and a kitchen. A bare-chested man was washing dishes at the sink, dressed simply in loose brown pants. A sparkle shone at his earlobe. He moved to leave, but Es'Sem shook her head at him, and he returned to the soapy bubbles.

"Because she looks young, but she's a great-grandmother in our world," Tommy said.

"Sounds like her," Es'Sem said. "Probably the same Kathryn then. Small universe." She sat on a bench, and the teens grouped themselves around her. "Small realms? Whatever."

"If only thirty years have passed in our world, but one thousand, two hundred and ninety years have passed here, how much time has passed on Earth in the one day we've been here?" Elyse asked.

Es'Sem shrugged again. "It's not an exact ratio." Then, when their faces fell, she added, "A few minutes, I would guess."

Carter felt a wave of relief pass over him and he sagged in his seat. "Oh, thank goodness. At least we don't have to worry about our parents."

"Yet." Elyse bit her bottom lip. "How long do you think we'll be here? How much will we age?"

"Stop thinking about worst case scenarios," Tommy advised. "We'll figure out logistics when we return home."

Greg had an odd expression on his face as he focussed on Es'Sem. "You're really over a thousand years old?" he asked, his voice catching a little on the number. "And it's not technology that extended your life?"

"Oh Goddess, definitely not! Everdome is a little behind when it comes to certain things, like technology, but very advanced when it comes to magic," Es'Sem said with a chuckle. She clapped her hands together. "We got a tad distracted. Why were the knights recalled? Do you know?" She sobered as Carter told her about the Icaryoe and the destruction of Gaulan's university building. "That's not good. The Great Beasts of Everdome are monsters in every sense of the word."

"What's the big deal about this Beast?" Greg asked. "People have been killing animals for millennia."

Tommy replied, "In the books, they were not only sapient but extremely clever. The six of them banded together and, even with a month's warning, were almost able to take down Pakaha Castle on their own. If it hadn't been for Kathryn, Emrys, and the wizard Daniel, they would have taken the castle and enslaved each and every Dome." Tommy looked at Es'Sem. "I've always wondered where they came from. They show up in the story with no explanation."

A dark shadow crossed over her face. "Some things are better not written down or talked about, even with impolite company like me. Let's just leave it at it needs to be stopped, or else it will release the others, and Everdome will be finished. It's gathering its strength right now, making a plan."

"I've never killed anything," Carter said, his stomach flipping. A glance at Tommy showed that he wasn't faring much better. "Let alone something that could fight back. I've trained to defend myself. I..." He ran a hand through his hair, anxiety coursing through his body. "What do I do?" he whispered. "I feel like killing it will be the only way to get back to Earth."

Es'Sem leaned back on her bench, her gaze fixed on him. "They're immortal, if that makes you feel any better." She rubbed her chin thoughtfully. "It's not easy for them to recombine if stored properly. I wonder where it was kept."

"Gaulan, I assume," Tommy said. "Since it attacked there first."

"Possibly." Es'Sem inclined her head in acknowledgement. "If not, why was it there?"

Why indeed? Carter wondered. *What's special about the university?*

He stopped listening as the others continued that train of thought. *I'm a rock giant. I live in a city filled with Aetherborn. Why is one mythical Beast freaking me out so much? Is this what Tommy felt like, when we told him about us?* Everything that had happened since arriving in Everdome caught up with him. He felt simultaneously exhilarated and terrified. *I bet Jason never feels this way.*

"Okay, so here's what I'm thinking," Elyse said. "We need to somehow get a message to Emrys, Morgana, or Kathryn."

"I just remembered something," Es'Sem put in. "Emrys doesn't always visit me in the same order."

"I'm sorry, I don't follow," Carter said, confused. "Like, he... I'm sorry, I got nothing."

Es'Sem chuckled. "Sometimes he's younger and sometimes he's older. He doesn't deal with time in the same way you or I do."

"Okay, so we need to send a message that will stand the test of time. Something that people will remember, like a prophecy." Elyse frowned. "How do we do that?"

"Music!" Tommy broke in excitedly. "We even know instrument makers. We can go back to Pakaha, and I can teach them a song. Then whoever our rescuer is will know when we got here so that they can come and get us at the proper time."

"I like that. Music lasts," Es'Sem said gravely. "What will the song be about?"

"I'm not sure yet." Tommy grinned. "I've got an idea, though."

"Great, we've got a message. But in case that doesn't work, we need to figure out how to defeat the Icaryoe. Any suggestions?" Elyse looked at the queen, but she was staring into the distance.

"Es'Sem, didn't you write about their destruction in *The Beasts of Everdome*?" Carter asked.

"Yes, but I don't remember. That was such a long time ago. Your best bet is to go to the library of Sartorna. They should have descriptions of the battle. But before you go, you should get some training. I'll train you for a week or so, and then you can go, but on one condition." Es'Sem glared at them.

"What is it?" Carter asked tentatively.

"You tell no one that I agreed to this." Es'Sem chuckled. "You all look so serious! If word got out that I was training young'uns, I'd be overrun in a month! Come on, I'll get Noah to take you up to the rest house and get you rooms." She looked them over. "Right, no luggage. I'll have him take you to the markets as well, get you some more clothing, toiletries, that sort of thing." Es'Sem shook her head and added bitterly, "Those Sisters. Not even the courtesy to let you contact your parents. Just like Everdome itself. I never get any warning when I'm ripped back from Earth." She slapped her knees and got to her feet. "That's enough wagging of my tongue for today. I should get back to training. I'll see all of you tonight for dinner at your rest house. Noah will collect you shortly." She left the room, leaving them in silence, other than the quiet splashes at the sink.

"Well, that was amazing," Carter said, feeling like all his energy had left with her. "Did I geek out too much?"

Tommy chuckled. "No, you were fine. Oh boy, I'd love to see Jason meet her!"

"Me too!" Elyse giggled. "He'd really lose his cool!"

"Was it just me, or did she seem a little absent-minded?" Greg asked.

"I mean, she's over a thousand years old!" Carter exclaimed. "I barely remember what I did last week!"

"When do you think Noah will come get us?" Tommy asked. "I can't wait to see more of the city!"

"And go shopping!" Elyse said enthusiastically. "The clothes here are beautiful. Do you think we'll be allowed to bring them back home with us when we go?"

"We might not have the option, if it's as abrupt as how we got pulled here," grumbled Greg, before mockingly adding, "Do you know, *Sir Knight*?"

"Stop that. It's not Carter's fault!" Elyse said, a scowl on her pretty face.

"He wasn't blaming Carter," Tommy said calmly. "Why don't we look around this building while we wait for Noah? Es'Sem didn't say we couldn't."

The man washing dishes dried his hands and cleared his throat. "I could give you a tour before we go to the city, but there really isn't much to see."

The teenagers all stared at him for a second before Carter started to laugh. "You're Noah, aren't you?"

"I am." Noah grinned. "Shall we?" He indicated the door with a thumb and fiddled with one earring.

On closer inspection, Carter could see that Noah wore white crystalline studs in his ears. *They look so cool.* His energy restored, Carter leaped to his feet and held a hand out for Tommy. "Yes, let's go!"

As they walked back the way they had come, Noah asked them questions. They found out that Wild Nations was currently about four hours ahead of Pakaha, so they had missed lunch.

"Do people get jet lag here, jumping between the Domes?" Elyse asked.

"I don't know what that is, but people don't cross Domes and expect to stay for long. The ones that do are tired for a day or two, but catch up easily," Noah replied.

"Sounds like jet lag to me," Tommy said. "Except without the exhaustion of travel!"

"That's always the worst part," Carter agreed.

"Would you like to see your rooms first or go shopping?" Noah asked.

The four exchanged looks. "Shopping," Tommy said. Everyone nodded eagerly.

"The market's this way," Noah said, leading them off the main road. "You need some everyday clothing, undergarments, training gear, and toiletries. Get enough to last you the week. Make sure to get some tunics that you can wear to other Domes. Here, you don't have to worry so much about covering up."

Carter nudged Elyse. "How do you feel about wearing something like that woman over there?"

Elyse turned to see who he was pointing at and blushed. The woman in question was only wearing a breast band and a mini skirt. "That's really not my style," she said.

"Too bad," Greg said, winking at her.

Carter suppressed a smile, seeing her blush even more and not getting angry. He raised an eyebrow at her, and she scowled at him.

Not a word. Her mindspeak came to him easily, surprising him until he remembered that Westmeath had a thick Aether barrier, and they weren't in Westmeath any longer. When they'd visited Toronto in May, his team had found it easy to mindspeak with each other.

I didn't say anything, he thought back to her, and she rolled her eyes.

Carter tuned back into the conversation just as Noah said, "We'll find you some bags for your things as well."

"Thank you for helping us navigate all this," Tommy said.

"It is my pleasure," the man replied with a smile.

The clothing stalls reminded Carter of Seams Likeable, where the tailors would have them try on clothing and then alter them to fit. The material for their everyday wear was a thin linen with embroidery around the neck. The shirts were a little longer than the ones from home, down to mid-thigh. The pants had drawstrings around the waist. Elyse's clothing options had more variety, but she chose the same style as the boys. Noah taught them the money system at the first stall and let them attempt to bargain on their own at the second.

Next, Noah brought them to a stall full of exercise clothing and equipment. He advised them to buy pants; although shorts would be cooler, they should avoid getting scrapes that could get infected. He also helped Elyse find a breast band that fit comfortably under a loose shirt.

"You'll be given leather tunics to wear if you do sword work. If you show proficiency in something, you'll be instructed to buy the proper equipment," Noah told them. "But until then, these will do."

Their training shoes would be ready after dinner. Carter was sure that they were rushing their order because of Noah being associated with the queen.

Last, they visited a stall with pharmacy items. Noah gave each of them a bag filled with things like toothbrushes, deodorant, and soap. The deodorant wasn't like at home but came in a little tub that could be scooped out and applied.

Greg picked up a jar of viscous liquid and tossed it at Carter, who caught it easily. "You might need some of this," he said teasingly.

Carter eyed the unmarked bottle. "What is it?" he asked, curious.

"That is lubricant," Noah explained. "It is safe to use for sexual activities."

"Oh." Carter blushed and put it back. "I'm not going to use Queen Es'Sem's money for something that isn't a necessity."

"You'll be given some pocket money," Noah said. "You can always come back for it later."

Carter exchanged glances with Tommy, who was as red as he felt. "Thank you for the explanation."

After all their purchases, Noah led them down the street to a long, low building.

The white stone used for all the buildings reminded Carter of pictures he'd seen of Greece. The inside was kept cool by many openings that allowed breezes to blow through.

"Four rooms?" Noah asked.

Carter tugged on Tommy's hand. "Do you want to share? No pressure." He hadn't finished his question before Tommy was nodding, a shy smile on his face.

"Of *course* I want to share with you!" He grinned. "If I get sick of you, I can ask for a separate room then."

"Hey!" Carter said with a laugh. "That's not supposed to happen!"

"Three rooms it is," Noah said with a smile. "See you tonight at dinner."

Chapter 15

Tommy tried not to stare at the tall towers of the large city they were now walking through. The portal had let them out on the banks of a large inland sea, which the city encircled. Though they had left the Wild Nations early that morning, it was the middle of the night in Sartorna.

"Why didn't they warn us?" Greg grumbled as they walked along the silent streets.

"Either Es'Sem forgot or thought it would be funny," Carter said with a chuckle. "Wild Nations has a more drastic time variation than other Domes because of its opposite rotation."

"Maybe that's why it's called 'Wild' Nations." Tommy grinned at his boyfriend. "It doesn't really matter. I read that the library never closes."

"I miss the stars we could see in Wild Nations, though," Elyse said mournfully.

Tommy looked up at the night sky, or rather, what he could see of it. The light pollution from the streetlamps of the city meant that few stars were visible. "I'm just glad that it's warm here, too."

"I would've thought you'd be tired of the heat after training for a week," Carter teased.

Tommy thought about his sore muscles from all the exercise he'd gotten and winced. "It's not the heat I'm tired of," he said with a groan. "I'm glad to have a break, that's for sure."

The day after they had arrived in Sydney, they were woken

before the sun. They donned their new clothing and set off with Noah for the training area at a jog.

Breakfast was waiting for them: a large egg of some sort, cured meat that tasted halfway between maple bacon and chicken, and an impressive variety of fruits. Then Noah ran them through basic stretches and endurance. After that, when Tommy felt like he was about to drop, they started martial arts.

For an hour.

And then archery. And more running.

All before lunch.

"I don't think I can do this," Tommy gasped, lying flat on his back in the shade of the house.

Carter sat beside him, hardly winded. "If we're really going to go up against the Icaryoe, I want you to stay in one piece. And if that means you have to learn defensive strategies, then that's what you have to do."

"I might hate you a little bit right now," Tommy grumbled. "You don't even sound out of breath!"

Carter chuckled. "How about I promise to give you a very *thorough* massage when we get back to our room?" he murmured, lying down facing Tommy. He walked his fingers up the middle of Tommy's heaving chest. "Work over every muscle in your body. Will you still hate me a little bit then?"

Tommy shivered despite the heat. "I don't think I could ever really hate you," he replied. Summoning up the energy, he rolled to face Carter. "Do you think I'll ever get used to this?"

Carter shrugged his shoulders awkwardly from his prone position. "I don't see why not. Besides," he smirked, "I like seeing you all sweaty and gasping for breath."

"Don't you dare turn this into something sexual!" Tommy complained, blushing. "I don't want to be thinking about *that* while working out. I also hope I'm a lot more graceful in bed than doing martial arts."

"I have no complaints so far," Carter teased. When Tommy stuck his tongue out, Carter laughed.

"Good."

"Come on, boys. Noah wants to talk to us over lunch," Elyse called, sticking her head out of the house.

Noah had come up with a training plan for each of them. For the rest of the week, they would start with the same routine as that day, but instead of archery, they would split up into their specialties. Greg would focus on boxing, Carter on knives, and Elyse on something called a rope dart, which involved a lot of graceful movements. Tommy would do defensive martial arts, which meant a lot of ducking and avoiding.

They would complete the routine with a run before lunch, and then after lunch, they would do the whole thing again.

The first couple of days felt like torture to Tommy. After they jogged home each night, he had a shower and ate dinner in a daze, falling asleep the instant his head touched the pillow.

But on the third day, he started to feel like he had more energy, and the exercises became easier to follow. His muscles still ached, but it was bearable. When he asked Noah about it, he was told that the drink they had with breakfast, a strong black tea with a mild taste of mocha, was a rejuvenating potion. He noticed his friends had more stamina as well and were faring better in their lessons than they had at the beginning.

Tommy was the only one who didn't need special equipment. Elyse bought a leather tunic, to protect herself from the rope dart, Carter got gloves, and Greg wore wrist wraps like the ones that Es'Sem had been wearing when they met her.

After a week of training, Es'Sem joined them for dinner again. "Looks like Everdome air is agreeing with you. How have you liked your training so far?"

"It's been educational," Carter said with a grin.

Es'Sem laughed loudly. "Good. Have you decided what to do next?"

"We're heading for Sartorna's historical archives first thing in the morning," Elyse supplied. "We want to read up on the Icaryoe, like where it was stored and how it was destroyed last time."

"Good idea. It will have learned from last time, so you'll have to come up with a new plan." Es'Sem took a sip of the alcohol she had ordered with her dinner. "Anything else?"

"We want to take a look at *how* it was stored, in whichever Dome it was in, and figure out how it got out," Tommy added.

"Excellent. How long do you expect that to take?"

"Hopefully not more than a few days," Greg said.

"But we're not exactly familiar with Everdome, so it could be up to a week," Carter finished.

"You'll be gone over Cataclysm Day. Make sure you partake in the merrymaking no matter where you end up," Es'Sem suggested. "It's a lot like Christmas on Earth, if I remember correctly. Gifts exchanged and all that." She reached into a pocket on her belt and withdrew four moneybags. "Here, this should be enough to feed yourselves and have some left over. Noah's been coaching you on how bartering works here, hasn't he?" When they all nodded, she said, "Good." She tossed a bag to each of them. "Now, Sartorna. The librarian won't let you touch his precious historical scrolls unless you give him some new information. Any details about Earth should do. The more forthcoming you are, the more helpful he will be."

Tommy looked up at the rough-hewn grey rock building that they were facing: the library of Sartorna. Counting the windows up the side, it was about seven storeys and was as wide as a city block. "This rock makes me think of some of the old houses in Upper Canada Village. We were told they were built two hundred and fifty years ago," he said, putting his hand on one. "Look at the size of them! And they're cool to the touch, even though the air is warm."

"What do you think it means?" Greg asked.

"Sartorna has some things in common with Canada, I guess," Elyse said. "Although I could be reaching because I miss home."

"I see the parallels," Carter agreed. "Let's go in and find this mysterious librarian. Do you think Es'Sem exaggerated? Or maybe the guy she's remembering is long dead, and we won't have to worry about exchanging information."

"Only one way to find out," Greg said, and pulled open the heavy wooden door.

They walked inside, and Tommy's jaw dropped. The hall in front of them stretched to the end of the building. His gaze followed the carved wooden balconies up both sides of the hall, counting six of them, until they reached the ceiling. Everywhere he looked, there were bookcases haphazardly filled with scrolls and books. He was sure there was a system, but it wasn't obvious. "Oh, wow," he breathed, awestruck.

"We are definitely going to need help," Elyse said.

The boys nodded slowly, reluctantly looking away from the spectacular library to see if they could find something resembling an information desk.

"Welcome to the library of Sartorna," said a chipper voice. "My name is Nanette. How can I help you today?"

The four teenagers spun around to face a girl not much older than they were, with copper-coloured skin and brown hair.

"Hello," Carter said, recovering first and introducing themselves. "We would like to know more about the Great Beasts of Everdome, please."

Nanette nodded and looked at them appraisingly. "You're going after the Icaryoe. I don't recommend it. That's what the knights are doing."

Tommy looked at Carter to see how he'd react to that. When he didn't say anything, Tommy nodded slightly and said, "We'd still like to read about it. If it attacks us, we might have a chance at defeating it, right?"

"Not much of a chance," Nanette said with a chuckle. "But I can show you where the scroll on the Icaryoe is kept." She led them to the back of the library and up five flights of stairs.

"What kind of information do you need in exchange?" Tommy asked nervously.

Nanette paused on the staircase. "You must be thinking of my great-grandfather. I don't need to take anything from you."

"Why did that change?" Elyse asked.

"I'm not sure." Nanette continued up the stairs. "I never met my great-grandfather. Maybe he liked gossip."

Greg snorted. "I guess Es'Sem's information is a little out of date."

"This place is amazing!" Tommy said enthusiastically, his fingers tracing the carving on the wooden railing as he climbed. "What is it like working here?"

"Exhausting sometimes," Nanette said. "There's a lot I need to know, like where to find the scrolls on the Great Beasts, without looking it up."

"How do you keep all that information in your head?" Elyse asked.

"Practise. I've been training for this since I was old enough to read. My family have been the librarians here since the library's inception."

"What if you want to do something else?" Greg was frowning. Tommy wondered if Greg was thinking about his own situation and how he was expected to be just like his father.

Nanette shrugged. "Some of my cousins have done other things, of course. The library isn't everyone's dream job, but it is mine." She stopped walking abruptly and examined the bookshelves around her. "Sorry, I got distracted. Here we go." She backed up one shelf and turned right, toward the balconies flanking the centre open space of the library. She pulled out several scrolls, looking for the right one.

After the third scroll, Tommy moved over to the railing, looking around at the massive library.

"This place really is something, isn't it?" Elyse whispered as she joined him.

"Sometimes I find it hard to believe that we're really here, in Everdome," Tommy replied, leaning his elbows on the balcony railing. "And then I see places like this, and yeah, I believe it."

"Because travelling through portals to different time zones isn't enough for you?" Elyse teased.

Tommy nudged her shoulder with his. "You know what I mean," he said with a chuckle.

"Here you go," Nanette said.

Tommy turned to see her handing a scroll to Greg.

"Let me know if you need anything else," she added.

"That's *all* you've got on the Icaryoe? Weaknesses, where it was stored, everything?" Carter's voice was laced with incredulity.

"I'm afraid so. It should all be in there." Nanette shrugged. "Good luck."

Greg waited until she had left before unrolling the scroll. They all bent over it.

"'Body of a four-legged dragon, head like a lion with the beak of a bird of prey, tail with sharp barbs like a porcupine,'" Tommy read aloud at a whisper. "This sounds like one of those monsters in Westmeath that the Phantom and Wraith were fighting back in June: the gorilla-bear and the moosequitoes."

Carter nodded. "The ones that were a combination of different animals. I see what you mean. But those were made by magic and vanished when killed. This Icaryoe keeps coming back."

"How do you know how those monsters were made?" Greg asked.

"Ummm..." Carter looked at Tommy with wide, panicked eyes.

"How else would they disappear once they were killed?" Tommy replied.

"Could've been a teleport," Greg pointed out.

"With perfect timing?" Tommy shook his head. "My sister killed a dinosaur at the Niche gala, and it literally *poofed* out of existence the second she pierced the brain."

"It doesn't matter," Elyse said, tapping the scroll. "We're here now. Focus. 'It has wings of fire that only appear when flying,'" she read.

"If it's a dragon, can it breathe fire?" Greg asked, his eyes flicking over the scroll. "I don't see any accounts of that here."

"It must have flown pretty close to the University of Gaulan, then," Carter said thoughtfully. "Perhaps even out of that building."

"That makes sense. We were on the second floor, and there were at least two floors above us," Elyse commented.

"It looks like they set a trap for it last time," Tommy said, pointing halfway down the scroll. "'The Beast stepped on the trigger, carefully concealed by leaves, and the mechanism snapped shut on its leg, preventing it from leaping into the air. The closing of the first mechanism triggered the second: a wall of blades that pierced upwards from the soil and sliced the Beast into large...' Oh, ew." Tommy stopped reading, a disgusted look on his face. "I don't want to read the rest. It's too descriptive."

Silently, the teens read about how all the parts of the Beast had been gathered up, making sure to leave none behind, and burned in stone basins. The ashes had been transferred to six spelled jars, each of which was stored in a separate metal and wooden chest etched with protective shielding.

"It says that these chests were stored in Gaulan's main castle," Elyse said. "Why would the Icaryoe appear in the university?"

"Maybe they were moved after this scroll was written, and they forgot to note it down," Greg suggested.

"I don't know," Carter said, frowning. "There are only six Great Beasts. You'd think they'd keep a careful eye on them. Perhaps it appeared initially at the castle and headed to the university."

"I can't believe that's all the scroll can teach us," Greg said, rolling it back up and shaking his head. "Next step, Gaulan?"

The others nodded in agreement. They left the library, the sun still not yet risen.

WEDNESDAY THE 26TH OF DECEMBER, 1290 POST-CATACLYSM - TÈNE, GAULAN

They made their way back to Gaulan via Pakaha. The blackness of midnight greeted them at their last portal, even though the first two looked as if the sun was about to rise.

"Switching time zones like this is going to give me whiplash," Greg complained. "How does anyone keep track?"

The official signing them into Gaulan chuckled. "Everything shifts constantly. Scholars predict the time zones for hundreds of years in advance, assuming there aren't any rogue asteroids. Would you like a chart?"

"Yes, please," Tommy said excitedly. "Thank you."

Greg whistled as they examined the chart. "The math involved in these calculations is immensely complex. Look, the gravity from other Domes needs to be considered, as well as the weight and rotational velocity of the Dome itself."

"It's beautiful," Tommy breathed. Elyse nodded in agreement.

Despite it being the middle of the night, the university was bustling with people. They found Todd easily enough, by heading straight for the storage rooms.

"What's happened?" Carter asked. "Did the Icaryoe attack again?"

Todd looked confused. "No. This is a normal level of activity for the university at this time of year. It's Cataclysm Day tomorrow, and lots of people are coming to celebrate here in Tène."

"Oh, that's right!" Elyse exclaimed. "Es'Sem suggested we take part in the celebrations. Is there anything we can do to help before the castle opens? We need to talk to someone about the Icaryoe storage."

"The castle?" Todd frowned. "The archivists and guards are there now. Why don't you run over and talk to them, and then you can come back and help. This will take much longer than that."

Elyse pulled out the map they had been given last time, and Greg easily found the castle. Todd gave them winter gear again, and they set out through the cold city.

There were fewer people on the streets the further they got from the university and Pakaha's portal, which were obviously the primary points of contact for visitors from other Domes. The shops and markets were few and far between the further away they got, becoming more residential.

They scuffed their boots through the fluffy snow until they reached the castle gates, guarded by two soldiers with long spears.

"Hello," Carter said politely. "May we please enter to speak with the guards of the Icaryoe? And can you tell us where they might be?"

The guard on the right replied, "The archivists would be the best people to speak to. They were the guardians."

"The archives are one floor down in the main castle keep," the guard on the left added. "One or two should be there right now."

"Thank you," Tommy said, and the guards stepped aside for them to enter.

"I wonder if any other knights have come here," Greg mused. "They seemed to know what we wanted."

They entered the main keep by a smaller door set inside larger doubled ones. The hall inside was huge, dominated by a massive staircase that split in two and wound upwards until it joined again at another set of double doors.

The stairs down were hidden in a shadowy corner behind a grey door.

"I guess they don't want people coming down here by accident," Carter murmured to the others as they walked down steep stone steps.

"If I were a lady in a ballgown and I found this staircase, I wouldn't touch it with a ten-foot pole," Elyse said, shaking her head. "The dust in the corners would get on the dress, and there isn't much light. It's obvious that this is not a place for entertaining."

"I see your point," Tommy agreed. "But it's perfect for exploring!"

Although the staircase continued past the first door they reached, they agreed that this must be one floor down, and they opened the narrow wooden door.

The room contained masses of shelving piled high with books

and scrolls. At the far end of the room there were two desks, each with a person bent over paper.

"Hello," Tommy said from the doorway, not wanting to startle them by getting too close.

Both heads lifted, and they could see that one was an old man, and the other was not much older than they were.

The old man shook his head when they asked about the Icaryoe. "I can show you where the chests were kept, but they were stolen a little over a week ago."

"Stolen?" Carter said, eyebrows rising in surprise. "How?"

"Lots of scholars come and go through here," the man said, waving his hand in the air. "We don't watch them all. Besides, who would want to recombine one of the Great Beasts?"

"You do realize that's exactly what happened, right?" Greg said scathingly.

"Of course I do. I've got ears, boy." The man shuffled slowly over to a stone wall and turned a brazier. The wall slid open, revealing a large room. There were six equidistant niches around the room, all of which were empty.

"Is there another entrance to this room?" Tommy asked. "How many people know how to get in here?"

"No other entrances." The man shuffled into the room and clapped his hands. Lights began to glow, making them squint their eyes at the sudden change. "This room is common knowledge. Who would want to recombine—"

"The Great Beasts. Yeah, you said that already," Greg said, rolling his eyes.

"Somebody came in here and managed to sneak out six large chests? How is that possible?" Tommy asked.

The old man stared at him for so long that Tommy started to wonder what he had said wrong. "You're not from around here, are you? They used magic, of course. A pocket dimension would work well, although expensive to purchase. And once inside, of course, the pieces of the Icaryoe would be close enough to each other to break through the protective shielding engraved on the chests and recombine. Then it would only be a matter of time before it exploded from the pocket dimension.”

“You've thought about this a lot. I'm impressed,” Carter said, and the old man seemed to puff up with pride. “Did you happen to hear where the Icaryoe was first seen?”

“At the university, of course,” the man replied.

The teenagers exchanged glances.

“Thank you for showing us this room,” Carter said.

“Well, that was a colossal waste of time,” Greg said once they were back on the streets.

“Now we know the Icaryoe was stolen,” Tommy pointed out. “Why would someone want to recombine it?”

“Reward money?” Elyse suggested.

They were all silent for a moment.

“Standard greed? I can see that happening,” Tommy said sadly.

“Back to the university we go,” Carter said with a sigh.

Chapter 16

They found Todd hanging strings of white lights in the same building as before and followed his lead until the sun peeked over the horizon.

"Do you ever go home?" Carter asked Todd, passing him the last decorative garland.

Todd laughed and climbed down the ladder. "I'll be heading home in about an hour, after breakfast. Join me?"

Carter's stomach rumbled loudly. They'd been up for well over six hours at this point. "Yes, please!"

The cafeteria staff had laid out a buffet feast full of freshly made bread, cooked meats, and cut fruit. Carter had no idea what most things were, so he grabbed a plate and took one of everything.

"The fruit is fresh from the Ruby Isles and Lefrane," Todd told them. "Came in on the most recent shipments."

"It's pretty cool that there's instantaneous transport between locations," Greg said. "Like, hey, I need a weekend getaway, I'll just pop over to that Dome with the beaches—"

"Ruby Isles," Carter supplied.

"Right, the Ruby Isles, and relax for the weekend, and then head right back to work, no flights, not much jet lag. Must be nice," Greg finished with a sigh.

Todd regarded him thoughtfully. "Do you know how Everdome came to exist?"

Greg scoffed. "Didn't it form the same way every other planet did, with pressure and gravitational forces? I mean, it's weird that it's all in pieces like it is, but every planet's different, right?"

"Come and sit, and I'll explain what Cataclysm Day means to us." Todd led them to a table set a little farther away from the others, and once they were all settled, he started his tale.

"The stories vary from region and people, but they all have a few things in common. The main one is that the planet, then called Everworld, was created by the old gods and that they had made it wrong. It was unstable and on the brink of falling apart. They used all their power to contain the destruction for so long that it built up, like steam in a boiler. Instead of falling apart over thousands of years, it was set to explode, killing everything.

"The last hope of Everworld was ten-year-old twin boys. Elric and Demetrius had incredible magical potential, and the gods saw in them the hope for our world. When they used their power to contain the inevitable explosion, it left them both powerless and signed their death warrant. With no other choice, and as gods are wont to do, they entrusted the fate of us all to two children. To Elric, they taught the spell needed to create the Domes. To Demetrius, they taught the spell to bind destructive energy into an object.

"The boys worked with the wizards of the time, and when the Cataclysm inevitably came; their combined knowledge saved our world but fragmented it in the process.

"It was the hope and strength of two children that saved us all. Cataclysm Day is the day we remember them and the sacrifices that all of Everworld made to ensure something survived."

Carter knew most of the story from the books, but to hear it told by someone from Everdome itself, whose ancestors had lived through it thirteen centuries before, was illuminating. It felt more real this way, and he could hear the pain in Todd's voice at the losses that Everworld had suffered so that Everdome could survive.

"I'm sorry," Greg said quietly. "I had no idea."

"It's alright. You're from another place." Todd started eating.

"We honour them tomorrow, December twenty-seventh, and then the following four days are days of celebration before the new year."

"How do you honour them?" Tommy asked. "Is there something special that you do?"

"Just before sunset, we come together as communities and light candles. Someone tells the story of the Cataclysm, or it's enacted by kids. When the sun sets, we blow out our candles and stand in the darkness for a minute of silence, during which we think about the story and are grateful for our blessings. Then someone lights the first candle, and each person lights their candle from their neighbour's candle until everything is bright again. We sing traditional songs during the re-lighting, which symbolizes the birth of Everdome." Todd smiled. "We gather as a community for a late dinner and exchange gifts with family and friends at that time. The king, or lord depending on the community, presides over the dinner and thanks us all for our work during the past year."

"That sounds really lovely," Elyse said. "Does the dinner take place at the castle?"

"No, the castle isn't big enough." Todd shook his head. "It takes place here at the university. These walls open, and there are two more rooms the same size as this to accommodate everyone. Are you interested in sticking around, or are you heading back to Wild Nations right away?"

Carter looked around the table at his friends. "Personally, I'd like to stay. Es'Sem *did* tell us to join the celebrations."

Tommy nodded eagerly. "I would love to stay. It would feel strange to celebrate something in December and there not be snow."

"Does it snow where you live?" Todd asked, leaning forward in interest.

"Oh yeah, up to my knees in February sometimes," Greg put in with a chuckle.

"Oh my gosh!" Elyse said, putting her hand on Greg's arm in

her excitement. "Don't you remember that one snowstorm this past February?" She turned to Todd. "Overnight, we got so much snow that the plows couldn't take care of it, so the streets and sidewalks were covered in the morning. I tried to walk to school the way I usually do, with snow pants on, of course, but I got to the end of my street and just couldn't do it! The snow came up to my *hips*! It was as if I was swimming, but with gravity holding me down, it was so exhausting. I sat in the snow until I got my energy back, and then I went home, and it was just as difficult because all my steps had been snowed in during my break!" She laughed. "I helped my parents shovel the driveway while we waited for the plows to do the streets. I made it to school after lunch."

"I remember that day really well," Carter put in. "I had a test in science that morning, and I was panicking because even though I only had three blocks to walk, I just couldn't manage it in time. I got to school halfway through first period, and I was the only person who had managed to show up! The test was postponed until two days later so that everyone had warning." He watched Greg's flushed face carefully. Elyse had yet to move her hand, and Greg was trying not to draw attention to it while maintaining his cool.

Greg coughed slightly. "Yes, I remember. I looked out my window and didn't even bother getting dressed. I just went back to bed."

Tommy laughed. "I would do the same thing, but our plows are generally equipped to deal with that much snow in a short time."

"Why?" Todd furrowed his brow. "You all know each other. Aren't you two together?" He indicated Carter and Tommy.

"Oh, we are together, but I don't live in the same area as them. My area gets a lot of lake-effect snow. That means a *lot* of snow in a short period of time is common. So, my bus would be a little late because I live out in the country, but it would still be running." Tommy grinned at Carter. "You city kids just don't know how to deal with snow."

Carter squeezed his hand gently.

"Well," Todd said, putting his fork down. "If you kids are staying for the celebrations, you need some place to sleep. How about the dorms?"

"That would be great!" Carter said. "How much are they per night?"

Todd gave him a quizzical look. "You don't pay to stay here. And even if they did charge, you wouldn't be, seeing as you're a knight."

"Oh." Carter felt his cheeks heat in embarrassment. "Thank you very much." He gazed wistfully at his empty plate. With all the conversation and how hungry he had been, he'd barely tasted his food.

"Not a problem. I'll lead you over to the main lobby and get you checked in. Then I recommend you check out the markets. You would appreciate some sweaters and thicker pants than what you've got on. Don't worry about the coats and boots. They're yours for as long as you need them." Todd grinned at their appreciative thanks, showed them where to place their dirty dishes, and led them down a couple buildings to the dorms. "Do you kids have any money?"

After they reassured him that Es'Sem had given them money and discovered that the money bags contained more than they looked like they should, Todd left them, striding down the street and whistling a merry tune.

They left their bags in their rooms, Elyse and Greg in singles and Tommy and Carter sharing a double, and headed for the nearest market.

The sun had fully risen. Tène was bustling with people decorating the buildings both inside and out. Shoppers carrying multiple bags stomped cheerfully through the snow, greeting each other happily.

They found a clothing store easily. The sweaters were the softest material that Carter had ever felt, and he realized that the yarn must come from the animals of Gaulan. "I wonder if there are textile workshops in Gaulan as well as the livestock business?" he whispered to Tommy as they wandered the aisles, looking for sweaters that appealed to them.

"It would make sense to have them here, wouldn't it?" Tommy replied. "Oh, look at that one. You look so good in orange."

"You need to get that green one, then." Carter indicated a sweater next to them.

Elyse had found an oversized red tunic sweater for herself, and Greg bought a thick black one with a high neck.

The next store had lined pants. They chose quickly, excited to move on to buying presents for each other.

They split into pairs, because they didn't think it was a good idea to separate completely, and Carter wandered the market hand-in-hand with Tommy, debating with him over whether Greg would appreciate a pocketknife or a scarf more.

When he spotted a health store like the one they had bought their soap at in Wild Nations, he paused, drawing Tommy out of the flow of pedestrian traffic. "I have a thought," Carter said, nodding his head at the store. "Remember that bottle of lube?"

Tommy blushed but smiled. "Honestly, I haven't been able to stop thinking about it."

"Me too." Carter bit his lip. "Should we maybe consider picking some up?"

"I'd like that, as long as you're okay with it." Tommy ducked his head, staring at his feet. "I guess you wouldn't have brought it up if you weren't."

"I am more than okay." Carter swallowed hard. "No pressure, yeah? Just because we have it doesn't mean we have to use it."

Tommy looked up at him and grinned. "Okay." He stepped closer, slipping his cold hands into Carter's warm ones. "I love you," he whispered.

Carter's heart skipped a beat. He pressed their foreheads together. "I love you, too." After a moment of intense eye contact, he reluctantly pulled away. "We need to get presents. Also, do you think they have condoms here?"

"Maybe not latex, but we can ask," Tommy said with a chuckle.

They made the rest of their purchases, finding a delicately woven leatherwork wall hanging and a set of winter gear in a pretty shade of red for Elyse and agreeing to get Greg a pocketknife, a black scarf, and a black leather jacket to replace his purple one since he didn't seem keen on staying with the Blue Bloods.

They met back up with the others for lunch, ordering several platters to share amongst them, including an egg dish that they all agreed was like quiche and a meat and pastry dish that Greg insisted was like Beef Wellington, but Elyse argued was more like Boeuf Bourguignon pot pie.

"I mean it's got spices kinda like tourtière, too," Carter said as they ate. "But does it really matter? It's delicious."

"I want to bring back recipes from every Dome for Jason to recreate," Tommy said. "It would be a great Christmas present."

Carter's mouth hung open. "Can I get in on that gift? It's perfect!"

"Why is it perfect?" Greg asked. "I get that your brother-in-law is super into Everdome, but why recipes?"

Tommy laughed. "I guess I haven't mentioned that he's the owner of a restaurant." To Carter, he added, "We should try to buy some spices for him, too. The ones that he won't be able to get back home. And maybe some seeds of the more unusual plants for Kennedy to grow at the ARC. She's an agricultural scientist," he explained to Greg, "so she'll know which ones will be safe to plant on Earth and won't take over everything."

"That is a fantastic idea!" Carter agreed enthusiastically. "We should pop over to Lefrane and get the seeds after the holiday."

"—thank Goddess for King Todric, or else we'd be going hungry this season!" a boisterous voice was so loud that it interrupted their conversation. As if by silent agreement, the four teenagers stopped talking to listen.

"Lord Bourges hasn't been paying *any* of his workers?" another man questioned the first.

"Not a single coin. Rumour has it that he has run out of money."

"How does a lord run out of money?"

"Frivolous spending, in my opinion. Too many parties and not enough investments. But I'm not a lord, and for good reason!" The first man laughed too loudly at his joke.

"Do you know, I saw Lord Bourges here in Tène the other week, acting all suspicious-like. Do you suppose he purposefully recombined the Icaryoe so that he could gain the reward money?"

Carter whipped around to look at the two men.

"Hush, don't you know it's treason to talk like that?" the other man hissed, looking furtively around the pub. He caught Carter's eye and flinched.

Carter leaned over the back of his chair and tapped the bigger man's shoulder to get his attention. "Hey, about the Icaryoe," he began, and the men turned to look at them. "Isn't it super easy for it to recombine?"

The bigger man shook his head. "Not as far as I know. The Beasts have never broken out of containment and spontaneously recombined before. The Kings of Gaulan have been looking after the remains of the Icaryoe since it was defeated. Something had to have happened for it to break out so suddenly. Why so curious, youngster?"

"He's one of the knights who were recalled to destroy the Icaryoe," Elyse told them.

The men stared at Carter and then burst into laughter.

"You? You're a knight? You're a scrawny little kid! Now I've seen everything," they said between their guffaws.

Carter rolled his eyes at Elyse, who winced. *Sorry,* she thought to him. *I forgot you wanted to keep a low profile.*

It's okay. It'll only be a problem if— He cut himself off as Greg stood up and crossed his arms defensively.

"He is a knight, and he'll prove it!" Greg said loudly.

Carter sighed. *And there's the problem.* "There is no need for me to prove anything to these people. Let's just enjoy our lunch and then maybe take a nap. We've been up for way too long already today."

"A test of strength?" the first man suggested to Greg.

"Do you have arm wrestling here?" Greg asked.

"Come on—" Carter started to say.

"I'll arm wrestle this youngster." The first man was bigger than the second. He flexed his arm muscles in front of the crowd that was gathering.

"Oh boy," Carter muttered under his breath. Louder, he said, "Really, I have nothing to prove to you. You don't have to believe that I'm a knight."

"Caught in a lie, are you?" The big man sneered. "Come on, little fella. Just say you're lying, and I'll ignore the whole thing."

"Leave him alone!" Elyse shouted defiantly.

"Yeah," Greg added. "He just doesn't want to embarrass you."

"Embarrass me?" The big man was getting angry now. He stood up, towering over Greg, who was large to begin with. "I lift heavy cargo all day long. There's no way I would lose to a twig like him."

"You aren't going to let this go, are you?" Carter said as he got to his feet. "Greg, sit down." He gave the boy a push toward his seat. He looked up at the man. "What would be adequate proof of my knighthood for you, since the ring of Gaulan isn't enough?"

Several of the bystanders looked taken aback at the ring Carter showed them, but the big man laughed, the smell of alcohol on his breath making Carter wince.

"An arm wrestle will do. If you can prove you're stronger than me, that will satisfy me." The man clapped a heavy hand on Carter's back, and he let himself be steered toward a table in the centre of the pub.

"All I wanted to know was more about the rumours around the Icaryoe," Carter said, sitting down at the table and rolling up his sleeves. "I would just like to state for the record that being drunk is not a good excuse when you lose."

"I am not drunk!" the man exclaimed loudly and put out his right hand.

You're going to wish you hadn't said that, Carter thought to himself. "No magic, only our strength."

"Pah! I don't need to cheat to win. Is there someone who can see magic here?"

When a wizened old woman came forward, the man nodded at her. "Make sure magic isn't used to win," he said rudely.

"Thank you," Carter said to her. He traded his knight's ring for Tommy's bracelet so he could still understand. "This is just the normal translation bracelet we were given at the university," he clarified, and the man nodded his acceptance. They joined hands.

The woman counted down from three, and then Carter started to press down. He appreciated that the man hadn't tried to start early and was obviously overconfident, but Carter's continued push didn't waver. The man's eyes widened as he realized he was going to lose.

"Do you believe me now, or do I have to win?" Carter said quietly, no strain in his voice.

"You're using magic! There's no way you can be this strong!" the man shouted, every word a fight to get out.

The old woman shook her head. "No magic is on this young man or yourself."

Carter paused an inch away from winning. "Do you yield?"

"Never!" The man's bicep bulged.

"One of your joints is locked," Carter said calmly. "I can feel the resistance. If I keep pushing, you're going to dislocate something."

"It's a trick! I'm fine!"

Carter sighed and rolled his eyes. "If you lift things for a living, you don't want a dislocation to prevent you from working."

The big man only sneered at Carter.

Ugh, why can't people just use their common sense? Carter thought to himself. He relaxed his arm muscles, letting the other take control. The joint finally unlocked when Carter's arm was past halfway, and he re-engaged his muscles.

The big man, who had been gloating over his inevitable win, fell silent.

"Your joint is fine now. I can win this in one motion. Or you can accept defeat," Carter said. The man strained to push him down, but Carter barely felt it. "I'm going to count to three. One, two..." He paused, hoping the man would stop this. "Three." In a fluid motion, Carter whipped his arm in an arc to bring the big man's hand down on the table, controlling his strength at the last second to not damage the other's hand.

The man released him reflexively, jaw hanging open.

Carter stood up, the legs of his chair squeaking loudly in the silence of the room. "I'm glad you didn't hurt yourself," he said, patting the man on his shoulder as he passed. "Thanks for the tip about the lord." He sat down at his table and took a bite of his lunch. "What?" he said to his friends, who were staring at him. "You knew I was going to win." He couldn't read the expression in Tommy's eyes. Carter's stomach swooped; was his strength too much for his boyfriend?

"Excuse me, Sir Knight?" a sultry woman's voice said, and Carter felt a hand trace along his shoulders. "Might I get your name?"

"I'm spoken for," Carter said, not even looking up from his dish.

"By whom? This *little* girl? I assure you, I'm more woman than she'll ever be."

"Wow, that's insulting," Tommy snarled, batting the hand away from Carter's shoulder. "And he's *mine*, so back off."

"Prove it," the woman said harshly.

"Oh my God," Carter muttered. "Is everyone done eating? I'm ready to leave."

The man who had served them hurried over. "On behalf of this establishment, your food is on the house, for the inconveniences you've suffered."

Carter waved his words away. "If you wish to make it up to us, we would appreciate the recipes for the two dishes we ate today. We'll be back tonight to pick them up." He pressed coins into the man's hand, enough to cover the meal and a tip, even though he wasn't sure if tipping was done here. "And in the future, maybe step in earlier to prevent this sort of thing from happening again." He stood, taking Tommy's hand tentatively. He was relieved that the returning grip was firm. Together, they brushed past the young woman who had been propositioning him. *She has pretty features,* he thought, *but she doesn't hold a candle to Tommy.* "Better luck with a different knight," he said to her.

Once they were outside, they huddled together against the wind.

"What was that all about?" Carter demanded of Greg, who looked mildly ashamed.

"He was making fun of you," Greg said defensively.

"I can take a little teasing. He would have gotten bored quickly." Carter sighed. "Instead, we made a fuss, and now people are going to remember us."

"I hate to break it to you, but you're incredibly memorable," Tommy said with a smirk.

"You're heavily biased," Elyse said, shoulder bumping Tommy. "What's the plan for this afternoon?" She yawned.

"I was thinking a nap," Carter replied. "I found gifts for the rest of you before lunch, so I don't need to shop any more. I'm exhausted from our early morning. Jet lag is real, even if there aren't any jets."

"After dinner, we should ask around, find out where Lord Bourges lives and how to get there," Tommy suggested. "Hopefully, we can make it there and back after Cataclysm Day."

"Agreed," Elyse said. "Shall we?"

They returned to their rooms. Carter was finally alone with the one person he wanted to speak to the most, and yet he found himself at a loss for words.

"Are you okay?" Tommy asked, rubbing a hand along Carter's back. "You've been pretty quiet."

"You're not afraid of me?" Carter whispered, looking at his boyfriend's dark grey socks.

"No," Tommy replied flatly. "You know why?" He tipped Carter's head up by his chin. "Because I trust you."

Carter searched the green eyes staring back at him. "I could break you in half," he murmured.

Tommy smirked. "You know what that means, don't you?"

It took a moment for Carter to catch up and then he flushed. "That's not what I meant, and you know it."

Shaking his head, Tommy reassured him, "I knew how strong you were before today. Nothing has changed, except I'm never going to watch arm wrestling without getting a little lightheaded." He tossed the bottle and packets on the bed and stripped off his shirt. "Come on, let's have a shower. See where things go from there."

Carter bit his lip as he trailed a finger over Tommy's bicep and down to his pectoral. "I want to be with you."

"You are." Tommy pressed Carter's hand over his heart. "I'm here."

Carter curled his fingers slightly, feeling the soft give of Tommy's tanned skin and the *thump-thumping* of his pulse beneath. "Okay."

"No pressure," Tommy breathed, moving in close and brushing their noses together.

"We'll see how this goes," Carter murmured in reply. He tilted his head and pressed their lips together. "Tommy?" he gasped, his knees feeling weak.

"I've got you." Tommy held him tighter as their kiss grew in intensity.

I love you, Carter thought to him, but there was no response in his mind. It didn't bother him too much. He knew Jason and Kennedy hadn't been able to mindspeak until just before their wedding. *We've got time.*

Chapter 17

FRIDAY THE 28TH OF DECEMBER, 1290 POST-CATACLYSM - GAULAN

I'm on a train! Tommy was almost giddy with excitement. Their little group was in a private room in one of the train cars, their faces pressed against the glass as they watched the countryside fly by. "I've never been on a train before," Tommy admitted to the others.

"Neither have I," everyone chorused, and then they all chuckled.

This particular train was powered by magic. The conductor had kindly showed them how it worked when they'd first boarded. The train was powered by a wind spell on a white gem. When it was activated, the wind filled the square sail at the nose of the train, which pulled the rest of the cars along behind it.

The slight rocking motion of the cars as they clicked along over the tracks was soothing, but all four teens were too excited to rest.

The day prior had been Cataclysm Day, and they had spent it at the university, helping various crews to get ready for the evening's ceremony. Gifts weren't exchanged until afterwards, so they left their presents for each other in their rooms.

They had looked for Todd but were told that he was getting ready for the ceremony.

Tommy chuckled out loud, making the others turn to him. "Do you remember how you felt when we first saw Todd yesterday?"

Greg rolled his eyes. "You mean *King Todric*? I almost fell off my chair."

"He looked so magnificent in his ceremonial robes," Elyse said dreamily. "That cape! And the jewels in his crown!"

"He must have had his reasons for not telling us," Carter said. "He obviously is very hands-on with his people. I like that. I'm proud to be one of his knights."

"But it was a girl who won in the show in Toronto," Elyse pointed out. "When you got your ring. The show must not be canon regarding names."

"I wondered about that," Tommy said. "I asked someone if Todd was native to Gaulan. He is. His family's been the royal family for generations. I guess the show made up the story."

"That makes sense," Carter said. "It would be easier to change things up if it's a completely made-up story."

"High King Pincas is a real person, though," Tommy added. "Es'Sem must have visited Earth recently, if someone was portraying him at the dinner theatre show in Toronto."

"Too bad we can't ask her," Greg said. "She probably doesn't remember."

The others chuckled a little at that.

"Just because it was recently in Earth time, doesn't mean it was recently in Everdome time," Elyse reminded them.

"I should try to work on the song," Tommy said with a sigh. "I've got a bit down, but it needs a lot of work."

"What's it about?" Elyse asked, leaning over to look at the folded paper Tommy pulled out of his pocket.

"The Phantom and the Wraith," Tommy said, putting his hand over it to prevent her from picking it up. "It's not finished. You can't look at it yet."

"Why them?" Greg asked, his nose wrinkled.

"Because they're unique to our world and the comics are awesome," Tommy said blithely. "Plus, people love a love story. Added to them being superheroes? This song will be remembered." He grinned. "To have a song pop up about them in Everdome will be anachronistic."

"Like 'Carol of the Bells' at the Cataclysm Day ceremony

yesterday," Carter said with a chuckle. "Wanna bet that's Es'Sem's favourite Christmas carol?"

Elyse laughed. "No bet!"

"You have to make it easy to remember, easy to play, and catchy," Greg said, bringing the subject back to Tommy's song.

"Yeah, I know. Like I said, I'm working on it," Tommy grumbled, fiddling with a pencil-like writing implement. "I only started last night."

"Why last night?" Elyse asked. "I thought you were going to write one when we first got here."

"I was going to just give the wedding song to Pieter the next time we saw him," Tommy said. He hesitated.

Carter added, "But then Es'Sem gave him a guitar for Cataclysm Day. And ideas started flowing."

"Yeah, that," Tommy said sheepishly.

They had been surprised upon returning to the dorms after the Cataclysm Day dinner to find packages waiting for them, each with a scrawled message; *May your fractured nights be followed by glorious dawns.* Es'Sem gave them each a present. Tommy's was a beautiful guitar made from a soft wood stained a deep bluc. The fretboard was black with each fret a silver metal. The strings almost glowed blue. It came with a matching soft leather case that could be worn on his back with his initials engraved in the same metal as the strings. Under the fretboard, in the case, was a compartment with a sleek metallic blue capo and a wide, braided leather strap that was the same colour as the strings.

Carter received a cross-body leather knife holster with two throwing knives, Elyse got a rope dart, and Greg opened his small package to find hand wraps of a light, breathable fabric.

"And then he started writing before I pulled him to bed," Carter said.

"Oh, really?" Greg smirked.

"To *sleep*," Tommy clarified, rolling his eyes. "We had an early start this morning." He exchanged glances with Carter, noting the light blush high on his cheekbones that matched the burning he felt on his own.

"Uh huh." Elyse didn't sound convinced, but she left it at that.

Tommy tuned out his friends and focussed on the paper in front of him. The last few lines made him think about how Carter had finally managed to distract him the night before. He clenched his fists and closed his eyes. It didn't help. He stood up and grabbed the song. "I'm going to take a walk. It's not fair to you to ask you to be quiet just because I can't focus."

He closed the door with a quiet *snick* behind him and let out a sigh. He met Carter's concerned eyes through the window of the door and offered a small smile in return.

He paced the length of the car twice before he finally felt calm enough to look at the lyrics he had written so far.

More ideas came to him, and he scribbled them down, leaning against the outside wall of the train. He rearranged some lines and counted syllables before reading it over from the beginning.

One of the private room doors opened, and Carter walked out, looking around. His posture relaxed when he saw Tommy, and he closed the door behind him. "It had been a while since I saw you walk in front of the door," he said once he got close enough. "I was worried."

"Sorry. I finished the song," Tommy said happily, waving the paper in his hand. "Now I just need to figure out the music."

Carter shook his head, a small smile on his lips. "I don't know how you do it."

"Well, it's a little easier without distractions," Tommy said playfully.

"Alright. I won't distract you anymore," Carter teased.

"Don't you dare stop!" Tommy said, stuffing the folded paper in his pocket. "I need breaks, too. Like right now, for example." He grabbed Carter's hand and tugged lightly. "There's a bathroom this way."

A sly grin bloomed on Carter's face. "Why Mister Fairfield, are you proposing we have sex in a bathroom?"

"I might be. Is that something you'd be interested in?" Tommy said, feeling bolder now that Carter was giving him that look, the one that meant he was mentally undressing him and wanted to do it in reality.

"Where is it?" Carter demanded eagerly, heading off down the corridor in the direction Tommy indicated. When he reached the bathroom, he whipped open the door.

Tommy pushed him in, crowding after him and pressing him against the counter.

There was a charged moment between them as they stood sharing breath, swaying with the motion of the train. Carter nudged his nose against Tommy's, tilting his head just enough to bring their lips together.

Tommy let him take the lead in the kiss, tongues stroking and dancing together, only for Carter to pull just far enough away to bite Tommy's bottom lip gently. Tommy slipped his hands under Carter's new sweater, working it up and over his boyfriend's head, careful to avoid catching on the silver chain around his neck. They had gifted each other silver box chain necklaces for Cataclysm Day the day before. Tommy admired the silver against his boyfriend's skin for a moment, touching it gently, before dropping the sweater on the counter beside them. His arms were practically vibrating, and his legs felt like jelly, and there was nowhere else he'd rather be.

Later, they returned to the private room a little rumpled but satisfied.

"Was he that *hard* to find, then?" Greg asked, raising one eyebrow.

"Nah, we just didn't want to bother you two with all our steamy kissing," Tommy said with a chuckle.

"Ugh, you two are the worst," Elyse groaned, rolling her eyes.

"Oh, I'm sorry, we didn't mean to take away your entertainment." Carter picked up the teasing where Tommy left off. "We all know Greg wants to know more about our relationship, but I didn't think you were into that."

"That's—That was before!" Greg protested. "Your business is your business."

Tommy relented. "It's okay. I get that you were trying to be all tough and macho."

Greg spluttered but didn't say anything, and Tommy grinned.

He pulled out his new guitar and strummed it thoughtfully. "This is a beautiful instrument," he said softly. "Listen to that sound!" He played over a few chords, enjoying the way they resonated through the small room. "Alright, let's see if I can figure out some chords before we get to Bourges." He pulled the song out of his pocket, flattening it on the seat next to him, and began to play.

By the time the train pulled into the station, Tommy felt confident with what he'd accomplished.

"Did you seriously just write a song in less than a day?" Greg asked when they were on the platform, a combination of awe and annoyance in his voice.

Tommy scrunched up his face. "I guess so? I mean, I didn't have a professional look it over first. That usually takes the most time. And sometimes it just... Flows. I don't know. It's not always that easy."

Carter chuckled. "You've written how many songs now?"

"Three." Tommy flushed. He knew where Carter was going with this line of questioning.

"And how long did the first one take?"

"Half an hour, but the rhymes are repetitive, and the lines don't have the same number of syllables—" Tommy stopped at Carter's raised hand.

"And the second one?"

"I wrote the lyrics in about fifteen minutes, but then my music teacher gave me feedback and I fixed things up..."

Carter was smirking at him. "And then you figured out the chords over a video call with me in, what, five minutes?"

"Yeah," Tommy whispered.

"What I'm getting from that is that this song actually took you a long time, by your standards," Elyse teased.

"Stop it," Tommy said, blushing. "We should probably find out when the return train arrives."

Carter slipped an arm around Tommy's neck, avoiding the guitar case on his back. "And then we'll get directions to the lord's house."

According to the chart on the wall, the return train would arrive in four hours, giving them plenty of time to explore the town.

When they found someone to ask for directions, they were greeted with a scoff. "Look for the most ostentatious house, and you've found it." The man immediately turned away.

"Okaaaaaay," Greg drawled. He shrugged. "If it's that easy, let's give it a shot."

Bourges was a small town set at the foot of a mountain range at the edge of the Dome. Where the mountain ended, the forest began, spreading out like the train of Kennedy's wedding dress. Right beside the station was a massive building with many large crates between them. The rest of the town, the houses, restaurants, shops, and other buildings, slowly sloped upward on the mountain. The highest house was large enough that they could see it clearly, even from a distance.

"Wanna bet that's it?" Tommy asked, nodding his head at it.

"No bet," chorused the others, grinning at each other.

"I guess we'd better start climbing," Carter said.

The walk through the town was lovely. Flowers were starting to bloom in gardens, and there was almost no snow. The teenagers shed their coats after a couple streets and carried them.

"I wonder why Tène is in the middle of winter, but Bourges feels like spring," Carter said as they passed yet another blooming tree. "I'm starting to regret wearing my new winter clothing."

"I think it has something to do with how close it is to the edge of the Dome," Greg pointed out. "Kinda like how Victoria, BC is on the edge of the Pacific current, so spring arrives in February."

"I see what you mean," Elyse said, staring at the Dome. "The sun's rays would refract more closely together here, making the edge warmer than the middle."

"Look!" Tommy said suddenly as they turned a corner, and everyone gazed back toward the train station. In the sky beyond it, another Dome was rising on the horizon, much closer than they'd ever seen.

He watched in awe, and partially in horror, because seeing something that huge in the sky was more than a little jarring, as the other Dome rose. Soon, they could see what it contained. Water.

"Is that... the ocean?" Tommy gasped. The angle of the other Dome didn't align with theirs, making it look like the water was going to spill out onto them. "That is so weird!"

"We should probably move away from the middle of the street," Elyse said, nudging the others. "And keep walking?"

"Right." With great reluctance, Tommy tore his gaze away from the sky and back to the ground. "That's one way to remind me we're not at home. Jeepers!"

They continued on their way, looking back occasionally to watch the Dome rise higher and show more of the depths each time.

"I wonder if people use telescopes to look at other Domes," Greg said.

"That would be a fascinating way to study deep sea fish," Carter agreed.

They unexpectedly found themselves in front of the highest house after one last curve of the road. By this time, the other Dome was almost directly overhead, casting a shadow that stretched as far as they could see. The streetlights flickered to life, even though it wasn't quite noon yet.

The house itself was a large wooden structure, heavily adorned with wrought iron decorative pieces. There was a cream-coloured wall of marble that surrounded it, with a fancy iron gate in the middle.

"None of the other houses had walls," Elyse whispered. "And it seems silly to have one so close to the mountain behind it. Even *I* could scale it, with a little help."

Tommy shrugged. "A show of wealth doesn't make sense." He pointed up at one of the towers. "See how that roof is rounded? It wouldn't surprise me to find that he has an observatory there, even though a public one for everyone to use would be more functional." He poked a button on the side of the wall. "Anyway, let's see if he's home."

The sound of the chime echoed through the walled courtyard. When they were about to ring again, hurried steps approached the gate from inside the wall, and a middle-aged woman appeared.

"Hello—" Tommy began, but she interrupted him.

"Lord Bourges is not at home," she said quickly. "Please go away." She turned to leave.

"Wait!" Carter called out to her. "We've travelled from Tène to speak with him. Can you tell us when he'll be back?"

She shook her head and glanced above the house at the Dome. "He's hunting the Icaryoe along with all the other knights."

"Really?" Tommy said, pretending to be awed. "He was one of the people summoned to Tène by the Sisters last week?"

"No, he was already in Tène. He had a meeting at the university with a professor." The woman wrung her hands together.

"Oh, so he must have returned right after that to collect his weaponry," Carter said brightly.

"No, he brought his lance with him."

"To see a professor?" Greg said skeptically. "Is that common here?"

"Well, his lance is specially made. It can change shape to that of a pen, so it's easily transportable." The woman stuck her hands in the pockets of her skirt. "If that's everything?"

"Do you happen to know the name of the professor he was meeting?" Elyse asked.

"No." The woman turned and walked away.

"Thank you for your time!" Tommy called after her.

"So he was already in Tène," Carter mused.

Elyse added, "And he was at the university."

"*With* his weapon." Greg scratched his chin. "Did she seem off to you?"

"Nervous and not very polite?" Tommy nodded. "Shall we get lunch? I think I noticed a little place just before the other Dome showed up."

"I think that's the Ruby Isles," Carter said. "I don't know of any other Dome with so much water."

"Ohana?" Elyse suggested.

"Hmm, maybe," Tommy replied. "I bet we could ask someone, and they'd know. This can't be the first time this has happened, or else a lot more people would be out here watching."

By the time they made their way back down the mountain to the restaurant Tommy had seen, the Dome had mostly passed over them, and the streetlights had turned off.

They were informed that it was, in fact, the Ruby Isles, and it orbited around them about once a week, depending on where the other Domes were and how much their gravity affected them both. The Ruby Isles had set behind the mountain range when they made their way back to the station.

They sank gratefully into the private room on the train.

"Should we try to find the professor as soon as we get back?" Tommy asked.

"It could take us ages. The university's huge," Greg pointed out.

"Maybe we should ask Todd for help. He knows everyone," Carter suggested. He stretched his arms over his head and draped one around Tommy's shoulders.

"Smooth move, loverboy," Elyse teased.

"Very smooth, and I wish I could cuddle up, but I should really practise some more," Tommy said regretfully.

"Can you play for four hours straight?" Carter asked mildly. When Tommy shook his head, Carter tugged him closer. "Relax for a bit first and then you can practise. You don't want to give yourself blisters or wear out your voice before your performance, do you?"

"That's true. This way you can help me memorize the lyrics!" Tommy pulled the paper out of his pocket and snuggled into his boyfriend's embrace.

"If we must," Elyse said with a sigh and a smirk.

Chapter 18

MONDAY THE 31ST OF DECEMBER, 1290 POST-CATACLYSM - TÈNE, GAULAN

The lead on the professor had proven fruitless; he had died in the initial Icaryoe attack.

The quartet had spent the last few days exploring Tène and Pakaha City, especially around the various portals and train stations, hoping to hear news of the Icaryoe's whereabouts. But the Beast had vanished.

It was now New Year's Eve.

Carter anxiously wiped the palms of his hands on his pants and glanced at the clock on the wall. Tommy was going on stage in less than five minutes. Carter wished he could be backstage with him but knew that he'd only be a distraction.

"We have one last song for you before we ring in the new year," the lead vocalist of the band playing in the great hall of Tène Castle said to the cheering crowd. "It was written by Tommy Fairfield, and it's a love song about two mythical superheroes, the Phantom and the Wraith. We fell in love with it the first time we heard it, and I know you will too. Put your hands together for Tommy!" He gestured backstage, and Tommy, pale and obviously nervous, stepped out.

The noise level in the hall increased, the cheers ringing through the large room.

Tommy cleared his throat and stepped up to the microphone set up for him. "Happy New Year to Gaulan!" he said, and the crowd applauded. "May 1291 bring us home."

He struck the first chords, and Carter stared, amazed; the instrument sounded as loud as if it was right next to him. The lead guitarist of the band, who had been preparing to give Tommy a magical amplification device like a microphone for his guitar, shrugged and nodded before joining in as backup.

The hero of Westmeath searches,
Desperate and alone,
Using the power of shadows,
Leaving no unturned stone.

Ooo-ooo-oooooo the heroes of Westmeath,
The Phantom and the Wraith!

His people keep being taken,
No one seems to notice,
Every clue, a new dead end,
He cannot lose focus.

He tracks them to a run-down house,
When a green glow appears,
The hero walks toward the wraith,
Calmly despite his fears.

Ooo-ooo-oooooo the heroes of Westmeath,
The Phantom and the Wraith!

"You are seeking them, too," she said,
A finger at her lips,
"They took my friends, we must save them!"
"And who are you?" he quips.

"No time to talk, they're coming now."
She ducked behind a shed.
The hero hid in the shadows,
And watched where they were led.

Ooo-ooo-oooooo the heroes of Westmeath,
The Phantom and the Wraith!

"They're being shipped out, I've got this."
He went to make his move.
"I've got an idea," she said.
"I'm sure you will approve."

"We wait until everyone's in,
And steal the train from them."
Hero smirked at the clever plan,
"On your mark, Lady Gem."

Ooo-ooo-oooooo the heroes of Westmeath,
The Phantom and the Wraith!

She glanced at the orb on her chest,
Laughing, she shook her head.
"We should do this again, Lord Shade.
Work as a team," she said.

They saved all the people that night,
Returning them back home,
Phantom and Wraith protect Westmeath,
Together now they roam.

Ooo-ooo-oooooo the heroes of Westmeath,
The Phantom and the Wraith!

Ooo-ooo-oooooo the heroes of Westmeath,
The Phantom and the Wraith!

As the last note died away, the audience went wild, demands of an encore filtering through until the entire room resounded with the chant.

"I think that went well," Carter shouted to Elyse and Greg, who gave him thumbs up in return.

The band had a quick conference, and then Tommy raised his hand, getting silence almost immediately. He was flushed now, with both the exhilaration of performing and mild embarrassment at his success. "After the countdown, we'll play it again for you, and I'll teach you the refrain. But it's too close to midnight right now, and I have a date."

Carter grinned as the crowd whooped.

Tommy slung his guitar on his back and jumped down from the stage, heading straight for his friends, the audience parting to let him through and eagerly watching to see who he was meeting.

"You were incredible up there," Carter said, and scooped Tommy up as soon as he was close enough. "My boyfriend is so cool."

"I'm really not," Tommy protested.

"Coolness is in the eye of the beholder," Carter misquoted.

Tommy chuckled, and Carter felt his laughter through his chest, still pressed tightly against his own.

The band started the countdown on stage, and Carter put their foreheads together. "Our first new year's kiss," he murmured.

"And it's only what, August?" Tommy teased.

"Three... Two... One!"

"Happy New Year," Carter said, and kissed Tommy gently.

Tommy tilted his head and tightened his grip on Carter's curls, making his scalp tingle. They slid their tongues together in an ever-deepening kiss that had Carter dizzy in seconds and dimmed the sounds of the hall.

"Do we get to wish you a Happy New Year, too?" Elyse's voice sounded far away.

The boys pulled apart with a gasp. "Yeah. Course," Carter rasped, eyes still locked on Tommy.

Greg chuckled. "If you do that every midnight, you're going to—"

"Don't finish that sentence. I don't want to hear it," Elyse said, putting a finger on Greg's lips and making his eyes grow wide.

Carter laughed and gave his other friends hugs. "Happy New Year," they said to each other.

Then Tommy was beckoned back up onto the stage, where he spent the next half hour playing his song on repeat for the enraptured audience, who sang along with the refrain.

"It's a good thing I like this song," Greg grumbled. "The refrain is such an earworm that I could sing it in my sleep."

Carter laughed. "As you said when he was writing it, that's kinda the point."

Tommy finally left the stage and joined his friends, his guitar safely stowed in its case on his back. "Shall we?" he said.

Carter offered his elbow, and Tommy linked their arms. "On to concert venue number two," Carter said with a wink. "Your entourage is ready."

"Ugh, that makes me feel like a snob," Tommy said, wrinkling his nose.

"It's okay, we know we're beneath you," Elyse said, grinning.

"Just lowly common folk," Greg said.

"Stop it!" Tommy frowned. "You don't really feel like that, do you?"

"No, of course not!" Carter exclaimed as they entered the university building with the portal to Pakaha. They returned their coats and boots, again, and headed for the portal courtyard. "It just feels like we're walking with a rock star."

Tommy laughed. "A rock star, I am not."

"You're just playing at three New Year's Eve parties," Greg said sarcastically.

"After which I'm not going on tour or making an album or any of that nonsense. We've got a goal: kill the Icaryoe. This is just a back-up plan in case we don't get to the Beast first." Tommy sighed. "Which, I'm not going to lie, I'm not sure is something we want to do. I'm terrified of going up against that thing, and I've only read a description of it."

Carter squeezed Tommy's hand. "That's why we're training first, so that if we do face it, we'll live to tell the tale." Carter signed in to access the Pakaha portal. "But I'm glad we have your back-up plan, just in case."

MONDAY THE 31ST OF DECEMBER, 1290 POST-CATACLYSM - PAKAHA CITY, PAKAHA

Pakaha City was bustling with energy. Carter sniffed the breeze and hummed happily, his stomach rumbling. "Shall we get dinner before we head to Aliyah and Pieter's?"

"How about we each pick a street vendor, buy four of whatever they sell, and split it?" Greg suggested.

"Great idea!" Carter agreed enthusiastically. "I'm dying to try the meat pies here."

"And get the recipes," Tommy said with a chuckle. "You get meat, I'll get potato. I see a dumpling slash perogi slash samosa type pastry over there."

"I'll get veggies. There's a shish-ka-bab barbeque vendor beside the meat pie," Elyse said.

"Does that mean I get to pick dessert?" Greg said, a grin on his face. "Don't worry, I got this."

Carter laughed. "I wasn't worried. Now I kinda am."

They met back up at a courtyard with tables and chairs and swapped their spoils, eating everything as if starving.

"We did have our last meal over six hours ago," Elyse pointed out when Tommy brought that up. "And you're performing."

"We should probably nap when we get to Wild Nations," Carter suggested, yawning. "We'll have been up for almost a full day by that point."

"I'll probably still be too pumped up to sleep," Tommy said, bouncing a little in his chair.

"The dark circles under your eyes say otherwise," Greg teased.

Carter brushed the back of his hand over Tommy's cheek. "You'll cuddle up with me, though, right?" He smirked in satisfaction when Tommy's eyes fluttered closed.

"Yeah, okay," Tommy said breathlessly.

"Ew, gross, go flirt somewhere else," Elyse said, pretending to gag over her veggie skewer.

"Yeah, get a room," Greg teased.

"We're not even... Gah!" Carter threw up his hands in mock frustration. "We don't have to take this! We can leave!"

"Greg has the pastries," Tommy pointed out, not budging from his seat.

Carter eyed the berry-filled tarts. "We can bring them with us," he said, uncertainly looking at the rest of his meal that he'd also have to carry. "Bah, too much work to be dramatic."

The group laughed.

Tommy's performance in Pakaha was in a sunken amphitheatre. He left the others near the entrance and disappeared backstage.

Carter sat down on a cushioned riser at the top of the structure and stretched his arms out beside him. "Oh yeah, this is the life: following my superstar boyfriend from one concert to another."

The band was currently playing a slow song featuring a violinist, the music filling the amphitheatre and spilling out into the night air.

"You okay with being on the sidelines?" Greg asked, sitting beside him.

"This is his time to shine and he's doing a fantastic job at it," Carter said. He waved at Tommy as he climbed the stairs back up to them. "Makes me fall in love with him all over again," he murmured, more to himself than his friends.

"Hey," Tommy said, throwing himself half on Carter's lap and half on the seat. "There's still an hour before they need me for the sound check, so I can hang out for a bit. Wanna know what they told me about my guitar?"

"Yes," Carter immediately replied.

"You'd tell us even if we didn't want to know," Greg teased.

Tommy stuck his tongue out at Greg. "You'll find this interesting, trust me." He cleared his throat and leaned in. "Apparently, there's a forest of musical trees in Wild Nations, and any instrument made with the wood from those trees has magical properties. My guitar is made of maple from that forest."

"You're pulling my leg," Greg whispered.

"How do they know the wood is from there?" Elyse asked.

"There's a stamp on the inside of the guitar. The guy in charge backstage told me."

"What kind of magical properties?" Carter asked, eyes wide.

"The tuning pegs never lose their tune," Tommy said. "And I can bend the volume to my will."

"But you don't have magic." Greg's face was white, the lines around his mouth tight with tension.

"No, I don't. But a musician in tune with his instrument can make magical things happen." Tommy shrugged. "In my case, that's quite literal. Did you notice I didn't need the amplifier for my guitar at the last venue?"

"I wondered about that," Carter said. "That's awesome!"

"So, on the train, you wanted to play quietly, but at a concert, you want to be loud," Elyse said. "Very convenient."

"I thought so." Tommy wrapped his arms around Carter's shoulders. "Do you think it'll still work in Westmeath?"

"We'll find out," Carter said and bumped their noses together. "We can test it at the community centre; try it out in the teen room and the main hall and see if there's a difference."

"Or we can try to convince Jason to have a live band one night for the dance!" Elyse said excitedly. "I bet Alicia would want in on that, and George too! You three were so awesome up on stage back in June."

"Would that be okay, you think?" Tommy asked Carter.

"The only problem I can see is that I wouldn't be able to dance with you," Carter joked, pulling Tommy closer.

"Ugh, are you going to get all sappy again?" Elyse said, rolling her eyes. "I don't remember Adrien and Arielle being like this when they first got together."

Carter laughed. "Oh my God, are you serious? They were *so* much worse than us! The number of times I spotted them...

Actually, Kennedy and Jason are like that, although I've never bumped into them other than at their house."

"You *saw* them..." Greg made an obscene hand gesture, his mouth hanging open.

"Not Kennedy and Jason." Carter shook his head. "They were just making out. But the others?" He whistled low. "At a distance, and I turned away as soon as I realized what was going on, but yeah."

"Dang. That's hot." Greg sat back, a smug expression on his face.

Carter chuckled. "You've got a thing for that, eh? Personally, I'd rather be one of the two consenting participants than be on the outside looking in."

"Stop goading each other!" Elyse said, giving their shoulders light slaps, Carter's a little harder, probably because she knew he could take it. "Gross."

Greg blushed.

"You guys are hilarious," Tommy said, snuggling into Carter's embrace. "Was it that place you showed me?"

"Yeah." Carter swallowed hard and tried not to think about the time he had brought Tommy up to the roof of the community centre in June. Now wasn't the appropriate time or place for that. The night had been magical, and not in the Aether sense.

"Oh, looks like they want me backstage now," Tommy said, pointing out a man who had emerged from the side of the amphitheatre and was looking around. "See you at midnight!" He pressed a quick kiss to Carter's lips and hopped up excitedly, almost bouncing as he took the stairs down to the stage two at a time.

"You've got a goofy looking grin on your face, you know," Elyse pointed out.

"Yeah. Don't care." Carter brushed her off. "He's so cute."

The performance went even better than the first; the crowd loved his song, begged to learn it, and Tommy had to disappear quietly out the side of the amphitheatre to avoid people swarming him.

While Greg and Elyse went to buy a snack for them to eat, Carter and Tommy kept to the shadows to avoid being spotted.

"Do you feel like your practise concert back at the school in June was leading you up to this point?" Carter asked quietly.

Tommy chuckled. "If you had told me then that I would be playing at three New Year's Eve concerts, I wouldn't have believed you."

"Especially since they're in August," Carter replied mischievously before joining his boyfriend's quiet laughter.

"We found a stall selling deep fried balls of meat and peas," Elyse interrupted them, bringing them each a battered ball on a stick. "It seemed pretty popular at dinnertime."

"And since it's dinner again for us, it makes sense," Carter finished her thought. He took a bite and moaned. "That is *delicious.* We *need* this recipe for Jason."

"Got ya covered." Greg held out a piece of paper. "They had a stack of these beside their napkins."

"It's super complicated," Tommy said, examining the instructions before slipping it into an outside pocket of his guitar case. "Jason's going to love this."

"Shall we make our way to the portals?" Elyse said. "People will have forgotten what you look like by now."

"If the guitar doesn't give it away," Greg said sarcastically.

"We'll just walk quickly," Carter said.

Monday the 31st of December, 1290 Post-Cataclysm - Sydney, Wild Nations

The sun was still high in the sky, and the air was heavy with humidity.

"Oh my gosh, the first thing I'm going to do when I get to my room is change into lighter clothing," Elyse gasped.

"No clothing," Greg added with a sigh.

"I wouldn't say it even if I was going to do that," Elyse retorted.

"I was talking about myself." Greg affected a haughty expression. "No better way to sleep in the heat than nude. Don't you two agree?" He looked pointedly at the couple.

Carter spread his hands wide and grinned. "Nice try."

"That's a bit personal, don't you think?" Tommy asked. "Would you ask that if we were single guys?"

"Yeah, to back me up on my opinion."

"Uh huh," Elyse scoffed.

"You know, this is tame locker room gossip at my school," Greg pointed out. "We're not measuring sizes or anything."

"Thanks for that," Carter said, rolling his eyes. "Poor Elyse would be scarred for life."

"Speak for yourself. I can handle turning away while you get rulers," Elyse said calmly. "But don't expect me to wait around for you. I'm exhausted."

"Me too," Carter said, proving his words with a yawn.

"I'm still really pumped up from performing, but I have no interest in knowing anything about your dick," Tommy said.

"Not the point," Greg grumbled when the others laughed.

"Hey, I had a thought while I was backstage," Tommy said, once they'd all calmed down. "My guitar is magic. Do you think your gifts are magic, too?"

They walked silently for a moment.

"We can ask Es'Sem," Carter said at last. "We'll probably see her tomorrow when we restart our training."

"And if we don't see her, maybe Noah will know," Elyse suggested. "He seems to be rather involved with both the yard and our training."

"And Es'Sem," Greg said suggestively.

"Greg!" everyone said at the same time.

He shrugged and said, "What? You were all thinking it."

"Guys and girls can be friends without their relationship being romantic," Elyse pointed out. "Look at me and Carter."

They had reached their rooms at this point, and Carter leaned against his door. "And you could hurt their reputations if someone overheard."

Greg paused midway through opening his door. His shoulders sagged. "Yeah, I guess you're right," he said, not looking at them. "Have a good nap." He closed the door behind him.

"Wow, no innuendo," Tommy said with a chuckle. "He must be tired."

"Sleep well, boys," Elyse said, going into her room.

Carter walked into their room, letting Tommy shut the door behind him, and immediately started stripping off his outer layers. Once he was down to his briefs, he climbed onto the bed on his back and shut his eyes.

"You're going to stop there?" Tommy's voice murmured, getting louder as he got closer to the bed.

"You're the one with energy. If you want it, you're going to have to do the work." Carter yawned, his ears creaking at the stretch. "Or we can nap first and then wake up the fun way. Your choice. But don't be offended if I fall asleep in the middle of the first option."

Tommy chuckled, and Carter heard his clothes softly hitting the floor. He wanted to look, really he did, but his eyelids refused to cooperate. The bed dipped, and a warm body draped across his own.

"It's okay. We'll sleep first and get our energy back," Tommy whispered in Carter's ear.

Soft lips pressed a kiss to his jaw, and then Carter knew no more.

Quiet beeping from Tommy's watch alarm woke him. Carter reached over to the bedside table and turned it off before it got any louder. The time read just before ten at night, which meant they had half an hour before they had to head over to the concert pavilion. They had spotted the tents being set up early that morning when they had dropped off their things. One large tent for the concert was flanked by several smaller tents for food vendors.

When asked, they had explained that the sides of the tents would be raised to allow for air flow but keep things in the shade.

Carter smirked at his boyfriend, spread out on his back beside him, one arm over his eyes. The sheet dipped enticingly low on his hips, and Carter reached out, tracing the muscles that arrowed down under the cover.

"A fun way to wake up, hmmm?" Carter murmured, pressing his lips to the pale skin of Tommy's collarbone. "Time to wake up," he said in a singsong voice, kissing lower and lower until Tommy woke up, and Carter brushed the sheet off them both.

Chapter 19

Tuesday the 5th of March, 1291 Post-Cataclysm - Teardrop, Ruby Isles

"What in the Aether..." Carter gasped when they stepped out of a mini portal in the Ruby Isles. They had travelled via the normal portal system to the capital city, Teardrop, and then after checking in, had taken the smaller portal to their private island.

Tommy felt more than a little overwhelmed himself, and he had arranged for Carter's birthday. His eyes were wide as he took in the white sand, the blue sky, and the clear water that stretched to the horizon. Several palm trees swayed in the light breeze, their red fronds rustling softly.

It felt self-indulgent to plan this surprise, but with no sign of the Icaryoe in three months, and them diligently training, they deserved a little treat. He just hoped that Carter saw it the same way. There was nothing they could do until Es'Sem's scouts found the Great Beast.

"As you can see, you'll have the entire island to yourselves. Menus are available in the hut; food is delivered privately. If you need anything, just write on this tablet, and all will be arranged for you. Do you have any questions?" The woman who had accompanied them smiled brightly.

"We can go in the water?" Carter asked, bouncing excitedly.

"Yes, of course." The woman indicated the hut again. "You'll find breathing necklaces on a shelf. They're good for a depth of up to ten metres and will flash orange when you get to nine. The reef on the left of the island has a wide variety of tropical fish. The beach gets the most sun on the right."

Tommy absorbed that information slowly. "Sorry, did you say, 'breathing necklaces'?"

"Yes. You wear them and can breathe underwater up to ten metres in depth," she repeated.

"Like a snorkel!" Tommy exclaimed.

"Except way better," Carter added. "Does it work for all species? I'm Aetherborn. Rock giant," he clarified further.

"If you will permit me to scan you...?" The woman held a device over Carter's chest for a moment after he agreed. "Your biology is similar enough to human. They will work for you."

"Awesome."

"There's a cavern within range of the breathing necklaces on the rocky side of the island. I suggest you bring the light bracelet with you if you want to explore it."

"Great idea. Thanks."

When they had no further questions, the woman left, leaving them alone on the small island.

Tommy watched Carter turn in a circle, taking in the view. "Good birthday present?"

"I can't believe this is the equivalent of renting a hotel room back home. There's only one problem with it," Carter said seriously.

"What?" Tommy's heart sank.

"I don't know how you're going to top this when we're back in Westmeath." Carter flung his arms wide and spun around before scooping Tommy up in a hug.

"Oh!" Heart restored and full to bursting, Tommy wrapped his legs around Carter's waist. "Just because I'll never be able to top this doesn't mean I won't give it to you now, when I have the chance. When else will we have the opportunity to spend the entire day together, by ourselves, on a private island?"

"If we're still here on your birthday, we can do it then. And our anniversary's coming up." Carter kissed Tommy hard. "Lots of opportunities to spoil each other."

"Want to explore?"

"Yeah, let's grab those necklaces and the bracelet, and then we can hop into the water whenever we want," Carter suggested.

"I bought us swim trunks when I went out yesterday," Tommy said, dropping his bag on the table in the hut and digging through it. "I thought you might look good in these." He held out a pair of burgundy swim shorts.

"How did you know my size?" Carter said with a wink, taking them. "I love this colour. Thank you."

"We both put on muscle so we're still the same size. I tried on mine and then bought yours to match." Tommy held up an emerald green pair.

"Nice." Carter grinned and wrapped his arms around Tommy's waist. "You know, we don't have to wear anything but our jewellery. We *are* alone out here."

Tommy opened and closed his mouth. He could feel a blush painting his cheeks. "Sand?" he managed to squeak. He cleared his throat. "Doesn't sound comfortable."

Carter chuckled. "Sand doesn't bother me that much. But I'm only teasing."

"And would you only be teasing if I'd said yes?" Tommy asked as he took off his shirt.

"I am always going to be enthusiastic about being starkers with you," Carter said, eyeing Tommy appreciatively. "We may both have put on some muscle from training, but simply saying that does not do your shoulders, abs, or thighs justice. You haven't bulked up or anything, but the toning is..." He whistled low. "I want to touch you, like, all the time."

"I'm in the same boat. Your body went from toned to rock hard," Tommy said with a teasing grin.

"Did you... Did you just pun on my heritage?" Carter gasped.

"I did, yes." Tommy waggled a finger. "Did you think I'd forgotten your comments at the STEM competition in Toronto? 'Sink like a rock' indeed! And your MSN handle? I just about died of laughter when I got home from the wedding, and you popped up. 'CarterIsARockStar?' Genius."

"You like that, eh?" Carter grinned and dropped his clothing on a chair. "I'll have to come up with something else, especially now that you've proven you're the rock star in this relationship."

"Jeepers, that so does not count." An idea came to Tommy, and he chuckled. "You could change your handle to 'TommyRocksMyWorld', and I'll do the same, but with your name."

Carter burst out laughing. "Oh my God, yes! That's perfect."

"People would get so confused about which one of us they're talking to," Tommy continued with a grin, delighted to make Carter laugh.

"I love you," Carter said, hugging Tommy close.

Tommy's heart did a little flip. "Love you, too. Shall we get to exploring the island? Because if I'm going to be honest, my willpower to pull away from you right now is almost gone, and we can do this anywhere." While he spoke, his hand traced nonsense patterns on Carter's back, getting lower while his voice got higher and ended with a squeak.

Carter grinned mischievously. "Yeah, alright."

The island was small, but just the right size for two. They walked along the beach first, admiring the blue-green of the water. At the pointed end of the island, they turned and followed the grassy, tree-lined side back to the hut, excitedly pointing out the different fish they could see darting about amidst the brightly coloured coral.

On the far side of the hut was rocky terrain. The boys hopped from one large rock to the next until they got to the end, which was higher above the water than the rest of the island.

"Oh man, if it's deep enough, this would be such an epic place to jump from!" Carter exclaimed. "Look, there's a path down to the water. Let's go scout it out!"

The water was warm when they slipped in. Grinning, Carter ducked beneath the lapping waves. Tommy touched his neck, feeling both the silver chain and the breathing necklace. He resisted taking a deep breath before following his boyfriend under the water.

Despite the water being clear from up above, Tommy was still surprised to find it easy to see once he was underneath. Carter grinned at him and blew out a stream of bubbles, sinking deeper in the water.

Tommy was still holding his breath. The water surrounding him made his instincts scream not to breathe, but his lungs were starting to protest the lack of oxygen. He touched the necklace again to reassure himself and took a tiny breath in, ready to kick to the surface if he started choking.

Nothing happened. Nothing, in the sense that he could breathe normally, as if he were above the water. He cautiously took a deeper breath and blew out, bubbles rising to the surface from his open lips.

Laughing, although it sounded more like a burble, he swam down to where Carter was floating.

Carter indicated the rocky tower he was looking at and made a gesture as if to stay away from it, and then pointed to the surface.

Tommy nodded, and they both swam upwards.

When they broke the surface, Carter said, "That was the only rock we have to avoid. It's off to the left, so it shouldn't be a problem. Wanna jump off a cliff with me?"

"I'd follow you anywhere," Tommy said with a grin. "Even to Everdome."

"Good thing!" Carter exclaimed, laughing as he hauled himself onto the rocks. He held out a hand for Tommy, who took it and let himself be lifted out of the water.

"I love how easy it is for you to pick me up," Tommy said admiringly, climbing back up the rocky path.

"You weigh about half what I can comfortably lift," Carter said. "Rock strength, remember?"

"*Hard* to forget," Tommy said teasingly.

Carter scoffed and chased Tommy the rest of the way to the top, the two of them clasping hands and launching themselves far into the air, shouting with glee as they hurtled toward the water.

They let themselves slowly sink further than they had investigated earlier. Tommy looked toward the island to see a large cavern in the side. He gestured to it, and Carter's face lit up with excitement as he nodded eagerly.

They swam toward it cautiously, examining the edges for signs of life. It was built like the rest of this side of the island, rock everywhere. It was pitch dark inside. Tommy gestured in, but Carter shook his head and pointed upwards.

Tommy looked expectantly at the stone bracelet next to the leather translation bracelet and shook it, but nothing happened until he stuck his hand inside the cave, away from the ambient sunlight filtering through the water. The cave lit up like he'd turned on a flashlight.

Carter pointed at the light bracelet and then at himself, indicating that he wanted to go first, and Tommy willingly gave up the bracelet.

Peering eagerly over Carter's shoulder, Tommy saw only a rocky passage leading into the island. He gave Carter's shoulder a little push to indicate that he wanted to go inside, and then followed Carter into the tunnel.

There was a turn to the right and then a sharp turn upwards before their heads popped up into an air pocket inside the island.

The bracelet showed them a low roof, a narrow ledge, and a different kind of rock than what they'd seen elsewhere on the island.

"What is this?" Tommy asked, picking up one of the rough shapes, about the size of his thumb. It was grey with speckles of red.

"It's pretty." Carter picked up one as well. "A nice way to remember this place." He lifted the bracelet in the air, illuminating the tiny cavern to make sure they hadn't missed anything on the first glance. "Shall we go order lunch? I'm starving."

After lunch, they swam with the fishes on the coral side of the island and then relaxed together on the beach, stretching out on the sand with their feet splashing in the water.

"Can I ask you something?" Tommy asked, popping a piece of fruit into his mouth.

"Anything." Carter opened his mouth, and Tommy fed him the next piece.

"Why were you comfortable telling the woman that brought us here that you're Aetherborn, but Greg is still in the dark about it?"

"Did you see some of the other guests when we checked in? Back on the main island, I mean." Carter asked. "I saw a dog person, and a fish person! If they get clientele that different, me being Aetherborn was unlikely to throw them. As for Greg, I know he's changed a lot, but will that stick when we get home? I'm not about to expose my entire Community to a Blue Blood just because he *might* have had a change of heart."

Tommy nodded thoughtfully. "That's the same conclusion Elyse came to about agreeing to a date with him."

"What?" Carter sat bolt upright. "He asked her out? How am I only hearing about this now?"

Tommy pulled Carter back down on the sand. "She only told me yesterday when we were shopping for a gift for you. She didn't want Greg to feel bad. He asked her out last week. She told him that if he still feels the same way when we get home, she'll go on a date with him then."

"Really?"

Carter was silent for a minute, and Tommy dug his toes into the soft sand, popping them up again and letting the water clean them off.

"She must think we're going to be able to go home soon then. Like, months, not years," Carter said slowly.

"I hope so. We've only been here for two and a half months and I'm homesick. She and I did the math, and if time passes at a regular speed, we think we've been gone for about half a day. Our families are probably worried sick about us." Tommy popped another fruit into his mouth and offered one to Carter.

"I really don't want to think about how worried they are," Carter said around his mouthful. "There's nothing we can do about it that we aren't already doing, like setting up that earworm at New Year's and training to kill the Icaryoe. But you're homesick? Do you think you would've been homesick in August, being in Westmeath for the whole month and away from your parents?"

"No. I'd still be with some family, and I could call my parents any time I wanted. When..." Tommy took a deep breath. "When I come to Oldtown High for grade ten, I won't feel homesick."

The silence was broken by the call of a sea bird up in one of the trees.

"I'm sorry, *what?*" Carter shrieked. "You're just bringing this up *now*?"

"It's not for sure yet," Tommy said cautiously. "I haven't received confirmation of the transfer of my transcripts yet. But everyone's fully on board. I wasn't supposed to tell you until everything was finalized, but it's been two and a half months of keeping this secret, and I can't do it anymore!"

Carter laughed. "Alright, I get it." He ran a hand through his curls, sand flaking away. "Wow. We'll get to be together for the whole year. We can go on dates!"

"And have sleepovers every weekend," Tommy said, cuddling into Carter's side before sitting up abruptly. "Oh! I almost forgot to give you my gift."

"I thought the day on a private island was my gift," Carter said dryly. "You didn't have to get me anything."

"I know, I know, but..." Tommy got to his feet. "You'll see what I mean when you open it." He hurried to the hut and dug through his bag for the small box at the bottom. Back on the beach, he sat himself down on Carter's thighs and placed the box on his chest.

Carter raised an eyebrow and shuffled around to sit up, the box between them. "This looks an awful lot like a jewellery box," he said quietly.

"It's not a ring," Tommy said reassuringly. "We're both a little young for that. Open it." Heart in his mouth, he watched Carter take the lid off and lift the silky cloth inside.

"Earrings," Carter said, a smile curling at his lips. "Ruby earrings. How did you know I wanted to get my ears pierced?"

Tommy grinned. "You stare at Noah's earrings enough. And here in Everdome, you might be able to. There's probably a spell of some sort that would soften your skin enough for a needle. And if there isn't, I can get them converted to clip-ons."

"There's an Aetherborn piercer in Westmeath. They use a diamond needle, and you're right about the softening spell." Carter closed the box carefully and pulled Tommy into a hug. "But I can get pierced before we leave the Isles. I saw a parlour near the reservations booth."

"I'm so glad you like them." Tommy told the butterflies in his stomach to calm down.

"I love them." Carter got to his feet, still holding Tommy. "Get in the water. I'm going to put this somewhere safe, and then we're going to make-out underwater, because that has been a fantasy of mine for, like, ever."

Tommy laughed. "You and me both." He walked into the water up to his knees and sat down, head and shoulders above the surface. "I'm going to need you to hold me down," he called to Carter. "I float too easily."

Carter grinned rakishly at him as he splashed through the water. "You know I love holding you down."

"Yeah," Tommy replied breathlessly. "About as much as you love when I hold you down."

Hovering over him, Carter smirked. "What can I say? I like both."

Tommy chortled with laughter, lying back under the gently lapping waves, floating an inch from the bottom until Carter's weight pinned him solidly to the sand. *Oh my God, yes,* Tommy thought, looking up at his gorgeous boyfriend. And then they were kissing, water swirling around and between them, caressing them gently in contrast to grasping, firm hands.

A shadow passing in front of the sun made them pause, Tommy mid-arch to get closer to Carter, and they sat up in the water to get a better look at the Dome passing between them and the sun.

"That'll never get old," Tommy whispered in awe. The Dome was facing them, the verdant greenery and lush plants easy to see despite the distance. "Jungle Dome is Ohana, right?"

"Yeah, that's right." Carter's voice was tense. "Hush. Get down."

Tommy obeyed instantly, ducking until only his eyes were above the waves. He followed Carter's gaze to see what was scaring him. For a minute, he couldn't see anything other than blue sky and water. He was about to relax when he saw it: a long smear of darkness with fire wings, leaving behind a trail of grey smoke. It flew higher and higher in the direction of the other Dome until Tommy thought it would hit the barrier between them.

It did, but then it melted through the barrier, passing into the space between the Domes for an instant, and then repeating the process into Ohana.

"Holy *shit*!" Carter cursed, getting to his feet, and heading for the hut. "No wonder it's still kicking! The Icaryoe can phase through the barrier! We gotta go, before it moves on again."

"Right," Tommy said, his mind still reeling from what he'd witnessed as he followed Carter back to shore. "We should ask back in Teardrop if they've seen it before. Maybe it only makes excursions out from its lair, rather than going from one Dome to the next, in constant motion. I mean, most predators need somewhere defensible to sleep, right? Especially if they're alone."

"Hopefully it's still alone." Carter passed Tommy the towel and started yanking on his clothes.

Friday the 15th of March, 1291 Post-Cataclysm - Nara, Ohana

The rough jungle surrounding Nara, Ohana's capital city, was beautiful to look at, but not so much fun to walk through. The heat in Sydney had been dry; *this* was oppressive. Tommy felt like he was breathing soup.

Es'Sem had equipped the four of them well, both in clothing and protective spells, and they were moving quickly and quietly through the wilderness of the lush, tropical Dome.

Tommy glanced to his left at Carter, reassured by his presence. A shaft of sunlight penetrated the canopy above them, making the red stud in his ear glimmer. After telling Es'Sem about what they'd seen, she said that it would take some time to prepare to track it down. That meant they'd had the time to return to Teardrop to get his ears pierced and finish their vacation.

Carter caught his glance and winked, putting a finger to his lips to indicate silence.

Greg pointed to the right and gave the hand signal for everyone crouch.

This was the fifth cavern the people of Nara had marked on the map they had given them, and Greg had proven to be an expert at reading it. The first four caves had been occupied by various wildlife, which they had left untouched.

Tommy crawled closer, inching between Greg and Carter, and peered at the mouth of the cave.

No birds or small animals, Tommy thought, heart beating so loudly he was sure the others could hear it. A wisp of smoke exited the inky blackness, only to dissipate in the breeze. *I think we've found it.*

Carter nodded at him, and Tommy backed away, carefully pulling his guitar off his back, and opening the case. He walked carefully forward again, the case returned to his back.

Here goes nothing, he thought desperately, and stepped out into the clearing in front of the cavern. He played a lullaby from Earth, one he loved to sing to his nephew Arthur, "Puff, the Magic Dragon".

The massive Icaryoe slunk out of the cave, his lion head low as though it was heavy with sleep. His body, long and lean, with dragon-like scales, took an entire verse to exit the cave, and the sharply barbed tail yet another. Altogether, it was approximately the size of two coach busses end-to-end.

Tommy tried to keep the terror out of his voice as he sang, trying to only convey the soft melody of the lullaby. He got to the end of the song and restarted it, afraid to change to something else or pause his playing.

Curling up like a cat in the sunshine, the Icaryoe put its large head on its forepaws and closed its eyes.

I think it's working! Tommy thought excitedly, keeping his fingers steady on the frets of the guitar. He heard his friends come out of the foliage behind him. One strong hand gripped his shoulder: Carter. They got ready to pounce on the Icaryoe, to tear it apart, and Tommy hoped that his music was strong enough to keep it asleep.

A spear sped past the teenagers, piercing the Icaryoe's side, causing an eruption of chaotic commotion. The Beast leaped to its feet, tail thrashing and flattening trees on the other side of the clearing. It grabbed the all-too-familiar spear with its teeth and ripped it out, spitting it onto the ground.

It stared right at them, nostrils flaring, and opened its mouth wide. Each tooth was longer than Tommy was tall. Its ululation made Tommy's insides shrivel with fear. His fingers stopped moving, frozen, and the music ended, the last chord echoing softly.

The Icaryoe whirled, the barbs on its tail flared out to strike at them, when an invisible shield sprung up between them, unbalancing the Beast. It fell over onto its side, body writhing as it tried to get back on its feet.

"This way!" hissed a voice.

Tommy looked around wildly for the source and spotted a hand gesturing to him from an opening in space that looked like a beach. He pointed it out to the others, and the four teenagers ran through the sliver of space.

Chapter 20

Carter sank to his knees in the black sand, knife falling from nerveless fingers. It vanished when it hit the sand, and he felt its weight return to the holster he wore across his chest. "I'm sorry," he gasped to the others. "I froze. I— We would have died. Thank you." He raised his head to look at their saviour, expecting to see Es'Sem.

Kathryn put her hands on her hips and raised an eyebrow at him. "What in all the Goddess' names made you think that four teenagers could take on a Great Beast of Everdome and survive?"

All four teens started talking at once.

"The Sisters said he had to—"

"We've been training with Es'Sem—"

"There was no other way home—"

"It was my duty as a Knight of Gaulan," Carter said, getting to his feet. He faced Kathryn calmly now. "I may have become a knight in an unusual way, but my duty to the people of Gaulan remains the same."

"Horsefeathers," Kathryn spat. "You're fifteen."

"Sixteen. My birthday just passed," Carter interrupted her, raising his chin. "And I don't appreciate the condescension."

Kathryn glared. "The greatest wizards and warriors of Everdome barely managed to defeat the Icaryoe last time. And *your* plan was to lead three barely trained teenagers against it, put it to sleep, and then what? Are you so sure you could handle killing it?"

Tommy let out a yelp, and Carter whirled to face the jungle, sand shifting under his feet. A snarling wildcat was creeping out from the dense jungle, its yellow eyes fixed on Greg. Each step it took, its shoulder blades protruded grotesquely.

Heart in his mouth, Carter unhooked a knife from his holster. "Greg, don't move," he whispered.

Greg raised his arms, hands loose. "It's okay, I can take it," he murmured. He rolled his shoulders and neck, maintaining eye contact with the animal.

Elyse let out a length of rope on her weapon.

"What are you waiting for?" Kathryn demanded. "It's going to attack your friend any second."

"It's hungry," Carter said. "That doesn't mean it deserves to die. I'm giving it a chance to realize that it can't win here." He growled deep in his chest, trying to mimic the way his dads could use their rock giant voices to make the air shake.

It worked, sort of; it sounded a little like he was purring. The cat didn't react.

Tommy chuckled. "Nice try, babe," he whispered.

"It was worth a shot," Carter muttered under his breath. He balanced his knife in his palm, comfortable with its weight after two months of intensive practice.

Noah had trained him to throw with both arms at moving targets with pinpoint accuracy. He had been about to start working on throwing with a blindfold when they'd discovered the Icaryoe was hiding in Ohana.

Carter released the second knife into his left hand in case the first missed and took his stance.

The wildcat pulled back on its haunches, readying to pounce, its front paws kneading the soft black sand.

The cat leaped, Carter's knives striking it midair: one in the heart, one in the eye.

The force of the hits knocked the wildcat off its trajectory, and it fell, black sand spraying up as it slid across the beach.

Carter felt the weight of the knives in their holster as they returned to him, and pulled one out again, ready in case the animal got up.

The wildcat vanished in the next second.

"That was very good," Kathryn said. "But not enough to kill an Icaryoe."

It took a moment for Carter to connect the dots, but when he did, he felt anger surge through him. He stomped up to her, meeting her calm gaze with fury. "You might be the Arikis' grandmother, but your testing methods are barbaric and unnecessary. If you're not going to help me protect Everdome from this vile Beast, *get out of my way,*" he snarled. Months of being told the only way to get his friends home was to kill this thing, only to be mocked and treated like a child made his blood boil. Carter spun and marched away from the group a few paces, not far enough to be out of range.

"Let him rage for a while," he heard Kathryn say. "He's had a fright."

Her words made his hackles rise even further.

"And you think making an illusion *helped*?" Tommy demanded.

"I had to see what he'd do. Just because Merlin gave him a ring doesn't mean he's qualified to be a knight. And just because some old biddies with more power than brains dragged you along doesn't make you three heroes. Heroes die," Kathryn said.

"You don't know what it's been like," Tommy said. "The amount of stress he's been under, all because the only way to return home was through killing the Icaryoe!"

"Well, I'm here now and I can take you home."

Silence met that statement.

Kathryn scoffed. "What? You don't think the rest of the knights of Gaulan can handle the Icaryoe, but you four—what was it that Nick called the new servers? Ah yes, *newbs*—will succeed? This isn't your fight."

"The hell it isn't!" Greg shouted.

"We've been here almost three months and we're the first ones to even *find* it!" Elyse said vehemently.

"Not to mention the intentional release of it, which nobody seems to care about except us," Tommy added so quietly that Carter had to strain his ears.

"Intentional? No one is that— That's impossible!" Kathryn said shakily.

"Then why did it appear at the university instead of in the archives of the castle where it was stored?" Carter asked, rejoining the conversation.

Kathryn looked grey under her dark skin. "The fool who chose to release such a monster would have paid with his life."

"Lord Bourges is still very much alive, as evidenced by his spear suddenly hitting the Icaryoe," Tommy said. "I saw the Bourges crest on the shaft of the spear just before we left the clearing."

Carter slapped his forehead. "Of course that's what happened! Bourges must have been following us."

"How did *you* find us?" Elyse said suddenly.

"And who *are* you?" Greg added. He looked around the little group and shrugged. "Just because you all know her doesn't mean I do."

Tommy laughed. "Sorry. Greg, this is my grandmother-in-law Kathryn Johnson. Kathryn, our friend, Greg Finch."

"Wow, okay. I thought they were kidding when they said you didn't age," Greg said, shaking her hand.

"What a silly thing to kid about," Kathryn said, shrugging off the comment. She then gave him an intense look. "I met your father yesterday. He was concerned about you."

"Really?" Greg gaped at her. "How did you meet him?"

"I guess I should start at the beginning," Kathryn mused. "That should answer Elyse's question too." She sat cross-legged on the black sand and waited until they joined her before she began her story. "When you four disappeared, I went with Jason to Door Technology. I met Mister Finch there. After watching security footage, we went to your classroom. The leftover magic was...” Kathryn winced. “Excessive. And recognizable. The Sisters’ magical signature was all over that room, so I immediately followed, knowing that there was no time to lose. Time moves much faster in Everdome than on Earth, so even though I left Earth less than an hour after you, I only arrived in Gaulan yesterday.”

“An hour?” Elyse said, visibly relaxing. “That’s a relief.”

“We’ve been concerned about our parents worrying about us,” Tommy explained.

“They *are* worried about you, but I’ll have you back in no time, whether or not I let you try to fight the Icaryoe.” Kathryn lifted an eyebrow at Carter, who had raised his hand.

“Why did they bring the others along with me? No other knights arrived in Tène with accompaniment. No offence,” he said quickly to the others.

They shrugged.

“I thought about that, and there are two options. Either there was a dilation effect from crossing between realms, or the spells on your ring made sure you had company. If I had to guess, I’d assume Merlin was worried about how you’d do alone.” He nodded, and she continued, “I arrived in the middle of a dissection lecture. They hadn’t seen you. I described you to a couple people on the campus, but none of them remembered you. I was about to go visit my friend in Wild Nations when a snippet of a song caught my ear.” She whistled the chorus of *The Ballad of the Phantom and the Wraith* and grinned at Tommy. “Clever boy.”

Tommy sat up straighter under her praise, and Carter took his hand, giving it a squeeze.

“From there, it was easy to follow your trail to Pakaha and then here to Ohana, thanks to the portal logs. Then I asked around for you in Nara until today, when I felt you channel your gift. It took a little bit of searching through the Quintessence, but you kept using your gift, which helped. I found you just in time, which brings us to now.”

"What do you mean, 'actively channelling my gift?'" Tommy asked. "My guitar?"

Kathryn hesitated for a moment. "You have the Fay gift of Luck. I won't explain why. That's a conversation for you to have with your family when we get home. But I can tell you that when you play your guitar, you are sharing your gift with your friends, making them lucky by extension."

"Back up," Greg said. "Fay gift?"

"As in fairies?" Elyse asked. "I thought they were just a myth."

Kathryn looked amused. "Most myths have a basis in reality. There is an entire realm, just like those of Everdome and of Earth, for the Fay."

"How do you know?" Greg asked, narrowing his eyes suspiciously.

"I've been there," Kathryn replied simply. "You've been awfully quiet, Carter."

"How big is Earth's realm? We see objects in deep space with our telescopes. Are they other realms? Are other realms alternate realities?" Carter asked all in one breath.

Kathryn laughed. "Earth's realm is the size of the universe. You cannot see other realms through telescopes, you can only travel there by magic. Alternate realities are something I know nothing about other than from Jason and Kennedy's favourite television show."

There was silence for a minute.

"Why should I let you fight the Icaryoe?" Kathryn asked quietly. "And don't give me any of that 'duty' nonsense."

Does everything hinge on what I say now? Carter thought anxiously. He resisted the urge to twist his fingers together. "We're the only ones who can defeat it because we're the only ones who have you," Carter said, attempting to be ingratiating. "Even if you come back here after you bring us home, another huge chunk of time will have gone by. It was laying low before, but now that it's pissed off, who knows what it'll do?

"You've taken lessons in persuasion from Jason, haven't you?"

Kathryn said wryly. She sighed, a deep sadness showing on her face. "Alright. Let's make a plan. I don't like winging it."

"Don't you mean playing by ear?" Tommy teased.

"She means improv," Carter said.

"I like rolling with the punches," Greg said, miming ducking and punching an invisible opponent.

"I hate this game," Elyse sighed. "I guess I could say freestyling?"

Carter grinned at her. "Yeah, that works perfectly."

Kathryn raised her eyebrows. "If everyone's finished...?"

It took them the better part of the morning to craft a plan, and it relied heavily on Kathryn's expertise.

She cast an illusion on a rock and gave it to Tommy to hide him. He put it in his pocket, and then Carter could no longer see his boyfriend; only the sand behind him was visible.

"Whoa, that's cool." Carter reached out until he could touch Tommy, and suddenly he could see him. "Do we all get one of those?"

"Unfortunately, no." Kathryn grimaced. "If one of us is touching the Icaryoe, it will be able to see all of us."

"Okay then." Carter let go of Tommy, who disappeared again.

Next, Kathryn gave Elyse and Greg several charmed stones. "The instant these touch the ground, they will create a fire. Make sure they are far apart before you cast them. They will make a good distraction and will be needed to burn the Beast."

Then she turned to Carter. "You and I will be the closest to the Beast. Can you handle cutting out its heart?"

Carter swallowed hard. "It's just like dissecting a worm, right?"

"Except that a worm doesn't have blood and was probably already dead," Greg snarked.

"Yes, thank you Greg," Carter snapped back. He took a deep breath and focussed on Kathryn again. "Is the skin tough? Is there a trick to cutting it open?" *Are you sure I can do this?* he thought but didn't ask.

"The Icaryoe is covered in scales, but they meet at the sternum. You'll be able to pierce your knife through at that point and then cut along the ribs. Our hearts are on the left side of our bodies, so I would assume the same for it." Kathryn demonstrated with her fingers on her torso. "You'll need to use force, and you'll have to be quick. It will start flailing almost immediately once the first incisions are made."

"Got it." Carter's stomach flipped.

"I will remove its head. Once those two parts are gone, we will toss them to the fires, and then take apart the rest of the body." Kathryn fixed Carter with her gaze. "Remember, you must burn every part you cut off, or else it will reattach. The Icaryoe has remarkable healing capabilities. Possibly the reason why it was taken: to be studied," she added, more to herself than the teenagers. She clapped her hands together. "Are you ready?"

"Bring it in," Carter said, putting out his hand. First Elyse, then Greg, then Kathryn, and last Tommy joined him.

"Oh, there you are!" Elyse beamed at Tommy. "Great illusion."

"Thank you," Kathryn replied, amused.

"Success on three!" Carter exclaimed. "One... two... three!"

"SUCCESS!" everyone shouted.

"Hold hands, please," Kathryn said. "Tommy? Oh, there you are. Good. Here we go."

Carter took a step and had to remind himself to breathe; it felt like he was walking through empty, foggy space.

"Where are we?" Greg asked as they walked through grey nothingness. "I don't remember this part last time."

"This is the Quintessence. I used a portal to rescue you from the Icaryoe. I was able to pinpoint your location thanks to Tommy channelling his gift. You walked through the portal from the clearing directly to the beach. This is a little different; I'm not certain that the Icaryoe stayed in the same place, so I'm following its essence through the Quintessence." Kathryn turned her head to the right. "This way."

She knows more about the Icaryoe than anyone we've talked to, and more than what was on the scroll, Elyse said to Carter in mindspeak. Out loud, she asked, "What is Quintessence?"

"It's a form of purified power derived from the souls of all living things," Kathryn replied absentmindedly. "It's easier to access than Aether. Get ready. It's here."

The Quintessence faded, and Carter found himself in another clearing surrounded by exotic plants. There was no cavern here, and, so he thought, no Icaryoe.

"Start playing," Kathryn muttered.

The next instant, music rang out, filling the clearing from no specific source.

"Fires," she whispered next, her mouth barely moving.

Carter watched Elyse toss her stone onto the ground, curious to see what would happen. The stone flared out into a wide basin with a fire in the centre. *Cool,* he thought.

"Ready?" Kathryn said calmly, only the tight grip on his hand showing her nerves.

Carter pulled a knife out of his holster. "Ready." He saw the eyes of the creature through the trees, but before he could blink, he was walking through Quintessence, and then he was underneath the hulking Icaryoe.

Now! Kathryn shouted in mindspeak.

Despite the plan having had the Icaryoe lying down, or at least somewhat within reach, Carter leaped into action. Literally. Using a nearby rock, he launched himself from there to a tree trunk, and then airborne underneath the Icaryoe. He grasped a large scale and punched his knife in where the scales got smaller, a spurt of blood jetting out and hitting him in the chest. *Ew,* he thought, dragging the knife down the Icaryoe's body. *Why isn't it reacting—? Oh, there we go.*

Carter clung to his scale as the Beast thrashed, crashing against the trees and falling to one side.

The legs! Kathryn shrieked in his mind.

The Icaryoe was curling up like a cat, but not to sleep this time; its claws were out, and it was kicking up, trying to dislodge him. He slipped a little in the blood that was now gushing from the cut in its chest and scrambled up the heaving rib cage to get out of range of the back claws. Ducking under a swipe from a front claw, he dug his knife in again, dragging it up between two ribs.

The Icaryoe bellowed its fury and flailed wildly, almost bucking Carter off. Blood poured freely from the gaping hole. He saw his chance when the Beast arched its back in pain.

I'm going for the heart! he announced to Kathryn. He leaped down, grabbed the exposed sternum, tried not to think about what he was holding, and peered inside.

This is so cool and will give me nightmares for months, Carter thought, watching the heart pulse rhythmically. He reached in and cut through the tissue running to and from it, adding to the disgusting amount of blood. He didn't want to touch the heart, so he stabbed it and pulled it out that way, trying not to gag.

Suddenly, Carter was flying, the wind knocked out of him by one of the Icaryoe's claws. He'd forgotten to watch his surroundings.

He hit a tree so hard that he went through it, breaking it in half, and he felt something crack in his ribs as he landed on the ground. Pain washed over him. *Shit,* he thought, from his prone position in the dirt. Then he noticed that the knife was back in his holster. He must have let go of it during his impromptu flying lesson. *I've lost the heart!* he alerted Kathryn.

Carter struggled to his feet, one hand bracing his ribs, and circled the fallen tree, searching the ground for the watermelon-sized muscle. He spotted it just as it rose into the air. "No!" he shouted, whipping out a knife and throwing it, neatly piercing the centre of the heart. It faltered but continued its journey back to the Icaryoe. "No!" Carter gasped, half running after it, trying to catch it. His lungs were screaming in pain, and he guessed one was punctured. *No time to deal with that now,* he told himself.

He gave one last burst of speed, the heart almost within reach, when he skidded on a patch of blood. He watched in horror as the heart zipped back into the Icaryoe and its chest stitched itself back up again in record time.

YOU DID BETTER THAN I EXPECTED. I'M IMPRESSED.

Carter screamed and put his hands over his ears, as if that would stop the voice reverberating in his mind.

I'LL REMEMBER YOU, ROCK GIANT.

With that foreboding declaration, the Icaryoe opened a portal and started sauntering through it.

"It's entering the Quintessence!" Kathryn gasped. "We have to stop it!"

IF YOU LIVE, was the Icaryoe's parting shot to Carter.

Carter saw the tail flick, saw the barb heading straight for him. He tried to avoid it, but he couldn't move fast enough.

The thick barb punctured through the right side of his abdomen, making him stagger back from the force of the blow.

He looked down at his belly, where the two-inch diameter barb was sticking out just above his hip bone like a javelin.

I'm a shish-ka-Carter, he thought fuzzily. *Ha.*

He heard Elyse's shriek, although he wasn't sure if it was out loud or in mindspeak. The jungle was spinny and his knees were shaking and was Tommy shouting something?

Carter blinked, trying to clear his vision. He could see people running toward him, leaping over the low foliage, but he couldn't hear their voices over the rushing in his ears.

He opened his mouth, about to tell Tommy not to worry, and felt warm liquid dribble onto his chin. *That can't be good,* he thought.

His eyes felt heavier than on New Year's Eve when they'd Dome-hopped. Carter fought to keep them open and found himself kneeling on the ground. He hadn't even felt the impact on his knees from the fall. He refused to look down and kept his gaze fixed on his friends.

Tommy's panicked face came into view, and Carter relaxed, knowing everything would be alright.

Darkness started to creep over his vision, and then he knew no more.

Chapter 21

FRIDAY THE 15TH OF MARCH, 1291 POST-CATACLYSM - PAKAHA CITY, PAKAHA

Tommy continued brushing his thumb over the back of a sleeping Carter's hand, resisting the urge to lift the sheet and see his fully healed abdomen again.

The last few hours had been a nightmare.

Tommy followed the screams of the Icaryoe into the forest, trying not to make any sounds that would draw attention to himself.

Not that the thrashing Icaryoe could have heard him over the noise it was making.

Tommy almost stopped playing, the scene he came across was so gruesome. Kathryn seemed to have the head trapped in some sort of a bubble that was getting smaller by the second, and Carter was hanging from the gaping chest by one hand. Tommy watched, horrified, as the Icaryoe's hind legs caught under Carter's body and flung him across the forest, straight through a tree trunk. Tommy had to run out of the way of the falling tree, and he lost track of the fight for a bit.

Kathryn landed close to Tommy, having been thrown away from the Icaryoe by a lucky toss of its head. She took a moment, hands on her knees, and then readied herself to rejoin the fray. She stopped abruptly. "It's entering the Quintessence!" Kathryn gasped. "We have to stop it!"

Tommy fished the stone Kathryn had given him out of his pocket. "You need this more than I do if you're going to follow it," he said, running toward her and pressing it into her hand.

She smiled tightly. "Thank you." Her hand slipped from his, and she vanished from sight.

The Icaryoe was almost completely gone at this point, and Tommy hoped that Kathryn would be able to defeat it on her own in the Quintessence. He flipped his guitar back around to his front and struck a G chord, his favourite, hoping that would send good luck with Kathryn.

The Beast flicked its tail just before it disappeared.

He heard a cry of pain, and Tommy looked frantically around for Carter. A horrifying sight met his gaze: Carter, covered in blood, had one of the barbs from the Icaryoe's tail sticking out of his abdomen.

Tommy shouted to the others for help and ran to Carter, slinging his guitar on his back again to get it out of the way. Carter opened his mouth and blood dribbled out.

"Stay with me!" Tommy shouted, picking up speed as he leaped over the fallen tree.

Carter fell to his knees, and Tommy panicked. "No no no! Carter!" he screamed. He only vaguely heard his friends behind him; all his attention was on his boyfriend. Tommy threw himself to his knees in front of Carter just in time to catch him before he collapsed forward onto the barb. Tommy struggled under Carter's weight.

"A little help?" Tommy gasped to his friends, arms around Carter's body. He could hear Carter's breath in his ear, faint and wheezing. "Please stay with me!" he begged, tears filling his eyes. He barely noticed Greg's presence until he pulled Carter away to lie him down on his right side.

"Do you know any first aid?" Greg asked.

Tommy shook his head, and they both looked at Elyse.

"Not me," she said through her tears.

Tommy got to his feet. "This is going to sound ridiculous, but hopefully if I play, Kathryn will be able to find her way back to us faster. I might even be able to give Carter some of my luck." He pulled his guitar around to the front again and cast about his memory for the right song to play. He struck a few chords and started to sing. *Please, please let this help,* he thought, his mind in a whirl of panic. They were in the middle of the jungle, nobody but Kathryn knew where they were, and she might not even make it back to them from her solo fight with the Icaryoe. He tried not to think that their situation was hopeless.

Elyse gave a weird half laugh, half sob. "Are you seriously playing The Cure right now?"

"Carter would appreciate it," Tommy said, interrupting himself mid-verse. He picked up right where he'd left off, his voice quivering with unshed tears. Carter needed him to be strong. He couldn't help if he fell apart.

"It's even Friday," Greg commented, wiping a hand across his forehead, and leaving a bloody streak. "Nice touch."

"It opened a portal into the Aether from the Quintessence. What's going o—?" Kathryn stopped abruptly as she got closer and saw Carter on the ground. She ran the last few steps and crouched over him, pressing her thumb to his forehead. "I've put him in stasis. It's like a coma and will keep him alive until we can get him to a healer. Do you have everything? We won't be coming back."

"The fires?" Elyse asked.

Kathryn snapped her fingers, and Tommy assumed she'd put out the fires. "Anything else?" They shook their heads. She closed her eyes and made a circular gesture at the ground around them.

The soft dirt vanished under Tommy's feet only to be replaced with hard floors. The familiar scent of antiseptic filled his nostrils, telling him that they were in a hospital.

A flurry of activity around Carter pushed them back against the walls, and Tommy breathed easier, knowing Carter was going to be treated quickly.

After Carter was lifted onto a bed and taken away to an

operating room, Kathryn looked the three teenagers over. "You look like you've been to the prom in *Carrie*."

Tommy blinked at her, not understanding.

"Both you and Greg are covered in blood," Kathryn said, gesturing at them.

"My guitar!" Tommy gasped, and sure enough, there were blood smears all over the strings and back of the instrument.

"Good thing I know a handy little spell to remove blood stains," Kathryn said, flicking her fingers at both boys. "Although I usually use it on underwear and bedsheets."

"Do you get stabbed often?" Tommy asked politely.

Elyse chuckled. "Don't you have three older sisters?"

"Yes, but I don't see—Oh!" Tommy exclaimed, embarrassed. "I might have sisters, but they've never really talked to me about menstruation."

"Is there any way you can teach me that spell?" Elyse asked Kathryn hopefully. "Or is there a charm I can buy?"

Kathryn shook her head. "Sorry. It's not like the spells on the stones I gave you, which anyone can use."

"Excuse me, Mistress Kathryn," a man in a clean white tunic addressed them. "The knight you brought in will be with the healers for a short time, and then he will need rest under supervision. Would you like to wait in his recovery room?"

"That's a polite way of saying that we're in your way," Kathryn replied, grinning. "Please, lead on."

"Is he going to be alright?" Tommy blurted out, almost stumbling over his feet as he followed the man.

"Our healers are the best in Everdome," the man said. "Your knight will be back on his feet very shortly. We will keep him for observation overnight, but he should be free to leave tomorrow morning."

Tommy let out a sigh of relief.

While they were waiting for Carter to be brought to them, Kathryn explained what had happened with the Icaryoe. "I followed it into the Quintessence. The Beasts learn and adapt at remarkable speeds. It must have seen how we exited and copied me. I was about to challenge it when it laughed at me. It could see through my illusion spell. Then it opened a portal from the Quintessence to the Aether. I am not a wizard, so I couldn't follow it there. The Aether would have torn me apart." Kathryn clenched her jaw. "This is not good news. The Aether connects the realms. If the Icaryoe breaks through into Earth…" She sighed. "We're in for a world of trouble."

"Wouldn't the Aether destroy it, too?" Tommy asked tentatively.

Kathryn barked a short laugh. "Wouldn't that be helpful! I doubt it. The Icaryoe is immortal. It will reform no matter what."

Greg shuddered. "That's disturbing."

"Indeed." Kathryn glowered at a spot on the floor. "After Carter has recovered, we must inform the Sisters. Perhaps they can do something."

Carter was brought into the room just then, sleeping peacefully on the bed. His earrings shone brightly under the hospital lighting, making Tommy think of droplets of blood against the white pillow. He swallowed hard, trying to get the lump in his throat to go away.

"He needs his rest. A magical healing like this is very draining for the patient." The healer glared at them. "You can return tomorrow morning."

"I'm not leaving him," Tommy said defiantly, crossing his arms.

"He's in good hands," Kathryn began, but Tommy shook his head.

"I'm sure he is, but I'm not going anywhere." He sat in a chair beside the head of the bed and put his hand in Carter's.

"Tommy," Carter breathed. His fingers tightened briefly on Tommy's and a small smile curled his lips before he drifted back into a deep sleep.

The healer checked his patient and nodded. "You may stay. The rest of you, out."

"We'll go back to Wild Nations," Elyse said quietly. "Sleep there tonight and bring your things with ours tomorrow."

Tommy passed her the key to his room. "Thanks. Everything's packed and on the bed."

"I want to go talk to my friend there, so I will go with you," Kathryn said.

"I'm sure Es'Sem will be happy to see you," Elyse said mischievously.

Kathryn chuckled. "Of course you'd have figured that out."

And so, Tommy had been left alone.

The first thing he did was reassure himself that there was no gaping hole in Carter's abdomen. The skin was smooth and unblemished; he had to run his fingers over it a few times to believe it was real. *Thank goodness for magical healers,* he thought. Tommy talked quietly for a while, just holding his boyfriend's hand.

Silence fell over the room. Outside, the sun was setting, lighting up the Dome with brilliant reds, oranges, and pinks.

"I'm so glad you're okay," Tommy murmured.

"Tommy?" Carter mumbled. "'Zat you?"

"Yes, I'm here," Tommy replied, squeezing Carter's hand, and scanning his face eagerly.

Carter slowly opened his eyes. "Did you get the licence plate of the truck that hit me?" he joked.

"I think it was you that hit a tree," Tommy said with a wet chuckle. "You don't know how happy I am to hear your voice. I was so scared."

"Sorry," Carter said. "I tried to move. I think it anticipated that."

"Not fair," Tommy grumbled. "All our planning, for what? You getting hurt and the Icaryoe entering the Aether."

Carter closed his eyes. "I'm going to pretend you didn't say that until tomorrow. Come up here." He patted the spot beside him. "You're not going to sleep in a chair."

"I won't hurt you?" Tommy hesitated.

"Other than tired, I feel fine," Carter said. "Actually, I should pee." He pulled himself up to a sitting position using the bar on the side of the bed, the sheet pooling at his waist. "Where are my clothes?"

Tommy chuckled. "They had to cut your shirt off you. Your pants are here."

"I'm glad my underwear wasn't destroyed. This is the pair from home." Carter swung his legs over the side and stood up steadily. "See, I'm fine. Strip and get in bed. Patient's orders. I'll sleep better with you."

"Alright, alright," Tommy said, obeying. "I'd probably have nightmares tonight if I didn't sleep with you."

"You and me both," Carter said from the small bathroom in the corner. He washed his hands and returned to the bed. "This is the way to have surgery."

"Magical surgery." Tommy hugged Carter close, burying his nose in brown curls. "Please don't ever do that to me again."

"Can't promise, but I'll definitely try my best," Carter whispered, breath tickling Tommy's collarbone.

"How... I thought you couldn't get hurt like that," Tommy said, choking a little around the lump in his throat. "How does rock get pierced?"

"The same way anything does," Carter said. "Enough force, plus magic, will go through anything. The Icaryoe is even more powerful than we realized. The way it kept us at bay like that?" He shuddered and rubbed his nose against Tommy's neck.

When he didn't continue his thought, Tommy said, "You were amazing. I'm proud of you."

"Thanks." Carter traced Tommy's necklace with gentle fingers for a moment before draping his arm around Tommy's waist. "Good night."

Tommy thought it would take forever for him to fall asleep, but Carter's deep, even breathing worked its magic.

SATURDAY THE 16TH OF MARCH, 1291 POST-CATACLYSM - PAKAHA CITY, PAKAHA

"Of course you would."

Elyse's voice woke Tommy abruptly from a deep sleep. He yawned, one hand over his mouth. "Carter asked me to," Tommy said, unrepentant. He stretched, shifting Carter as he did so.

"Five more minutes?" Carter mumbled, pressing closer to Tommy, and tightening his grip.

"I need to examine the patient," the healer said, raising an eyebrow.

"Do I need to be awake for that?" Carter asked sleepily.

"Preferably."

"Listen to your healer," Tommy said, sitting up.

"I brought your things." Elyse put their bags on the chair Tommy had been sitting in the day before. "Es'Sem says goodbye and that you both did her proud. She also gave me a package to mail. Something about blueprints for the castle of Pakaha?"

"Thanks, and blueprints? Seriously? That's hilarious." Tommy got to his feet and rifled through his bag, pulling out clean clothing. "I won't be long," he said, disappearing into the bathroom.

"Take as long as you want," Carter called after him. "I'll join you."

Tommy started the shower, enjoying the feeling of the warm water. They'd slept outside in Ohana's jungle the night before last, and he hadn't had a proper wash since they'd left Wild Nations.

The door opened, and Carter squeezed in. "I've been given the all clear," he said, beaming. "Even for strenuous physical activity." He winked.

"Awesome." Tommy grinned. "You can carry your own bag."

Carter laughed, water droplets clinging to his eyelashes and curls.

Tommy leaned in and kissed him gently. "I love you. For too long yesterday, I thought I wouldn't be able to hold you ever again."

"As if I'd leave you," Carter scoffed. "Broken ribs, punctured lung, shish-ka-Carter and all, is nothing compared to my determination to stay with you."

Tommy stared. "Shish-ka-Carter?" he said at last, trying not to laugh and failing. He sobered quickly. "That's a lot of injuries. Are you sure you're alright?" He ran his hands over Carter's ribs as if he'd be able to tell if they were still broken.

"I'm a little dirty. Can you wash me?" Carter murmured, eyes dark.

Shivers rippled over Tommy's skin despite the warm water. "I'll be extra thorough."

"You'd better."

SATURDAY THE 16TH OF MARCH, 1291 POST-CATACLYSM - TÈNE, GAULAN

After thanking the healers for their help, the small group travelled to Gaulan. Carter's ring was sending him the message that he was to return to the courtyard the Sisters had first addressed the knights.

"I hope we're not too late," Tommy worried.

"We won't be," Kathryn said. "They like a big fanfare. Since we were the ones to drive the Icaryoe away, they will be waiting for us."

King Todric met them in the portal building and insisted he accompany them to the courtyard. "The knights have all returned; you're the last. I've been hearing some interesting rumours," he said, but wouldn't say any more about it.

The walk through Tène was quiet. Very few people were on the streets, and most of the shops had closed signs hanging in the doors.

"Where is everybody?" Greg asked. "This is disturbing."

"I'll protect you," Elyse teased.

Tommy and Carter exchanged amused glances.

"They're probably all at the courtyard," Todd replied.

The Sisters started speaking the instant Carter's feet entered the courtyard.

"Creepy how they do that," Carter muttered to Tommy, who nodded.

"Knights and citizens of Gaulan, your Icaryoe problems are over!" the Sisters said in unison.

"I, Lord Bourges, am your saviour!" the lord shouted, interrupting them, and turning to face the crowd in front of the golden Sister. "I tracked the Beast to Ohana. I trekked through the hot and dirty jungle, searching the ground for hints of the monster's passage. At last, I came upon its cavern, where I lured it out with a song. The music put it to sleep, and that's when I, Lord Bourges, threw my spear. My aim was true; the spear lodged into its heart. The Great Beast Icaryoe is dead!"

The crowd cheered loudly, and the lord gave them a grand bow.

Carter crossed his arms over his chest. "Then what did *I* fight, a glorified porcupine?" he said with a sneer.

Kathryn raised her voice when the cheers died down. "If you killed it, where are the sealed chests with its ashes?"

"I didn't burn it," Lord Bourges scoffed. "I told you; I lanced it through the heart."

"You killed an immortal Beast without burning it?" Kathryn rolled her eyes. "Did you even stick around to see what happened after you threw the spear, or did you run away immediately like the coward you are?"

Lord Bourges's jaw dropped. "Who are you to spread such lies?"

"This is Mistress Kathryn, better known as the Scholar," the Sisters said. "If she doesn't know something about the Great Beasts, it's not worth knowing."

Deflating, the lord backed away from the crowd. "I saw my spear pierce through the dragon's scales. It flailed…"

"And pulled the spear out. You're lucky it was so focussed on us. You know, the knight you followed into the jungle," Carter said, getting angry.

Kathryn put a hand on Carter's shoulder, and he quieted. "The Icaryoe escaped into the Aether," she said.

A murmur rippled through the crowd.

The Sisters raised their hands. "Then all is well. The Icaryoe is no longer in Everdome and is, therefore, no longer under our jurisdiction. Three cheers for the young knight who delivered us from the Great Beast!"

Carter frowned. "But it's still out there!" he shouted over the cheering. "It could come back or go somewhere else and cause even more destruction! It's not gone!"

Ignoring him, they continued, "Your name will go down in the history books, and you have earned your reward. You wished to be returned home?" The Sisters looked smug.

"My *wish* is for you to find the thief who stole the Icaryoe from the castle and released it on purpose. And then I want you to raise a search party to chase the Icaryoe and get rid of it," Carter demanded. "I'll find my own way home."

"We cannot scry the Beasts. Their magic is too powerful, even as ashes."

"Who would release the Icaryoe on purpose?" Lord Bourges said scathingly. "What folly!"

"Someone who wanted the reward money?" Tommy said pointedly.

Lord Bourges's throat bobbed as he swallowed. "What are you implying? I had nothing to do with it escaping at the university!"

"We didn't say anything about it *escaping* at the university," Greg said mildly.

"Knights, seize him," the Sisters said, indicating the lord. "We may not be able to see the Icaryoe, but if we see that you walked into the castle and not out, you are culpable."

Three big knights took hold of Lord Bourges while the Sisters turned inward and grasped each other's hands. Above them, a swirl of clouds appeared, Lord Bourges clearly visible within. The lord walked into King Todric's castle and vanished from sight. The clouds blurred for some time, and then the lord was visible again, clearly exiting a building at the university.

"Ugh. Such drama queens," muttered Kathryn.

"Since he wasn't visible during the time between the castle and the university, he had the Icaryoe on him?" Greg whispered to Tommy, who nodded.

King Todric stepped forward. "You are stripped of your title and your lands, and shall await your trial for treason against Everdome," he said.

The lord vanished with a wave of the Sisters' hands.

"That was abrupt. Where did you send him?" Carter asked.

"To the dungeons of Pakaha." The Sisters turned to him. "We are not able to fulfil your second request. Until we meet again, Sir Carter of Westmeath." They bowed and vanished.

"I hate when they do that!" Carter exclaimed.

"It never gets less annoying," Kathryn agreed.

"What now?" Tommy asked. "Who's going to look after Bourges now?"

Todd stroked his beard thoughtfully. "By rights, Carter could claim it. He did expose the previous lord's treachery, albeit unintentionally."

"Me?" Carter squeaked. "I don't know anything about running a city! Besides, I've got to get home. My dads, my school, and my life are there."

"I could arrange for a steward to look after it in your place. Then, whenever you do return to Everdome, you will have a home to come back to," Todd said, a neutral expression on his face.

Carter shook his head. "Thank you, but I'm going to respectfully decline. The person in charge should be present and really care for the people of Bourges. If I do return to Everdome, I expect it'll be on another quest. Just, make sure that the new lord is better with their money. There's a lot of repairs that need to be done right now."

Todd grinned and shook Carter's hand. "You are a good soul, Sir Carter. I hereby appoint you a Hero of Gaulan. If ever you do return to us, no matter how many years have gone by, you shall have refuge here."

"Thank you, King Todric," Carter said, bowing deeply while the crowd cheered. "I think it's time we returned home."

FRIDAY THE 1ST OF AUGUST, 2003 - WESTMEATH, ONTARIO

Jason's familiar bungalow was the first thing Tommy saw when they stepped out of the doorway Kathryn had made between the realms. "We're home!" he breathed, squeezing Carter's hand.

"You sound as though you doubted me," Kathryn said wryly. She chuckled when all four protested. "Everdome has noticed you now, and you will surely be recalled again. The next time you go, it could be a week has passed, or six months, or a hundred years. You won't know until you arrive." She sighed heavily. "I'll make each of you a ring that will allow you to contact me across the realms should you get pulled back in. Never take it off."

Tommy was relieved. "Thank you. I'm glad I don't have to write another song."

Carter laughed. "As if you can stop yourself from writing songs!"

Kathryn led them up the stairs to the front door, but Greg hung back, hefting his bag over one shoulder.

"I'm just... going to go," he said, stumbling over his words and pointing down the street.

"Nonsense," Kathryn said. "Your father's waiting for you."

"Here?" he asked, eyes wide.

The front door flew open, and they were pulled inside the house. A giant man brushed past Tommy, heading for Greg, and scooping him up in a hug, still on the front lawn.

In the front hall, Tommy threw himself at his mother and Kennedy, hugging them tightly.

"Wow, look at you!" Kennedy exclaimed. "You're so tanned! And where did these muscles come from?"

"Are you alright?" Lilah asked, holding his face in her hands. "How long were you gone?"

"We have so much to tell you," Tommy said, shaking his head

with a smile. He looked around Jason's living room. Elyse's parents and sisters were still hugging her, Carter's dads were beaming at him proudly, and Jason was hugging Kathryn tightly.

"Thank you for bringing them home safely," Tommy overheard Jason say.

"We brought back souvenirs!" Tommy said loudly. "Why don't we go outside in the driveway and get chairs, and then Zoe and Gabrielle can hear all about it too?"

Epilogue 1 – Kathryn

FRIDAY THE 1ST OF AUGUST, 2003 -
WESTMEATH, ONTARIO

Kathryn drove down Yakabuski Drive in Jason's old car, leaving the happily reunited families to hear the teenager's experiences. She'd already heard it all from Greg and Elyse when they'd told Es'Sem their last night in Everdome. Veronica had arrived just as Kathryn had pulled out of the driveway.

She bit her lip in anxiety as the walls of Door Technology came into view. The extra two days she'd had to figure out what to say to Margery hadn't helped in the slightest.

After parking the car, Kathryn sat for a bit, drumming her fingers on the steering wheel. Finally, she sighed. "Sitting here isn't going to do anything except delay the inevitable," she told herself. She pulled out the guest pass she'd stored in a pocket dimension and headed for the main entrance.

It would have been rude to enter Margery's pride and joy without announcing herself. The walls around the facility made Kathryn think of the metaphorical walls between the two women. She hoped the conversation they were about to have would at the very least create a door. Kathryn snorted at both her whimsy and the unintentional pun.

The guard at the entrance barely glanced at her visitor's pass before waving her in.

Kathryn hoped that Margery would be in the same building as last time. Security met her at the door.

"Ms. Door is expecting you. Right this way."

They led her to an elevator and up twelve storeys to a floor with many offices and labs. Kathryn wished she could see into the numerous rooms they passed, but all the doors were closed.

"Here you go." They gave her a short bow and left her alone in front of a translucent glass door.

Kathryn dug her short fingernails into her palms, working up the courage to knock.

She heard a faint, "Come in," and opened the door to find herself facing a secretary behind a computer.

"I was hoping to see…" Kathryn began, the door closing behind her with a soft click.

"Margery is expecting you, Mrs. Johnson. You can go right in." The woman flashed Kathryn a smile.

Facing yet another door, but this time with an audience, Kathryn closed her eyes briefly and thought about how Carter had instantly reacted to her directions when facing the Icaryoe. If he could face that Beast while terrified, she could face one of her closest friends.

Margery was pacing the floor and whirled to face her the instant the door opened. "Are they alright?" she asked immediately.

"All four of them are safe in the arms of their families," Kathryn replied.

"Thank you," Margery said and collapsed into one of the armchairs at the side of the room.

"You really care about these kids," Kathryn remarked.

"Of course I do!" Margery gestured at the other armchair. "I may have only gotten to know them recently, and I know we're not supposed to pick favourites, but all four of them impressed me in Toronto. I have spent the past two hours very anxious."

Kathryn sat in the offered chair. "Just to warn you, they spent three months in Everdome training for an impossible task."

"Really?" Margery sat up straight. "Everdome?"

"Do you not believe me?"

Margery raised an eyebrow. "Seriously? We spent twenty-five years together in Robin's Fay Kingdom, and you think that I don't believe you?" She shook her head. "I had no idea that Everdome existed. That is fascinating. How did they do?"

"At the task?" Kathryn nodded thoughtfully. "They almost succeeded. They came awfully close."

"Why them? How were they chosen?" Margery asked.

Kathryn's mouth twisted. "Merlin himself knighted Carter back in March. When the Sisters recalled the Knights of Gaulan, it pulled him, and those around him, into Everdome."

Margery laughed and clapped her hands delightedly. "That's amazing! I have a knight of Everdome in my summer camp!"

Kathryn chuckled along with her. "Margery," she said at last, her gaze fixating on a loose thread from her tunic that her fingers were playing with. "I want to thank you for looking out for Hammond."

"I didn't start looking for him right away," Margery said apologetically. "I was, selfishly, still very upset with how things ended in Fay." She covered Kathryn's hands with one of her own. "We all had our own reasons for what we did then. I understand now that everything you said and did was out of love. I've missed you, my dear Kathryn."

A tear escaped Kathryn's eye. "I've missed you, too." She brought Margery's hand to her lips, pressing a light kiss on the back. "We should make a trip out to Baker to see Denise, hole up in a hotel, and catch up on all we've missed."

Margery looked taken aback. "You've found Denise?"

Kathryn grinned. "Wouldn't you know? Her granddaughter married my grandson in June." She watched the wheels turn behind Margery's beautiful brown eyes and waited for the penny to drop.

"Tommy is Denise's grandson!" Margery gasped. She burst into gales of laughter, throwing herself back in her chair and holding her stomach. "Oh, oh! No wonder he looked so familiar! That's amazing!"

"If you'd seen Kennedy, you wouldn't have had a problem. She's the spitting image of Denise, but with her father's eyes. Tommy's got a slightly more angular jaw. That probably threw you," Kathryn said, grinning.

"My goodness! I met MacKenzie, their older sister, in Toronto too. Yes, I can see it now." Margery slapped the arms of the chair. "This is hilarious. Yes, let's go to Baker. Maybe next weekend?"

"I'll talk to Denise about it tonight."

"I can't get over the fact that Tommy is Denise's grandson." Margery slapped her forehead. "Of course! Luck!"

"He has had quite a string of good luck, hasn't he?" Kathryn said, amused. "Just the fact that he got into the Westmeath-only March Break camp when he doesn't live here should've been enough."

"Denise was always a clever one. Her asking for Luck as her Fay gift was genius."

"No more or less so than you asking for Cleverness or me asking for Power. Look at the empire Ellen has built!"

"And your descendants do very well being in charge of Oldtown. Despite its age, the people there thrive, and there is practically no crime ever reported there," Margery said thoughtfully.

Kathryn stood up. "It has been so good to see you."

"You, too." Margery leaped to her feet and held Kathryn tightly. "You'll have to tell me how you haven't changed. I thought we were supposed to age when we returned to Earth?"

"I did. And then I reversed it a bit." Kathryn smiled sadly. "It had a steep price. I don't recommend it. You look beautiful."

Margery blushed. "You're just saying that."

Kathryn linked their fingers intimately and leaned back in, whispering a few choice words in Margery's ear that made the redhead's knees buckle.

"Ohh," Margery gasped. "Alright then."

Kathryn smiled. "I'll talk to you soon."

"Yes," Margery said dazedly. "Wait! You need my number." She grabbed a business card and scribbled a number on the back. "This is my personal cell."

"I'll take good care of it." Kathryn had a bounce in her step as she returned to the car. *Today is a good day.*

Epilogue 2 - Carter

THURSDAY THE 14TH OF AUGUST, 2003 - WESTMEATH, ONTARIO

❝ Today, we're going to be doing something a little bit different," Margery Door said as she stood at the front of the classroom.

The students quieted their chatter the instant she started speaking.

Carter and Tommy sat up straighter and shot each other excited glances. Whenever Margery showed up at the camp, everything got turned on its head.

"I have been given a riddle by Ellen, one that the best minds in the world haven't been able to solve. But I've always found that young minds think in new ways, and so I want you to have a crack at it. Work in small groups of four or five. If you succeed, the prize is the newest model of the Door Tech phone, the DT-74656." Margery smiled when a low murmur started up. "You have access to whatever you need to solve this. You have until the end of camp, but today is the only camp day that we will dedicate to the riddle."

"Sweet!" Tommy said. "Five is perfect for us."

Carter nudged Greg, who was sitting next to him. "You in?" he asked.

"Yeah, of course." Greg squeezed Elyse's hand, and she nodded enthusiastically before looking at Faith on her other side.

"Why would I join any other group?" Faith asked, smiling. "I'm still annoyed that I wasn't here early enough to join you on your adventure to Everdome. There's no way I'm going to let you do something else exciting without me."

Carter laughed. "We would have loved to have you with us, you know that."

They accepted the paper from Quinn, and all bent over it eagerly.

"It looks like you and Elyse are going to be leading on this," Carter said to Tommy, whistling at the impressively complicated math equation on the paper.

"Leading?" Tommy asked, frowning. "I can't make heads or tails out of this."

"What are you talking about?" Carter was confused. "Math's your strongest subject."

"Math?" Elyse chimed in. "All I see are a bunch of weird symbols."

"There's numbers all over this worksheet!" Carter exclaimed. "I mean, sure, there are some odd-looking variables as well, but…"

Tommy took Carter's hand and removed the knight's ring. Instantly, the numbers were replaced by symbols. "Ah," Carter said sheepishly. "That makes more sense."

Greg chuckled. "Don't you mean 'less sense?'"

"I mean, it didn't make much sense to me with it on either," Carter joked, watching Tommy put on his ring and scan the paper. "What do you think?"

"There's a lot of really complicated math here. It reminds me of the calculations for Everdome's time zones," Tommy said. "I think the first step should be to transcribe it so that we can all see what it says without passing this back and forth."

"Go ahead," Elyse said, passing him paper and pencil from the end of the desk.

Tommy bent over the paper, and Carter watched as the equation he had seen bloomed under Tommy's careful copying. "I think that's it," Tommy said. "Elyse, can you please check my work?"

Elyse took the ring and papers and went over them slowly.

"This *does* look like the Everdome time zones. Great observation. It all matches." She passed Carter back his ring. "Now let's try to solve this."

"Ms. Door said we had access to whatever we need for today," Faith said thoughtfully. "Does that include *whomever* we need?"

"Excellent question," Carter said. "I think we're going to need all the help we can get." He raised his hand, and Margery came over.

"Don't tell me you've solved it already," she said with a light chuckle.

"Not yet. We need some help with the math. Who would you recommend for this sort of thing?" He showed her the equation, and her jaw dropped.

"I..." She lowered her voice to a whisper. "How did you get this?"

Carter smirked. "Let's just say it 'rings a bell' and leave it at that." He spun his ring around his finger, and Margery nodded thoughtfully.

"I know just the person. Bring your work and follow me."

After a full day of math that went mostly over his head, the equation was solved, and Carter was relieved to step outside the main building. He stretched his arms over his head, feeling his spine pop. "Wanna hang out at the community centre?" he asked the others.

"I want to call my parents and tell them about my new phone," Faith said excitedly.

"There's a quiet room on the first floor for phone conversations," Elyse said. "I'd like to stop at home first and grab my bikini and sunscreen. I'm starting to lose my tan from Everdome, and I'd like to lay on the roof in the sun for a while."

"Good idea," Carter said. "I'll practise my Katas and keep you company."

"I'll work on my boxing forms, but I'm not sure how much attention I'll be able to pay to them," Greg said with a chuckle.

Elyse smiled and looped her arm through his.

"I'll get my guitar?" Tommy said tentatively and was met by a resounding chorus of yesses. He smiled bashfully. "Alright then. I've been working on a new song that I want you to—"

He cut off as a shadow passed over them. Carter squinted up at the sky, expecting to see a drone, or maybe a spaceship, anything other than what met his gaze.

The Icaryoe was hovering just above the Door Tech wall, its huge fire wings sending washes of stifling air over them. "I HAVE FOUND YOU, KNIGHT," it said, the words sounding strange coming from its beak. "PREPARE—"

The sky flashed with lightning, all of it converging on the Beast. It howled in pain as the five of them covered their ears and huddled together, and then, it vanished.

They stared at where the monster had been, unsure what to do next.

"I think you understated its size and how terrifying it is," Faith muttered.

Carter raised the ring Kathryn had given him to his lips, ready to call for her, when Margery exited the building behind them.

"Are you alright?" she asked. "It didn't strike at you before it was banished?"

"We're fine," Tommy reassured her. "Banished?"

"Banished back to the Aether. We're still working out the kinks. Kathryn helped design it. Did you think we wouldn't protect you?" Margery said.

"What happened?" Carter asked, still shaken.

"We channelled the entire Eastern seaboard power grid into it," Margery said, as if that wasn't a big deal. "We'll be without power for a few days, but I think we can figure out how to fix that little problem for next time."

"*Entire?*" Greg squeaked. He coughed, blushing.

"Thank you," Carter said quietly.

"This is only temporary. You need to figure out a plan to make the destruction of the Icaryoe permanent." Margery smiled. "You should be able to figure it out. We'll buy you enough time until you do."

"How long until it comes back?" Carter asked.

"Kathryn estimated a couple months."

The five teenagers walked home in silence. It was strange having no lights at intersections. All the shops were closed, and there were groups of people everywhere discussing the unusual power outage.

"Any ideas?" Carter said at last.

"I think that instead of going to the community centre, we should go to the park," Elyse said.

Everyone stared at her.

"The community centre will be filled with people who have nowhere else to go," she said with a shrug. "And the wading pool might be open at the park."

"The water would be nice, especially if there's no AC at home," Tommy agreed.

"But the Icaryoe?" Faith asked, her face grey under her tan.

Carter finally understood what the others were saying. "We're not going to solve the Icaryoe problem today. We need to relax, spend some time with each other, and figure it out once we've recovered from our shock. Besides, we don't need to keep this to ourselves. We can ask Jason and Kennedy for help, and the STEM team, and the entire Community! Thousands of heads are better than five."

The five of them huddled together, and Carter focussed on each face. "We can do this. We have warning, and we have help. I'm terrified, but I'm confident. You?"

One by one they all nodded their agreement.

"We're with you," Tommy said. "Bring it on."

Cast of Characters

EARTH CAST

Adrien: Aetherborn elf/Vulcan, OAC student at Oldtown High School

Alicia: Aetherborn muse, grade 11 student at Oldtown High School

Amita Dubois, Dr: Aetherborn dryad, agricultural expert, Kennedy's boss

Angie: student at Oldtown High School

Arielle: Aetherborn wind spirit, OAC student at Oldtown High School, cousin to Lauryn, girlfriend of Adrien

Arthur Fairfield: human child, son of Phillip and Sarah

Brent DuLac: Aetherborn morgens, Oldtown Council member

Brooke Johnson: Aetherborn with water powers, daughter of Zoe and Gabrielle

Bryan: human, grade 12 student at Parry Sound High School, brother of Cindy Lou

Captain Herrington: Canadian Indigenous astronaut

Carol Jenkins: archeologist expert

Carter Batudev: Aetherborn rock giant, grade 9 student at Oldtown High School, boyfriend of Tommy

Chris: human, OAC student at Parry Sound High School

Cindy Lou: human, grade 9 student at Parry Sound High School, sister of Bryan

Claude: Aetherborn, honorary uncle of Jason

Denise Lake: human, grandmother of Kennedy

Doctor Rhys Sallah: Aetherborn Norse god, doctor in Oldtown

Dominic Peters: nanotech expert

Donald Johnson: Aetherborn, Jason's grandfather, husband of Kathryn

Eliza Fairfield: human, sister of Tommy

Ellen O. Door: human, CEO of Door Tech, daughter of Margery

Elyse Garrido: Aetherborn succubus, sister to Rachel, friend of Carter and Tommy

Emily: Aetherborn, grade 10 student at Oldtown High School, friend of Lauryn

Evanna Swan: alien with healing powers, daughter of Michelle

Faith Roi: human, grade 9 student at Parry Sound High School, friend of Tommy

Gabrielle Johnson: Aetherborn elf/Vulcan, wife of Zoe

Gerard Fairfield: human, father of Tommy

Greg Finch: human, grade 9 student at Westmeath High School, Blue Blood member

Hammond: Aetherborn, Jason's father

Jason Johnson, the elder: Aetherborn, Jason's great-grandfather

Jason Johnson, AKA The Phantom: Aetherborn with shadow powers, co-leader of the Oldtown Aetherborn Council, proprietor of The Hawaiian, fiancé of Kennedy

Jesse Mortimer Wells: wizard, owner of Mortimer's Diner

Judy Fauche: Aetherborn Iwa, trainer of Carter

Julien Trevino: geology expert

Karine: grade 9 student at Oldtown High School, Elyse's friend

Kathryn Johnson: Aetherborn changeling, grandmother of Jason

Kennedy Fairfield, AKA The Wraith: human, Agricultural scientist, fiancée of Jason, sister of Tommy

Lauryn: Aetherborn wind spirit, grade 10 student at Oldtown High School, cousin to Arielle

Leo: human, friend of Carter

Lilah Fairfield: human, mother of Tommy

Lydia Turgeneva: Aetherborn hag, co-owner of Seams Likeable

MacKenzie Fairfield: human, sister of Tommy

Margery Door: human, founder of Door Tech, runs the summer camp for grades 10-11

Maria: Door Tech employee

Michelle Swan: alien with fire powers, mother of Evanna, friend of Kennedy

Mr. Coolidge: teacher at Oldtown High School

Mr. Finch: Greg's father, Blue Blood member

Mr. Gordon: music teacher at Parry Sound High School

Mr. Travese: science teacher at Parry Sound High School

Ms. Chang: principal at Oldtown High School

Ms. Rubens: science teacher at Oldtown High School

Ms. VanCamp: vice-principal at Oldtown High School

Naomi: human, grade 11 student at Parry Sound High School

Nick Potnia: Aetherborn nymph, manager of The Hawaiian

Oldtown STEM group: Adrien (Arielle), George, Alicia, Lauryn, Elyse, Carter (all Aetherborn)

Parry Sound STEM group: Chris, Bryan, Naomi, Sabrina, Tommy, Faith (all human)

Patricia: Aetherborn, grade 9 student at Oldtown High School

Phillip Fairfield: human, brother of Tommy

Quinn: Door Tech employee, TA at the summer camp

Rachel Garrido: Aetherborn succubus, sister of Elyse, friend of Kennedy

Reverend Patrick Mitchel: Aetherborn watcher, Anglican minister, uncle of Veronica

Robin: Fay Lord

Sabrina: human, grade 10 student at Parry Sound High School

Sam Batudev: Aetherborn rock giant, co-owner of Oven Baked, husband of William, father of Carter

Sanaa: Aetherborn cambion, friend of Kennedy

Sarah Fairfield: human, wife of Phillip

Steve: Aetherborn cyclops, friend of Carter

Sylvie Therien: human, girlfriend of Veronica

Tommy Fairfield: human, boyfriend of Carter

Veronica Giles: Aetherborn watcher-wizard, best friend of Jason, robotics expert

Wayne Edgerton: biology expert

William Batudev: Aetherborn rock giant, co-owner of Oven Baked, husband of Sam, father of Carter

Zhanna Turgeneva: Aetherborn hag, co-owner of Seams Likeable

Zoe Johnson: Aetherborn with water powers, co-leader of the Oldtown Aetherborn Council, sister of Jason

Appendices

Shadows Live For the Light

Capo (3)

Verse 1:
```
G                          Em
Crunching through the leaves,
C                    D
Your hand clasped in mine,
G          Em
Life lines interweave,
C             D7
Winding like a vine.
```

Chorus 1:
```
C                    E
This journey's just begun,
G                D
We're ready for some fun,
C                    E
Our hearts are taking flight,
G        Em A      Am
Shadows li-ve for the light.
```

Verse 2:
```
Run across the snow,
Leap into my arms,
You will never know,
How much my heart warms.
```

Chorus 2:
```
This journey's just begun,
G                       D
Kisses, need more than one,
Our hearts are taking flight,
Shadows li-ve for the light.
```

Verse 3:
Dance amidst flowers,
Twirling in a spin,
Sunshine and showers,
Life is never dim.

Chorus 3:
This journey's just begun,
G   D
Play fights, who cares who won?
Our hearts are taking flight,
Shadows li-ve for the light.

Verse 4:
Lying in the sun,
Counting grains of sand,
Our life has begun,
Keep hold of my hand.

Bridge:
Fmaj7   C
Press you up against a wall,
Em   Am
I come undone,
Fmaj7   C
More in love with you I fall,
Em   Am
Hearts beat as one.

Chorus 4:
This journey's just begun,
G   D
Shine brighter than the sun,
Our hearts are taking flight,
G   Em A   Am Am7
Shadows li-ve for the light.

THE BALLAD OF THE PHANTOM AND THE WRAITH

Capo (3)

```
Em                    C
The hero of Westmeath searches,
G              D
Desperate and a-lone,
Em                 C
Using the power of shadows,
G                  D
Leaving no unturned stone.
```

Chorus:

```
Am   C  E        Am        C
Ooo-ooo-oooooo the heroes of Westmeath,
      E              C
The Phantom and the Wraith!

Em                    C
His people keep being taken,
G                 D
No one seems to no-tice,
Em               C
Every clue, a new dead end,
G                D
He cannot lose fo-cus.

Em                      C
He tracks them to a run-down house,
G                 D
When a green glow ap-pears,
Em                   C
The hero walks toward the wraith,
G                D
Calmly despite his fears.

Ooo-ooo-oooooo the heroes of Westmeath,
The Phantom and the Wraith!

Em                         C
"You are seeking them, too," she said,
G          D
A finger at her lips,
Em                            C
"They took my friends, we must save them!"
G                   D
"And who are you?" he quips.

Em                        C
"No time to talk, they're co-ming now."
G                D
She ducked behind a shed.
```

Em   C
The hero hid in the shadows,
G   D
And watched where they were led.

Ooo-ooo-oooooo the heroes of Westmeath,
The Phantom and the Wraith!

Em   C
"They're being shipped out, I've got this."
G   D
He went to make his move.
Em   C
"I've got an idea," she said.
G   D
"I'm sure you will ap-prove."

Em   C
"We wait until every-one's in,
G   D
And steal the train from them."
Em   C
Hero smirked at the cle-ver plan,
G   D
"On your mark, Lady Gem."

Ooo-ooo-oooooo the heroes of Westmeath,
The Phantom and the Wraith!

Em   C
She glanced at the orb on her chest,
G   D
Laughing, she shook her head.
Em   C
"We should do this again, Lord Shade.
G   D
Work as a team," she said.

Em   C
They saved all the people that night,
G   D
Returning them back home,
Em   C
Phantom and Wraith protect Westmeath,
G   D
Together now they roam.

Ooo-ooo-oooooo the heroes of Westmeath,
The Phantom and the Wraith!

Ooo-ooo-oooooo the heroes of Westmeath,
        E   Am
The Phantom and the Wraith!

CATACLYSM DAY GIFTS

To Tommy from
- Es'Sem: guitar, case, and accessories (magic guitar that projects at the volume needed, never loses tune)
- Carter: silver chain necklace
- Elyse: Everdome astronomy book
- Greg: a galaxy projector of Everdome's stars

To Carter from
- Es'Sem: throwing knives and holster (magic returning knives)
- Tommy: silver chain necklace
- Elyse: martial arts book
- Greg: a collapsible model of Everdome

To Elyse from
- Es'Sem: rope dart (rope cannot be cut, both a dart and practice weight)
- Tommy and Carter: red winter set (hat, mitts, scarf) and leather wall hanging
- Greg: magical jewellery box

To Greg from
- Es'Sem: hand wraps (magically feel like the wearer has full gloves on) and magic puzzle game that is never the same answer
- Tommy and Carter: pocketknife, black scarf, and leather jacket
- Elyse: an abridged book on magic and a fancy watch

Family Tree

TOMMY'S FAMILY

André Lake (1920-1992) and Denise Lake, née Lance (1924)
- Lilah Lake (1946)
- Arthur Lake (1977)

André Lake (1920-1992) and Charlotte Lake, née Pelletier (1928-1974)
- William Lake (1954)
- Nancy Lake (1957)

Lilah Fairfield, née Lake (1946) and Gerard Fairfield (1946)
- Phillip Fairfield (1972)
- Eliza Fairfield (1976)
- MacKenzie Fairfield (1976)
- Kennedy Fairfield (1980)
- Thomas "Tommy" Fairfield (May 11, 1988)

Phillip Fairfield (1972) and Sarah Fairfield, née Weber (1972)
- Arthur Fairfield (2001)

Arthur Lake (1977) and Mary Lake, née Landry (1978)
- Randal Lake (1998)

CARTER'S FAMILY

William Batudev, née Baturak (1940) and Sam Batudev, née Kaydev (1940)
- Carter Batudev (Mar 5, 1988)

Songs in order of appearance

"Boom Boom Boom Boom" by VengaBoys
"Slide" by The Goo Goo Dolls
"You're Still The One" by Shania Twain
"Survivor" by Destiny's Child
"Je n'attendais que vous" by Garou
"Get Down" by B4-4
"Can't Help Falling in Love" by Elvis
"Stomp to my Beat" by JS16
"Shadows Live For The Light" by Tommy Fairfield*
"Carol of the Bells" by Peter J. Wilhousky
"The Ballad of the Phantom and the Wraith" by Tommy Fairfield*
"Puff, the Magic Dragon" by Peter, Paul, and Mary
"It's Friday, I'm in Love" by The Cure

*Artist is fictional

Spotify Playlist
www.jeneric-designs.ca/playlists/#WingingIt

Acknowledgments

First and foremost, I need to thank my husband, Éric Desmarais. Thank you for your patience when I was working through a tough spot, and helping me with plot ideas. Allowing me to play with your world of Everdome was going above and beyond.

My kids, for letting me talk about my characters nearly nonstop while I was writing this (and before and after, tbh). I hope they're as real to you as they are to me.

My music mentors. My dad, David Coderre, who encouraged me to try his guitar and brought me to buy my own when his proved to be too large for me to handle. You also provided the spark; I have such fond memories of you playing your guitar for us when I was little, letting me strum while you changed chords and sang. Many thanks go out to Cait Gordon, for her editing and tightening up the lyrics, and Bruce Gordon, for assisting with the music and teaching me how to fit music to lyrics.

Tasha Kalbfleisch, for answering my million and one questions about what teenage boys were like, and LGBTQ+ experiences, and just generally reliving high school with me. I can't think of anyone else that I could ask about this stuff without being even more awkward than I already am.

My beta readers (alphabetical by first name). Ann Birdgenaw, for analyzing the book like a librarian. Your feedback was so helpful. Daniela Neri Barberena, your enthusiasm was contagious. I appreciate all the time you spent talking with me about this book. Jamieson Wolf, I appreciate how thorough you were with your comments and didn't shy away from pointing out when things didn't work for you, and you loved it despite those flaws. Sonia Carrière, you pointed out problems I didn't even know were there, which is much appreciated.

The cover artist, who wishes to go by pinkpiggy93, who took "give Tommy a guitar and put them outside...oh, and add a dome in the sky from this world you've never heard of" and made it reality. This cover blew me away. I can't wait to hold it in my hands.

We would like to acknowledge that this book was written on the unceded, unsurrendered Territory of the Anishinaabe Algonquin Nation, and we pay our respects to elders both past and present.

Last but certainly not least, the entire team at Renaissance Press, from the acquisitions committee who approved the acceptance of my book, the editors who polished it up (especially Max!), and to most especially Nathan Fréchette who was there for me every step of the way. I am so honoured that you are publishing it.

About the Author

Jen Desmarais is the creator of the sex education game Blush, co-author of Assassins! Accidental Matchmakers and Monsters! Incidental Wedding Guests, and author of Crushing It and Winging It.

Co-founder of JenEric Designs, she creates unique geeky crocheted items. Her blogs The Travelling TARDIS and How I Taught My Dragon have been nominated for the Prix Aurora Awards over 2018-2024.

She lives in Ottawa with her author husband, daughter, son, and their library of over 3000 books.

Other Works

The Gates of Westmeath
1. *Assassins! Accidental Matchmakers*
2. *Monsters! Incidental Wedding Guests*

Lucky in Love
1. *Crushing It*
2. *Winging It*

Short Stories
"The Summer of '95" in *The Mystery of the Dancing Lights*
"Semper Ubi Sub Ubi" in *Nothing Without Us Too*

About Renaissance

Canadian Renaissance Press has been in business since 2013 and has published over eighty books in that time, most of which genre-bend in unexpected and fantastic ways.

Many of our authors are members of marginalized groups, and we delight in uplifting their voices and provide a platform for them to speak to the rest of the world through their work.

At Renaissance, we are passionate about books! We care about our authors' enjoyment of the publishing process and about our readers' enjoyment of a great Canadian read.

Renaissance books are available on the platform of your choice.

pressesrenaissancepress.ca

pressesrenaissancepress@gmail.com

Crushing It

After an epic grounding for some bad decisions with even worse friends, Tommy is lucky to even go to the Door Tech March Break camp. There, he crosses paths with Carter Batudev, and chemistry isn't just for the classroom. With love and a renewed interest in STEM, Tommy returns home to Parry Sound, where, to the relief of his parents, he makes better friends, and joins the STEM club.

When the club goes to the province-wide competition in Toronto, he's reunited with Carter, whose team is also competing. Thus ensues a wild long weekend full of romance, hijinks, STEM, and singing.

Includes a novelette from Carter's POV at the dinner theatre show Knights of Everdome.

This book takes place in an alternate world where technology is more advanced, especially in Westmeath, due to in-universe reasons.

Everdome

S.M. Ardwur's epic ten novel series and the world's biggest MMORPG is a world fractured by a magical disaster and saved from destruction by a brave king and mad wizard. It is now formed of twelve floating continents with magical domes protecting them.

For thirteen lucky contestants, when a man dressed as a knight offers them the opportunity to visit their favourite fantasy world as an immersive reality show, there's only one answer they can give: YES!

The level of impressiveness is beyond anything they can believe and some of them start to wonder why.

Abigail, James, Krista, Nicole, Richard, and Megan have to learn how to play the game and win; the fate of Everdome depends on it.

The Baker City Mysteries

A Study in Aether

Elizabeth Coderre has always known that there was something strange about her home town, Baker Ontario, but it isn't until her English teacher disappears that she starts to find out how strange. Getting through classes, killer kitten swarms, and bullies are going to be the easy parts of surviving at Sir Arthur Conan Doyle High. Elizabeth and her best friends, Jackie and Angela, are up to the challenge... they hope.

The Sign of Faust

Elizabeth Coderre solves mysteries. Magic, wizards, and killer kittens didn't stop her last semester. Now someone is trying to kill her in absurdly complicated ways, she's hearing voices, her best friends are constantly fighting despite being madly in love, and the desires of Baker City's residents are becoming reality. Can she find out who's trying to kill her and discover the source of everyone's luck, while navigating dating, concerts, school, and competing in the science Olympics? She can only wish... and you know what they say about wishes!

A Case of Synchronicity

Elizabeth Coderre loves mysteries. She's faced down deranged Hags, killer kittens, wiley Artificers, and evil Genies, all with the help of her two best friends. Now she's stuck in summer 1985, Jackie is in a coma, and Angela is quarantined. Can Elizabeth cope with her inner demons, the 80's, and a new voice in her head? Can Angela save Jackie and the entire Bytown Memorial Hospital? This is going to be the least relaxing March break, but can they solve the mystery... in time?

The Mystery of the Dancing Lights

Mysteries are Elizabeth Coderre's life, and after wizards, hags, artificers, vampires, kobolds, genies, and killer kittens, she thinks she's seen everything. She's wrong! And when she goes to Riding Thorpe summer camp, which is built on an old government experimental facility, she discovers that there's a lot she doesn't know.

Can she solve the mystery of the dancing lights, save her friends, and escape a time loop? Or is she cursed to relive her friends' deaths forever?

The Gates of Westmeath

Assassins! Accidental Matchmakers

Kennedy Fairfield just graduated in the class of 2002, and is now trying to find her purpose in life, or at least a job in her field. When she saves Jason Johnson, the leader of a secret Community of supernatural people called Aetherborn, from an attempted assassination, they embark on a whirlwind epic romance and adventure.

For Kennedy and Jason to discover why people are disappearing in time to save her friends, they'll have to face teleporting assassins, grumpy wizards, gossiping hags, mafia robots, and secret military groups, all in the city of Westmeath, Ontario, which has more secrets than residents.

The first book of four in The Gates of Westmeath series.

Monsters! Incidental Wedding Guests

The week before Kennedy and Jason's wedding is busy. There are cake tastings, dress fittings, a formal ball, and, as their superhero personas the Phantom and the Wraith, fighting monsters.

These behemoths are destructive, smell like snack food, and are only after one thing: Door Tech Industries technology.

Adding to the chaos are their friends and families; Jason's grandmother has returned after having been missing for half a century, Kennedy's mom is dead-set on keeping things traditional, and Jason's best friend is kidnapped before the rehearsal.

Kennedy and Jason just want to get married, preferably before the next monster attack.

The second book of four in The Gates of Westmeath series.

Murder at the World's Fair

The year is 1893, and airships cloud the skies over the bustling metropolis of Toronto. The city is set to host the world's fair thanks in no small part to the work of two fantastical inventors. The New World Exhibition is to be a celebration of cultural and technological marvels; roving automatons, clockwork contraptions, the world's biggest steam-powered paddle boat, all to be fully lit by the wonder of electricity!

On the day of the grand opening, young Norwood Quigley, aspiring journalist, photographer and scion of a world-famous airship magnate, stumbles onto the scene of a murder; the victim: a Prussian Ambassador; the perpetrator: a Chinese assassin, or so the powers-that-be say. In truth, the suspect is Jing, a roguish but amiable youthful delinquent.

Concerned by Jing's claim of innocence and his assumed guilt by higher powers, including the British Empire's military, Norwood is thrown into a grand intrigue that hinges on Toronto's world fair. As chaos consumes the celebrations, he fears that his influential family is being manipulated in a plot to create an international incident that will lead to a war that spans the world.

Mrs. Victoria buys a Brothel

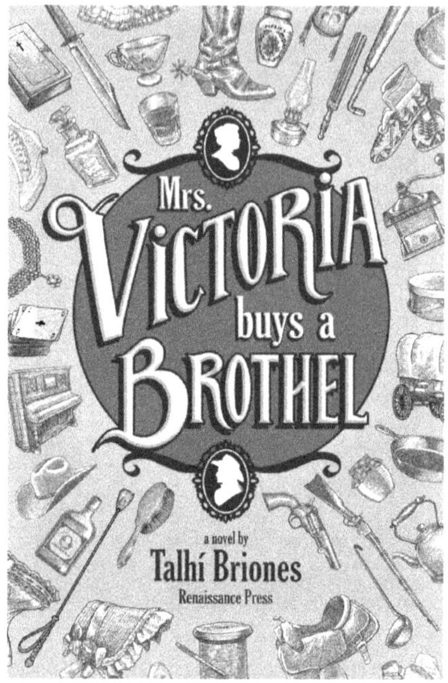

1865, United States— It took thirty years and a dislocated arm for Victoria to leave her abusive husband. Heartbroken, she has to choose her own life over the hope of ever seeing her son again. She escapes the manor in the dead of night, only bringing with her a white wedding dress.

She ends up in Swainsburg, a minuscule town in Wyoming, where she's adopted by the local prostitutes. To save them from expulsion, she buys the building and learns that in these parts, entertainment is worth more than gold. It's almost easy, even fun, to organize piano recitals and cancan shows for the cowboys of the area, but being a Madam comes with responsibilities and dangers she isn't ready to face. Her husband, after all, has contacts everywhere.

It's hard to navigate the delicate tensions between respectable ladies and whores, between white society and the 'others.' Her new friends are women who carved their place in this merciless life; people who, like her, ended up in Swainsburg when they got tired of running.

Victoria falls in love. She doesn't notice, she can't even imagine the possibility. The townfolk say the widow Díaz is strange. Natane is actually incredibly awkward, kind, and very lonely. Victoria has no name for this burning friendship, but the feeling grows and demands to be acknowledged.

This is a story about women who age, gossip, drink, love, and help you hide the body of your dead husband.